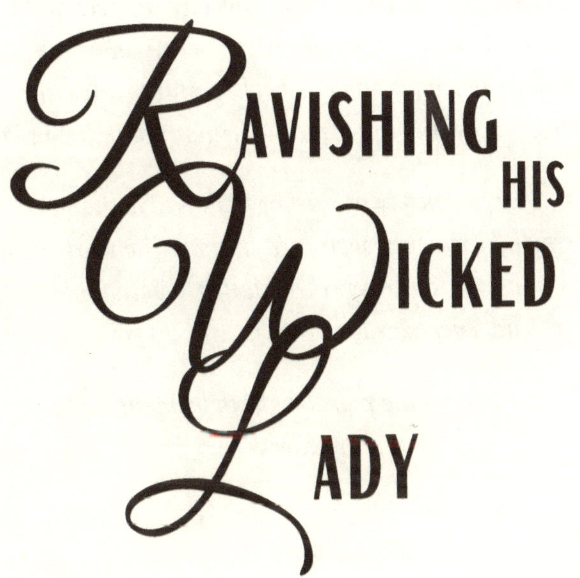

Ravishing His Wicked Lady

SADIE BOSQUE

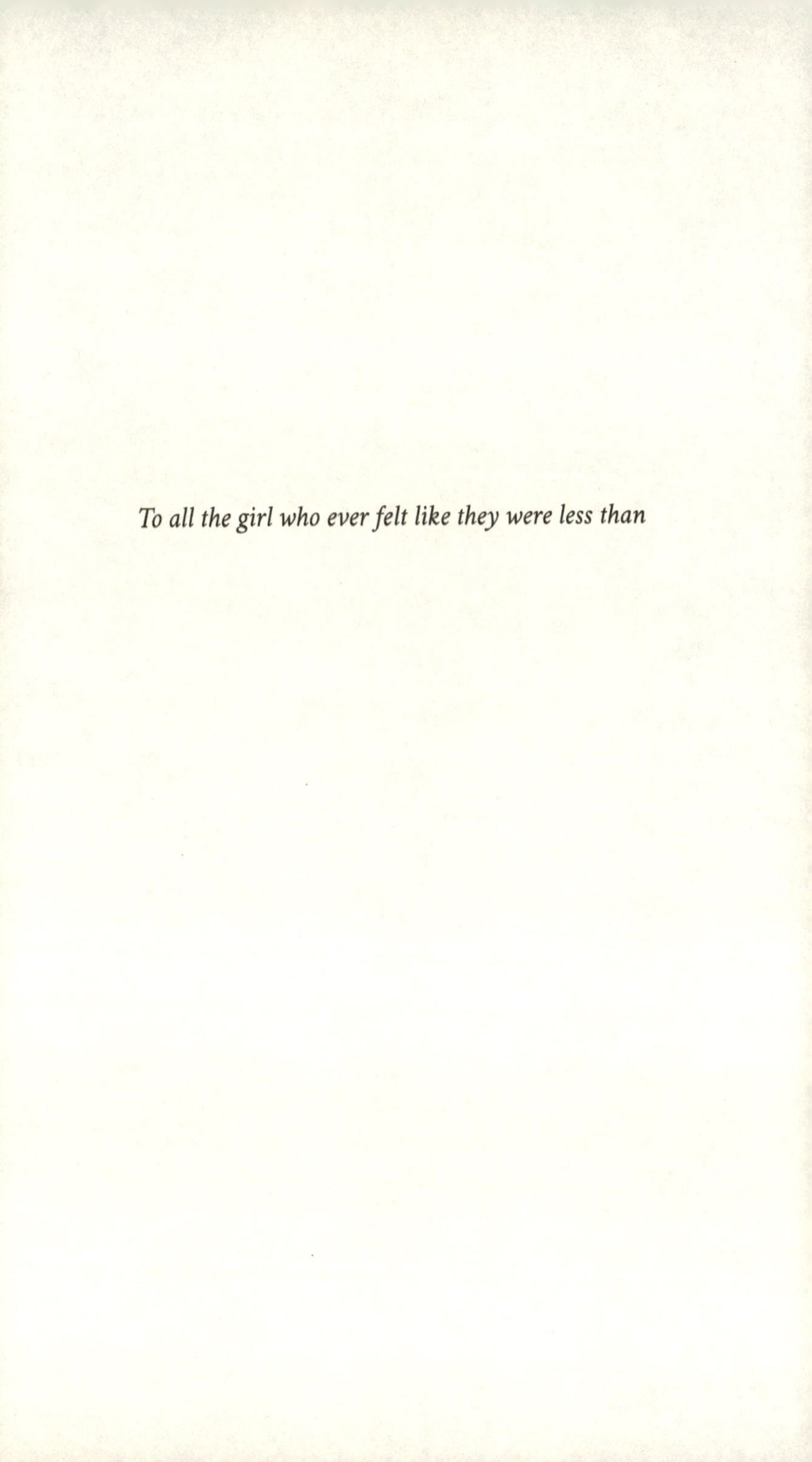

To all the girl who ever felt like they were less than

Contents

Acknowledgement

Special thanks to:
My awesome beta readers Nicole Yost and Michelle Lokeigh.
The story would not be the same without you.
And
reader and author friends in the Brazen Belles facebook
group.

Chapter 1

Autumn 1741

Lady Lavinia wasn't one to give in to panic easily. In fact, in the friendship between her and her oldest friend Annalise, Lavinia was the levelheaded one. When they were children, she was the one who caught frogs and chased away the bees without being frightened. Once they grew up and Annalise married, Lavinia was the one to constantly wipe away her friend's tears and give her advice.

And when Annalise needed it most, Lavinia was willing to give up the man she loved for her best friend.

Losing things and thanking the lord that she hadn't lost more, handling difficult matters without breaking to pieces, were things that defined Lavinia. She was rational and was always willing to make sacrifices. The panic had never caught her off guard.

Until now.

I know what you did.

Lavinia stared at the note she received a few moments ago with glassy eyes. Those five words made her heart race and her vision blur to the point she thought she was going to swoon.

Lavinia knew there was only one thing this note could have alluded to, and if she was right, she was in deep, deep trouble.

She placed her hand to her heart as it beat wildly, her eyes roaming about the room, unable to find a place to settle her gaze.

She was in Annalise's drawing room, the room she'd been in countless times, yet it felt foreign at the moment. Her friends sat in a circle not far from her, but she felt completely alone.

Somebody knew.

And that somebody had followed her to Annalise's home.

"Lavinia?" Annalise stepped closer, startling Lavinia out of her skin. "You seem unwell. Are you feeling faint?"

Yes, yes, I am! I am in a blasted panic! Lavinia's hands shook, but the only thing she could say was, "I am well, thank you."

Annalise peered into her face, unconvinced. "I shall bring you a glass of wine."

Lavinia nodded and stood there, reading and rereading the words on the paper as if expecting them to change. She turned the note and twisted it, hoping the paper itself would give her some clue, any clue, but her attempts were in vain. Other than the words and indecipherable signature under them, there was nothing to indicate where it came from and who'd written it.

Annalise returned a few moments later with a glass of wine. "Here, drink."

Lavinia took a sip and let the drink calm her as it traveled through her mouth and down her throat. Only it didn't help.

She bunched the note in her hand and discreetly put it in her pocket. Her breaths accelerated, and her eyes watered. Lavinia blinked the tears away.

"Annalise," she whispered, without looking at her friend. "I am in big trouble."

There was a slight pause as Annalise searched Lavinia's features for a clue as to what had happened, and when she didn't find her answers there, she asked, "What do you need?"

Lavinia was ready to cry. How easily her friend offered her help without even knowing what the issue was. If Annalise knew the issue, her reaction would not be much different, Lavinia was certain.

"I want to tell you everything but"—Lavinia looked at the two women quietly conversing in the sitting area—"it will not be a short conversation. And I don't want to keep your guests waiting."

Annalise followed Lavinia's gaze. "Dear, you know Olivia would be happy to help. Perhaps you should—"

Lavinia shook her head, cutting Annalise off. "I know Olivia would be happy to help. But she is not alone. And her poor cousin lost a husband recently. She doesn't need someone else's problems thrust onto her."

Annalise nodded. "Then, if you wish, I can just tell everyone that you are not feeling well."

Lavinia needed a moment to think it over.

She didn't want to go home yet. She wasn't ready. She'd rather stay among friends and speak to Annalise after. "Thank you, but I'm… I think I'd rather stay here awhile. Just… please, let's pretend that nothing is amiss."

Annalise nodded again, put on her radiant smile, and

proceeded to the sitting area.

"And how are you, ladies?" she asked brightly.

"I am incredibly well. Thank you for asking," Olivia answered with a broad grin.

Olivia's cousin just offered a polite smile as she sat with her hands demurely folded on her lap, handkerchief in hand.

Helen, Olivia's cousin by marriage, was a frail, slight lady, with a pale complexion and big brown eyes. She wore all black since she was in mourning for her recently departed husband. He had died only a little over a week ago under bizarre circumstances, and this was the first outing Helen had been on since his death.

Helen was obviously still in pain, but Olivia was determined to help her cousin rejoin the world.

Lavinia conceded that for the first outing after a great tragedy, a quiet nuncheon with a few lady friends was a perfect choice. But she could not imagine how Helen must have felt at the moment. Losing the man she loved was not something to easily get over.

Helen looked like a ghost. Lavinia had never noticed her much before, but looking at her now, she wondered if she had suffered long before her husband's passing. But who was she to pass judgment? Nobody would suspect the turmoil of Lavinia's life, and here she was, sitting during a nuncheon, pretending to be content.

"How is married life, Olivia?" Annalise asked, and Lavinia turned toward her newly wedded friend.

"It is incredibly, surprisingly fulfilling. I didn't think I would enjoy it—"

"You didn't? Why not?" Annalise asked with a chuckle. "You seem rather fond of your new husband."

"I am… It's just…" Olivia suddenly turned a slight shade of pink. "I was not used to sharing a room with another person. And I have a… Well, I am used to doing things one way, and he—let's just say that the adjusting period wasn't easy."

"You share a room?" Lavinia asked, aghast. Didn't the viscount and viscountess have their separate chambers?

Olivia blinked up at her and then turned to Annalise. "Is that wrong? My parents also share a room. I thought—"

"It isn't wrong," Annalise said with a soft smile. She turned to Lavinia and repeated firmer, "It isn't wrong. Blake and I share a room, too. I mean, I have my own chamber, but I only go there to change my clothing."

Lavinia frowned. Was that common? She turned toward Helen. "Did you and your husband share a bedroom?"

Helen blinked and shook her head. "No."

"Oh." Lavinia was more confused than ever. What was the difference? And why would one want to share a room with one's husband when one had a perfectly spacious chamber of her own?

"It is simply a preference," Annalise said as if reading her mind.

The butler stepped into the room and lightly knocked on the doorjamb. "Her Grace, the Duchess of Kensington," he announced with a flourish.

Everyone's heads turned toward the door while Lavinia's insides tightened. She found it difficult to breathe.

Caroline, their mutual friend, entered the parlor room with a smile on her face. She was as composed as ever, dressed in a beautiful midnight-blue gown, an intricate coiffure adorning her head.

Caroline had always been a fashionable lady. But now

that she was a duchess, her appearance seemed grander. She looked almost like a queen.

Annalise threw a worried gaze toward Lavinia before getting up to greet her new guest. This was the first time both Lavinia and Caroline were present at the nuncheon since the day Caroline had announced her betrothal.

That day was one of the worst days of Lavinia's life.

The reason for that was simple. Lavinia had been in love with Dane, the Duke of Kensington, for as long as she could remember. They'd been friends for a long time, but just a few months ago, Lavinia had decided to try to make him see her in a new light. Not as a friend, but as a woman and a potential wife.

But all her dreams had shattered when Caroline announced that she was betrothed to the duke.

Lavinia had pleaded with Caroline not to go through with the marriage. She had even told her why. She had confided in Caroline about her feelings, hoping that would change her mind. But Caroline had married him, nonetheless.

This decision had created a rift between the women. And they had not occupied the same room together ever since.

Annalise had been a good friend of Caroline's, and although she was prepared to plead with Caroline again to change her mind, Lavinia had insisted that neither she nor Olivia meddled.

Lavinia did not want her unrequited love for Dane to break the group apart. But she knew that things between Caroline and her would never be the same.

"My apologies, I am late," Caroline said. "I've had to deal with packing up the house to prepare for the country."

"We're glad to see you," Annalise said as she greeted the

duchess.

Olivia stood and extended her arms toward her friend. Caroline took her hands in hers and studied her with an appraising gaze. "Marriage agrees with you, dear," she said with a warm smile.

"Yes, as it does you."

Helen performed a perfect curtsy. "Your Grace."

"Oh, please." Caroline waved a dismissive hand. "Friends call me by my Christian name. And if you are here, it means you are a friend. So, call me Caroline."

"Oh, I couldn't," Helen answered shyly.

"I insist."

Lavinia sucked in a deep breath. Now it was her turn. She stood and curtsied lightly. "Caroline," she said, barely keeping a demure smile on her face.

Caroline turned to her, and her face changed. Lavinia could not quite read her facial expressions. Unlike the open Annalise whom she could read in a second, Caroline had always been closed off. But her eyes softened, and perhaps Lavinia could see remorse in them. Or maybe Lavinia just hoped that's what she saw.

"I am glad to see you," Caroline said with a smile. "It's been too long."

"Indeed."

Silence turned uncomfortable for a brief moment, then Caroline looked around and put on her regular, bright smile. "Well, is there any news I've missed?"

The chatter resumed, and Lavinia let out a breath of relief. She did not want the group to be uncomfortable because of the little tiff between her and the duchess. But she shouldn't have worried. Caroline had always known what to say and what to do to make everyone comfortable in her presence. She was only too perfect for the role of the duchess. Dane had made the right choice in marrying her, Lavinia had to agree begrudgingly, even though her heart bled every time she thought of it.

"And then we were discussing husbands and a wives sharing a chamber. Lavinia found it strange that we do. Do you share your bedchamber with the duke, Caroline?" Olivia—always direct, and sometimes inept in social interactions—turned toward the duchess.

Caroline threw a brief glance toward Lavinia before answering. "No. And I find it quite rare for a married couple of noble stature to share anything beyond the title and the house."

"That's how it was for my parents," Lavinia said quietly.

"And that's far more common than what you are describing, Olivia. It does not mean your arrangement is wrong, however, as long as you're comfortable with it. But love matches are… rare, to say the least," Caroline continued.

Lavinia closed her eyes. Yes. And she would never get a love match. She might never get any match at all under the current circumstances. Suddenly, the air turned suffocating. The room became much too small, and the conversation turned dull. No, she couldn't just sit here listening to her friends talk about their perfect lives and pretend as if all was well in her life. Nothing was well.

"Lavinia?" Annalise's voice cut through the fog of her despair. "Are you unwell?"

"Yes." Lavinia stood. "Apologies. I thought my headache would pass, but it did not. So I think I shall retire."

Caroline stood also. "Do you mind if I see you out? I would

love to—"

"No," Lavinia answered too quickly. She composed herself and smiled at Caroline. "Truly, my headache is splitting my skull, and I would rather leave this house in solitude. But thank you."

Lavinia hurried out of the room, her breathing labored. She put on her cloak and dashed out of the house. *Blast.* She couldn't even manage to be civil among her friends. She truly had no place in this world anymore.

She drew the corners of her cloak closer together. It was a rather warm day, but she felt chilly nonetheless.

Now that she was away from the comfort of her friend's home, her previous fears had returned. She looked both ways to see if anyone was lingering nearby. A few carriages were passing by, a man was walking his dog, and a boy rushed past them, but nothing out of the ordinary. Nobody suspicious was in sight.

She swallowed. Perhaps she should have left the townhouse right away. At least then she might have had some luck in noticing if anyone suspicious was nearby. Someone who might have followed her from her home and handed her the note.

It was unlikely. Whoever sought to threaten her was probably too smart to lurk around the house. They probably paid someone else to deliver the message. But perhaps they were watching, gauging her reactions.

In that case, she needed to act as composed as she normally would. She took a deep breath, looked both ways one more time, and ascended into her carriage.

As the vehicle jolted to a start, she opened the note again.

It was still the same, not that Lavinia expected it to change.

Five words written in a precise scrawl, and then a mangled signature that looked like it spelled *Everly* or *Erelius*? Nothing made sense.

And why would a nefarious person sign their real name, anyway? They were probably trying to throw her off their scent. Or perhaps that wasn't a signature at all. Maybe that was a threat? *Ever die*? What kind of threat was that?

Lavinia turned out the window and watched the changing scenery for the rest of her journey.

Even if she deciphered the text, what were her choices, truly? In the world she lived in, without a man to offer her assistance, she was completely helpless. And she had no man to save her. Especially not after what she'd done.

Dane would, her heart whispered. *Dane would protect me.*

Dane—the Duke of Kensington—would offer to help her in a heartbeat. He had been the one to save her from her troubles ever since he'd walked into her life. And a helping hand from a duke would be invaluable in her case. But what she wanted from Dane was more than a helping hand. And if she could not have that, she'd rather not have him at all.

The carriage drew to a halt, and Lavinia jolted forward. She fixed her hat on her head, drew her gloves tighter onto her hands, and exited the carriage.

She looked around again, but no one suspicious was about. Or at least, she didn't notice anyone.

Lavinia entered the dank old house and slowly ascended the steps. The closer she came to the family wing, the slower her steps became. She finally stopped before the door to her father's chamber.

Her heartbeat accelerated, and her breathing was erratic.

What if he'd awakened? What if he was awake, and he

remembered everything?

She reached for the handle, carefully twisted it, and opened the door.

Chapter 2

Lord Birch's chamber was as dark and musty as always. The windows were draped tightly, not letting in even a sliver of light. A couple of candles were burning on the bedside table, adding to the musky scent.

The doctor had insisted it was imperative for Lord Birch's recovery that there was neither draft nor the sun.

Lavinia stepped inside the room, closed the door behind her, and had to wait for her eyes to adjust to the darkness. She blinked a few times, and then scanned the room.

Her father lay sprawled on the bed, covered with blankets. He looked gray, almost wax-like. Was he even still alive?

Something shifted in the shadows, and Lavinia shivered from fright before realizing it was Matilda, Lavinia's stepmother, sitting by his bedside.

Lavinia only saw Matilda's outline. She was wrapped up in a shawl in a warm room, but she always had a shawl around her to hide the bruises. She was only a few years older than Lavinia but had the unfortunate fate to marry a man twice her age, who had a propensity for drinking and losing his temper.

"Has he awakened?" Lavinia whispered.

Matilda shook her head. "No, dear. He mumbled something in his sleep, just as he did before, but nothing intelligible. The doctor came to check on him, though."

"Did he say anything new?"

"No. Just the usual. To keep Lord Birch comfortable and warm, wait for him to be lucid again." Matilda's voice broke on the last syllable, and she wiped away the tears. "I know that he'd been a monster, but I do not want him to die."

Lavinia hurried toward her stepmother. "He shall be fine, I am certain," she whispered, although she was lying. It didn't look like her father was going to recover and one part of her was glad for it. Another part was utterly terrified.

"I don't want that sin on your soul," Matilda whispered again, looking directly into Lavinia's eyes.

Lavinia's heart squeezed. She didn't want it either. She couldn't believe any of this was happening at all. Her fingers touched the note, still lying crumpled in her pocket.

"Matilda, did anyone else come by the house while I was gone?"

"Besides the doctor, you mean?" Matilda wiped her tears again. She thought for a moment before shaking her head. "No, no one else. Why?"

Lavinia chewed on her lip, wondering if she should tell her distressed stepmother about the note. "No reason," she finally said, not being able to conjure the words to speak her worries aloud. What would it help? Matilda was so distressed that the note would just send her into a catatonic state.

Matilda took Lavinia's hands in hers. "Did you speak to

Annalise about this? About your father's state, I mean?"

"I wanted to, but…" Lavinia shook her head. "The other ladies came earlier than I anticipated. And Olivia brought her cousin by marriage with her. That woman has gone through a lot recently. Her husband died, and well, she needs a distraction, not more problems piled on top of her. I did not think it was appropriate to bring up my woes at that moment."

Matilda nodded and looked at her husband's body. "So, what are we to do now?"

There was a beat of silence as Lavinia also studied her father's withered form. Formerly big and strong, with a rounded stomach and a frown on his face, he did not look threatening at all in his current state. "I suppose we can wait," she finally said, thinking of all the possibilities that awaited them ahead. "We don't know who will inherit the title next… Perhaps it will be someone good. Perhaps we shall not have to suffer after all."

Lavinia did not believe her own words. When had luck been on her side?

"Perhaps," Matilda agreed with the same dry tone of voice. She did not believe Lavinia's reassurances, either.

* * *

A thin, tall man in a snow-white wig and overly colorful clothing approached the table and looked around. "May I join you, gentlemen?" he asked jubilantly.

Sebastian gave him a quick glance. The newcomer's dark green coat might have been called fashionable a couple of decades ago, but the bright orange waistcoat and golden ornamentation at the sleeve edges were just a perfect example of poor taste. As a connoisseur, Sebastian found the fashion sense of most of the English aristocracy lacking at best and ridiculous at worst. However, what did he care about another's fashion sense as long as the gaming table was full and so were his coffers?

Sebastian tipped his head and leaned back in his chair. The more players, the more coins he would win. The man did not seem like he had a lot of money, not based on his clothing, anyhow. But Sebastian was ready to give him the benefit of the doubt. Once.

"I do not think you want this one joining us," William, one of Sebastian's oldest acquaintances, said from his seat. The golden-haired devil grinned widely. "Do you have anything to pay for your losses, Atwood?"

The man whom William called Atwood sat gingerly and called for whisky. "I am here, am I not?" he asked in an offhand manner.

"That doesn't say much to me," William retorted.

"Let us play, shall we? I do not have all night to…" Sebastian paused and chewed on his cigar while searching for the right word, "banter. I only came here for your money."

All the men around the table laughed.

"Touche," Lord Ian McAllistair, a profligate drunkard and a notorious rake, cried, then hiccuped and asked for another glass of whisky.

Sebastian, the new Marquess of Roth, was neither joking nor exaggerating when he had claimed that he was there only for the money of the men sitting at the table. He was a very talented gentleman, if he claimed so himself, and was good at everything he decided to apply himself to. And that was his curse.

He was a good student at school, which helped him get into the Academy of Science in Paris; he was an expert swordsman and he was lucky at gambling, if you considered calculating odds either gambling or being lucky.

Sebastian pushed the fish into the middle of the table and sat back. He'd win this hand as well, he knew.

Lord McAllistair and the other gentlemen, Lord Cunningham and Mr. Townsend, were simply too drunk to care. Well, Lord Cunningham and McAllistair had an added distraction keeping their attentions occupied: the rounded bosoms of the ladies of the night. That's what gaming hells counted on. Get a curvy wench and a couple of bottles of drink in front of a gentleman and he'd forget his own name, let alone the game he was playing. Any gentleman, that was, except for Sebastian.

The only other person at the table who was lucid and alert enough to pay attention was William. But he always let his opponents win. On purpose. And that was part of his charm.

William was a duke's bastard, and as such, he was scorned by high society. Nevertheless, he always found a seat at their table and an invitation to their soirees, mostly due to his charming disposition. Either that or by blackmail.

Sebastian had known William for many years. He wasn't a friend exactly. But in England, he was the closest thing Sebastian had to one.

Sebastian steepled his fingers as he waited for the dealer to turn over the last card. *The valet.*

"The valet of spades," the dealer announced and everyone groaned, while Sebastian swallowed a smirk. He collected his winnings and let the dealer deal another round of cards, now including the newcomer to the table.

Yes, Sebastian was good at everything, but only one thing ever brought him joy, and it wasn't gambling.

Despite his winning streak, sitting in the smoke-filled gaming hell was not where he'd rather be at the moment. Of course, he enjoyed winning money, but he was here tonight more out of boredom than anything else.

Since Sebastian was young, the thing he enjoyed doing most was painting. Everything else was just a distraction. And he'd rather be in his studio painting at the moment, except that ever since he had returned to England, he had never once picked up a brush.

It could have been that the heavy weight of the responsibility to his newly inherited marquessate was crushing him. Or it could have been the burden of trying to marry off his niece while protecting her from the damaging influence of her other relatives. Perhaps moving to England from his beloved France was misery enough. Either way, his muse was gone, and there seemed to be no way of getting her back.

So, here he was, counting cards, and winning money from the drunken fools.

"Say, Sebastian, how is it that you win every hand?" William asked, chewing on his cigar. "Or am I supposed to call you Roth now that you are an earl?"

"A marquess," Sebastian said in an offhand manner.

"Right, right, I always forget."

One side of Sebastian's mouth kicked up in a smirk. "No, you don't. You never forget. You know everything about everyone."

"Wrong," William said as he sipped on a glass of whisky. "I know everything about the people whom I might profit off. *You* are useless to me."

"And isn't that splendid news?"

"Which means," William turned toward Atwood, "that I know you have not a penny in your coffers."

"Then you do not know everything, after all," Atwood bragged. "But if you are curious, I am about to come into a hefty inheritance."

Sebastian wasn't curious, nor was he the least bit interested, but he noticed McAllistair's eyes glint with intelligence and comprehension for one brief moment before he asked, "What is that?"

He immediately downed another drink and turned toward the wench on his lap, so perhaps that glint Sebastian thought he saw was a figment of his imagination.

"Have you not heard?" Atwood sniffed. "Lord Birch is gravely ill, and I am next in line to inherit. That's why I am back in London."

William scoffed. "Birch? He doesn't have two pennies to rub together. He might be the only person who owes more people than you do. And I should know; he owes me too."

Atwood chuckled. "That's not what his solicitor told me tonight."

"Spoke with him already, did you?" William chuckled.

"I'm out," Lord Cunningham said and asked for more whisky. "The game is not loving me tonight."

"The game is never loving me when Roth is at the table," Townsend said. "But deal me in one more time. Wouldn't want Atwood losing by himself."

Everyone laughed again. Sebastian pulled on a tight smile and asked for another drink.

The last deck dealt and cards turned over revealed another win by Sebastian. Well, this wasn't exactly the exhilarating feeling he had expected, but at least his coffers were still full.

He stood and tipped his head. "Gentlemen."

"You can't be leaving! The night has just begun," McAllistair protested with a deep slur.

"Did you not lose enough, my friend?" Sebastian asked with a slight smile.

"Perhaps I did"—a hiccup—"but Atwood certainly didn't."

"I'll win from Atwood when his inheritance is actually… inherited." It was late. Sebastian's mind refused to work properly.

William laughed. "You need to learn the proper use of English if you want to stay in England for a long time."

Lord forbid. Sebastian smiled tightly.

"I'll play you some other time, Roth," Atwood said.

"If you don't run out of things to wager off," William supplied.

"Oh, I would not worry about that." Atwood waved a hand. "As soon as old Birch kicks the bucket, I will be in possession of a beautiful young ward who will bring me a lot of golden coins."

Everyone laughed while Sebastian paused. "What do you mean? It's not like you can wager off a lady."

Atwood winked. "She is like a prized mare. Birch might not have known what to do with the brat, but I will certainly find a use for her. And for her small but lucrative estate."

"Is that what Birch's solicitor told you?" William asked, pretending boredom. Sebastian knew better. William was never bored. He was always paying attention to information that might be beneficial to him someday.

"Perhaps." Atwood grinned unpleasantly. "Who would have thought that old and greedy Birch left anything for his daughter, but here we are." The man winked and then called for a wench to come and sit on his lap.

Sebastian averted his nose from the display. Whoever the poor lady was who had the unfortunate fate to become Atwood's ward, he only felt pity for her. As for the men like Atwood, who treated their dependents like cattle, he only felt disgust.

But he couldn't waste his energy on the scum, or on the poor soul who was under his care. Sebastian's only priority now was to give away his niece in marriage to a man who was not as callous as any of the gentlemen sitting around the table. Once he'd done that, he'd be free to travel back to the Continent where he belonged.

Chapter 3

Lavinia clutched her skirts in her hands as she ran up the stairs.

"Don't you run from me, you stupid chit!"

Lavinia clasped the banister and looked over her shoulder, her breathing labored. Her father, the old, heavy drunkard, was taking two steps at a time and was gaining on her really fast. "Please, Father," Lavinia pleaded, although she knew it wouldn't do any good. Her limbs felt heavy, and she could not move any farther.

"Please, what? Do not punish you for acting like a strumpet? For defying my orders?"

He grabbed Lavinia by her hair and pulled so hard that Lavinia let go of the banister and fell backward. The moment felt suspended in time as she fell for a few long moments that seemed like forever.

Finally, she landed with a loud thump but not on the floor. On something soft. Lavinia scrambled to her feet and looked down at her father.

He was lying there in a pool of his own blood.

"This is not how it happened," she whispered to herself. Some-

thing was off.

"You killed me, daughter," her father croaked, looking at her with bloodshot eyes.

Lavinia took a breath to scream, but no sound emerged. She reached to grab for the railing, but there was nothing there. She was caught off balance and fell into an abyss, nothing but darkness surrounding her.

"You killed me, daughter!" Her father's voice sounded around her, echoing in the void.

Her head was spinning as she kept on falling and falling until she was shaken by an earthquake or thunder... a knock?

Lavinia jumped awake and hit her elbow against the back of the chair. She rubbed the aching place and looked around the dark, dank room.

She was still in her father's sickroom. The curtains were shut as they had always been, not letting in the light, so she had no idea what time of day it was.

Another knock.

Lavinia glanced in her father's direction before hurrying toward the door.

"Lady Lavinia. Lady Payne is here to see you," the butler said as Lavinia opened the door.

"Oh… Good. Thank you." Lavinia swept a lock of hair away from her face. "I'll be down in a moment."

She threw one last look at her father's body on the bed and walked away to take her morning ablutions.

A few moments later, she entered the parlor, where her friend Annalise paced restlessly. She turned as she heard Lavinia come in, and her face split into a wide smile. "Oh, good, Lavinia. You are well."

Lavinia smiled and walked toward her friend. "Of course,

I am well." She stretched out her arms and took Annalise's hands in hers.

"I was so worried. I am sorry I couldn't come yesterday, but I was so tired after the guests left. I just wanted to take a short nap before coming to you, but—"

Lavinia shook her head with a smile. "No apologies necessary. Truly. Please, sit."

With a nod, Annalise settled on the settee. "Thank you, darling, but you looked so distressed. I wanted to come as soon as I could, but…" She placed her hand on her slightly rounded stomach. "Blake doesn't let me out of the house if I am feeling even a little out of sorts."

Lavinia bit back a smile. "I am glad that he is so protective of you. How are things with Blake?"

"Meow!" A little black cat sauntered into the parlor as if she owned the place. She walked lazily across the floor, then rubbed her body against Lavinia's skirt.

"Oh, Miss Gale! How glad I am to see you!" Annalise exclaimed.

The animal didn't pay any attention to her former mistress. Instead, she jumped and effortlessly settled on Lavinia's lap. Lavinia scratched her silky fur, and the cat started to purr.

"Well, I see that I made the right decision in leaving Galinthias with you."

"I have to say, I am glad you did. She got me through some very difficult times."

Annalise peered into Lavinia's eyes, but she tried to evade her friend's perceptive gaze. "Will you tell me what is wrong?"

Lavinia swallowed. "It's my father… He is dying."

"Oh my God!" Annalise looked very perplexed. "What happened?"

"He… He fell… Two nights ago, after Lady Carlyle's ball."

"Oh! I am so sorry, Lavinia." Annalise scooted to the edge of the settee. "I know you have no love for the man, but he is your father."

Lavinia nodded frantically. "You are right. I have no love for him, and I am not exactly grieving. Perhaps it makes me a horrible person, but—"

"It doesn't. The man treated you like a rug. He beat you!"

Lavinia grimaced. "I know. It's just… I don't know. I still feel…" Lavinia bit her lip and looked away.

"Guilt?"

Lavinia's head snapped up. How would Annalise know?

"It is natural to feel guilty that you're not feeling grief for your father," Annalise assured her, and Lavinia let out a breath of relief.

"Thank you. And yes, you might be right. This must be the guilt I am feeling, or at least it could be a part of it. But to be honest, I am very confused at the moment. But also if he dies…" Lavinia shuddered.

"Someone else will take over the title."

"Yes, and knowing my father, I will be left with nothing but the clothing on my back. Both my stepmother and I."

Annalise stood and started pacing the room. "Are you certain your father is going to die?"

Lavinia shook her head. "The doctor doesn't know how to help him now. He tried a few remedies, but nothing seems to work. I fear he might perish soon, although I am not certain fear is the right word for what I am feeling either."

Annalise stopped and faced Lavinia directly. "We need to tell Kensington. He will be able to help. He always—"

"Please, do not involve Dane in this," Lavinia said, her heart squeezing at the mere mention of him. There was a huge boulder stuck in her throat, and tears burned at the back of her eyes, threatening to erupt. "He has always been the one to save me my entire life. And I-I just don't want him to be involved in this."

Annalise nodded, understanding clear on her face. Her brows were drawn over her eyes, and she bit her lip. She was concerned for Lavinia. She always had been. Annalise was like a sister to her. But this time, her expression held a note of pity, which Lavinia hated. But how could anyone not pity her? The man she loved, the only person who could make all her problems go away, was the man she could no longer look in the eyes because he had married one of her closest friends.

"Very well. But if we do not involve Kensington… There is only one solution that comes to mind, and I am not certain you are going to like it." At Lavinia's inquiring expression, Annalise continued, "We need to find you a suitor… A husband."

Lavinia expelled a breath. It wasn't a surprising conclusion at all. Lavinia had thought about that numerous times while sitting beside her ailing father. Of course, she'd have to marry sooner or later. But she didn't expect it to be this soon and under these ghastly circumstances.

She had always thought that if she ever had a husband, it would be Dane. She had spent her life waiting for him and, in the end, he had married someone else. And now that he was wed, she did not even have time to properly grieve the loss of her dreams.

The pain was still raw to the point it felt as if Lavinia was bleeding from the inside. But what was the alternative? Spending her life as a penniless spinster? Finding work?

There was nothing she was trained to do but be a lady. And even in that, she wasn't perfect. No, she could not put it off any longer. She needed to marry someone soon.

But whom could she marry on such short notice? It wasn't as if suitors were beating down her door. She was unmarried for a reason.

Not that Lavinia had ever applied herself to find a suitor. She had been waiting for Dane to ask her for most of her life, and she was grieving the rest. Now that she had no other choice, she would have to apply herself. Because whether her father died or awakened, being married and away from her home was her only salvation.

Her gut tightened as she remembered the note lying in her dresser. Well, she'd have to figure out what to do with that later. For now, her first priority was to leave home as soon as she could.

She inhaled deeply. "I agree."

Annalise's eyes rounded. "You do? I thought you would resist the idea."

Lavinia shook her head. Now it was her time to start pacing. "I know why you would think so, but despite everything, I am not foolish. I cannot afford to cry into my pillow now that my future is in jeopardy. And in the world we live in, the only protection I can count on is finding a powerful husband. Or any husband, for that matter."

Annalise chewed on her lip thoughtfully. "I shall ask Payne to help me. He has many friends, albeit most of them are either married or rakes. However, I am certain we can find at least one proper gentleman for you."

"Thank you," Lavinia agreed with a nod. "I don't know what I would do without you."

"That you never have to worry about." Annalise stood, approached Lavinia, and took her hands in hers. "I shall talk to my husband and then we can arrange for an intimate dinner party and introduce you to a few decent men. I am certain Caroline can help, too. Her cousin, the new marquess—" Annalise's eyes lit up, but Lavinia could not even continue listening. The idea that she could marry Caroline's cousin, while Caroline was married to Dane, was sickening.

"Please, Annalise." She raised a staying hand. "Please, do not involve Caroline in this either."

"Lavinia…" There was that look of pity again in Annalise's eyes, and it pained Lavinia to see it.

"I am not against Caroline helping me. I… Despite everything, I am not angry with her or with anything, for that matter. But I can't wed someone related to Dane even by marriage. And I'd rather Caroline didn't know of my predicament."

"But she could help." Annalise's features were troubled, and Lavinia wished she didn't worry her friend.

"I know she can. And she is a good friend. But we do not know what her relationship with Dane is like. I do not want him to know of my woes. And I do not want him finding out. Confiding in his wife is a risk I cannot take. I do not want either of them involved. My heart will not take this."

Annalise nodded, although Lavinia could see the doubt in her friend's eyes. "Very well, we shall not involve Caroline in this. But… she is worried about you. She was heartbroken when you left the nuncheon so soon. I realize now it probably had nothing to do with her, but that's what she thought."

It had everything to do with her. Lavinia bit her lip. "I do not mean to make her suffer. Despite what transpired between us, I just want to move on from this pain and grief, but it is not easy, Annalise."

"You won't be able to avoid her forever, dear. Especially if you start attending social events."

Annalise was right. That moment in Annalise's parlor had been awkward and uncomfortable. But cutting Caroline out of her life was almost impossible if she intended to continue being in the same social circle with her. Caroline and Dane were constantly at every function and avoiding them would be like avoiding the rain in England.

However, if Lavinia failed to secure herself a powerful husband, this issue would simply cease to exist, because if everything failed, she would not be part of anyone's social circle. "I shall make peace with her, I promise. But right now I have bigger things to worry about."

"Very well," Annalise agreed slowly, as if not quite ready to concede to Lavinia. "If that's what you think is best, I shall respect that. But having a duchess by your side in times of difficulty is not the worst thing in the world."

"I know. And I've had a duke by my side most of my life. I think it's time I've dealt with my issues on my own." *At least for now.*

Lavinia had too many issues to concentrate on. It felt as if everything was spiraling out of control. She'd deal with everything later.

One issue at a time. First, she needed to find herself a husband.

Chapter 4

If one wanted to get married in London's high society, just like in any other major European city, one needed to host a ball.

Balls, soirees, and dinner parties were not things that Sebastian enjoyed. He preferred a small, dank studio smelling of oil paints, a tiny, filthy laboratory stinking of dead animals and sometimes even rotting human flesh, or a fencing club smelling of human sweat.

Incidentally, most of Sebastian's favorite activities brought with them an unpleasant smell. Not to say that the crowded ballroom was as fresh as the outdoors, because it was not.

Mixed in with the sweet flowery scent were the odors of human sweat, unbathed flesh, and rotten breath. Everything to make him miss his laboratory.

No, the issue here was the number of people surrounding him.

Sebastian quite preferred his solitary existence. True, fencing required a partner, but even then there was just one person to concentrate on, to vanquish, and get on with his day.

This… this was torture.

But before he could return to his life of solitary leisure, there were a few things he needed to take care of.

First, he needed to put the marquessate back on its feet and hire enough managers to look out for things in his absence; second, he needed to hire someone to watch over his aunt if she refused to return to the Continent with him, and third, although, technically, this was the most prominent matter, he needed to marry off his niece, Victoria.

And that's precisely why Sebastian was in his current state of irritated boredom. He was throwing the last ball of the Season in his niece's honor.

"I can't believe I haven't been here before." The familiar, deep voice sounded close behind him. A little too close.

Sebastian stepped away in irritation. "Do you make it a habit to sneak up on people?"

"Only when it is easy to sneak up on someone," William said with a wide grin. "You used to be a difficult one to catch off guard. England does not become you."

"That we agree on. And I shall cheer the day I finally leave this dreadful place."

William raised a curious brow, but he didn't say anything, for at that time, the butler announced from the top of the stairs, "Princess Victoria Mecklenburg-Schwerin."

All eyes turned toward Victoria, standing there in her cerulean blue gown with golden ornaments, white ruffled sleeves, and an intricate coiffure topped off with a feathery ensemble. Her attire was truly ridiculous, but Victoria managed to make it look elegant. She could be wearing a burlap sack, and nobody would bat an eyelash.

She smiled widely and floated down the stairs.

The stunned silence in the ballroom was quickly replaced by whispers and exclamations of surprise. A princess! And a marquess's niece! And beauty to boot.

Victoria had everything to recommend herself: looks, intelligence, an enormous dowry, and high standing in society. No, Victoria truly should not have any issue finding a prosperous match. Even if this was the last event of the Season.

He didn't expect her to get betrothed tonight. But every guest at the ball was invited to his house party that would take place a week after the ball. And Victoria's introduction made it clear that his house party would be teeming with guests.

Sebastian had planned everything just so he would be able to find his niece a match as efficiently as possible.

"So, that sweet little bird is the niece of yours I've heard so much about?" William watched Victoria with a predatory glint in his eye, and something about the note in William's voice made Sebastian's spine crawl unpleasantly.

Sebastian turned on him sharply, almost knocking over his wine glass. "Do not even think about it," he warned.

"Think about what?" William asked, innocently sipping on his wine.

"Charming my niece, or talking to her, or even looking her way."

"Why not?" William asked carelessly. "She is of marriage-able age. She is out in society."

"She needs an advantageous match," Sebastian growled. *The last thing she needs is a bastard, a rake, and a criminal to boot.*

"Who is more advantageous than me?" William smirked,

still looking at Victoria.

Sebastian cocked his head so he would catch William's gaze. He looked him squarely in the eye and made his expression as serious as he could. *"Everyone."*

Without waiting for William to retort, Sebastian turned on his heel and stepped closer to the stairs to greet his niece.

As soon as her feet touched the floor of the ballroom, a swarm of gentlemen surrounded Victoria, asking for introductions, to fetch her a cup of ratafia, or to squeeze their names onto her fan for a dance.

No, marrying off Victoria would not be an issue at all.

As Victoria made her way to the middle of the dancefloor with her first partner, the flock of gentlemen around Sebastian dispersed and, in turn, a group of young women with their eager mamas took their place.

This wasn't the first ball Sebastian had attended, and he was already used to all the attention, but today was different somehow. Perhaps introducing his niece into society made him more respectable in some people's eyes. The fact that she was a princess, a duke's daughter, even if a foreign one, perhaps spurred people's interest. Either way, the crowd was even more suffocating than usual.

Sebastian fiddled with his cravat, hoping for more air, as he watched Victoria dance with her suitor and tried to ignore the women surrounding him in as polite a manner as possible.

Lucky for him, Frau Elinor, his aunt, made her way toward him and engaged the guests in a conversation, leaving him free to spy on his dancing niece.

Victoria had already been adept at dancing when she arrived in England. She spoke several languages and was quite well-read. But the English aristocracy had its own rules.

And while Sebastian was excused for committing *faux pas* from time to time, society looked with a much harsher eye upon a lady. And Sebastian didn't want anything to stunt Victoria's progress.

As such, Victoria, who was already past the age of coming out, had to spend a few weeks with the Duchess of Kensington before her first foray into society and learn English versions of dances and polite manners. This was also the reason Sebastian anxiously watched his niece, fearing a slight misstep would ruin her chances of an advantageous marriage.

But his fears disappeared as he saw her glowing on the dancefloor. She was confident, and she was enjoying herself.

The Duchess of Kensington had done well.

"Look at all these beautiful ladies," Frau Elinor said by his side. "I know you are worried about Vicky, but she is incomparable. She will not have trouble finding the right suitor. You, on the other hand, need to start improving your behavior."

Sebastian raised a brow. "Do I?"

"You just rudely dismissed a few very agreeable young ladies by ignoring them and their mothers. You must have an interest in at least one of them. If we are to stay in England—"

"But we are not to stay in England, Frau Elinor," he said firmly.

She threw him a sidelong glance. "I am too old to travel anywhere."

"You traveled here well enough."

"Not well enough," she enunciated clearly. "Do you not remember how tired I was? You might still remember me as a young, energetic woman who took care of your household back in France, but I am getting old, Bastian, dear. And feeble."

Sebastian scoffed. "You might be adding in age, my dear aunt, but you are anything but feeble."

"Flattery will get you nowhere, Bastian. Besides, you will not leave Vicky all alone, will you?"

Sebastian threw a glance toward his glowing niece. She was enjoying all the frivolities of the ball; it seemed. Or else she was extremely hot and needed a breath of fresh air.

The thought of leaving Victoria behind didn't cause him joy. He had been looking after her since she was in leading strings—or at least it seemed that long—and he was not about to let any harm come to her. But he wanted what was best for her. And best for her meant to keep her as far away from her relatives on her mother's side as he could.

Perhaps, the best course of action would indeed be to wed her to some titled, wealthy man, who would worship the ground she walked upon. And by the looks in English gentlemen's eyes, it wouldn't be difficult to find that person here.

Sebastian threw a dark glance toward an old, stocky lord who watched Victoria with a lecherous gaze.

"Excuse me, Frau Elinor." He made two steps toward the offending gentleman and discreetly, but painfully, jabbed him with an elbow.

The man blinked up at him, looking confused.

"I think you dropped something," Sebastian said darkly.

The man looked around. "I don't think—"

"Your manners, perhaps. For I do not think it is entirely polite to ogle a young lady the way you are doing."

A lady, who was probably his wife—though she could have been his daughter—gasped by his side. Sebastian returned to his aunt's side and continued to scan the crowd.

"With your rude behavior, you are bound to frighten away not only your prospects but Victoria's too," Frau Elinor said crisply.

"I do not need any prospects. And any man easily frightened away by me is not worth Victoria's pinky finger, much less her hand in marriage."

Frau Elinor pursed her lips. "So, you are determined to bundle me away and leave poor Victoria all alone as soon as she marries, then?"

"No, she won't be alone. That's why we are here, are we not? To find her the perfect husband."

"Perfect? No such thing. In your stead, I would pay attention to—Oh, good evening, ladies." Frau Elinor's mouth split in a feigned smile as three women approached them. A mother with her marriage-aged daughters, no doubt.

Sebastian tipped his head in greeting and turned toward the dancefloor. He was glad that his aunt was interrupted from her diatribe as he had no interest in listening to more of her complaints. He would rather watch out for Victoria than verbally spar with his aunt on whether he should remain in England after Victoria's wedding. Sebastian had made his plans. Now it was a matter of ensuring Victoria played her part in them.

Another lady approached them with her young daughter. After the greetings were exchanged, Lady Cunningham turned toward Sebastian. "Lord Roth, how lovely for you to sponsor your niece into English society. Is it true then that your brother is a duke?" She fanned her red cheeks, studying him carefully, sizing up his worthiness to marry her daughter, he presumed. The other ladies leaned in closer to hear his answer.

"I am sorry to disappoint. Alas, the duke is only a cousin on my mother's side. However, I think of Victoria as my niece."

"Oh, and she is no doubt very lucky," the woman said, still eyeing Sebastian as if he were a piece of fish and she the cat. Was she looking for a husband for her daughter, or perhaps a lover for herself?

Either way, Sebastian was not interested.

"I see you are not dancing," the woman continued.

"You have quite the observation skills," he replied drily.

She frowned but didn't relent. "My daughter is an excellent dancer. Perhaps you two should take to the floor."

It was rude to turn down such a blatant invitation, but the last thing Sebastian needed was to dance with a simpering debutante and try to hold an intelligible conversation with her.

"I am afraid my duty is to chaperone my niece today, not to dance."

Frau Elinor raised a haughty brow. "And am I a potted plant? Please, do not refuse a dance on Victoria's behalf. I am a more than capable chaperone. I raised her, did I not?"

Sebastian stifled the urge to raise his eyes heavenward. "Of course, my dear aunt," he said and offered his arm to the young lady.

She gleefully accepted, and they both ventured onto the dancefloor. Sebastian only hoped the majority of the dance was over, so he could bow out soon.

Chapter 5

Nobody had expected Lavinia to be here at the last ball of the Season. Actually, nobody would have expected her to be here if anyone paid any attention to her. But here she was at the periphery of the ball and not an eyeball directed her way.

Perhaps nobody knew about Lavinia's father's condition. And even if they did, would they care? Gossips certainly would have found a word or two to describe Lavinia's impetuous actions. How does a lady go gallivanting around ballrooms when her father is on his deathbed, after all?

Annalise didn't give Lavinia much of a choice, however. Determined to help Lavinia avoid a worse fate, she brought her to Lord Roth's ball, hoping to find her a suitor. In one night.

Lavinia would have scoffed if she had any strength left. At the moment, all she could do was follow Annalise's instructions and drink awful ratafia, just to keep her hands busy.

She needed to keep her mind busy, too, but that was a more difficult task.

Her mind kept circulating around three issues, one thing buzzing louder in her mind, and then quieting down only for her to torment herself with the other issue.

The note, her father's condition, and the Duke of Kensington.

The three issues kept plaguing her, although she could not do anything about them at the moment.

She looked down at the beautiful purple gown she wore, remembering the day she'd bought it.

Caroline had helped her pick out this gown. She had selected the color, the design, the bodice, everything down to the petticoats to help Lavinia win over a suitor. What neither of them had realized at that moment was that the suitor Lavinia had been trying to impress was already Caroline's betrothed. Oh, how amusing fate was sometimes.

And now Lavinia wore the same gown as her last attempt to ensnare another man. Any man.

How would she ever be able to flirt with anyone when Dane was in attendance? How was she to walk around him, laugh, and smile while he was there with his wife on his arm?

Tears threatened to erupt from her eyes, and her fingers bunched into fists by her sides. There was nothing she could do about that, just like there was nothing she could do about the gown she was wearing. It was the only piece of clothing that was remotely appropriate for the occasion. All her other gowns were overworn, dull, and did nothing to flatter her figure.

Lucky for her, Dane had not made an appearance at the ball yet. It didn't mean, however, that he would not and not knowing was driving Lavinia slightly mad. She would rather be prepared.

"Oh, Lord, this was a mistake," Lavinia whined out loud.

"Why do you say so?" Annalise asked, sidling closer to her.

"There is no way I am going to find myself a husband in one night."

"Perhaps not, but you might find a suitor who will start courting you just as the Season closes. Otherwise, how else are you going to find a husband once the Season is over?"

"It's not only that, Annalise. I cannot concentrate on anything. I am afraid that—" *my father will wake up while I am away, or worse, die.* Although she wasn't sure that his death was the worse of the two possible eventualities. She wasn't going to say any of this to Annalise, either. As luck would have it, she didn't get to finish her sentence anyway, because just then the butler announced the arrival of the Duke and the Duchess of Kensington, and all eyes were directed toward the main staircase.

Dane, tall, broad-shouldered, and positively handsome, appeared at the top of the stairs in all black, except for his white stockings, shirt, and cravat. His wig was fashionably trimmed and hung about his shoulders, a shocking contrast to his bronzed face. Lavinia knew that he spent a lot of time outdoors, riding and visiting his tenants. Even in London, he had never been idle. Lavinia knew too much about his activities. She used to collect every piece of information about him and then asked him everything she didn't know on occasions when he came to visit her household.

Seeing him made Lavinia's heart sore, but it sank as quickly as it rose, for by his side, hanging on his arm, was his wife.

Caroline had a demure smile on her lips as they glided down

the stairs. She was wearing a fashionable golden gown with ocean-blue overskirts and bodice. Her hair was collected on top of her head, and a few strands crowned her face in soft waves. She had thick mahogany red hair that glinted and glimmered in the candlelight, shimmering into gold from one angle and dark brown from another. Combined with her marble-white complexion and her soft rosy lips, she looked stunning.

Damn her. She and Dane looked absolutely gorgeous together.

Tears sprung to Lavinia's eyes, and she blinked them back, unwilling to cry in front of the entire ballroom—not that anyone was paying her any heed. All eyes were on the newly arrived couple. And who could blame them?

The perfect couple. Everybody whispered behind their fans, talking about just how well suited they were. Lavinia's breaths accelerated; she would not be able to hold on to her tears any longer.

"She looks crushed," Annalise whispered softly by her side.

Lavinia blinked and turned toward her friend. Was Annalise speaking of Lavinia in the third person?

No, she was carefully observing the new arrivals, too.

"Who are you talking about?"

"Caroline," Annalise said simply, then turned toward Lavinia. "Dear, I know that Caroline is not your favorite person right now, but just look at her. She isn't happy at all."

"Well, she didn't have to marry him," Lavinia said, with a little too much bitterness seeping into her voice. Why would Caroline be unhappy? She got what she wished for. Hell, she got what Lavinia wished for.

"She thought she did," Annalise insisted. "I truly think you need to speak to her."

"I can't, Annalise. Please, do not start with your mission to get us to be friendly to each other again. I am not angry with Caroline, I promise. I am just—" Lavinia swallowed and clenched her fingers into fists by her side.

"Grieving. I know. But so is she. Do not forget that she'd lost the uncle she adored a few months before her wedding."

Lavinia looked at Caroline again. She was smiling politely and speaking to people approaching her. She did not look crushed to Lavinia. But she didn't look happy either.

However, Caroline had always been able to mask her true feelings. She only showed whatever she wished to show. Was there truth to Annalise's words? Was Caroline unhappy?

But Dane placed a hand on the small of Caroline's back at that moment and smiled down at her. That look in his eyes could not have been a lie. They were close.

Devil take it. Of course, they were close. They were husband and wife. They shared a life, a duchy… a bed.

Lavinia turned away and squeezed her eyes shut. "I can't," she whispered and pushed her way out of the ballroom.

She needed some air. Perhaps in time, she would find the grace from deep within her to make peace with the entire situation. Perhaps in time, she would be able to look Caroline in the eye and smile… genuinely, or at least insincerely. Perhaps in time, she could forget about Dane and squash the love she had carried for him for over a decade.

Perhaps someday. But that day was not today.

* * *

Sebastian stood on the balcony, looking into the distance,

his gaze unfocused. He had barely finished the dance with Miss Aurora Cunningham when more ladies surrounded him—mothers wanting to introduce their daughters and asking for a dance.

He had managed to leave the ballroom and found refuge in the gentlemen's retiring room, only to be accosted right outside the door.

He couldn't take it anymore, so instead of returning to the ballroom, he had evaded everyone and slipped onto the balcony, hoping for some privacy.

He could only hope that Frau Elinor was doing a good job of chaperoning Victoria. Sebastian didn't need some leech taking hold of his niece while he was cowering on the balcony.

Sebastian took a deep breath of fresh night air. The darkness enveloped him and, for the first time in days, he finally felt as though he was back in France.

Perhaps if he stood there for a few more moments, the same calmness as the one that had lived within him throughout his entire life—but which deserted him in England—would return. All the noise that came with becoming a marquess crushed Sebastian's mind and left him feeling winded and tired even if he hadn't been doing much all day.

The constant communication with members of the aristocracy, conversing with managers, attending balls and other social events, all the while preparing Victoria for her coming out and fending off advances of marriage-minded young ladies just crushed Sebastian's spirit.

Now, standing on the balcony, he wished more than anything that he could be back in his little studio, back in his home in France. He would lock the door, block out all the noise, and paint.

Only even if he did lock himself in the studio right now, he wouldn't be able to draw a straight line. The muse had deserted him at the same time as the peace of mind left him.

The door to the balcony squeaked open, followed by the swishing of the skirts and chaotic breathing.

Wonderful. Someone had followed him here.

Sebastian slowly turned toward the lady, who had so rudely disrupted his peace, when she crashed full-body into him.

Sebastian caught her against him, his hands on her arms. He froze for one long moment as the lady flailed, trying to disentangle herself from him. Or at least he hoped that was her aim, for she had enticed an entirely different reaction from him.

Sebastian knew that he needed to push her away, demand her to leave, or perhaps, chastise her for rushing onto dark balconies without a chaperone, no less! But to his shame, he couldn't quite make himself move.

Well, one part of him was happily moving in an upward direction. *How typical.*

A simple press of a woman's ample bosom against his shirt, the scent of lilies emanating from her hair reaching his nose, and his male flesh hardened as if he were an untried youth.

How predictable indeed.

After a moment of brief enjoyment, Sebastian's brain returned to its functioning self, and he took the young lady by her arms and pushed her away from him.

"It is truly unbecoming how brazen young ladies have become in pursuit of a title," he said as he pulled his frock closer together to avoid the young lady seeing the effect she'd had on him.

"Pardon me?" Her voice was breathless, and she seemed

truly confused.

"You are pardoned," Sebastian said drily. "But please, make haste and find your chaperone before we become miraculously compromised."

"I beg your pardon?" the lady repeated again, but this time louder, her expression growing astonished. "Are you insinuating that I came here in hopes of ensnaring *you* as my husband?" She waved her hand toward him, and her face held a note of confusion.

"Are you professing your innocence, then?" Sebastian cocked his head to the side and finally studied the woman in front of him.

She was a tiny little thing. Her head barely reached his sternum. But she was deliciously rounded in all the right places; her breasts almost spilled out from her bodice, her body was tightly hugged by the fabric, and although he couldn't see it, he was certain her bottom was filling her skirts perfectly, too. No wonder his body had reacted to her the way it had. She was every man's dream.

Her face was shaded so he couldn't tell exactly what she looked like, but the light from the ballroom outlined her in such a way that would make her a perfect subject to paint. The glowing curls on her head crowned her face just so, the golden line of light emphasized the side of her neck and traveled down to her milky white breast tops, illuminating the perfect little birthmark, just above the edge of the bodice, leaving the mind to imagine what view awaited him under the clothing.

"Let me assure you that marriage, especially to you, was the last thing on my mind upon coming here."

Sebastian's eyes snapped back into focus as he met the lady's defiant gaze. "Then why did you come here, unchaperoned, to a balcony clearly occupied by a lonesome gentleman? *A marquess.*"

The lady crinkled her nose adorably. "I have not seen you, and contrary to what you might believe about yourself, there is no halo around your head with the word marquess written over it." She gestured with her hand, exactly where in her opinion that writing should have been located. "The truth, however unpleasant to you, yet clear to everyone else, is that you are just as invisible as any other mortal man. I have not seen you before entering the balcony and I wish I wasn't seeing you now."

A halo! What a wonderful idea. Sebastian could easily imagine it being painted over the lady's head. Come to think of it, the lady would be a perfect model for an angel, leaving out the fact that she was currently aggravated, and her words resembled a devil's more than an angel's. However, Sebastian was not angry with her anymore.

Perhaps she came here to ensnare herself a rich husband. Could he fault her? No.

But should he stand here and contemplate her heavenly visage and her viper-like sharp tongue? Probably not. That way lay disaster.

"Let me disappear out of your way then," he said and stepped toward the doors.

"Splendid," she bit out and leaned her hands against the balustrade.

She didn't even glance his way. Perhaps it was true. She hadn't come here seeking him out. She came here seeking solitude. Just like he had.

Disappointment filled Sebastian's chest.

Why disappointment? Wasn't it what he had wanted? To

be invisible to marriage-minded misses?

In this case, for some unfathomable reason, he wished it was the reverse.

* * *

The sound of footsteps and the swishing of a skirt alerted Lavinia that someone had entered the balcony. A female someone. The scent of lavender preceded its owner. Lavinia wiped her tears discreetly just a moment before Annalise appeared by her side.

Thank god it was Annalise and not some gossipy matron bent on chastising her for leaving the ballroom, or worse yet, Caroline.

Something squeezed at the center of her chest just thinking of that possibility.

"I am sorry this is so difficult for you," Annalise said quietly.

Lavinia swallowed the bitterness inside her. "I wish I did not feel this way. I want to be supportive of Caroline, I really do. I haven't even congratulated her on the wedding. I am such a terrible friend. But I can't... I just can't look at her at the moment."

Annalise stared into the void for a moment before saying, "You are not being a terrible friend. You need to take care of your feelings, too. Caroline is very understanding, trust me. Whenever you're ready, she will hear you out."

That just made it worse. Of course, Caroline would be understanding. Of course, she didn't approach Lavinia, because she knew Lavinia needed space. Of course. Caroline was perfect. While Lavinia... Well, at the moment, Lavinia was bitter, and she loathed herself for it.

Why can't I be just a little bit like Caroline?

"But I saw you talking to Lord Roth," Annalise added cheerfully.

Lavinia furrowed her brows and turned fully toward her friend. "Who?"

"Lord Roth." Annalise blinked innocently.

"The Marquess of Roth? Caroline's—" *The marquess.* Lavinia paused, her features frozen in surprise. That rude, arrogant man who'd accused her of following him onto this balcony was Caroline's cousin! Well, *he* certainly was far from perfect.

"Yes, you just stumbled upon him on this balcony. It looked like you conversed."

A burst of nervous laughter left her lips. "Conversed. Yes. The man accused me of trying to ensnare him in marriage."

"He… What?" Annalise's mouth hung open in shock.

"Yes." Lavinia nodded and turned back to look out over the grounds below.

"Well, I suppose it was warranted. You should see how he is being hounded today by unmarried young ladies."

"Well, not by me," Lavinia whispered.

There was a beat of silence. "Maybe he should be."

Lavinia stared out into the void, not quite hearing or comprehending Annalise's words. "What?" she asked absently.

"Perhaps he should be hounded by you. He is young, very influential, and handsome."

Lavinia's face scrunched up in disgust. *Are you serious?* "He is Caroline's cousin. And more than that, he is rude and unpleasant company."

"Maybe today, but you would be too if you had to elbow your way through a throng of young ladies hunting him down like a dog. He is having a house party in a week. And every guest at tonight's ball is invited. Perhaps we could go, and it would be a perfect place for you to get to know him better. Perhaps—"

"Annalise… Just… no."

Annalise didn't protest. She didn't say anything else, but she didn't leave Lavinia's side either, while the latter continued staring into the night, enjoying the light autumn breeze.

Lavinia wished there was a world beyond this one where she didn't have to marry, where nobody was threatening her, and nobody wanted anything from her. A world where she could just enjoy herself without worrying about anything.

She would love to disappear into a world like that.

The orchestra started another melody, reminding Lavinia that the world she dreamed about was out of her reach.

"Annalise… Please, take me home."

Annalise wanted to protest, but she must have seen the resolution, or perhaps a deep sorrow, in Lavinia's eyes, so she smiled and nodded.

Chapter 6

Lavinia stood outside the door to her townhouse, breathing deeply. Before, at the ball, she'd thought that staying there, watching Dane dance with Caroline, worrying about her fate while everyone was oblivious to her plight, was the worst kind of torture. But now that Annalise's carriage had driven off, leaving Lavinia behind, there was no recourse but to enter her father's townhouse, and she couldn't make herself move.

What Lavinia realized—what she should have realized earlier—was that she didn't want to go to her father's residence, she'd just wanted to leave the ballroom. It hurt watching Dane and Caroline together. It hurt being lonely when all her friends were happy with their spouses. And it hurt having nowhere to come home to.

Yes, she did have a roof she resided under, but it wasn't home. Anywhere Lavinia went, she was a burden. Of course, her friends didn't think of her that way, but they had their new lives now. She was just a part of their former life, a part that still kept them miserable when they could have been gloriously happy if they'd just left her alone.

So she stood on the doorstep of her father's house, wondering if another blow waited for her inside. Had her father awakened and spoken, or was she to spend another night grappling with the unknown?

Annalise was right. It would be better for everyone if she just married.

But finding any suitor who would be willing to wed her required a concentrated effort on her part to seem agreeable. That was a state she was not sure she could achieve under the circumstances.

Lavinia took a fortifying breath. She couldn't stand outside of the townhouse forever. She needed to enter.

The door swung open as soon as she knocked, and her butler's pale face stared at her gloomily.

"My lady," he said as he took her cloak. "The new master has arrived."

Lavinia's entire body tensed. "The new master?"

"Yes. Lord Birch's successor."

Lavinia froze, her mind going blank. The new master. She hadn't thought he would be here before her father's death. She hadn't thought about what awaited her when he arrived. *Oh, Lord.*

But before she could ask anything from the frightened servant, light steps sounded in the hall, and then a tall, confident-looking gentleman appeared before her.

"Ah, you must be Lady Lavinia," he said with a smile. Laugh lines appeared at the corners of his eyes, and he seemed genuinely delighted to meet her. "Pleasure to finally make your acquaintance."

Lavinia sank into a slow curtsy. "The pleasure is mine."

"I know you must be tired, but I wish to speak to you, if you do not mind. I shall not take much of your time, gentleman's promise."

The smile never left his face, but goosebumps crawled up Lavinia's spine. Something about the gentleman did not inspire trust. It might have been his good-natured countenance, for that was something extremely rare in the Birch residence. Or it could just have been Lavinia's natural mistrust for any man—any man except for Dane, that was.

"Of course." Lavinia tried for a smile.

The gentleman waved a hand, silently asking for Lavinia to proceed. "We can speak in my—Pardon, in Lord Birch's study, if you please."

With a slight nod, Lavinia hastened to the indicated room.

Lord Birch's successor pulled up a chair for Lavinia, and once she settled in, he rounded the desk and sat opposite her.

"I arrived a few hours ago," he said. "And I wished to speak with you right away. I was surprised to find out that you were out, not that I can blame you. Having a sick relative is definitely a chore, is it not?"

Was this his way of chastising her for leaving her ill father's side? "I have been spending my nights by my father's bed. My stepmother and I alternate. It is impossible for one person to be cooped up in a sickroom all day long without earning a migraine."

"I do not disagree. My mother—her name was Rose—passed away just a few months ago. It was a trial," he said. "We lived in a small coastal town, and I was the one looking after her until her final day…"

"My condolences."

"Thank you. " He cleared his throat and steepled his fingers on the desk as he watched Lavinia under hooded eyes.

Lavinia shifted uncomfortably. "When did you say you arrived in London?"

"I arrived in London last night. But I didn't want to bother you so very late, so I came to call upon you today. A few hours ago, as a matter of fact. Lady Birch told me that I had just missed you, so I assume I arrived a few minutes after you left for the ball. How was it?"

"Pleasant enough." Lavinia made her face expressionless.

She felt as though she were being studied. Judged. She didn't want to divulge any information to the person in front of her. Granted, she had no reason to distrust him. But she couldn't tamp the feeling of dread creeping up her spine... It made her shudder. Perhaps it was just the result of her eventful—if short—night at the Roth ball.

Now that Lavinia sat in front of her new guardian, she wondered if she'd needed to apply herself more during the ball. Perhaps she'd have to travel to Lord Roth's house party in search of a husband, after all. But what if this gentleman in front of her wasn't an adversary at all? Perhaps he would help her with her woes.

Lavinia tried to squash the hope inside her.

"Well, I would like to speak to you about the situation at hand," her guardian said.

Lavinia blinked innocently. "Of course, Mr..."

He smiled one of his slow smiles. "Apologies. Where are my manners? I'm Mr. Atwood. But you can call me Cousin George."

Lavinia swallowed. "A pleasure... Cousin George."

"Splendid. I do not mean to tire you, but I do have some

concerns I'd like to address as soon as possible. For instance, I have to tell you that I scoured the books today, and I found that your father was—is in dire straits."

"I am aware of that," Lavinia said calmly.

"Well, were you aware that he was on the precipice of landing in debtor's prison?"

Lavinia licked her dry lips. This did not sound good at all. "I am afraid I wasn't aware of that."

"And now that I am your official guardian, I find it my duty to control Lord Birch's expenditures until or if he ever awakens."

"I understand. To be honest, I wish someone had done it sooner. That way, perhaps I would have a dowry."

Mr. Atwood studied her carefully, from the top of her coiffure to her skirts that disappeared under the desk. "I have to say that I am very surprised to see you enjoying such nice silks if your father was in as dire circumstances as his ledgers indicate."

Lavinia swallowed and crossed her arms across her chest. "This was a gift from a friend."

"And if your father does not awaken," her guardian continued as though she had not spoken, "I might have to make some very difficult decisions."

"Such as?"

"Such as marrying you off to one of the men your father owed the most."

Lavinia's eyes widened, and her heart chilled. What did he say? *He* would marry her off to one of her father's creditors? Lavinia knew most of the people Lord Birch owed money. She had met them on a few occasions, and none of them were pleasant enough to speak to for five minutes, let alone marry for her entire life. There was a buzzing in her ears as Mr. Atwood continued speaking.

"I know these are not the most perfect of circumstances. I understand you were unaware of most of the issues in the household, but I will not keep you in the dark. I think you are intelligent enough to know the truth and make your own decisions."

"Make my own decisions?" Hadn't he *just* said he was about to force her to marry the man her father owed the most?

"Yes. I am not a cruel man. And I would never do anything to hurt you. But I am not about to land in prison for something your father is at fault for. However, I am certain you won't resist marrying an earl, an heir to one of the oldest dukedoms. He is widowed and would appreciate—"

A widower. An old earl… One of the lecherous gaming companions her father owed money to. Lavinia barely heard the rest of Mr. Atwood's words, before blurting out, "But I am already betrothed."

Lavinia clamped her lips shut, but it was too late. The words were out, and there was no way back. Did she want to take her words back? What else could save her from her nefarious guardian's plans?

"To whom?" He drew his bushy brows over his eyes. He was obviously taken aback by her announcement and not too happy with it, either.

Lavinia squirmed inwardly. She should have known that this question would follow, and perhaps she would have dwelled on it if the lie hadn't slipped so easily off her tongue. But what else was she to do?

Either way, she needed to give this vile person a name, or he'd know she'd made everything up. Suddenly, all the names of people she knew disappeared from her addled mind.

The only name that echoed through the chambers of her empty heart was the name of the man she could not call. *Dane...*

No, Dane was married. Were she to name him, her guardian would know that was a lie. Who else did she know who was unmarried? Well... there was another gentleman whose name came across her mind, but she would be damned before she named him. The rude and arrogant marquess who thought she was out to ensnare him.

She tried really hard to remember someone, anyone else, as using Caroline's cousin's name was the worst idea ever.

"Well?" Mr. Atwood prompted.

"It's the Marquess of Roth," Lavinia blurted and then put on a tight smile. *What have I done?*

Mr. Atwood sat back and steepled his fingers, studying Lavinia carefully. "Is that so?"

"Yes," Lavinia hastened to add. "It's a rather new circumstance, and I didn't want to announce it prematurely."

"Prematurely?" Brows drew over those calculating eyes.

"By that, I mean that no official announcement has been made. We were going to do that during the upcoming house party." Suddenly, all her lies were falling into place.

Lavinia was glad she had attended the ball, for if she hadn't, she wouldn't have known who to name as her sham fiancé. However, then she wouldn't have locked herself to the arrogant marquess who happened to be Caroline's cousin!

Couldn't she have named someone else? Anyone else!

Her head was splitting from conflicting thoughts, and she placed her fingers against her temples.

"Hmm, that explains the secrecy. However, I find it rather

strange that I do not see a marriage contract between you two, and I looked through all the documents in this study." Mr. Atwood waved his hands at the surrounding books.

"Right." Lavinia nodded, frantically searching her brain for an explanation that would suffice. "We didn't have time… in fact, he only received my father's permission the night before the accident. He-Father was supposed to speak to his solicitor the morning of… of…" Lavinia choked and closed her eyes.

"I understand. I did not mean to make you upset," Mr. Atwood said in the driest of tones. "One more question if you please, and I shall not deter you any longer."

Lavinia blinked up at him just as he extended her a crisp white handkerchief. Lavinia looked at it strangely before taking it. Did he think she was crying? Mr. Atwood didn't pay her any attention, so she folded the handkerchief on her lap. It had a tiny rose embroidered at the corner, and Lavinia found it soothing to run her finger over the stitching.

"What question?" Lavinia asked quietly.

He drummed his fingertips on the desk and watched Lavinia with narrowed eyes for a moment. "So Roth did not mind that you have no dowry?"

Did he wait for her to disprove the fact that she had no dowry? Hadn't she just told him that she indeed had none because of her father's spending? Did the man think that was a lie? That she had a hidden treasure somewhere? She almost scoffed aloud.

However, there was more to Mr. Atwood's interest, and she decided to be cautious with her answers. She crushed the handkerchief in her hands and answered in as composed a manner as she could, although her voice was shaking. "I-I am not privy to these kinds of details, I am afraid. This discussion was between Lord Roth and my father. But since I have not heard otherwise, I assume everything was settled."

Mr. Atwood held her gaze for one long moment before leaning back in his chair. "Thank you. I do not have any further questions. I didn't mean to deter you, but some things cannot wait." He flashed a toothy grin. "You are probably tired, so feel free to… Well, have a pleasant night. I shall deal with your wedding plans accordingly. I shall need to discuss things with my… Lord Birch's solicitor, of course, before any papers can be drawn. And of course, I shall call on Lord Roth—"

"Oh, but he's already left," Lavinia hastened to interrupt. "I mean… He said that he'd leave for his country seat with the light of dawn, right after the ball. For the house party. If you wish to speak to him, it'll have to be there." *What are you doing, Lavinia?*

"A house party?"

Lavinia nodded. *Blast!* Now he'd want to attend a house party with her. "Yes, we planned to announce our betrothal at the end… Although I am certain it's in bad taste to do it while my father is ill—"

Mr. Atwood suddenly perked up. "Oh, you are right, my dear. There is no need for any haste. Surely Roth would not make an announcement without papers being drawn. Yes. Go to the house party. Enjoy yourself while I tend to things here… There is no reason for haste. After all, old Birch might wake up any day and walk you down the aisle himself. Wouldn't that be splendid?"

Lavinia stretched her lips into a parody of a smile. "Indeed."

Something about everything that transpired just now didn't sit well. But Lavinia stood, curtsied, and left the study.

"Oh Lord," she whispered to herself as she hurried up the stairs and toward her room. "What have I done? *What* have I done?"

Lavinia berated herself for the lie she'd told. She then berated herself for telling Mr. Atwood about the house party. There was a calculating glint in his eyes, and if his goal was to marry Lavinia off to someone Lord Birch owed money to, she was certain he would plot to do just that.

If she'd thought that getting married was a necessity before, now it had become an eventuality. She needed to marry and fast.

But whom? Certainly not Lord Roth.

She needed to speak to Annalise. If only morning would come sooner so she'd be able to call on her friend. Annalise would know what to do. She always did. She'd help her get out of this horrid situation. Because no matter what happened next, Lavinia wasn't getting out of it unscathed.

Lord Roth would not marry her. That was obvious enough. But when Mr. Atwood found out that there was no betrothal, there would be hell to pay.

Chapter 7

"Please make haste, my dear aunt. Otherwise, we shall be late," Sebastian said as Frau Elinor slowly applied butter to her toast.

"How can we be late to our own estate, pray tell?" she asked in a croaky voice. "The house party is not for another week, and we had made all the preparations necessary before we left for London. The Duchess of Kensington made sure of that."

"Yes, I am aware. But I shall not put it past our staff to forget something. Unless I check on it myself, I shall not trust it. And you haven't even prepared your valises. I told you to let your maid prepare them yesterday. Now the poor thing has to wait for you to eat before she can help you do that."

"I am not going to hurry while I eat, Bastian. I was not raised in a stable. I cannot rush the process."

Sebastian pulled out his pocket watch for what seemed like a hundredth time that morning. He looked at the time and promptly forgot what it was. Not that it mattered. The light was getting away from them.

In truth, Sebastian was irritated because he hadn't slept well the entire night. He had been plagued by the visions of an angel-faced young lady with the body of a goddess he had briefly come across during the ball. He didn't even know her name. But her features outlined by the candlelight lived vividly in his mind.

Sebastian had spent the entire night fantasizing about putting her onto the canvas, mixing different colors of paint to come up with the perfect golden halo to adorn her face. Line after line, he had imagined painting her until he finally couldn't take it anymore. So he had gotten up, had climbed the stairs to his studio, had found an empty canvas, and had started painting.

Only with the light of dawn had he stopped.

No, his painting wasn't finished. There were too many missing pieces. He hadn't seen his mysterious lady's facial features, her body had been shrouded in shadows. So he had to abandon his painting unfinished.

And now, his eyes red and smarting, he sat by his aunt, who wasn't at all hurrying to get on with the trip. But if they didn't leave soon, Sebastian would fall asleep right there at the breakfast table.

Sebastian took out the timepiece and glanced at it once more. "What could be taking Victoria so long?"

"She is young. Let her rest!" Frau Elinor said with a wave of her toast.

Victoria flew downstairs at that exact moment wearing her morning gown, her hair disheveled but her eyes shining like two bright stars. "Is there breakfast? I am starving!"

"Of course, there's breakfast, *Kindchen*," Frau Elinor cooed and snapped her fingers at a footman standing by the wall. "What would you like? Oh, mayhap we should ask the cook to make you the warm buns she made a few days ago, do you remember? They were lovely!"

"We are late!" Sebastian enunciated, but there was no point. The women were chattering away happily, not paying him any heed. "Frau Elinor, I think I explained that it is imperative—"

"How wonderful, *Kindchen*!" Frau Elinor exclaimed and put her hand to her heart. She turned to Sebastian. "Our dear Victoria is in love!"

"You are?" Sebastian frowned.

Victoria's cheeks flushed red. "I wouldn't say in love, no. But I found a gentleman worthy of my attention."

"Oh! I thought this day would never come!" Frau Elinor said dramatically.

"But I've only had my come-out yesterday," Victoria protested with a frown.

"Now, now, *Kindchen*. Eat. You need your strength for the trip."

"Frau Elinor is right. Please, eat." Sebastian pulled up a chair. "And who is the lucky gentleman, may I inquire?"

"No, you may not inquire," Victoria said carefully. "Or at least, you can inquire as much as you like, but I shall not answer."

Sebastian's frown turned thunderous. "Why not?"

"Because, my dear uncle, you shall just frighten him away. I've only just met him."

"I am not a brute." Sebastian was slightly offended but also proud of Victoria's remark. She wasn't wrong. He *would* frighten them away.

Frau Elinor raised a brow. "Indeed."

"What? I do need to know who he is so I can investigate him and tell you if he is a worthy man to waste your time on."

"And that is why I shall not tell you," Victoria said and sipped on her tea unhurriedly.

"Victoria," Sebastian growled.

"Yes, Uncle?"

"You are not to fall in love without my approval."

Victoria chuckled into her napkin until her chuckle turned into a coughing fit.

Frau Elinor tapped her on the back. "There, there, *Kindchen*. Why women want to marry is beyond me. Then they get stuck with these unbearable creatures their entire lives!"

Victoria straightened and cleared her throat. "I know why *I* need to marry," she said calmly.

"Are you still so determined to carry out your family's wishes?" Frau Elinor asked with a worried frown.

"You know that I am," Victoria said softly.

"And for your goal, you need an advantageous match. Which brings us back to the gentleman you met yesterday," Sebastian supplied.

"He is of noble birth, so please, do not fret, Uncle. I am not as dimwitted as I might seem."

"I know you are not dimwitted!" Sebastian threw up his hands.

"Let Victoria bask in the light of her infatuation for a little while, Bastian. You do not need to threaten her right away."

"Threaten?"

"Uncle, Frau Elinor." Victoria looked from Sebastian to his aunt. "I might be young, but I know my goals. I know what I want, and I know exactly the kind of husband I need. But this gentleman hasn't even started courting me yet. I shall tell you his name as soon as the occasion warrants it."

A footman brought a plate full of breakfast foods and placed it in front of Victoria, while Sebastian pondered her words. Victoria was young, bright, and impressionable. At nineteen years old, she did not know her mind and could be easily manipulated, especially by the people she trusted, like her family. That was an issue for another time. But meeting an influential older man in England had the potential to lead to a disaster. Truly, whose idea was it to marry off women at such a young age?

Of course, he knew whose. Men's. Because young and impressionable were exactly the kinds of ladies the majority of them needed in order to persuade anyone to marry them. Otherwise, the vast majority would end up without wives.

"You might think that you know what you want, Victoria, but I know what you need and, more importantly, whom you do not need. I know these men."

Frau Elinor let out a burst of hoarse laughter. "My dear, nephew. You think you know everything," she said, then winked at Victoria conspiratorially. "Now remember something about men, *Kindchen*. Men always think they know better. While they are as lost as babes when it comes to the affairs of the heart."

"Thank you, Frau Elinor." Victoria chuckled and continued eating heartily.

"For example, did any lady catch your eye last night?" Frau Elinor finally turned to Sebastian.

"As I said, I am not here to seek a bride," Sebastian grumbled, while he mentally ran through every man Victoria had danced with the night before.

She'd smiled at everyone and was polite and gracious, but

he hadn't noticed any special attention she paid to anyone. Was Frau Elinor right? Was he so clueless as to not notice when Victoria bestowed her attention on some unknown man? Or perhaps it had happened when he was evading all those marriage-minded ladies, or hiding out on the balcony with his beautiful muse…

"But if you do, you will tell us first, will you not? Because you might think you know more about men, while we definitely know more about women," Victoria added with a giggle.

"Yes, we shall find you a perfect bride," Frau Elinor chimed in.

Sebastian raised his eyes heavenward. Thank the Lord he was not looking for a wife. Dealing with two women was difficult enough.

* * *

"I am in big trouble!" Lavinia announced from the doorway of Annalise's parlor.

"Lady Lavinia for you, my lady," the butler said behind her back.

Drat. She'd flown past him in the hallway, forgetting all her manners or anything, really. Her cheeks and ears heated in embarrassment. It wasn't like her to act so rudely.

"Thank you, Crane," Annalise said with a sheepish smile and a nod toward the servant. She looked at Lavinia, and her expression immediately turned concerned. "Please, come in. What's the matter?"

"I am in deep, deep trouble," Lavinia repeated quietly as she walked into the parlor room and plopped onto a settee.

"Oh, if that's the case, then we shall need some tea. And perhaps brioches? They always put a smile on your face, and it seems like your day could use a bit of brightening," Annalise said with a smile in her voice.

Lavinia covered her eyes with her palms. "I can't think about brioches or tea or any other pastry. I can't think about anything!"

"No pastries? The matter does sound dire."

Annalise tried to lighten the mood. Lavinia understood that, but she didn't have an ounce of humor left in her at that moment.

As soon as Annalise ordered the servants to bring them some tea, she sat across from Lavinia, and prompted gently, "Tell me."

Lavinia lowered her hands to her lap and directed a pleading gaze toward Annalise. "I met my new guardian."

"Oh." Annalise grimaced. "Blake told me he'd heard rumors that he arrived. And by the look on your face, I can deduce that he is not a pleasant fellow?"

"No!" Lavinia stood and started pacing. "He is even a bigger monster than my father ever was. He pretends to be nice and caring, but he told Matilda that if Father doesn't awaken, she should clear out her room and leave."

"He said that?"

Lavinia paused and looked out the window, her gaze unfocused. "Not in so many words, but his implications were clear. And he dressed it up as though he had so much concern for her, as though he was being benevolent. He implied that my father was the monster for not leaving her a widow's stipend—which is true, he is a monster—and that he was saying this only to give her time to collect her belongings.

Because once my father passes, she will not have a home anymore."

"Oh, no! Well, tell your stepmother—actually, I shall just tell her myself, so she'll know she is not imposing—but she always has a home with us. Here."

"Thank you, my dear friend. But it seems like she is not the only one who would have to impose upon your hospitality."

"What are you talking about?"

Lavinia raised her eyes to her friend. "My guardian… He said that my father owes quite a lot of debt… And upon inheriting the title, Mr. Atwood would be taking on that debt, which could potentially land him in debtor's prison. And that the only way to avoid that would be for me to marry the man my father owes the most!"

Annalise's face whitened, and she seemed as if she was about to swoon. Lavinia hurried toward her friend and sat next to her. "Oh, please, Annalise. Do not swoon. I shall not let him send me off to an old, lecherous, and greedy man."

Annalise placed her hands on her stomach and swallowed. "Of course not. We shall not allow that. And Blake will threaten your guardian if need be—"

Lavinia smiled and placed a hand over Annalise's. "Let's not make hasty decisions, shall we? I"—she grimaced—"I actually made enough mayhem on my own."

Annalise blinked up at her. "How?"

"Well…" Lavinia inhaled a deep breath. "When Mr. Atwood told me about this… um… prospect. I… uh… Well, I told him that I was already betrothed."

Annalise opened her mouth to say something, then shut it and smiled. "Quick thinking."

Lavinia threw up her hands. "Too quick! My brain didn't

even process the thought before it was on my lips. What have I done?"

The maid entered at the moment with a tray of tea, sweetmeats, and pastries. She settled them on a small table, and Lavinia took this time to compose herself and sit across from Annalise. At the sight of brioches, her heart soared. She'd refused them a moment ago, but now that they were in front of her, her mouth watered.

The Birch house was always lacking pastries, because of her father's frugality when it came to his daughter. That's why Annalise made sure to supply Lavinia with treats every time she came to her house.

"And what did your guardian say to your statement?" Annalise asked as she poured them each a cup of tea.

Lavinia took a pastry in her hands and fiddled with it before putting it down on her plate. "He asked me who I am betrothed to, and I… Well, I panicked, and I told him the first name that came to my mind." She bit her lip and grimaced.

Annalise leaned forward. "Whose name did you say? Don't tell me you said Dane! Because bigamy is still a crime in England."

"Of course, you're right." Lavinia folded her hands on her lap and looked down, unable to meet her friend's gaze. "You are correct. Dane's was the first name that came to my mind, but I resisted. I told him the second name that came to me…"

"Well?"

Lavinia licked her lips. "I said I am betrothed to Lord Roth."

"Wha… Why?"

"I don't know!" Lavinia stood and covered her face with her palms before starting to pace again. "I don't know. But

I panicked, and the only thing I could think of was our conversation before and how I said Lord Roth would be the last person I'd want to marry. But when I panicked, my brain just stopped working, and I got stuck with his name on my lips, and when Mr. Atwood demanded I answer… Well, what was I supposed to say?" Lavinia finally drew a breath. "Who else was I going to name?"

Annalise bit on the tip of her thumb in thought. That action from the proper Annalise meant that she was truly distressed. And that was the last thing Lavinia had wanted to do. Especially since Annalise was in a delicate condition and wasn't in the best of health. And now Lavinia had poured down all her worries onto her. But who else was she going to tell this to? Not Caroline, that's for certain. And Olivia was dealing with her cousin's problems. She didn't have time for anyone else's.

"I should… I should just tell him the truth. Or I should tell him that I decided to break off the betrothal."

"Do not be ridiculous." Annalise's words were soft, almost a whisper, but Lavinia heard them nonetheless.

She stopped pacing and looked at Annalise's frowning face. "Pardon me?"

Annalise looked up at Lavinia. "Sit, please." Once Lavinia complied, Annalise continued, "The lies you told might not have been ideal—"

"Indeed," Lavinia scoffed.

"However, it does buy you some time. But first, tell me everything you told your guardian."

Once Lavinia recited her conversation with Mr. Atwood verbatim, Annalise tapped her lips with the finger and then focused her gaze on Lavinia. "Here's what we are going to do.

We are going to go to that house party. And you are going to try and seduce Lord Roth into proposing."

"What? But I don't want… And even if I did… To seduce? I don't even know—"

Annalise lifted a staying hand. "Who is better, Lord Roth, or whoever your guardian has prepared for you?"

Lavinia grimaced. "Neither?"

"You might not have a choice. Lavinia, all my life you have always been the rational one, the sane one," she said with a chuckle.

"Compared to you, perhaps." Lavinia's lips curled in a smile, but she quickly sobered. "But I cannot be rational about this, please, understand."

"You *can* be rational; you can be stone-hearted. You gave up the man you loved for me, when Payne disappeared, or did you forget?" When Lavinia didn't answer, Annalise scooted closer to her and covered her hand with hers. "You have to be rational in this, my dear. I want you to be happy more than anyone else. Perhaps even more than you." They both chuckled, and Lavinia shook her head.

"It was easy giving up Dane for you. But it was painful seeing him marry Caroline. It was easy contemplating my life alone. But marrying Lord Roth? Caroline's cousin? I just… I can't imagine it, Annalise. I can't imagine those visits to Kensington's townhouse, the teatime with the family, seeing Caroline carrying Dane's babe… It's just… it's too painful to contemplate." Her heart squeezed, and her stomach churned at the mere thought.

Annalise nodded thoughtfully. "Well, there might be an alternative."

Lavinia looked up at her friend in surprise. "Alternative?"

"We could go to that house party under the guise of announcing your betrothal to Lord Roth, and while we are there, you'll find someone else to charm. But, Lavinia, I do not see any other option for you."

"How about running away to France?" Lavinia said with a feigned smile.

She was only half-joking. Truly, leaving England seemed like the only feasible plan at the moment. Especially considering the note...

If someone truly knew what had happened that night in her father's townhouse, there was no telling what they could do. They'd warned her once, and she dreaded what the second note would say if she ever received one. Given time, they could make her life a living hell. She needed a more long-term plan than a sham betrothal. But Annalise was right. The house party would give her time to plot.

Chapter 8

Lavinia had spent the first few days of the journey looking out the window and worrying about things she had no control over. She worried about Matilda and if Lavinia's new guardian would harm her in Lavinia's absence. She worried if Matilda would receive a missive from the same people who sent Lavinia that ominous note. And she worried about Annalise, who was riding beside her, jolting in the carriage and feeling sick.

Matilda had insisted that Lavinia go to the house party and find herself a husband. She had insisted that marrying someone, anyone other than whom Atwood had in mind, was the best course of action for both Lavinia and Matilda. And in a way, Lavinia agreed. Only she was not confident in her feminine charm, and she thought that Matilda had more chance of entrapping a husband than Lavinia did.

However, Matilda was not a widow yet. Lavinia was their only hope.

Lavinia did not tell her stepmother about the note. She

didn't tell anyone about it, because she did not want to worry everyone even more than she had already had. As it was, she already felt guilty for burdening everyone around her with her problems. Even poor Miss Gale, Lavinia's cat, was currently jolting in her basket on the seat next to Lavinia, looking irritated and not comfortable at all.

Usually, while riding in the carriage with Annalise, the two women chattered away, discussing anything and everything, but this time, it had been different.

Annalise was ill, and the carriage was forced to halt every few hours so she could empty her stomach and walk around. This was a blessing for Miss Gale, who preferred to run around the field rather than jolting in a carriage, but it also worried Lavinia and Annalise's husband.

"You shouldn't be on this trip at all," her husband muttered for the tenth time after another unplanned stop.

Annalise settled closer to him and burrowed into his side. Payne was right. She shouldn't have been. Lavinia was the only reason she was.

Lavinia felt terrible for forcing her friend to attend the house party while she was feeling this unwell. But Annalise was stubborn and nobody, not even her husband, was able to tell her what to do. After all, if Annalise didn't go, Lavinia would not be able to go either. She needed a chaperone. And since Matilda was looking after the sickly Lord Birch, Annalise was the logical answer. The only answer.

"I know myself, Blake," Annalise said quietly. "This shall pass, and all will be well in a few hours."

Lord Payne ran his hand over Annalise's forehead, then pressed a kiss to the top of her head. "Sometimes I wish you weren't this stubborn."

"Isn't that why you love me?" Annalise asked with a soft smile.

"Yes, against my better judgment." Payne pressed another kiss to the top of her head.

Lavinia smiled, watching the couple snuggle on the plush carriage seat as Payne cooed over his wife and tried to make her feel as comfortable as he could. Annalise lay her head on his shoulder, took Payne's hand, and rested it on her slightly rounded stomach.

"I feel better already," she whispered.

Lavinia looked out the window. She felt as though she was imposing on the couple's private moment, which she was. But she also loved seeing how tender Payne was with Annalise, how much he cared for her, and how much he didn't care if *he* was uncomfortable as long as Annalise had everything she needed and desired.

Lavinia wanted that. She craved that connection, that tenderness, such care from another human being to the bottom of her soul. A large boulder settled in her throat because she knew she wasn't going to get that.

At best, she would get a cold marriage of convenience. At worst, she'd end up alone. Because the only hands wrapped around her that would give her comfort, the only voice saying her name that would sound soothing, were those of a man who was unattainable to her.

Lavinia shook her head and blinked back the tears. She needed to stop thinking about Dane. And she'd better start preparing herself for a marriage that would simply save her life, and not the one that would bring her happiness. Because at the moment, her priority was surviving.

On the last day of the journey, Annalise miraculously came

down to breakfast, rested and rejuvenated. She felt well enough to send her husband outside to ride on horseback so she and Lavinia could chat privately.

"Oh, this happens all the time," she said to Lavinia once they were back in the carriage and on the way to the house party. "One day everything is bad, and I am casting up my accounts, pardon for the gruesome description. But the next day I am well and strong. I just hope the babe is born healthy and not with these strange bouts of illnesses." She covered her stomach with her hand.

"You shouldn't have traveled," Lavinia said softly.

"Nonsense!" Annalise waved the issue away. "I would have been just as ill at home."

"But you would have been at home, in your bed. Comfortable."

"Everything turned out fine, did it not?"

Lavinia grimaced. "Well, not yet. We haven't even arrived."

Annalise chuckled good-naturedly. "Oh, you worry too much."

"And you worry too little," Lavinia chastised her friend.

"I think you and Blake worry about me enough for all three of us. Besides, somebody has to worry about you. That reminds me. I wanted to speak with you about something."

Lavinia raised her brows. "Yes?"

"Well, I've been thinking about your predicament since the last time we saw each other, and I think I have a solution for you."

Lavinia furrowed her brows in thought. What predicament was Annalise talking about? Lavinia had plenty. "Apologies, my mind is scattered. What problem are you talking about?"

Annalise gave a short laugh. "About your betrothal, dear. If you do not want to marry Lord Roth, I have another suitor for you."

"You do? Who?" Lavinia scooted closer to Annalise.

"Marcus." Annalise smiled, clearly very pleased with herself.

"Marcus?" Lavinia scrunched up her face in thought.

"Yes, Blake's cousin."

"Oh, the Earl of Payne—I mean, the gentleman who was the Earl of Payne, while your husband—"

"Yes!" Annalise interrupted giddily. "Him. Anyway, you know that he came to London from the Continent to take care of the Payne earldom when Blake disappeared. And, as soon as Blake returned, Marcus became very adamant about going back. Only he can't, since he invested all of his funds into Payne's lands when he inherited them. Long story short, Blake had promised to help him get his investments back, including his art collection. But until then, he is forced to stay in England. But perhaps if he had a wife, he'd consider staying—"

"No!" Lavinia exclaimed excitedly. "No, it's perfect."

And it was perfect. If Marcus were to marry Lavinia and move back to the Continent, that would be the most perfect solution to all Lavinia's woes. No strange notes would follow her there, or so she hoped. She would avoid running into Dane and Caroline at every function. Why didn't she think of this earlier? She should marry a man who would leave the country shortly after their wedding!

Of course, Lavinia would miss her friends, especially Annalise, and quirky Olivia. Oh, who was she trying to fool? She would miss Caroline as well. But she did not have a future in England. She had to come to terms with that. Without realizing it, Annalise had just given her the perfect solution.

"Yes, that's perfect," Lavinia repeated. "I already know him. I mean, we've met a handful of times, but he is a pleasant enough gentleman. He is your relative, and he and your husband get along, which is an added boon. And he is not hideous to look at, neither is he too old. He is perfect."

"I am so glad you agree!" Annalise exclaimed in glee.

He is perfect.

And now was the time for self-doubt to start plaguing Lavinia.

Of course, he was perfect. Which meant that he would not look Lavinia's way. How in the world did she think she could ensnare a man who was that splendid while she… well, was not.

"And the best part is," Annalise continued, not realizing Lavinia had shifted from excitement to utter terror, "he is going to the house party, too! Blake convinced him to come under the pretense of discussing business. He should arrive today, or perhaps he has already arrived. Ample time for the two of you to get to know each other and fall in love!"

Lavinia's smile died on her lips. *Love.* That was not in the cards for Lavinia anymore.

* * *

The first—and Sebastian hoped from the bottom of his soul that it would also be the last—house party hosted by the Marquess of Roth was underway. Caroline, the Duchess of Kensington, had hosted one house party on his behalf, but this time, he was all on his own.

The carriages had started arriving in the early morning, and a few more families were expected to join the party on the morrow.

Sebastian and Victoria had spent most of the day greeting the visitors, smiling, and making idle conversation with the new arrivals.

Frau Elinor joined them from time to time, but due to her health, she opted to lie down and rest for most of the day. She had not lied when she'd said that travel had started becoming more difficult for her. Perhaps it truly wouldn't be easy for her to travel back to the Continent. And if that were true, Sebastian's own plans of leaving were under question.

Sebastian did not want to think about that. He'd find a way to turn things toward his advantage. He always did.

If Victoria's chosen husband proved to be pleasant, perhaps Sebastian would be able to leave Frau Elinor under his and Victoria's care.

Victoria, in her own cheery way, had spent all of this time looking outside and peeking behind every newcomer to see if the man she had met at the ball—the man she'd become infatuated with within a matter of minutes—had arrived at the house party. So far, it seemed like he had not. But Victoria's youthful enthusiasm didn't die down even with dusk. He could still arrive on the morrow, after all.

Sebastian ran through the guest list in his mind, trying to remember everyone he'd invited who hadn't arrived yet, and of them, who Victoria could be so infatuated with. There were a few married couples and a young gentleman who was not titled. Could it be him?

Victoria insisted that she needed a gentleman, but not one burdened with too many responsibilities. A man who was a leader, and yet who could afford to leave England for long periods of time. Not a duke, but a man who could inherit a title. She had a long list of attributes dictated by her sister, and Sebastian only hoped that she would listen to her heart more than the words of her relative, whom she had not seen since she was ten years old.

Sebastian knew Victoria's soft heart, and he knew she was not up to all the plotting her sister was involved in. And as much as Sebastian didn't buy into an idea of love so strong it could sever familial ties, he certainly hoped it would become true for Victoria.

Sebastian did not care who she was infatuated with, as long as this someone convinced her to stay in England where she was safe and would not be sucked into any political drama.

But her relations aside, Sebastian also worried that Victoria was too young and naïve. She had lived a sheltered life, and she could have been easily tricked. What if the man she had fallen for was already married? That was a road leading to a disaster.

No, Sebastian would not allow that to happen. He would watch Victoria's every move and make certain that her paramour was worthy of her affections.

If only Sebastian knew who it was who caught her fancy, he could steer her away from him, or at the very least investigate the fellow and make certain that he was a perfect candidate for a husband to Sebastian's beloved niece.

Victoria sailed past a few more people and sat across from Sebastian.

"You seem particularly gloomy today, my lord," she noted.

Sebastian narrowed his eyes at her suspiciously. "Since when are you calling me *my lord*?"

"I am to call you that in public, am I not?" She crinkled her brows adorably.

She always did that when she was confused, ever since she was a little girl. Actually, he'd seen this exact expression on her face a lot more often when she'd moved in with him and Frau Elinor all those years ago. Sebastian smiled. It seemed just like yesterday.

"Yes, you are right. I am just not used to hearing that from you. And I am not gloomy in the least. I am just trying to guess who is the man who caught your attention."

Victoria smiled broadly. "As if I would be careless enough to give you or the gossips in this room any indication of who he is."

"Ah, so he is here," Sebastian said, leaning forward and watching Victoria with narrowed eyes.

Victoria raised her brows as she watched him in challenge. She didn't break eye contact, but her eyes narrowed slightly. "Why are your eyes red-rimmed?"

Sebastian leaned back with a sigh. "I haven't been sleeping well."

"Ah." Victoria smiled knowingly. "Did some lady catch *your* fancy?"

Sebastian grinned. "What would you know about that?"

"Oh, nothing. How could I know anything about falling in love, my lord?"

"I am certainly not speaking about falling in love, Victoria." He avoided Victoria's gaze now because even though she wasn't fully right, she was at least partially correct.

He had spent the night thinking about, or rather drawing, a lady. Not that it was any kind of indication of his feelings. Muses were just that, muses. They came to provide inspiration and once the portrait was done, the interest would disappear. The only thing of note was that it was the first time since his arrival in England that he'd found any inspiration at all.

Well, it was bound to come sooner or later. The lady was just a catalyst. If it wasn't her, it would be someone else. But if he admitted as much to Victoria, there would be no end to her teasing. So he kept his lips pursed as he scanned the room.

Hadn't he given out invitations for this house party to every guest of the ball? If so, then why hadn't his muse arrived?

"So, who is it?" Victoria's voice cut through his thoughts.

"Who is what?"

"The lady who caught your attention," she said with a smile.

"There is no one," Sebastian answered irritably. "And even if there was, it is of no importance. Far greater importance should be granted to the gentleman of your choosing. Because while I am not interested in taking a wife, at least not in England, you, my dear niece, have to marry. Appropriately."

"I thought you found most gentlemen in England rather… boring. And undeserving of my hand."

"Undeserving of you, yes. Boring? No. In fact, I find it quite entertaining winning money from them in Vingt-Un." Sebastian flashed Victoria a smile. "Now, shouldn't you be the one socializing and charming men, luring them into a wedded trap?"

Victoria stood with a light giggle. "Indeed. You just seemed slightly troubled, and I wanted to lighten your mood. It seems like I have achieved my goal, so I can go back to my other mission. Luring men into a trap."

She winked and sailed away.

Chapter 9

Deep purple silk crushed under his fingers as he yanked it away from the creamy white skin. He ran his fingertip over round, soft flesh.

He leaned down, his hot breath causing goosebumps to appear on the perfect, silky skin. He picked up a brush and smeared the ivory color to mix with the bone-white complexion.

The next thing he knew, the living, breathing woman turned into the canvas as he stood over it with a brush in his hand and the scattered art supplies around him.

Perhaps he should add a shade of golden honey to replicate the kiss of the candlelight playing on her neck.

No! That wouldn't do at all. He needed something else, something to depict how soft her skin was. Was it even possible? How does one paint softness?

Sebastian rolled over and almost fell out of bed in agitation. He opened his eyes and realized he was lying in bed with a very awkward feeling of arousal and inspiration.

He blinked in confusion. He hadn't had a woman in some months, and he hadn't painted even longer. His inspiration and desire were all mixed up in his head now, unwilling to let go.

And even in his lucid state, the visions of his muse weren't leaving his mind. He needed… no, he *craved* to paint her. His first attempt back in London had not been successful enough to quench his thirst for putting her likeness to canvas. Especially because her form evaded him. And for some reason, that fact didn't give him a moment's rest. What did she look like, his mysterious lady?

He threw back the covers and sat up. No, he wasn't going to get any sleep tonight either. He ran his fingers through his hair. Perhaps he should try to paint. Anything was better than nothing.

After months of being in a painting drought—the artist's hell—now he was in a different agony entirely. But at least he wanted to paint.

Sebastian stood and slowly padded to the chair by his bed, which held his clothing. Yes, perhaps he'd paint a little again, and then hopefully, his lady would grace his house party with her presence, and he'd be able to finish what he'd started.

He threw on his clothing and exited his room. With soft footsteps, he left the family wing and almost ran into someone in the dark. He halted and reared back.

"Bloody hell," the other gentleman muttered. The voice sounded familiar.

"William?"

"Bastian?"

"What are you doing roaming around in the middle of the night?" Sebastian asked, irritated.

"I might ask you the same thing."

Sebastian raised a brow. The hall was dark, but a thin line of light from the moon crept from behind the clouds, illuminating the man in front of him. Now that Sebastian's eyes had adjusted to the dark, he noticed that William was half-clad, not a waistcoat in sight, just his shirtsleeves under the cloak. "Ah, so you are coming from a clandestine affair, I presume?"

William shrugged. "Actually, no. At least not yet. Haven't roped the ladybird into an affair yet. But you do not have to worry. I am not about to make a nuisance of myself. You will barely see me at the house party. I shall keep to myself, join the lords on your manly activities, and spend nights chasing after my bird."

"Hm." Sebastian tied the banyan tighter around him.

He was grateful that William would try to avoid his guests. William was not invited to many house parties, and when he was, scandal followed. The only reason Sebastian had invited him at all was because he had been present at the ball when the invitations were given out. And even if William was not a close friend, he did not want to make an enemy of him.

"And you?" William asked.

"Actually, I was going to try and paint."

"Are you? Didn't you complain just recently that you haven't picked up a brush in months?" William craned his neck as if to peek over Sebastian's shoulder.

"I haven't…" Sebastian followed his gaze, but there was nothing there. "But I had an inspiration. What are you—?"

"Could it be? Bastian Devis is painting again?" William asked excitedly.

"I wouldn't say so, no. I started, but the vision is eluding me.

I can't seem to finish the damned painting." Sebastian heaved a sigh. There was a rustle behind him. He looked back, but nothing was out of place. Only the curtains at the end of the hall moved in the night breeze.

"Perhaps you need a model," William threw out carelessly.

Sebastian's attention snapped back to his companion. *A model!* Why didn't he think of it himself? Suddenly, he was grateful he'd met his friend in the hall under bizarre circumstances in the middle of the night.

The idea seemed so simple now. Sebastian had an inspiration. All he needed to find was someone to paint. Perhaps that was why he had bits and pieces of the flesh come to his mind. He needed to fill in the blanks with a real-life model.

Not that models were just hanging about his house in the middle of the night… Even worse, he was in the middle of the countryside. In London, perhaps he could just go to the Royal Academy of Arts and seek out a model there, or if worse came to worst, go to a brothel. But not here.

"Well, in that case, I'll probably need to wait until morning." Sebastian turned to leave and paused. "But where will I even find one out in the country?"

"Don't look at me," William exclaimed with a chuckle. "You would have to pay me a lot of money to convince me to pose for you naked."

"Lord forbid." Sebastian leaned his back against the wall, suddenly tired. "Why would I want to paint you?"

"Why, I am the fairest of them all. Besides, who else are you going to find at this hour?"

A hoarse chuckle left Sebastian's lips. "I thought you didn't want me to paint you."

"I do not. I am just saying that I might be your only choice."

Sebastian raised his eyes heavenward. "Well, you're right on one thing. I will likely not find a model here. Perhaps in the village... A bar wench?"

William let out a bark of laughter. "Do not be ridiculous. With so many *virtuous* women present under your roof, all you have to do is ask. Trust me, they will be grateful, and they will probably reward you handsomely for your talent." William waggled his brows.

Sebastian cocked his head to the side. "Perhaps the ladybird you are trying to catch? I mean, if she is interested in you, there's not much she'll say no to."

William choked on his laugh and then proceeded to cough into his fist. Sebastian frowned and clapped him on the back.

"Are you well?"

"Yes, quite well," William croaked between fits of coughs. He straightened a moment later, wiped at his tears, and cleared his throat. "Apologies. But I do not think I am in the mood to share my most recent conquest. You'll have to find someone else. But I am quite certain you'll not have any trouble."

Sebastian shrugged. "Perhaps."

"Well, as much as I loved our little discourse... I better go." William tipped his head and hurried away in the opposite direction.

Sebastian looked at the disappearing William and then back at the hall where he came from. Where was William going before Sebastian ran into him? He was acting quite strangely, not that Sebastian had ever known William to not act strangely. Was he trying to steal something? Or was he following someone in hopes of gathering some scandalous information?

Sebastian looked around but didn't notice anything out of place. The curtains still rustled in the wind, the moon still illuminated a slight patch of the hall. Otherwise, it was dark and lonely.

He heaved a sigh. And now back to torture himself in bed with the visions of his muse without the ability to actually paint her.

* * *

When Lavinia, Annalise, and Payne arrived at the Roth estate, the house party was already in full motion. The weather was wonderful, so the gentlemen had gone out hunting, while the ladies were frolicking in the gardens or otherwise going about their business.

Payne's carriage got delayed because of all the unplanned stops they had to make due to Annalise's condition, and by the end of the trip, even Lavinia felt nauseous. Now, as they finally stepped into the house, she expelled a breath of relief. Their journey was over.

"Welcome to the Roth estate," a thin, elderly woman with a turban over her head and a cane in her hand said from above the stairs. She slowly made her way down, accompanied by a much younger, beautiful ebony-haired woman.

Lavinia remembered the older woman to be the Marquess of Roth's aunt, Lady Elinor. And the lady by her side must have been Princess Victoria, the young lady who had just made her come out. Lavinia was ashamed to admit that she didn't remember her at all. But then she was preoccupied with other issues during the last ball.

"Good morning." Lavinia executed a curtsy and watched

the women's unhurried approach.

The princess moved with fluid grace. Her head was raised, her neck perfectly balanced, like a swan. Come to think of it, she did remind Lavinia of a beautiful swan. Compared to her, Lavinia probably looked like a clumsy, large duck.

Lavinia threw a glance toward her friend. Even tired and sickly, Annalise looked perfectly composed and graceful.

Lavinia sighed with all the sadness accorded to women in her position. Now, women like Annalise and Princess Victoria were born to become countesses and duchesses. There was a reason Lavinia was always overlooked. And how was she to compete with the likes of a graceful swan gliding toward her when she was an odd duck?

"A pleasure to have you here, Lord Payne, Lady Payne," the older woman said, with a slight European lilt Lavinia couldn't quite discern. She turned toward Lavinia. "And…"

Of course, she didn't even remember her.

"Lady Lavinia, my lady," Lavinia said with another curtsy.

"Ah. Delighted to introduce you to my great-niece, Princess Victoria."

The princess smiled an innocent smile and performed a perfect curtsy. "A pleasure," she said with a slight accent.

"I trust your journey was smooth?" Lady Elinor asked.

"As much as could be expected," Payne answered with a smile. "But we are rather tired."

"Of course. Let me show you to your rooms. Lady Lavinia, Victoria will show you to your chambers."

Lavinia smiled at her friends as they shuffled away after Lady Elinor. As soon as they disappeared behind the curve of the staircase, Princess Victoria grabbed her arm.

"I am so pleased to meet you, truly!" she said excitedly.

Lavinia blinked. "You are?"

"Of course! Caroline speaks so highly of you."

"She does?" Lavinia was so taken aback by the princess's uncharacteristic friendliness and more so by what she said about Caroline that the only thing she could do was repeat the statements back to her.

"Yes. And about Lady Payne as well. But my aunt is very strict about etiquette. I did not dare show my emotions in front of her. Not that she would punish me for it, but I have to pretend to be a proper English lady when I am around her or she is afraid I shall not find a husband."

All Lavinia could do was smile at the flurry of words leaving the young princess's mouth. Her speech was very cultured, but something about the way she spoke gave away the fact that English was not her native language. And the accent became more and more noticeable the more she spoke.

"It's a genuine pleasure to meet you," Lavinia said, for the lack of a better reply. "Is Caroline here?"

"Yes." Princess Victoria turned and beckoned Lavinia to follow. Of course, Caroline was here. This had been her house, after all, and the marquess was her cousin. "And I left you the perfect room right by her side. It is in the family wing, obviously. After all, according to Caroline, you *are* family."

Perfect. Just what Lavinia needed, crying her nights away, imagining what Caroline was doing in there with her husband. It was understandable why Princess Victoria would want them to be nearby, but Lavinia wished she could be in the furthest corner of the guest wing. She couldn't very well say that to the princess, so she followed her silently.

"See, I do not know anybody here. But Caroline was so nice to me, and we became fast friends. I do hope we can be friends also. Yes?"

Lavinia smiled. "Of course, we can. I would be delighted, Your Highness."

Princess Victoria let out a musical laugh. "Please. Nobody calls me that, least of all my friends. Call me Victoria."

"Oh, I couldn't!" Lavinia exclaimed.

"I insist."

They walked in silence for a moment. "So, are you here to secure yourself an advantageous match for political reasons? I mean, does your father want to gain allies by marrying you into the British aristocracy?" Lavinia asked.

"Do I seek an advantageous match? Yes. Is it for the benefit of my father? No." They stopped in front of the doors to a chamber. "This is where you will reside. The door to your left is where Caroline is, and the door further up is where the Paynes are staying."

Lavinia opened the door and entered a beautiful, spacious chamber. She had never stayed in a chamber such as this. In her home, her room was small and dark. And when she stayed at house parties, she always had a smaller room, which she had to share with her maid. Which reminded her that she didn't have a maid this time.

She turned toward Victoria, who followed her inside.

"I will need a maid," she started uncomfortably. She wasn't used to asking anything, but she needed someone to help her dress.

"Of course. I shall notify our housekeeper right away," Victoria said with a smile.

Lavinia placed her basket on the floor and opened the lid. Miss Gale immediately jumped out and started licking herself in irritation.

"Oh, you have a cat! How lovely!" Victoria picked up Miss Gale and sat down, forcing the poor cat on her lap.

"Please, be careful. She doesn't take well to strangers. Actually, she is usually quite gentle with women, so I am not surprised she hasn't scratched you. But she does not like men at all."

"Oh, truly?" Victoria laughed earnestly. "I love her already."

"I hope it is not a trouble that I brought her with me. I know, cats are not usually kept as pets. But she is not feral... mostly. She is quite friendly with ladies and... I couldn't leave her at home for fear she might run away without me."

"Oh, do not worry about it. I wouldn't want to leave my cat either if I had one. I imagine the journey was not easy for her. I shall let the servants know to take good care of her. And will mention that she prefers female caretakers."

"Thank you so much!" Lavinia felt a load lift off her shoulders. It felt nice to connect to a young lady this quickly. It had not happened to her before. Not since Annalise. Sure, she was friends with Caroline and Olivia, but they were Annalise's friends first. Annalise was the one who introduced her to them. Making a friend on her own was... tough.

"I am very glad you are here," Victoria echoed Lavinia's thoughts. "I was quite famished for the company. Not to say that the company of my uncle and great aunt is lacking. But..."

Lavinia smiled. "You wished for the company of someone closer to your age."

"Yes," Victoria said with a sigh as she stroked Miss Gale's fur. "See, you understand me so well. I knew we would get along. And it is rather difficult navigating through society, especially having no one to discuss things with. But you have friends. It must have been easy for you."

Oh, lord… If you only knew. Lavinia sat opposite Victoria and folded her hands on her lap. "I have just finished my second season, I am still unmarried, and on the brink of losing everything. Trust me, it has not been easy."

Victoria's eyes grew wide. "Oh, no. You might be in even more dire straits than me. But how… why…?"

"Well, I'll start with how…" Lavinia said with a chuckle. "I've always wished for a love match."

"That's where the trouble begins!" Victoria said cheerfully. "See, my sister told me to marry for status, and then just keep lovers for love. That's what she did."

"Oh." Lavinia blinked. There was truly nothing she could say to that. "You have a sister then?"

Victoria waved a hand. "Yes, but she is married and happily living with her lovers."

Multiple lovers? "And you wish to follow in her footsteps?"

Victoria's smile turned coy. "I truly thought I did, but now I am not so certain. Perhaps I can have it all."

Victoria's optimism was infectious, and Lavinia found herself smiling in turn. "You are young, beautiful, rich, and quite clever. I can't see why you can't have it all."

Victoria bit on her lower lip playfully. "You might be right. But what about you? You wished for a love match, and then what happened?"

Lavinia inhaled deeply. "And then he married someone else."

"Oh, no!" Victoria's face scrunched up in a frown. "And now what do you want?"

What did she want? Except for Dane, that was… "I want a marriage to a respectable lord, who would take me away from all my miseries, of which I have plenty. I am not looking for a love match anymore. An amicable union would do."

Victoria narrowed her eyes. "Is that truly all you wish for?"

Something between a snort and a chuckle left Lavinia's lips. "I am not going to lie, I would love to meet a man who would see me for me and instantly fall in love. I would love to meet a man who would appreciate my intellect and wit and whatever else a gentleman might find appealing in me. And perhaps he would not care about my full, unshapely figure, clumsiness, and all that uncertainty I carry around with me daily. But this is not possible. Such a man does not exist. Not in this life."

Victoria pursed her lips thoughtfully. "Not in your life thus far. But it doesn't mean that this could never happen."

Lavinia shook her head. "If it hasn't happened to me before, why would it happen to me now?"

Victoria leaned closer toward Lavinia. "There is something my sister told me, which I carry with me to this day. I think it will help you, too. She said that if you want to have something you've never had, you need to do something you've never done."

Lavinia furrowed her brows in thought. Such a simple yet poignant statement. How did Lavinia expect to win over a suitor if she hadn't won anyone in her twenty years? To find a husband this time around, she might need to plot something outrageous. "She sounds very wise."

"Beyond her years," Victoria agreed. She handed Miss Gale to Lavinia and jumped up. "But I am wasting your time. You need to rest, get refreshed, clothed, and out onto the suitor hunt. And I," she continued as she skipped toward the door, "shall go and make certain you get the very best lady's maid."

"Thank you," Lavinia said with a smile, her mood lighter.

"Oh, but we should take afternoon tea together, all four of us! I shall tell Caroline my brilliant idea! Oh, how lovely!" Victoria said and slunk away excitedly.

Yes. Lovely. Lavinia expelled a breath. Surely she knew she was going to share a house with Caroline and Dane when she agreed to come to this house party. But she hadn't quite imagined being forced to socialize with either of them.

I suppose I better start preparing for it.

Chapter 10

Lavinia received her summons to the afternoon tea with the ladies a few hours later. She had managed to take a bath, rest, and get dressed by that time, ready to take on the world. But the thought of meeting Caroline still didn't sit well with her. She ran the possible conversations she'd have in her head over and over again and still hadn't come up with anything good. She wasn't even certain if she'd be able to genuinely smile in Caroline's presence.

Oh, how truly sad she was.

There was a knock on the door, and Lavinia went to open it. Annalise stood on a threshold in a clean day gown, her hair swept up, her cheeks rosy. She looked relaxed after the hard journey and quite healthy.

"It seems I have no reason to be worrying about you," Lavinia said with a smile.

"I told you, everything is well. You, on the other hand, look a bit… pale."

Lavinia stepped outside the door and entwined her arm

with Annalise's. "I suppose I am awaiting our afternoon tea like I would the gallows."

"Oh, Lavinia. Are you still upset with Caroline?"

Lavinia shook her head. "I am not certain upset is the right word, but you have to imagine that this is difficult for me."

Annalise nodded and patted Lavinia's hand. They started walking toward the main staircase in silence.

"I suppose I hoped that time would heal you. Besides, you have more pressing issues to worry about," Annalise said.

"Yes, I know… finding a husband."

"Oh! And as our luck would have it… Look!" Annalise pointed down.

Lavinia peeked over the railing. There in the hall stood Marcus, Lord Payne's cousin. He was speaking animatedly to someone who was obscured by the column.

Lavinia turned toward Annalise, resolute. "Annalise, I have a favor to ask of you."

"Of course, anything."

"I know you're my chaperone, but… for the duration of the party, I need you to look away and give me a bit of freedom."

"Lavinia, I don't think that's the best idea—"

"If I am to secure myself a husband and quickly, you shall have to indulge me with slight freedoms. I can't go through the rigmarole of courtship. There just isn't enough time."

Annalise frowned, obviously confused. "What do you mean? What do you want me to do?"

"Well, for one thing, I want you to express my apology for not joining you for afternoon tea."

Lavinia peeked down to where Marcus had stood just a moment ago. He seemed to have disappeared somewhere.

"And what are *you* going to do?" Annalise studied Lavinia's face under her furrowed brows.

"Do not worry about me," Lavinia said and disengaged herself from her friend. Then she added quietly to herself, "I shall do something I haven't done before."

* * *

Sebastian put away his hunting rifle in his study, took off his hat, and washed his face and hands in the small basin before venturing back out into the hall.

He'd never enjoyed hunting. A barbaric activity if he'd ever participated in one.

He was not a gentleman who loved the outdoors, and he had never been successful with guns. Now hand him a rapier, and he would challenge any deer to a duel and be certain to win. But hand him a rifle and he was completely lost.

There was a certain detachment to wielding a gun that Sebastian had never liked. He preferred to engage with his subject, whether he painted it, dissected and studied it, or healed it. Killing was never his first instinct.

But hunting was a common activity during house parties, and as a host, he couldn't get out of it.

Sebastian shook out his hands as he walked toward the stairs. He didn't have to think about hunting for the rest of the day. He needed to change and—

He was about to ascend to his chamber when he noticed a gentleman observing one of the few paintings he'd brought with him to England.

The gentleman was Mr. Marcus Townsend if Sebastian was not mistaken. One of the men who'd arrived late to the house party, making him the prime suspect as the recipient of Victoria's affections.

Sebastian slowly backed away from the stairs and made his way toward the gentleman.

Mr. Townsend darted his eyes toward Sebastian as he noticed him. "Rather beautiful brushwork, wouldn't you say? Bold and evokes the summer mood perfectly."

"What an astute observation." Sebastian smiled. "Do you paint?"

"Oh, no. Well, I used to. I lived in Italy for a while, but I haven't picked up a brush since I came back."

Sebastian chuckled. "England seems to knock the brush out of people's hands, doesn't it?"

"Do you paint?" Mr. Townsend had a note of astonishment in his voice.

"I do. You are looking at my work."

"No," the gentleman said confidently. "I can't be. This is the work of the great Bastian Devis. A French painter. I used to own a few of his paintings."

Sebastian pursed his lips to not let his self-satisfied smile give him away. It was always nice to be recognized. "Indeed."

"You are Bastian Devis? The author of the legendary piece *Les Saisons?*"

"One and the same." Sebastian gave a small bow.

Mr. Townsend blinked, unable to utter a word for a long moment. "A pleasure," he finally said and stretched out a hand.

Sebastian shook it. He was glad to finally meet a person who was equally interested in art. This was the conversation he'd rather have than endure more hunting expeditions. "Would you like to see some more of my art? I do not have a lot of it here. I moved only my most favorite pieces with me."

"It would be an honor," Mr. Townsend said with star-stricken awe.

Sebastian waved a hand. "Follow me."

"I used to have at least half a dozen of your paintings," Mr. Townsend said as he followed Sebastian into the hall, which Sebastian had transformed into a mini-gallery.

It was the corridor that led from the main hall and into the gardens. Openly lit with wide windows, it was a perfect place for a gallery, and a perfect place to paint, too, not that Sebastian had used this place for that particular purpose.

"Used to?"

Mr. Townsend grimaced. "Yes. I had to sacrifice my small collection for the sake of my lands."

"Are you a titled lord, then?" Sebastian furrowed his brows. His research indicated that Mr. Townsend was the cousin of an earl, but did not own lands himself.

Mr. Townsend cleared his throat. "Not exactly. I inherited a title when my cousin was missing—presumed dead. It's a long story, but fortunately, he returned, healthy and ready to resume his seat. I, on the other hand, was left with no lands and without my collection."

Sebastian remembered the story. He hadn't witnessed these events himself, but Caroline, his cousin and the current Duchess of Kensington, was friends with the earl's wife, so he knew a little of that story. "Quite unfortunate," Sebastian said.

"He did promise to buy it back for me, but it is not that easy when my collection is now scattered around the Continent. But perhaps I can buy some of the paintings from the hand of the great Bastian Devis?"

Sebastian walked into the gallery hall and waved his hand

once again. "These are all the paintings I brought with me. Aside from a few more which are in my studio. Unfortunately, none of them are for sale. But you can certainly look."

Townsend walked deeper into the hall, admiring Sebastian's work.

Sebastian was glad to have the company of a man who understood composition and appreciated how much work it took to complete a painting. Sometimes people thought it was so easy. As if simply by having talent, you could draw anything you wanted. No, it wasn't that simple.

It was painstakingly hard work, long hours, tweaking the painting into perfection, and irritation if one wasn't getting it the way one saw it in one's head. And then there was the matter of a muse. Or, in Sebastian's case, lack thereof.

But this wasn't about Sebastian. He needed to find out more about Mr. Townsend, and he needed to figure out if he was the gentleman Victoria fancied.

"Are you a part of the Society of Dilettanti, then?" he asked.

Mr. Townsend shook his head. "I attended their gatherings a couple of times, but no. Are you?"

Sebastian snorted. "Oh, no. I've visited once, and it was quite enough. Something about young men who visit the Continent once and proclaim themselves connoisseurs does not sit well with me."

Mr. Townsend grinned. "I did not think you would enjoy it either."

Sebastian liked this gentleman already. But what could he ask to figure out if he was interested in Victoria? Of course, he was interested. The man seemed to be in possession of good taste. But was he the one Victoria fancied?

"I would love to continue this conversation," Mr. Townsend

said as he looked at the setting sun. "But I am afraid I won't be ready for tea."

Right. Afternoon tea was fast approaching. But then they'd have dinner. And that's when Sebastian would be certain to observe Victoria's attention toward Mr. Townsend. "Understandable. We can continue our discussion later, perhaps, during the port."

"That would be splendid!"

"There's an exit further down. It's actually a closer way to get to the guest wing rather than going back through the main hall," Sebastian supplied.

"Perfect. I shall be looking forward to our dinner conversation," Mr. Marcus Townsend said and hurried away.

"As shall I." Sebastian tipped his head and was left alone, staring at his paintings.

Would he ever be able to finish another painting? Or was his career as the famous Bastian Devis over so soon?

He walked slowly past the ghosts of his models, looking at his work, and heaved a long sigh.

There was a clatter somewhere down the corridor. He peeked out and saw a lady straightening the painting she must have knocked over.

No, not *a* lady, *the* lady.

His muse.

Sebastian stared at the woman he had been dreaming about for the past few nights. His feverish dreams all rushed up to his head, making his cheeks heat. She was truly a vision with her soft, round bosom, her cherry pink lips, and her full apple cheeks. She looked around in confusion as if searching for someone. *Him*? Was it possible she was indeed looking for him?

Sebastian cleared his throat, and she turned toward him. She placed a hand softly to her chest, as if he'd startled her, then smiled and walked up to him. There was no glimmer of recognition in her eyes. So she hadn't come here for him. *What is she doing here then?*

"Apologies, I did not mean to impose… I thought I saw a gentleman enter through here." She glanced back at the door.

Sebastian didn't say anything, he just continued watching her carefully. In his mind, he was picking out colors to paint her with.

She was wearing a simple, beige day gown that almost blended with her skin in the worst sense. The color was different enough to not encourage lurid thoughts but not different enough to make a striking contrast. Quite simply, the gown did nothing to complement her complexion. More than that, her bodice was too high, hiding her glorious bosom, her sleeves were too tight on her arms, bunching the fabric and emphasizing her soft, full figure, and the skirts were… He paused while looking her over; were they torn at the edges?

In short, this gown was nothing like the lavish one she wore at the ball when he'd seen her first. He returned his gaze to her eyes. She was still looking at him inquiringly.

"I must have been mistaken. Are you alone here?" she asked.

Sebastian frowned in thought. "No." After all, this was not a lie. He wasn't alone. He was with her. But the truth was, he knew that if he said they were alone, she would have left the room immediately, and he wanted a little more time to study her. He slowly shifted toward the portraits area. "Are you an art enthusiast? A connoisseur?"

She looked around the gallery. "I have to admit, not at all."

He raised a brow. "You are not interested in art?"

She shrugged lightly. "I never truly thought about it. And isn't being a connoisseur a male occupation?"

"Anyone can appreciate the beauty around them, can they not?"

His muse slowly walked toward him and peeked at one of the paintings, incidentally, of a half-naked woman. Her cheeks burned, and her eyes rounded. "This is what you find beautiful?"

"And you do not?" Sebastian hid his smile.

"I have to say that I do not quite see the splendor in naked female flesh. Especially so much of it." She was still blushing.

"Perhaps you prefer naked male flesh?"

Her mouth half opened in surprise, but she quickly composed herself. "I do not find the display of utter lack of inhibitions beautiful. I prefer modesty and decent human decorum."

"People were not meant to be hidden inside those contraptions." Sebastian waved his hand to indicate her clothing. He knew she would find fault in his behavior again. But he quite enjoyed making this lady uncomfortable.

She crossed her arms over her chest, her lips pursed. "Perhaps in France, this passes for a decent conversation with a lady, but here in England, it is different. Women are not allowed to ogle human flesh while in the company of a strange man."

"How boring," he drawled. "But let us be strangers no more. My name is Sebastian."

She straightened. "And yet another *faux pas.* You are to introduce yourself with your title, not your name."

"Since we've already broken etiquette by discussing naked human flesh, I thought we could skip the formalities."

"I am afraid it is not possible." The lady was simply tiresome.

"What is it that prevents you from having a conversation with me about art? Is it truly the restrictions of your society? Your own moral uptightness or the fact that you're blushing?"

"I am not blushing," she countered immediately, although her cheeks were cherry red, and her eyes held a curious glint.

Sebastian grinned. "Perhaps you rather like these paintings. You are just not willing to admit the truth."

She straightened. "These women were not painted as objects of art; they were painted as objects of male lust. See how her bosom is accentuated, and her thin waist? The way her legs are…" She paused as if realizing she'd gone too far. Wasn't referring to body parts just as scandalous as being alone with a gentleman? She cleared her throat. "If you wanted to express your appreciation of human nature, you would buy a painting of an old man, all wrinkled and weary, or a woman who is tired from her daily chores, her calloused fingers, with a crying babe at her side. And they would *not* be naked."

"What if I want to appreciate human form, not human nature?"

"Then you should pick someone less perfect."

Sebastian smiled slowly. *Ah, now we are getting somewhere.* "And who would be less perfect?"

"Someone with uneven features and a disproportionate figure. We are not all like this under our corsets," she said, not realizing where that would lead Sebastian's mind. Yes, he'd love to see exactly what she looked like under the corset.

"But, see, therein lies the problem," he said softly as he stepped closer to her. "People who feel like they are less than perfect rarely allow themselves to be painted."

"Perhaps you weren't looking hard enough." She tilted her chin up stubbornly.

"Would you like to prove me wrong?"

"I am certain London has many people who—"

"No, prove me wrong right now. Allow me to paint *you*."

She let out a gasp. "You have no idea how insulting you are being at the moment, do you?"

"I think it is an honor—"

"You are not even a real artist! You pretend to be a connoisseur to gape at naked female flesh and then insult other ladies by trying to get them to disrobe in front of you to prove something. Well, I do not need to prove anything to anyone. And I have spent an inordinate amount of time conversing with you tête-à-tête, which is not allowed in our society, so I bid you a good day."

Sebastian blinked, for he did not have the time to do or say anything else before his muse was gone.

Just like that.

Sebastian felt his blood simmering in his veins and his heart beating wildly. For the first time in a long time, he felt... alive.

Chapter 11

Lavinia walked out of the corridor feeling hot and flustered. Her cheeks were burning, her hair stuck to her forehead, and her clothing clung to her. What was that strange feeling? Why was she burning up from the inside?

She rushed toward her room, unwilling to discern what she was feeling. Those lurid paintings, the marquess's callous words, his gravelly low voice…

Wait… What did his voice have to do with what she was feeling? Lavinia picked up her skirts and started ascending the stairs when she heard the steps behind her.

She didn't want to talk to anyone at the moment, so she hurried her step. The footsteps behind her picked up their pace, too.

Cold shivers ran down Lavinia's spine. Was someone following her? She glanced back as she turned the corner and noticed a dark, shadowed man behind her. She couldn't make out his face and she didn't want to turn again and make it obvious that she'd noticed him.

Drat! Who was it? Was it the rude marquess? Or was it the person who'd sent her the ominous note?

Lavinia's breath accelerated, and her fingers grew numb from fear. Before she made it to the corridor of the family wing, she thought she heard someone call her name.

"…Lavinia!" Now she was certain someone had called her name.

She froze on the top staircase landing and slowly turned around.

Dane.

Her heart soared as her stomach made a flip inside. It was Dane.

Lavinia's relief was almost a physical being at that moment. Her lips spread in a smile. Oh, how she'd missed him.

"Lady Lavinia," he said, as he stopped before her and tipped his head.

"Your Grace." She dipped into a curtsy.

"I've heard about your father. How are you feeling?"

Just like Dane to sidestep the small talk and jump right into the issues.

"I am well, thank you," she said with a smile, while her heart beat violently in her chest. Dane was here. Right in front of her. His deep gray eyes glinted with kindness, and his full lips were pursed into a thin line. No matter. She loved his lips in any shape or form.

"I am sorry. This must be difficult for you. But if you want, I can look into his affairs—"

Just like him, to offer her help. Her knight in shining armor. She swallowed a lump that formed in her throat. "Actually, you don't need to worry. His heir, Mr. Atwood has already arrived, and he is looking into everything. It is all taken care of to the point that I am here instead of back at home." She forced a smile to her lips.

"Mr. Atwood? The name is familiar, but I do not think I've met him." Dane furrowed his brows. "Well, I can call on him when we come back."

"There is no need, truly."

"There is every need. Your father is ailing, and there is no one to look out for you, not that he ever did." The concern in his eyes was real, and Lavinia's insides tightened. Why did he care so much, and yet clearly not enough? He would never be able to give her what she really wanted from him. So, she needed him to stop.

"You are right. He was never concerned about me. And I thank you for everything you've done, Your Grace, but I am a grown woman now. Without my father's interference, I can take care of my life myself."

"I never said you couldn't," Dane countered. "But I shall feel better when I meet with your guardian. Have you spoken to him about your marriage prospects? There is a matter of your dowry—"

Lavinia squirmed inside. Her marriage prospects were the last thing she wanted to discuss with him. When he was around, she couldn't think of any other prospects.

"I–I need to change for dinner. Please, can we talk about this later?"

"Of course." Dane tipped his head. "I shall not keep you any longer."

Lavinia bobbed a curtsy and hurried toward her room.

* * *

Sebastian felt incredibly uneasy. As he watched his muse fiddle with her skirts and avoid looking anyone in the eye, guilt crept into the dark corners of his soul.

He'd acted ungentlemanly in the gallery hall.

She was a debutante, and apart from Victoria, whom he still treated like a little girl—because for him she was still a little girl—Sebastian did not have many interactions with debutantes.

He'd had mistresses, he had dallied with widows and models who were anything but modest. Therefore his jests might have come off too strong for the young lady.

As he watched her sunken face, he wondered if their earlier interaction was the reason for her current dejected state. His heart squeezed, and he wanted to drop to his knees and beg for forgiveness. Except, that would cause even more of a scene, so he stayed away, observing her silently.

"Lady Lavinia Birch," Frau Elinor said by his side. "An earl's daughter. I believe no dowry was announced for her, but we truly do not need that nonsense."

Sebastian turned his head toward his aunt. Was he that obvious? "I am not interested in marrying her. She just seems... sad."

Lavinia... What a beautiful name. It quite suited her.

Her last name did sound familiar though. Where had he heard it before?

Frau Elinor harrumphed. "In that case, perhaps, you should act a gracious host and sit her next to you at dinner. Today is an informal dinner, but even if it wasn't, she is high enough in rank to warrant it."

Sebastian didn't protest as Frau Elinor led him toward his muse.

Lavinia.

His aunt was hoping to marry him off, he knew. He wasn't about to fall into her trap, but he also wanted to be properly introduced to his muse. And there also was this deep-seated need to make her smile. Although there was a bigger possibility that he'd make her frown or storm off by saying something inappropriate again.

Frau Elinor paused and breathed in deeply before they reached their destination.

Sebastian frowned down at her. "Is something amiss?"

"No, no." She resumed her step. "I am just getting tired a lot quicker these days. And I keep falling asleep in all sorts of inconvenient situations. One day I might just fall asleep standing up." She laughed, but Sebastian didn't find her lack of energy charming.

She was in her seventies, and not many people lived this long. But she'd seemed strong and healthy until this blasted trip to England. The voyage had tired her out. But the country air was bound to do her good.

"Lady Lavinia," Frau Elinor said. "Allow me to introduce you to my nephew, the Marquess of Roth."

Lady Lavinia turned, and a smile froze on her lips.

Sebastian sketched a bow. "A pleasure."

She sank into a curtsy, although her eyes were shooting daggers at him. "Pleasure's all mine."

"Look at that, Victoria needs me!" Frau Elinor exclaimed and slowly went in the opposite direction from her grand niece.

Sebastian swallowed a chuckle. She was not subtle at all. "My aunt, ever the matchmaker, decided that I should escort you to dinner."

"Why did you not protest?" she asked with a sigh, looking fatigued and rather defeated.

To cheer you up? "I never say no to my aunt."

"You probably do not say inappropriate things in her presence, either."

A surprised chuckle left his lips. So she was still upset about earlier? "Believe it or not, I do. But she loves me just the way I am."

"Lord Roth—"

"Sebastian."

She threw him a sharp, reprimanding gaze. "I do not know why you decided to make me the center of your amusement, but I shall be quite dull company."

Something was amiss with his muse, but Sebastian was not about to give up easily. "Then how about I try and provide the amusement for you instead?" Sebastian offered his arm.

She looked at him from under the furrowed brows. She was so tiny, just a fraction of his height, which was why her expression was more comical than threatening. Her eyes darted to the side for a second, before she nodded to herself and placed her fingers on his sleeve.

* * *

The dinner was a disaster. The entire house party was not going the way Lavinia had planned either. Instead of spending time with Mr. Townsend, she was constantly accosted by Lord Roth. If that wasn't bad enough, seeing Kensington, speaking with him, pulled the rug right out from under her feet.

So Lavinia sat there concentrating on her food instead of

the conversation around her. People made her anxious. Food made her feel better, if only for a few moments.

"I enjoy a woman with a hearty appetite," Lord Roth said by her side. "But if you continue ignoring me in favor of your plate, people will think that you prefer venison to my conversation."

Lavinia licked the remnants of the venison's juicy flavor off her lips. "But I do indeed prefer venison to your conversation," she said quietly.

"You wound me," Lord Roth placed a hand to his chest in mock offense. "I am trying to be a gracious host."

"By offending me? Offering to paint me as an excuse to—" Lavinia clamped her lips shut, realizing that she spoke too loudly. What was it about this man that could so easily arouse the flames of ire within her?

"It is a compliment, I assure you," the wretch said with a grin.

He bowed his head, dark hair glinting in the candlelight, now, more than ever, standing out, in contrast to other gentlemen surrounding him with stark white wigs. And then to her horror, he turned to his other side and called for Mr. Townsend, who happened to be sitting a few seats down. "Wouldn't you agree, Mr. Townsend?"

Lavinia froze in horror. Her eyes darted to the gentleman in question. What was Roth doing?

"Apologies, my lord. I must have missed the question."

"Wouldn't you say that an offering to paint a person is meant as a compliment?"

Lavinia was ready to collapse from shame. What was he doing?

"If the offer is extended by you, then no doubt," Mr.

Townsend replied. "Lord Roth is one of the greatest con-temporary artists of our time."

The gasps and whispers of surprise ran down the table, while Lord Roth turned toward Lavinia. "See, *ma petite* Lady Lavinia? I would not dream of causing you offense. On the contrary."

Petite? Lavinia raised her brow.

Uncommon for most dinners where people only talked to the people beside them, their side of the table started animatedly discussing art, a buzz of conversation enveloping the entire room.

"Very well," Lavinia allowed. "Perhaps you are not a lecherous old marquess on the prowl for a young, gullible soul."

Lord Roth's dark, forest green eyes twinkled in merriment. "Coming from you, that is a high praise indeed."

Chapter 12

Lavinia entered the parlor the next day in higher spirits than before. The dinner last night was lively, and she seemed to have replenished her strength after the soul-sucking conversation with Kensington. If she could just avoid him and Caroline for the rest of the house party, and if she were able to corner Mr. Townsend and have an actual conversation with him, then perhaps the time spent here would not be in vain.

Lucky for her, neither Kensington nor Caroline was in the room. Unlucky for her, Mr. Townsend was absent, too. And so was Lord Roth.

Why was she looking for Lord Roth? She shook herself and headed toward Annalise.

"Well, how was your evening, darling?" Annalise asked as she saw her. "I saw you sit close to Marcus at dinner. Your entire side of the table was engulfed in an animated discussion. Did you have a chance to converse with him at all?"

Lavinia stretched her mouth into a smile. "We did converse,

but not a lot, because he and Lord Roth were discussing art most of the night."

"Oh." Annalise looked at her strangely. "I thought it was rather kind of Lord Roth to escort you into dinner."

"Yes, well, he only did that because his aunt insisted upon it. He has no interest in me at all." Brows drew over Lavinia's face. Why did she care? "Neither does Mr. Townsend," she hastened to add. "I am afraid I am still no closer to getting a proposal out of him than I was before the house party. And time is running out."

"Well." Annalise pursed her lips. "There is always an option of—not that I am endorsing it—but something to think about, perhaps…" Annalise put a hand to her stomach and breathed out as if she had a hard time getting out words.

"Annalise? Are you feeling unwell?" Lavinia placed a hand on top of her friend's arm.

Annalise chuckled. "No. I am just trying to say that perhaps being caught in a compromising position might expedite things."

It took a couple of moments for Lavinia to fully understand the meaning of her friend's words. And when she did, she didn't believe she'd heard her right. "Are you honestly suggesting this?"

"Well, not right away." Annalise swept a strand of hair away from her face. "But after spending a few evenings talking and sitting side by side during dinner, this would be a perfect way to speed things up. I thought that's what you meant when you said you needed lax chaperoning during the house party."

That wasn't exactly what Lavinia meant, but the crux of it was, she needed to seduce Mr. Townsend if she wanted to marry him. And she needed to do it fast. Except she didn't know the first thing about seduction.

Lavinia's eyes drifted across the room in despair, as if hoping that the answer to all her earthly problems would materialize itself right in front of her if she just looked for it hard enough.

Then her eyes fell upon Victoria. She stood by the column in one corner of the room, talking to… a fern? Lavinia looked around but didn't see anyone paying Victoria any heed. She turned toward Annalise. "I'll let you rest now. But let us talk about this later? Hopefully, when I have come to some sort of decision about what to do next."

With a swift smile at Annalise, Lavinia walked toward Victoria.

Lavinia craned her neck and noticed a shadow disappearing behind the column.

"Who are you talking to?"

Victoria jumped as she turned around, her hand on her chest. "Oh, my! You frightened me," she said with a nervous laugh.

"Apologies. I did not mean to startle you. You seemed in a deep conversation with a… fern?"

Victoria blinked and looked back at the place a gentleman—for it must have been a gentleman—had just occupied. "No, of course not. I was just… rehearsing a-a speech."

"About?"

Victoria shifted uncomfortably, then clasped her hands together. "I a—well, you know that English is not my native language. I have to practice." She fidgeted and refused to meet Lavinia's eyes as she blushed.

"If you intend to keep your relationship with a… fern a secret, I propose that you practice the lies you are to tell people. It is not my business, surely. But I assume it is not me from whom you intend to keep your... er... friendship?"

Victoria nodded demurely. "My uncle can be a little obnoxious when it comes to gentlemen." Ah, the infamous Marquess of Roth, standing in the way of all relationships, it seemed. "And before I tell my uncle about this... um... friendship, yes, I want to be certain of the gentleman's feelings and that of my own. Before my uncle has a chance to frighten him away, that is."

Lavinia let out a chuckle. "Is he very stern then, your uncle?"

"Oh, no, he is very kind. He is the one who raised me most of my life. But... he doesn't trust gentlemen in England."

Lavinia scoffed. "Are the men on the Continent much more upstanding, then?" Considering his own behavior, Lavinia doubted it very much.

Victoria made a barely discernible shrug. "I wouldn't know. He is very protective of me. And he didn't let me socialize with gentlemen there."

"Typical." Lavinia raised her eyes heavenward. While *one of the greatest contemporary artists of our time* engaged in all sorts of scandalous behavior, she had no doubt. "But I'd wager he spent his entire time in brothels or at his studio with all his naked models."

Victoria's eyes grew wider with each Lavinia's word. And then there was a light clearing of the throat just behind Lavinia. *Of course.* This would be the moment he showed up to eavesdrop.

"Do not sound so jealous, Lady Lavinia."

Goosebumps covered Lavinia's skin at his low, gravelly voice. She slowly turned toward him and had to crane her head all the way back to look him in the eyes. "I wouldn't dream of it." Her voice came out breathless. Surely, because it was a chore talking to a man who was so much taller than herself.

This was the first time she'd noticed how truly large he was, or perhaps he'd just never stood as close to her as he was standing now.

"Besides, I offered you the honor of modeling for me, but you refused."

"Uncle Bastian!" Victoria gasped, horrified by his brazen statement.

Lavinia sucked in a breath, her cheeks and ears burning in embarrassment. "You didn't offer it as a compliment, I am afraid. You said I could be one of your deficient subjects."

"I didn't say that. And I would never say that," Roth countered.

"But you meant it."

Victoria's head turned this way and that as she observed their little exchange. "I believe I shall… speak to Frau Elinor. Over there." Victoria smiled and scurried away.

Lavinia pursed her lips and narrowed her eyes on the insolent marquess. Her cheeks burned, and her chest heaved with labored breaths. He always managed to ruffle her. She had never had a conversation with him after which she did not feel bothered, but also, oddly… alive.

"Here's your issue, Lady Lavinia," he said in his low voice that made her shiver. "You have ideas about yourself—which are wrong, by the way—but you have certain ideas about yourself and you assume that everyone agrees with you."

Lavinia resisted rolling her eyes. "What kinds of ideas do I have? Please, do enlighten me."

"That you are not as attractive as everyone else."

She looked into his deep, green eyes and wondered if he was mocking her. "I am not as attrac—"

"That every other lady is perfect. That you are too big, too clumsy, too—"

"Very well!" Lavinia put up a staying hand. His directness was irksome. But even from him, Lavinia did not wish to hear the truth she knew about herself. "Thank you, I understand now. Do you have a point?"

"I do have a very good point," the wretch said with a charming smile. His eyes glinted like emeralds, and laugh lines appeared at the corners.

"Then please, do go on," Lavinia said unenthusiastically.

"My point is that you're wrong."

She sighed, her lashes fluttering down. Why must he mock her so? But if he insisted on continuing this discussion, she wouldn't back down either. "In your response to my innocent observation that you should paint people who were anything but perfect, you asked to paint *me*."

"Yes."

"Then how am I wrong in assuming that you think me deficient?"

Lord Roth's smile turned sensual. Lavinia had to blink a few times to be able to concentrate on what he said next. *Damn*, but the scoundrel had a lovely smile. Full, soft lips curved in a perfect arc, showcasing white, straight teeth, but that wasn't why his smile was lovely.

No.

He had an adorable little dimple on his cheek that made his smile boyishly innocent, no matter how depraved he truly was. "Because, my dear Lady Lavinia, in my opinion, no lady—no person for that matter—is perfect. And that's the beauty of it. Beauty is in imperfection."

Lavinia opened her mouth to retort but couldn't think of anything to say. *Beauty is in imperfection.* How utterly lovely. And how absolutely untrue. "If that was true, then considering all my imperfections, I would be the most beautiful lady in England."

Lord Roth pursed his lips to hold on to his laughter. And the rascal still managed to seem charming as he asked, "What if you are?"

Lavinia emitted a sad sigh. "Ah, my lord, I knew you not to be kind, but there is no reason to be cruel."

His brows instantly furrowed over his eyes. "I wasn't—"

"My apologies for the interruption."

Lavinia jumped at the sound of a familiar voice by her side. Dane's voice.

She hadn't noticed his approach.

Usually, she was always aware of his presence. She was the first to notice when he entered a room. She felt with the back of her neck what corner he occupied. But this time, she was too busy sparring with Lord Roth, and it was too late to escape.

Damn both of these men.

"Do you mind if I steal Lady Lavinia for a moment?" Dane addressed Lord Roth.

It was the last thing Lavinia needed. Dane would start to speak about her marriage again, about her nonexistent dowry, and just cause her more heartache. She didn't want any heartache.

Since sparring with Roth was the reason Lavinia hadn't noticed Dane's approach, she decided he would be the man to get her out of a conversation with Dane.

"Actually," she said and turned a brilliant smile toward the marquess. "Did you know that Lord Roth is a very popular artist? Yes, last night, at dinner he was offering to paint a portrait for every lady, and today happens to be my turn. But I am afraid we are losing light. Can't it wait?"

Dane watched her suspiciously, then turned toward Roth, as if his decision was the one he waited on. As if Lavinia's word didn't matter.

Roth looked from Dane to Lavinia, and her heart sank. Nobody said no to the duke. Especially not in her favor. Especially not when she was lying.

"Lady Lavinia is absolutely right," Lord Roth said, surprising her. Lavinia's heart soared and she observed Dane's annoyed grimace as the marquess continued. "We have but minutes to capture her in the perfect light. And since I am booked for the rest of the house party, if you lead her away now, Lady Lavinia would be the only lady without a portrait. You would not be the one to blame for that injustice, would you? I am certain you two can discuss whatever you want to discuss later."

Roth took Lavinia's arm and gently weaved it through his.

Lavinia was still reeling from excitement and gratitude, and she could only smile at Dane as they left the room.

She was so tense and full of disbelief that she was truly saved from having a conversation with Dane that she was able to let out a sigh of relief once they exited the parlor. "Thank you. I didn't think you'd agree to my ploy," she said heartily.

"A ploy?" Lord Roth raised a brow. "I agreed to no such thing. I am about to paint you. I did not think you'd be amenable to it, but—"

Lavinia tugged her arm out from the crook of his. "I am

not amenable! It is insulting that you think—"

"*Calmez-vous, s'il vous plait, ma petite.*" The retch had the gall to laugh at her. "Just a portrait. Out in the gardens, if people are about. I am not about to break etiquette, and I am not about to put us in a compromising position either. The last thing I need is getting stuck with a wife."

He offered his arm again.

Lavinia looked at it suspiciously. But she was probably too harsh in her assessment of him. He was a little too forward, and perhaps, slightly arrogant, but he did save her from an uncomfortable situation just now. And for all his talk of painting her nude, she should have realized earlier that he wouldn't risk it.

Perhaps Lavinia was too jaded from evading indecent offers from her father's lecherous friends. She'd become too distrustful.

She remembered the first encounter she'd had with Lord Roth and how tired and irritated he had been because he was being hunted by marriage-minded ladies. He was not in need of a wife, therefore he would not risk being compromised with her.

Lavinia nodded and cautiously took his proffered arm. "A portrait is fine, I suppose."

Roth tucked her hand in the crook of his arm again and led her away. "This is the least that you owe me. After all, I did save you from the big, bad duke."

Lavinia swallowed but didn't say anything. He wasn't wrong.

"What did I save you from, exactly?"

Lavinia sighed. "Nothing. The duke just worries about me, and I prefer to do things my way."

"Ah."

Lavinia threw him a side glare. "What does that mean 'ah'?"

He shrugged. "Just that."

"No, you don't seem to believe me."

"Listen, it is none of my business, so if you don't want to tell me, I am not about to insist. It just seems a little more than a rebellion toward independence. *That* I know a lot about. My niece is doing it right now. She wants to choose a husband on her own." He scoffed as if the idea was utterly ridiculous.

"And why wouldn't she choose a husband on her own?" She watched from the corner of her eye, as his features turned grave.

"Because she is young and naïve and can fall for all sorts of lies. Gentlemen in England are not honorable."

Now it was Lavinia's turn to scoff. "As opposed to you?"

"I am in England, aren't I?" He raised a brow and smiled his charming smile again. The wretch.

Lavinia forced herself to stay indifferent. "So, you admit that you are dishonorable."

"Did you have reservations about that? Because I think offering to paint you unclothed sealed my title as a scoundrel."

Lavinia threw him a side-eyed glare. "You weren't serious when you offered that, were you?"

"Oh, I was very serious, but that is not what we were talking about, is it? I know a rebellious spirit when I see one, and you are *not* it."

"What am I then?" Lavinia stopped in her tracks, forcing him to halt too.

Roth looked her over under his hooded eyes. Lavinia's breath hitched in her lungs, and her cheeks heated as she forced herself to stand still under his rather rude perusal. "I think you and the duke were involved," he finally said in a matter-of-fact tone of voice. "And since he is here with his wife, you are avoiding them."

Lavinia wrenched her hand away from his side. "How dare you?" she seethed.

He looked at her in bewilderment. "How—?"

"What do you take me for? A fallen woman? A-a mistress? Is that why you offered to paint me? Because if you think—"

"I did not mean to insult."

"You did not mean to insult me by calling me a light skirt? Pardon for overreacting then!" She tossed her head back. "And thank you, but I do not need saving. Least of all by you. I'd rather face the wolves than be in proximity to you."

"My lady—"

Lavinia turned on her heel and walked away.

And to think that she'd started to like him, to sincerely enjoy his company. What an idiot she was.

Chapter 13

The dinner was a boring affair. Sebastian didn't want to cause gossip by sitting Lady Lavinia next to him for the second evening in a row, especially after their fight earlier in the day, because he was certain to get a set down or two from her.

So instead, he had to endure boring conversations and suffer through watching Lady Lavinia flirt with Mr. Townsend. Was Sebastian the one who'd encouraged their acquaintance with his question the night before? Or were they friendly even before? Sebastian remembered Lady Lavinia entering his gallery hall, looking for someone… Could it have been Mr. Townsend? If so, Sebastian didn't understand what she saw in the lad.

He studied the man with narrowed eyes. He wasn't an expert on masculine beauty, but Marcus's features were even, his nose straight, his manner polite. He could see how women would find him… tolerable if they liked boring men.

Sebastian heaved a sigh. He was being unfair. Mr.

Townsend was dependable. He had lands, he had money, he had looks. He wasn't a debauched bounder, nor was he a gambler. He was a reliable sort, and perhaps everything that Lady Lavinia needed.

He shifted uncomfortably in his seat. He needed to get his mind off of the chit. He wasn't looking for a lover, and neither was he looking for a wife. So whatever this obsession with Lady Lavinia had become, it needed to end.

Sure, she had inspired him to paint again, but was it truly an inspiration if he could only paint her and nothing else?

He needed to get out of England and for that, he needed to safely marry off his niece.

Ah, yes. Another stubborn woman who was dead set on torturing him. He looked across the table at Victoria, who was having a lively conversation with an elderly earl.

Sebastian frowned.

Who was the gentleman she was interested in? She never showed any indication of who it could be, or perhaps Sebastian didn't pay enough attention to her. He was too preoccupied with Lady Lavinia.

His gaze traveled back to the lady in question just as she laughed, throwing her head back, exposing her neck for all to see. Sebastian's breeches tightened, and his breathing quickened. He gulped and looked away before he made a fool of himself.

His gaze landed on the Duke of Kensington, who was also admiring Lady Lavinia.

Oh, for God's sake! Could he be more obvious? His wife sat just a few places away, conversing with her companions.

Everyone spoke about how perfect their marriage was. And by society's standards, it was perfect.

They attended all the same social events, held the most lavish balls, and despite always arriving together, they never spent a minute in each other's company in public.

There were no longing gazes. Hell, they barely even spoke.

Was it too much of a stretch to conclude that the duke had a mistress? And that said mistress was a lady he couldn't take his eyes off of?

Sebastian's fingers tightened on the silverware. He had an undeniable urge to throw something at the insolent duke. And Lady Lavinia had the gall to pretend affront when he'd suggested she'd had a liaison with the man.

Not that he could blame her for seeking comfort in the arms of a powerful duke.

"You've been quiet all evening, Lord Roth," said Lady Carlyle, a young, blonde widow, who sat by his side.

He cleared his throat and forced his gaze away from the other side of the table. He'd been completely rude to the ladies by his side. "My apologies," he said with a smile. "I am too preoccupied with my efforts to marry off my niece. You understand."

"Oh." Lady Carlyle waved the issue away. "A lady in possession of such beauty should not worry. Add to that her dowry and her status… She'll be married in no time."

Sebastian smiled. "I suppose. But I want her to choose wisely."

Lady Carlyle fiddled with a lock of her golden hair. "If she has as much charm as she has wit, it won't be a problem."

Sebastian inclined his head. "She is quite clever. I suppose you are right. I should trust her a little more."

Lady Carlyle leaned in, drawing his gaze to her ample bosom. "And perhaps if you trust her more, you shall have time for far more pleasurable activities than watching your niece like a hawk."

Sebastian blinked. He'd heard plenty of rumors about the lovely widow who loved spending her time with different gentlemen each night. Somehow, he hadn't even thought of arranging a tryst with her.

Did he want to have a tryst with her? She certainly was enticing.

His gaze drifted across the table to Lady Lavinia. She smiled shyly as she fiddled with her silverware. She seemed nervous and out of place. More than that, she was a debutante.

Whether his speculation about her and the duke was true or false, he couldn't have a liaison with her. He risked ruining her reputation and his own.

She needed to remain a muse for him and nothing more. As simple as that.

Sebastian returned his gaze to the beautiful widow by his side. "What do you think about modeling for a painting?"

Lady Carlyle licked the corner of her mouth. "What kind of painting?"

Sebastian studied her features intently as he spoke. "The kind that would require a great deal of privacy."

Her mouth drifted into a sensual smile. "I shall let you know."

* * *

The dinner was the liveliest of affairs. For the first time since Lavinia had arrived at the house party, she felt as if everything was going well. Mr. Townsend was charming and a good conversationalist. There was never an awkward pause in their interactions.

Lavinia would go as far as to say that this was her favorite evening of the house party if she ignored the fact that the owner of the estate was throwing dark glances her way the entire meal.

Lord Roth was scowling most of the evening, quietly sitting at his place, barely acknowledging the ladies sitting beside him. What darkened his mood? And why was he watching Lavinia?

Was he trying to figure out whether she was lovers with Mr. Townsend as well? The lout had the gall to tell her to her face that he thought she was Dane's mistress!

The nerve of the man.

Lavinia had to admit that it was slightly flattering that he had thought she could ensnare a man such as Dane… But it was mostly insulting that he thought her a light skirt.

Did he truly approach her because he thought her loose? Did he want her for himself?

The thought startled her.

Was she, in fact, desirable to a man? And not just any man, but a titled, handsome, strong man with long fingers and blazing green eyes…

What? When did she notice that he had long fingers?

Lavinia had to shake her head from her involuntary thoughts. Just then, Lady Elinor invited all the ladies to join her in the drawing-room while the men partook in port.

Thank God, a distraction! Her mind was going in a direction she did not like at all.

Annalise reached her side and weaved her arm through hers. "Well, it seems like things are going well for you," she said with a smile.

Lavinia nodded. "I think so. I think… Annalise, this might sound strange, but I think Mr. Townsend actually likes me."

"It is not strange at all, my darling." Annalise chuckled, her hand on her chest. "Marcus is a clever man. He can see how wonderful you are."

Lavinia squirmed inside her gown. Her corset was laced too tight, and she felt slightly flustered. "I am not certain that is enough for a proposal, though."

"Do not worry, darling. I spoke to Caroline and—"

Lavinia halted in her tracks. "Annalise!"

"Not about you." Annalise tugged her forward. "And do not stop, you will attract more attention. I wouldn't do that, dear. I wouldn't speak to her about you without your permission. But… I talked to her, and I suggested that we play some parlor games tonight after dinner. And she became very excited and scribbled a ton of ideas."

Lavinia gulped. "Aren't those scandalous?"

"Some are, some aren't. But they are a perfect way to get two people together without making it obvious. And then, of course, dancing does that too, and the ball is coming up in a few days." They reached a settee, and Annalise sat down gingerly. "Apologies if it seems like I am pushing you, but aside from everything going on in your life, this babe is growing too quickly. I don't think I'll be up to attending more house parties. "

Lavinia smiled and sat beside her. "It must be a wonderful feeling."

Annalise's smile turned tender. "The best."

"So, tell us, Princess Victoria," Lady Carlyle said loudly. "Did you find a man you fancy?"

Every eye turned toward Victoria. She smiled widely. "Do

I have to choose during my first house party?"

"You certainly do not," Lady Elinor said sternly. "You can have as many seasons as you need."

Victoria's family truly cared about her, and it made Lavinia feel warm inside.

Lavinia never had a family that cared. Well, that was not true. Matilda cared about her. But aside from the fact that she was eighteen when she'd married, now the poor woman had too many problems of her own.

And she hadn't been there for Lavinia when she was a young girl. Back then, she had no one to rely on except for Annalise, who was a young girl herself from a loving family and who did not completely comprehend all the woes Lavinia went through.

And then there was Dane…

Lavinia expelled a deep sigh. The conversation around her buzzed while she was just lost in her maudlin thoughts.

A few moments later, men joined the room, and the conversation grew even louder.

Payne walked straight toward his wife and sat next to her. Annalise, in an unfashionable show of affection, placed her head on her husband's shoulder, and he took her hand.

"Oh, how scandalous," Lady Carlyle said to Victoria, who stood nearby. "I truly hope you do not think this is how most marriages in the English aristocracy are." She averted her nose.

Victoria looked at the Paynes and shrugged. "What is so wrong with a loving relationship?"

Lady Carlyle scoffed. "Feelings are for the bourgeois. If you want to model your marriage after a perfect couple, you won't find anyone better than the Kensingtons."

Lavinia closed her eyes, although she wanted to shut her ears. She couldn't listen to this.

Lucky for her, Caroline spoke loudly, commanding the attention of the entire room. "How about a game?" she said cheerfully. "I think it is time to start some parlor amusements."

The entire room cheered, and people started suggesting games.

Victoria appeared by Lavinia's side. "Come," she said with a cheerful countenance.

Lavinia stood, and Victoria weaved her arm through hers.

"Let us get as far away from Lady Carlyle as we can. We do not want to sit next to her once the games start," she whispered into Lavinia's ear.

Lavinia tightened her hold on Victoria's arm and chuckled. Lady Carlyle was notorious for dragging people into scandalous situations and then gossiping about it. Lavinia was eternally grateful to have a new friend like Victoria.

Annalise was constantly too tired because of her babe, and Lavinia was happy for her. As well as terrified for her. So she didn't want to bother her too much. But she needed a companion. And Victoria was a lovely soul who made Lavinia smile.

"Thank you," she whispered back.

"Very well, deer hunter it is!" Caroline announced.

* * *

"As host, wouldn't you say that Lord Roth should be the first to play?" someone suggested from the crowd.

"Then I volunteer to play the deer," Lady Carlyle said

suggestively.

"Knowing how good of a hunter Roth is, this game will go on forever," Lord Cunningham noted with a bark of laughter.

Roth sketched a theatrical bow.

It was true; he was a terrible hunter, and quite honestly, he didn't want to play a foolish game. He wanted to paint.

Perhaps if he ensured that Victoria was entertained, he could slip away from the crowded parlor, whisk Lady Carlyle away, and spend the evening quietly.

He wasn't certain if the ploy of swapping out his muse for Lady Carlyle would work, but as long as he had the inspiration to paint, the subject didn't matter. Did it?

"Lord Cunningham is right, I am afraid," Sebastian said. "If we want the game to run quickly, we need to pick the best hunter. Kensington, perhaps you'd show us all how this is done."

All eyes turned to the duke. He just tipped his head in agreement. He was not a man of many words, and neither was he known to be an emotional fellow, which just made his exchanges with Lady Lavinia all the more interesting to Sebastian.

"Perhaps the duchess would indulge us in playing a deer?" Lady Carlyle said with a giggle. She'd definitely had a little too much champagne.

Caroline smiled widely. "Oh, I would never play the part of a prey."

The entire room fell into heaps of laughter.

"Perhaps you would want to switch and play the hunter, then?" Lord Cunningham offered and guffawed.

Caroline looked at her husband in a challenge, and he just tipped his head again in agreement.

"Now we'll all see the reenactment of how Her Grace ensnared the Duke of Kensington into marriage," Lord Sutton said, and laughter filled the room again.

Caroline's jaw tightened.

Sebastian was friendly with the duchess. After all, she became his ward when he'd inherited the title. But no matter how warm and welcoming Caroline was, they'd never become close.

Perhaps it had something to do with the fact that she'd been in mourning when he'd arrived. Or that she'd married soon after. She was very helpful with Victoria, and she was essential in helping Sebastian settle in, but Roth did not know anything of substance about his cousin.

The marriage between her and the duke was an enigma to him. Beyond the fact that the marriage had been prearranged by Caroline's uncle, Sebastian didn't know anything about the duchess's feelings toward her husband.

Perhaps Sebastian should have paid more attention to everyone around him, but he was too busy with his responsibilities. And too busy pouting that he couldn't go back to Europe.

He heaved a sigh. He needed to make certain he didn't make the same mistake with Victoria. He needed to make certain she made the best match she could.

Sebastian searched the room for Victoria and found her standing arm in arm with Lady Lavinia, laughing and exchanging whispers.

Were the two friends? When did that happen?

Sebastian inched his way toward them while the footmen moved a long table to the center of the drawing-room. When he reached their side, Lady Lavinia stood fiddling with her fan and nervously watching the Kensingtons as Lady Payne covered their eyes with a dark cloth.

"My lady," he said by her ear.

She jumped in reaction. She was easily spooked, he noticed.

"Unc—My lord," Victoria exclaimed with a smile. "I do not think you should have foregone—forewent?" She waved her hand in irritation. He and Victoria had a shared frustration with the English language. Because even though Sebastian was born in England, he'd spent most of his life in France. Whereas Victoria had only started learning English a few years ago.

"I don't think you should have given up your chance at playing the game," she finally finished her sentence. "It looks like quite a lot of fun!"

Sebastian shrugged. "I do not advise you to play it either. These games can get quite scandalous quickly. And we don't want any gossip following you around."

Lady Lavinia threw him a sidelong glance. She leaned closer to him, the scent of lilies permeating his lungs, and spoke so softly that he could barely make out her words. "Is that why you came here? To rid your niece of the scandalous influence of a fallen woman?"

Sebastian blinked at her, startled. Ah, she was still upset about his earlier remark. "You are a very suspicious person, Lady Lavinia. Why is that?"

She took a deep breath. "Perhaps it is because you constantly say the most scandalous things, and I am now conditioned to act suspicious around you."

Sebastian stifled a smile. "Trust me, out of all the influences in Victoria's life, you might actually be the least scandalous even if you *were* keeping company with the duke."

Lady Lavinia looked at him sharply. She opened her mouth

to say something but was interrupted by Lady Payne's loud voice. "Let's begin!"

The entire room erupted in shouts and cheers as the Duke and Duchess of Kensington stood across from each other on either side of the long table.

"To the left!"

"No, go right!"

"He is standing still!"

The crowd went wild, misdirecting the hunter—the duchess—while Kensington, in fact, did stand completely still. Wasn't the point of the game to move?

Any conversation became quite impossible though, so Roth had to contend himself with standing next to his muse silently.

Just then, from the periphery of the eye, he noticed Lady Carlyle fanning herself as she looked directly at him. Sebastian turned his head and met her gaze. Lady Carlyle lowered her fan just below her eyes and quirked her brow.

The invitation was clear.

Victoria was occupied with games, so he wasn't afraid of leaving her in the parlor. And Frau Elinor sat by the wall with a smile on her face.

Nothing is holding me in this room.

The crowd jostled, and Lady Lavinia staggered to his side. Sebastian caught her hand in his.

Or perhaps something is.

Chapter 14

People around Lavinia shouted and jostled from side to side. Lavinia instinctively tried to make herself as small as possible and occupy as little space as she could. Somehow she found herself sidling closer and closer to Lord Roth, to the point that their hands were almost touching.

Lavinia's left side burned from his closeness. She felt slightly uncomfortable, yet she didn't want to move away.

She couldn't quite reconcile her feelings toward this strange gentleman. He didn't repulse her. On the contrary, she felt a strange tug toward him. Sometimes it felt as though she had a thread tied to her bodice that was also tied to his waistcoat, and that it pulled her toward him every time he was in the room. Or every time he looked at her.

She was constantly aware of his presence, and it was quite unnerving. Someone waved a hand as they screamed toward the players, and Lavinia shrunk before staggering to the side.

She knocked against Lord Roth's solid shoulder, and he caught her hand in his. He looked at her as she straightened with an apologetic smile, then squeezed her hand.

Lavinia's heart jolted in her chest. The warmth from his hand traveled up her arm and then up her neck until she was blushing earnestly. He wasn't looking at her though, and neither was he looking at the players. His gaze was troubled as if he was lost in thought. And in his distracted state, he must have completely forgotten that he was still holding her hand.

Lavinia shifted uncomfortably in place but didn't pull her hand away. It was nice, she mused, having someone hold her hand. Was it the first time a gentleman had done that outside of dance? Very likely.

If anybody saw they were holding hands, she would be completely ruined, wouldn't she? She looked around. Nobody was paying them any heed.

Would it be the worst thing in the world to get ruined by Lord Roth?

She peeked at him from beneath her lashes. He was quite handsome, she had to admit. Not that that had ever been one of her requisites for a husband. But he was wealthy and powerful. His name would give her the protection she craved.

But she didn't like him… Did she?

No. He was insolent, arrogant, brash, and quite shameless. And aside from these adjectives, she knew nothing about him at all. Well, except that he was Caroline's cousin.

"Excuse me," he whispered closer to her ear, disengaged his hand, and walked in the direction of the exit.

Lavinia reeled as he left her side, feeling bereft and slightly chilly. How could she feel chilly in such a warm room with so many people around her?

Turning toward the players, Lavinia forced herself to

concentrate on the game.

Caroline ran her finger along the table as she walked slowly toward the other side, while Kensington walked in the counterclockwise direction.

How could Lavinia even have contemplated the possibility of marriage to Lord Roth? He was Caroline's cousin, and therefore, Dane's relative!

No. She should stick to her plan and try to get Mr. Townsend to marry her.

Where was he? She turned her head just as there was a high-pitched yelp, a gasp, cheers, and sounds of excitement.

Lavinia turned toward the players once more. Caroline was holding Dane by his arm as she tugged the cloth from her eyes. Her skirts were still swishing around her legs as if she'd made a rash move. Dane likewise tugged off his cloth and looked Caroline in the eyes.

She whispered something to him, but before he could answer, she turned toward the crowd. "Who is next?"

Dane stood there frozen, studying his wife in shock or admiration. She had never seen that expression on his face before.

Was she wrong? Was everyone wrong about their marriage? Did Dane harbor tender feelings toward his wife, after all?

A huge boulder settled in her throat, and she struggled to swallow around it. There was a time she'd wished Dane would look upon her in that unfathomable way instead. Just then, he raised his head, and his eyes met hers.

Lavinia blinked. What a way to have her wish granted.

"Did you see that?" Victoria exclaimed in excitement. "Cousin Caroline is so fast! I would have never thought."

Lavinia turned a polite smile toward Victoria. "Yes. Splendid."

Victoria raised her hand and took a step. "I want to play next!"

As Victoria rushed to play the game, the Duke of Kensington moved toward Lavinia.

Lavinia dreaded the conversation that might have followed. She felt alone and abandoned without Victoria or even Roth by her side. She didn't have anyone to cower behind. So before Dane reached her side, she ducked her head and slipped out of the room.

* * *

"Lavinia!"

Lavinia stopped in her tracks. She'd managed to scale the long staircase and even turn toward the family wing, but she should have just hid somewhere instead. There was no way she could outrun Kensington or anyone for that matter. As it was, her breath was rapid, and her heart felt as though it was about to jump out of her chest.

She slowly turned toward him.

His gaze was hard as he looked straight into her eyes, trapping her in place. "I've been trying to speak to you for the entire duration of this house party, and yet you always manage to elude me. Is something amiss?"

Lavinia took a moment to catch her breath. "No, everything's perfect."

"Then why are you avoiding me?" His voice was hard.

"I am not." Lavinia tossed her head defiantly.

"Truly?" Dane narrowed his eyes at her and took one step closer. "Then how come every time I want to speak with you,

I have to chase after you?"

"Perhaps you shouldn't have chased me," Lavinia breathed, breaking their eye contact. She couldn't look at him anymore. Not when he looked at her as though she were the only thing that mattered in the world. He had a way of looking at a person like that. Lavinia had to remind herself that she wasn't special. He just made everyone feel that way.

"Lady Lavinia." His voice gentled. "I only worry about your well-being, I always have. The duchess also expressed her concern—"

"Please," Lavinia said quietly, tears prickling in the back of her eyes. She raised her hand to keep him away.

She couldn't listen to this. He was always soft toward her when he was hard with everyone else. He was constantly worried for her when no one else was. And that was why she loved him.

But now that he was married, her heart bled just a little every time he showed her any sign of affection. Because if before she had harbored a hope that he could have loved her back, now that hope was dead. And every time he mentioned Caroline—his wife—Lavinia died just a little inside, too.

"Please, can you just let it go?"

"How can I let it go?" Dane furrowed his brows. "If I do, who will be the one to help you?"

"Your help is the last thing I need. The fact that I am avoiding you should have made you realize that!"

Dane stiffened. "The only thing it made me realize is that you are, in fact, in trouble."

"I am not," she lied brazenly. "I am quite well."

"Truly? Is that why you are here at a house party while your father is on his deathbed?"

Lavinia stilled. "It is not for you to criticize how I decide to spend my time, Your Grace. You, of all people, know how he treated me. He has never been there for me in my time of need, and he doesn't deserve me by his side in his."

Dane stared at her intently, making her feel uncomfortable. "You are not telling me something."

"Perhaps I am not. But why should I?"

"Because I am trying to help you," Dane gritted out.

"Well, I don't need your help, Dane!" Lavinia took a few deep breaths to calm herself. She licked her lips and repeated, calmer now, "I do not need your help, Your Grace. I do not need your meddling, and I do not owe you any explanations. Please, I would love for you to leave me alone."

"I shall leave you alone when you look me in the eye and assure me that you are not in trouble."

Lavinia's head felt heavy. She couldn't raise her eyes to him, let alone look him in the eye and lie. Not again.

"You'll be of age soon," he continued. "If your new household is troublesome, you can stay with us. The duchess can take you in as a companion."

To live with them under the same roof? Lavinia would rather die. "I won't—"

"We've been friends for too long for you to refuse my help now," Dane insisted, and it was just too much. Lavinia felt fear, resentment, frustration. All the feelings she'd managed to hide in the deep, dark corners of her soul bubbled up inside her.

"We were never friends!" She cried, then burst into a bout of nervous laughter. God, men were clueless. "We were *never* friends, Dane. I was in love with you! I *am* in love with you! Always have been."

There was a prolonged silence while neither of them spoke. Dane just stared at her as if seeing her for the first time. Self-deprecating laughter burst out of Lavinia's lips. Once she'd started, she might as well tell him all of it. What did she have to lose? "Do you remember the first day we met? My father had been…" she closed her eyes briefly against the memory and swallowed, "unkind that day. Then you came—large and strong—like a prince from the novels… And you saved me. You were the first man to ever show me kindness. And I have loved you for that. I loved you then, and I have loved you my entire life."

Tears freely slid down her cheeks now.

Dane cleared his throat. "Why didn't you tell me earlier?"

Lavinia raised her eyes to his. "Would it have mattered? Would you have married me if I told you?"

Dane looked away, his expression pained, his hands fisted by his side to the point of his knuckles whitening, and it was the answer if she ever got one. Of course, he wouldn't.

He swallowed. "Then why are you telling me this now?"

"Because you're married!" Lavinia wiped at her tears. "Because you are married to one of my closest friends. And for all your good intentions, seeing you now just… hurts. It hurts, Dane. And I don't want to hurt anymore. I am telling you this"—she wiped her tears with both her wrists—"I am telling you this so you will cease looking for me and just leave me alone. I can't accept your help, I cannot even look Caroline in the eye because of it. And the only solution for me now is to marry. And I can't do that if you're following me around and trying to interfere in my life."

"I only want what's best for you," he said quietly.

Lavinia nodded, tiny self-deprecating laughter leaving her

lips. "Yes. And what's best for me now is to be as far away from you as possible."

There was a beat of silence as Dane processed her words. It was obvious he wanted to say something, to protest, but Lavinia was tired of molding herself to his wants and needs. If he was her true friend, he would leave her alone. It seemed like Dane came to the same conclusion as he gave a sharp nod and walked away.

Lavinia's strength left her, and she leaned against the wall, lest she crumble to the floor.

It felt strange… During long, dark nights she had imagined having this reckoning with Dane, and she'd expected to feel free, happy even. But she didn't. What she felt was a gaping emptiness inside her. She felt as though she was surrounded by nothing… a void, or she was the void and nothing existed anymore. Her mind was completely blank.

Lavinia heard the soft noise of someone coming toward her, but before she could react, a crisp white handkerchief appeared before her face.

"Well, I think that was rather brazen of you." Lavinia immediately recognized Lord Roth's voice.

"Should I thank you for your observation, my lord? Was it meant as a compliment or chastisement?" she asked bitterly but took his handkerchief and wiped her face.

"Definitely a compliment," he said softly. "But there's no need to thank me for telling you what I think. But for what it's worth, I think you handled it splendidly. Very passionate, rather reminded me of French women. Definitely not like the simpering English debutante I've come to expect." There was a smile in his voice, and Lavinia couldn't help but smile, too.

"I thought you expected vultures, impinging on your title."

He let out a hoarse chuckle. "Or that. Yes. But you just told off a duke, so I don't think I have to worry about either of that with you. Come, I'll give you some wine that is not watered down."

Lavinia threw him a suspicious gaze. "You are not going to speak of nude art again, are you?"

He smiled widely, making her knees quiver and her heart skip a beat. "I shall try to restrain myself."

Lord Roth stretched out his arm, and she placed her hand in his. The moment he encircled her fingers with his, Lavinia felt steadier than she'd had since she'd encountered Dane in this corridor. Was she a fool to trust this man?

Whether she was or wasn't, there was no point in contemplating, because in the next moment they were ascending the steps of the servants' stairs. A moment later, they entered a small, stuffy chamber filled with canvases and other art supplies that smelled putrid like oil paint.

Lavinia looked around, but aside from three or four paintings, there were a few canvases with sketches on them which he had likely started but hadn't gotten around to finishing.

Lord Roth sat her on the padded chair by the window. Then he brought a bottle of port and two glasses.

He opened the bottle and poured them each a drink. "If you don't mind," he said as he moved away from her, "I will paint you while you drink. After all, you did promise to pose for me."

A hoarse chuckle left her lips. She had no idea why this gorgeous man would want to spend any time with her, let alone paint her. Her! The clumsy, unshapely lady with mousy brown hair and an unremarkable face. But if he wanted to, she wouldn't tell him no.

So she smiled and took a sip of the port. The sweet drink with a slight bitter pang traveled down her throat, making her feel lighter somehow. She took another gulp. Yes, the port was exactly what she needed right now. "Paint away, good sir," she said with a smile as she reached for the bottle to top her glass.

Chapter 15

When Sebastian agreed to meet Lady Carlyle in her chambers, the last thing he expected was to accidentally witness the dramatic argument between Lady Lavinia and the Duke of Kensington.

Lady Lavinia was so desolate after the fight, that Sebastian couldn't help but offer her wine. Surely, her sadness was the only reason for his invitation.

If following Lady Carlyle into her chambers felt like a journey to the gallows, inviting Lady Lavinia into his studio felt easy.

Easier still was sending a note via his discreet footman to convey to Lady Carlyle his apology.

Even easier was painting Lady Lavinia as the sun was setting and bathing one side of her face in red. The shadows played perfectly on her cheeks, accentuating her dimples as she smiled while drinking wine and recounting her life story.

Sebastian knew he wouldn't capture her likeness under this perfect light in one session, but he wasn't sure he'd get another try, either. As it was, he was courting trouble by hiding away in his studio with an unmarried young lady.

"…And then Caroline told us she was betrothed to Kensington," Lady Lavinia breathed and took another sip of wine. "It was the hardest day of my life. Well, one of the hardest…"

"You didn't mind Lady Payne marrying the duke before, yet you felt strongly about him marrying Caroline?"

She took another sip. "You do not understand." Her voice was slightly slurred, and she swayed in her seat. "Annalise is like a sister to me. We've known each other since early childhood, and she saved my life from becoming a complete tragedy. I love her, and there is nothing I wouldn't sacrifice for her."

"But not Caroline?" Sebastian asked as he painted cherry-red brushstrokes over her cheeks. The sun was setting rapidly, and quite soon he wouldn't be able to paint anymore.

"Caroline and Annalise became fast friends during Annalise's come-out ball. I'd been friends with Annalise forever, and suddenly all I heard from her was Caroline this and Caroline that—"

"You sound jealous," Sebastian noted with a soft smile.

Lady Lavinia sniffed and took another sip of wine. "She is beautiful, rich, beloved by many—including my best friend—*and* is married to the man I love. Yes, of course, I am jealous. I always have been. But it doesn't mean that I don't love her, nor does it mean that I don't want her to be happy."

She crinkled her brows as if she wasn't certain she was making any sense.

"Here's what the issue is," she said with a wave of her glass. "Caroline is happy and would be happy without Kensington.

She didn't *have* to marry him. Annalise was a penniless widow. So there's the difference. I would give Caroline everything I have in a heartbeat if she truly needed it. But I wasn't ready to give up Dane, because I thought I needed him more. And perhaps that is selfish, I know… And perhaps I haven't been the best friend to her lately, but… It is difficult to be the only one who is miserable."

The sun set completely while she spoke, enveloping his studio in darkness. Sebastian squinted at his canvas, illuminated by the lone fireplace in the corner of the room. No, it was too dark to continue. He put the brush down and lit a few candles.

"For what it's worth, I don't think you are being selfish," he said, as he perched his hips against the table with art supplies.

"You don't?"

"No, you have a right to fight for your happiness. You have a right to feel sad and angry when you lose. You can't just expect the feelings to disappear. It will take time."

A breath whooshed out of Lady Lavinia's lungs. Did she expect him to judge her and condemn her for her behavior?

"But tell me about you," Lady Lavinia suddenly said. "I feel like I've been talking for hours."

Sebastian crossed his arms across his chest. "What would you like to know?"

"Everything. I do not know a thing about you. How does a French gentleman and a Princess of Mecklenburg-Schwerin's uncle become an English Lord?"

Now, wasn't that a question requiring a two-hour answer? Well, Lady Lavinia seemed to require a distraction. "Do not let my accent fool you," Sebastian said with a smile. "I have no French blood in my body, although I love the country endlessly. My mother was the Duke of Mecklenburg-Schwerin's daughter. Frau Elinor's sister. She married an English gentleman against her family's approval and fled to England before I was born. The English gentleman was not titled, you see."

Sebastian shifted uncomfortably. He didn't like remembering the past. "She didn't quite fit in England either. So when my father died—I was about eight at the time—she moved to France with me. So that's where I grew up."

"Is that why you dislike England, so?" Lady Lavinia studied his face with rapt attention.

A chuckle left his lips as Sebastian contemplated his answer. "I apologize that this is the impression I made. I do not dislike England, I just prefer France."

"You seem, at least to me, to hold the English aristocracy in contempt."

Sebastian grimaced. Had he been this forward in his frustrations? "I do not. I suppose I am annoyed that I have to be here, but you have to understand that I have not been part of the aristocracy for most of my life. Even though I was born to a duke's daughter and an English gentleman, that was not how I was raised. I am a man of science and art. I've spent most of my days locked in tiny, dark rooms tending to my business. Having to interact with so many people is… difficult for me. It took a toll on my sanity, and I lost my peace of mind when I came to England. So if you think you saw contempt, I apologize. It was mainly my frustration."

"Do you wish you never came here?" Lady Lavinia trailed her finger over the edge of her wineglass, lost in thought. He wondered if she'd even hear his answer, but he answered still.

"No. I am grateful to have inherited this title, if only

for Victoria's benefit. If my being here helps her find an advantageous match and keeps her out of trouble, then I shan't have any regrets. It does not mean, however, that I do not feel out of place, because I do. I simply do not fit in."

Lady Lavinia laughed, her musical voice, wrapped Sebastian in a warm embrace. "You are handsome, rich, titled, and talented. Every woman in England would love to be your wife, and every man would love to be your friend. And if you do not fit in, then there is no hope for me."

She stood, swaying, and gingerly walked toward him. "Is my portrait done?"

Sebastian shook his head. "Not yet. I am not certain I'll be able to finish it, but—"

She stopped just beside him, her warm breath fanning across his arm. "Oh. this is amazing," she said softly as if mesmerized.

"Isn't it?" he asked with a wide smile. "Now imagine that… Except nude."

Lady Lavinia laughed merrily and pushed him on his arm. "You promised!" She swayed as she said it, and he put a hand on her shoulder to make certain she didn't fall.

"No, I promised to give it my best effort."

She chuckled, then turned back to the portrait. "I look at myself in the looking glass every day," she said thoughtfully. "But this is not what I see."

"What do you see?"

She narrowed her eyes at the portrait in concentration, the tip of her tongue peeking between her lips. "Not this," she finally said and laughed.

He took the empty glass from her hand. "How many of these did you drink?"

"When I look at myself," she said, staring into his eyes, ignoring his question, "I suppose I see all my imperfections."

Sebastian shook his head. He had had enough of that. Who in the world had convinced this beautiful woman that she was less than? Perhaps she didn't need to be convinced, perhaps the fact that the man she loved chose another played a major part in how she saw herself.

He placed his palm against her soft, warm cheek. "And all I see is your beauty."

She didn't answer for a long moment. Instead, she looked deeply into his eyes, as if trying to solve a puzzle. She licked her lips. "Do you know that I have never been kissed before?"

Sebastian blinked. He didn't expect the conversation to take this turn. He cleared his throat before he could speak. "No, I did not know that."

"I wonder if it's nice," she slurred lightly. "Is it nice?"

His eyes lowered to her lips without his conscious thought. She licked her lips slowly, and Sebastian's groin hardened. *Damn.* "Very nice."

"Show me," she breathed.

Sebastian realized that he was still holding her cheek in his hand. He stepped away. "I don't think you should be asking strange men to kiss you when you're alone in their studio, extremely, top-heavy drunk."

"I absolutely agree." Lavinia took his face between her palms and planted a kiss on his lips.

Sebastian couldn't help it. He instantly opened his mouth and kissed her back. She was enthusiastically lapping at his mouth, and Sebastian couldn't help but smile. But then her hands traveled to his hair, her fingers scratching against his scalp, bringing feelings of pleasure he hadn't felt before.

The wine must have gone into his head, too, because surely if he'd been sober, he wouldn't allow a young, unmarried lady to be fondling him brazenly, pressing her soft, ripe body to his length and kissing him ardently—albeit inexpertly.

He put his hands on her waist to push her away, but she moaned, and instead, his palms circled her waist and settled on her back, pressing her closer to him. He opened his mouth and took over the kiss.

She tasted of port, sweet, with the hint of fruit and raisins. Her mouth was warm and welcoming, her lips soft and silky. She moaned again and pressed herself even closer, cradling his hard cock with her warm flesh.

Sebastian's hand traveled up and cupped her soft, rounded breast. They both moaned at the contact.

Suddenly, Sebastian wished they had no barriers, no clothes on. He wanted to see her naked body, and not for the sake of art, but for his own carnal pleasure. He wanted to run his tongue along her skin and taste her… everywhere.

Her lips were sweet, but how would her breasts taste? He wanted to fondle her nipple not with his finger, but with his tongue. And he wanted to taste not only her breasts but everywhere; her neck, her belly, the soft skin on the inside of her thigh… He wanted to taste the sweet nectar of her passion and smell the scent of her desire.

The thought sobered him, and he pulled away from her.

What in the world was he doing? She was a virgin. An unmarried young lady! If anyone knew what they had been doing—hell, if anyone knew she was alone with him at all—she'd be ruined.

She swayed as he stepped back, and Sebastian steadied her. Lord, she was barely standing on her feet! And here he'd been delighting in her kisses, forgetting himself in the taste and feel of her while she was not comprehending what she was doing.

Sebastian closed his eyes in disgust. He never thought he'd be the one to take advantage of a helpless young lady.

"That was nice," she said dreamily.

One side of Sebastian's mouth kicked up in a smile. She was a delight, for certain.

"Now let me take you back to your chamber before anyone realizes that you've been missing this long."

"Nobody will be looking for me," she said with a sad lilt in her voice.

Lord, he'd taken total advantage of a lady who was clearly broken-hearted and vulnerable. He was the worst sort of scum.

He cleared his throat. "Can you walk?"

She looked at him, affronted. "Of course, I can walk."

"Good. Then let's go. I'll escort you through the servants' stairs so nobody notices you."

She nodded, so he took her arm and weaved it with his. She leaned slightly against him, either to keep herself upright or dare he hope because she wanted to?

They walked silently down the stairs, her warmth at his side giving him comfort. He liked having her by his side; he realized. There was no need to speak, nor to paint. She was just there, and he felt peaceful.

They reached her chamber, and Sebastian opened the door for her. She stumbled, caught herself on the doorjamb, and laughed. Sebastian shook his head. "Will you make it to your bed without incident?"

She giggled again. "I don't want to call my maid... But I

suppose I can manage."

Sebastian raised his eyes heavenward. "Fine, I'll help you."

He entered the room and barely had time to close the door when a tiny, black little demon with glowing green eyes jumped on top of him.

Wait… no, it wasn't a demon. A cat?

"Oh, no!" Lavinia exclaimed. "Careful, Miss Gale doesn't like…"

She didn't finish her sentence but just watched him with a strange expression on her face as he cuddled the cat close to his chest and she started purring.

"…men," Lavinia finally said. "Or at least she never liked a man before. Are you certain you are a man?"

Sebastian barked a laugh. "Perhaps it's just Englishmen she takes exception to."

"Perhaps." Lavinia watched him as Sebastian rubbed the kitten behind her ears and lowered her to the floor. The cat rubbed herself against his legs, unwilling to step away.

"Traitor," Lavinia whispered, and Sebastian gave a bark of laughter.

"You needed help?"

She cleared her throat. "Yes. Would you mind helping me out of my clothing?" She turned with her back to him and started working on her bodice and stomacher. "I can remove my front, but I'll need help with my corset."

Sebastian watched her as she shed the top of her dress and then the overskirts and petticoats. He gulped, watching the expanse of her back that now opened to him above the corset. His lips itched to kiss her, bite her, lick her.

He touched his fingers to her corset strings while trying to divert his mind. "Does Miss Gale spend her days in this room?" Miss Gale, as if hearing her name, started purring.

"Victoria was nice enough to assign me a maid since I haven't brought mine with me. A lovely girl named Beatrice. She takes Gale out for walks, feeds her, and takes care of her."

"Well, I can ask my other servants and they can take turns watching her during the day and perhaps let her roam around even more. These lands are vast. And perhaps she will appreciate hunting on our grounds." Sebastian's breathing quickened as the corset gave way and all that was left between his fingers and her flesh was the thin fabric of a chemise.

Lavinia caught the corset against her chest and turned toward him. "It is strange that she took an immediate liking to you. You are the first male she ever did that to."

One side of his mouth kicked up in a smile. "Perhaps she senses my noble character."

Lavinia looked down her undressed length and then raised her brow at him.

"Fair enough, but I am not undressing you for my personal gain… Well, maybe a little. But mostly I am helping you."

He walked toward the bed and threw back the sheets. "Get in."

She placed her clothing on the chair beside the bed and climbed under the sheets. Miss Gale immediately jumped onto her and settled on her chest.

Sebastian sat next to them on the bed, a sudden thought plaguing his mind. "She didn't like *any* man she came into contact with?"

Lavinia shook her head.

"Even Kensington?"

Lavinia let out a chuckle. "Even him."

"Hm, she must have known he was not good for you."

Lavinia smiled, then looked away for a moment before meeting his gaze again. "Will you kiss me again?"

Sebastian swallowed hard. "I don't think it's a good idea. I already took advantage of you—"

"Did I take advantage of you?"

"It's not the same." He placed his hand against her cheek, and she covered his hand with hers. So warm… So soft. So small. *Damn.*

Sebastian leaned down and placed a soft kiss upon her mouth. He licked slowly between her lips until she opened to him, then swept his tongue inside for one lingering kiss.

Just one.

He pulled away, his breathing frantic.

"Good night, Lady Lavinia," he whispered hoarsely.

Before he could turn away, she caught his hand. "Maybe you don't have to go."

Sebastian blinked, not sure he'd heard her correctly. She wanted him to stay? That would not end well.

"Just… sit with me for a while."

Sebastian had to summon all the willpower he had not to say yes to her at that moment. This would be most inappropriate. And if he stayed, they were not going to just lie there and talk.

No.

He would kiss her.

Everywhere.

He kissed her softly again and murmured against her lips, "Good night."

Sebastian stood sharply and ran out of her bedchamber as though the hounds of hell were on his tail.

Chapter 16

Something small and wet poked Lavinia in her face. She squirmed, unwilling to wake up, and then… lick. Lavinia turned her face away.

"Meow!"

"Oh, Gale," Lavinia croaked. "Why can't you give me a few more minutes to sleep?"

She opened her eyes and was greeted by the shimmering sun.

"Oh, Lord." She groaned, took Miss Gale into her arms, and cuddled her against her neck. Miss Gale was so warm and soft, and Lavinia didn't want to get up at all. Her head ached, her throat was dry, and her eyes itched.

There was a knock at the door and then the maid Victoria assigned to her, Beatrice, walked into the room.

"Ah, you're up, my lady. Just in time. Breakfast will be cleaned up in about an hour, and you need time to dress."

She looked around the room, and her gaze fell to the heap of clothing on the chair by the bed. "How did you get undressed without me?" She tsked and went to collect Lavinia's clothing.

How did I? The memories came flooding in, and Lavinia shot up. "Oh my God!"

Miss Gale jumped from the bed and licked herself irritably as if regretting letting Lavinia touch her at all. Lavinia could sympathize with that, for at the moment, she was feeling something remarkably similar.

Beatrice turned to Lavinia, wide-eyed. "Is something amiss, my lady?"

Lavinia bit her lip. "No. It's just… I didn't realize how late it was."

Beatrice smiled. "Well, you go wash up, and I shall prepare your morning gown."

Lavinia scurried from the bed and went to perform her morning ablutions.

"Oh, God," she whispered to herself, as she scrubbed her face.

Had she really kissed Lord Roth last night? Was he the one who undressed her? *Please, let it be a dream, let it be a dream.*

Miss Gale meowed and walked into the closet, rubbing herself against Lavinia's legs.

"His Lordship said to take your cat and keep it with us during the day," Beatrice said as she walked into the dressing room to pick out Lavinia's attire.

Blast!

So that wasn't a dream. *Oh, no. Oh, no. Oh, no.*

Lavinia smiled and nodded to the maid while she squirmed on the inside. She'd acted like a complete wanton! *And* she had invited him to stay the night!

She would never drink port ever again!

Lavinia squeezed her eyes shut and then took a few deep

breaths, trying to calm herself. Her hand went to her face, and she touched her lips, remembering his kisses… He was so tender with her, so sweet. She quite enjoyed the kisses. Did he?

What are you thinking, you fool?

She had flirted with Mr. Townsend during dinner, told Dane she loved him after the parlor games, then got drunk and kissed the marquess!

She covered her face with both her hands, and they almost burned from the heat in her cheeks. What had happened to her?

She took the toothbrush, peppered some powder, and brushed her teeth violently, hoping that it would help her forget everything that transpired the night before and wash away the shame.

She could fix it. She would apologize to Lord Roth for her brazen behavior and tell him that she'd never acted like this before and never would again. She would go to Dane, and… no. There was no salvaging that relationship.

Lavinia groaned and shut her eyes. She didn't want to get dressed. She didn't want to leave her chamber or even her dressing room.

She whimpered.

"My lady? Are you feeling unwell?"

Yes! Yes, that's a perfect excuse. She was unwell and would be for the rest of the house party. That would be the perfect excuse for her to never face any of those people ever again!

The idea was too tempting. But she couldn't do it. Annalise, Caroline, and even Victoria would be worried about her. And once they saw she wasn't ill, they would drag her out of her room to join the house party again.

More than that, not even taking into account all the trouble Lavinia was in, she couldn't hide away in her chamber while Matilda sat by Lord Birch's side, looking after the ill man. Matilda was on the precipice of being thrown out onto the street. She depended on Lavinia and her successful betrothal.

Hiding in her room would not solve Matilda's or Lavinia's own problems.

"I am well, thank you," Lavinia finally said. "Just a little headache, but that shall pass."

Beatrice nodded. "I shan't dress your hair tightly then."

Lavinia tried for a smile.

Oh, but she was in deep, deep trouble.

Now that she'd made up her mind about rejoining the house party, the gravity of what had happened the night before hit her.

How in the world was she going to face Dane after her outburst? How was she to continue flirting with Mr. Townsend after what happened with Lord Roth? And most importantly, how would she ever be able to look Lord Roth in the eye?

Beatrice helped her change into a fresh chemise and then started dressing her in her corset and the petticoats. But Lavinia could barely comprehend what was happening around her.

"Are you sure you don't have a fever? You are warm to the touch," Beatrice said.

Lavinia just smiled and shook her head. No, she had no fever; she was burning in shame.

"I am well, Beatrice. Please, do not fret."

Beatrice nodded and led her toward the vanity table, and as soon as Lavinia sat down, she started working on her hair.

Lavinia bit her lip nervously. She had to get out of this

house party as soon as she could. But the only way she could leave the house party and continue with the rest of her life was to marry and quickly.

Her fingers moved toward her face, and she touched her lips again.

Oh, but those kisses were divine.

She sighed deeply.

And then another thought hit her. Lord Roth had kissed her... Willingly.

She had been flirting with Mr. Townsend, but so far, he had yet to exhibit any interest in her. Whereas Lord Roth had kissed her!

More than that, she'd stolen away with him to his studio, and if anyone were to know what happened, she'd be ruined.

Annalise's words rang in her mind. *Being caught in a compromising position might expedite things.*

She hadn't considered him before as a viable marriage prospect because she didn't want to spend her life in proximity to Dane and Caroline, but he spoke extensively about how he missed the Continent, so perhaps she could convince him to leave England once Victoria was married. Either way, she was far closer to a compromising position with him than she ever was with Mr. Townsend.

The immorality of what she was contemplating didn't escape her. But truly, did she have another choice?

If she were a titled rich man, then she would just do as she wanted. She would leave England on her own and escape all the troubles. As an impoverished young lady, she did not have such a luxury. She depended on men, so in order to secure herself a future, her only choice was to act immorally.

"Please, God, forgive me," she whispered to herself.

"You're ready," Beatrice said, and it took Lavinia a moment to realize that she was talking about her hair, not her plan to entrap the marquess. Either way, Beatrice was right.

She was ready.

* * *

Lavinia came down to breakfast, hoping to run into Lord Roth. She needed to arrange an assignation with him, she needed to arrange for people to find them in a compromising position, *and* she needed to do it fast before she started having second thoughts about the entire scheme.

She had no time for second thoughts. The sooner she got betrothed, the sooner she could go back home and save her stepmother from the company of Lavinia's vile guardian. Matilda had sent her a note, saying that Lord Birch's condition had not improved and that there was no change. She had urged Lavinia not to worry about her, but Lavinia couldn't do that. Time was ticking away.

Lavinia needed to marry, and she'd found a perfect way to do it. All she needed was to execute said plan today. Her palms perspired, and her entire body started to get clammy.

No. I have no time for nerves.

Lavinia had a cup of coffee as she sat smiling at everyone in the breakfast room. Her stomach churned so bad she was not able to swallow a single piece of toast. She scanned the room, but Roth was not there, nor were either of her friends.

She wanted so badly to speak to someone, anyone, about her outrageous plan, but nobody was about.

After a few minutes of staring down her empty coffee cup and not finding any answers there, she left the room and went in search of Lord Roth.

She couldn't seem to find him anywhere. She was even so brazen as to go to his studio, but the door was locked, and there didn't seem to be anyone inside.

Lavinia roamed the mansion in frustration, starting to doubt her plan altogether. What if this was a sign? What if this was a sign from God? Perhaps she should turn away—

There were sounds of footsteps coming from the gallery hall.

Right. Gallery hall. *Of course.* That's where he'd be!

She made her way toward the hall, but instead of running into Lord Roth, she collided with Victoria.

Lavinia caught Victoria by her arms. "Apologies, I wasn't looking."

"No." Victoria smiled and started repining her hair. "The fault is mine. I was in a rush."

Lavinia studied Victoria's face. Her cheeks were flushed, her eyes glowing, and her lips were slightly puffy. Lavinia would say that she was coming down with a fever, except her clothing was disheveled and her hair... Lavinia furrowed her brows.

"Victoria, is everything well with you?"

"Um, yes. Everything is perfect." Victoria smiled widely.

"Are you certain? You seem... unwell."

"Do I?" Victoria raised her knuckles to her cheeks. "Must be a sunburn. I should have brought a parasol with me."

Lavinia narrowed her eyes. "To the gardens?"

"Mhm... I... um... wanted to spend a moment outdoors."

Lavinia bit her lip. "Victoria... Please, let me know if I am overstepping, but I thought we were friends. We are, aren't we?"

Victoria's eyes widened innocently. "Of course, we are friends."

"Then I need to ask you this question, and I expect an honest answer… Were you having an assignation with a gentleman in the garden?"

Victoria's color deepened and her eyes shifted nervously from side to side. Then she leaned closer to Lavinia. "You won't tell anyone, will you?"

Lavinia took her hands in hers. "Of course not. We are friends."

Victoria's lips swam in an indulgent smile. "Oh, Lavinia, I am in love!"

"Truly?"

"Yes! And it is the most beautiful of feelings. And he is the most wonderful, tender man I've ever known." Victoria tugged on Lavinia's arms and swept her in a giddy twirl.

Lavinia looked around as they stopped and spotted a bench by the wall of the corridor. She tugged Victoria toward it, and they both sat down. "If that is so, why are you not open about your love? Why do you not tell your uncle about him?"

Victoria's smile turned into a grin. "Oh, I will. I mean, he will. He told me that he is going to speak with my uncle. Mayhap before the end of the week."

Lavinia frowned. "Why not earlier? Why not today?"

"He is very thoughtful, and he wants me to be certain about my affections. Isn't he wonderful?" Victoria clasped her hands in front of her chest, her gaze dreamy.

"Yes." Something inside Lavinia rebelled at the idea that a gentleman would be sneaking around with the lady he claimed to love. Wouldn't he want to claim her as his?

Oh, who am I to judge?

Nevertheless, she knew from her recent experience that although women were eager to wed, gentlemen didn't mind dallying without the thought of serious intentions. "Victoria. I don't want to discourage you, trust me. But I do worry about you. What if this gentleman doesn't have honorable intentions toward you? How do you know that he even shares your feelings?"

Victoria chuckled. "You are very pragmatic. And I am certain you wouldn't do anything as foolish as sneak around, stealing kisses with the gentleman you fancy. But I am a romantic."

Lavinia squirmed in her seat. Pragmatic, indeed. The memories of last night came unbidden, and her entire body heated.

"I just don't want you to regret it in the future."

"Do not worry, Lavinia. He is a perfect gentleman. He stole a few kisses, which I didn't mind. But we spend most of the time just… talking."

"You do?"

Victoria's smile softened. "Oh, Lavinia. We can spend nights discussing the most fascinating things. I love how his mind works. I love to listen to him talk. And he doesn't find my opinions and ideas foolish at all. But it isn't just conversation. I can spend hours with him in silence, and I will never get bored."

"How interesting." Lavinia turned to fully face Victoria. "Well, tell me more about him."

"Oh, Lavinia. My heart sings every time I see him! He is made of dreams and fairytales and all those novels I've been reading, which my sister recommends to me."

"But what do you know about him? And is he titled? How

old is he?"

Victoria bit her lower lip. "He is not yet thirty. And no, he is not titled. But he is a duke's son! That should be enough, shouldn't it?"

A duke's son was still a potential heir to a dukedom. Who would have any reservations about that? "I think it is wonderful," Lavinia said softly. "But are you certain you are in love?"

Victoria nodded vigorously.

"How do you know it's love?" It wasn't up to Lavinia to question Victoria, but for some reason, Lavinia felt very protective of her, and she wanted to be certain of her feelings. Especially since the gentleman was giving her that freedom.

"Oh, it is simple," Victoria answered excitedly. "I feel this pull toward him. Every time I walk into a room and he is there, I can feel him before I even see him. And when we lock eyes, the entire world disappears around us and nothing else matters. Something beckons me to come closer to him, be closer to him always. It is like a... magnet, do you know? It's like that. Love pulls two people together."

Lavinia contemplated Victoria's words. She'd loved Dane for longer than she remembered and yes, there was a pull she felt toward him, but he'd never felt the same. "But how do you know that he feels the same? What if the love is unrequited?"

Victoria laughed. "Oh, it is not love then."

"How do you mean?" Lavinia frowned.

"Love can only be between two people. You can have admiration, affection, even tenderness toward another person, and love is that, too. But for it to be love, there needs to be a mutual pull toward each other." She paused. "It is not love unless reciprocated."

Lavinia was about to protest, but she was distracted by Lord Roth's low voice. "Victoria! I've been looking for you for the last half hour!"

Lavinia and Victoria hastily stood. Victoria turned toward her uncle, but Lavinia could not look his way. He moved closer, and she could feel every step he took like a lightning bolt.

"Lady Lavinia." His voice was as soft as silk.

"My lord." Lavinia forced herself to look his way, but she couldn't look into his eyes. So, she concentrated on the intricate knots of his cravat.

The marquess ran his gaze down her length before turning back to his niece. "Where have you disappeared to?"

Victoria threw a quick glance toward Lavinia. "We were chatting, and I suppose we completely lost track of time."

Lord Roth's gaze returned to Lavinia, and she lowered her eyes to his waistcoat. She could hardly stand still under his burning perusal.

"And what were you two chatting about?"

"Love," Victoria said innocently, and Lavinia's cheeks might as well have been on fire, they burned so hot.

"Really?" His voice was lower than usual, and Lavinia felt butterflies rioting in her stomach.

She cleared her throat. "Well, Victoria is looking for a love match. It is only natural that our discussion veered in that direction."

"And you are not?"

Lavinia finally met his eyes. Her entire body trembled, but she felt confident in her answer. "I am not."

Victoria looked from the marquess to Lavinia and back again. "Well, did you want something particular from me, or were you looking for me for no reason?"

Lord Roth turned his hard gaze toward his niece. "I am to chaperone you, Victoria. I need to know where you are at all times."

Victoria, the soft-mannered lady that she was, rolled her eyes. "Then I shall go and make myself known at the assembly, shall I?"

She bobbed a curtsy and hurried away.

There was a charged silence between the marquess and Lavinia as they both refused to either move or speak.

"I trust you slept well?" he finally asked, and Lavinia squirmed from the inside.

"Very well, my lord."

He gave a sharp nod and turned toward the disappearing Victoria. But before he could take a step, Lavinia grabbed him by his sleeve.

She had a plan to execute. She couldn't tarry.

"Apologies," she said and winced. *For more than you will ever know.* "I wish to speak with you. In private."

He looked at her hand and then raised his gaze to her face. "We are in private. If you wish to speak, now is—"

"No." She shook her head vigorously. She needed time to direct the gossips to where they'd be meeting, so they would be caught in time. "Not now. Not here. But meet me in the gardens in half an hour?"

He looked at her suspiciously for a moment before his gaze fell to her lips. Did he think she was proposing an assignation? Well, in a way, she was.

"Very well. In half an hour," he said and walked away.

Chapter 17

Sebastian's heart drummed in his chest as he sneaked away from the drawing-room once more, this time not to find Victoria, but to join his muse in the garden. She looked coy and dare he say shy when she'd asked to speak with him, but he had a feeling she had more in mind than just a conversation. His cock moved just thinking about it.

When he came to bed the night before, he could not sleep. He kept thinking, dreaming of her.

He knew he couldn't have her. She was an innocent.

When he'd thought that she'd had an affair with the duke, he'd contemplated making her his mistress. He'd thought of spending nights with her, painting her, painting on her. Licking her all over…

But this was different. In her innocent, guileless way, she'd admitted to him that she'd never been kissed, and he could not ruin that innocence. But he could not avoid the pull she had on him, either. He couldn't avoid his rabid desire to possess her.

He wouldn't possess her, of course. But he wouldn't say no to stealing a few more kisses and perhaps making her feel needed, wanted. Making her feel as desirable as she was to him.

And perhaps he could make her feel something else she'd never felt before.

He swallowed and paused just as he saw her pacing behind the rose bushes. She seemed anxious and out of sorts.

Of course, this must have been the first rendezvous she had arranged. He smiled at the thought. The sun glinted off her brown hair as she walked back and forth. She puckered her lips, and there was a frown between her brows.

No matter, he'd smooth out the wrinkles on her face in no time.

He stepped out of the shadowed corner, and Lavinia jumped and placed her hand on her chest. She did that a lot. She was very easily spooked.

Sebastian smiled and stepped further into the alcove. "You wanted to speak to me?"

Lavinia wrung her hands nervously in front of her. "Yes."

Sebastian nodded. "Very well. But first—" He took one long step, and he was right in front of her. Sebastian lowered his head and caught her mouth in a soft feather of a kiss.

Lavinia instantly melted into him, and he had to weave his hands around her to keep her upright. She took him by the lapels of his coat and tugged him closer as she kissed him ardently.

"You feel so good," he whispered against her lips.

Lavinia moaned and rose on her tiptoes, pressing herself closer to him. Her soft curves enveloped his body in a warm, delightful feeling.

Sebastian took her face between his palms and angled her face for better access. She welcomed his tongue and moaned into his mouth, pressing herself even closer to him.

Sebastian tore his mouth away and trailed kisses down her face, then buried his face in the crook of her shoulder. "You are so beautiful, so—"

Sebastian was about to draw her even closer, but she jumped again, in her characteristic spooked way, and frantically looked around.

Her chest was rising and falling with her every breath, drawing his attention to her breasts. Sebastian tugged on her hand. "Do not worry, we are alone."

"For now," she whispered and stepped away from him.

"What?"

He didn't want to let go of her hand, but she pulled away from him.

"We shouldn't be here," she whispered, still frantically looking around. "Please, we have to go."

Sebastian scowled in confusion. "What's wrong?"

Lavinia covered her face with her palms. "People are coming, please."

She looked at him with such misery in her eyes, so he complied. They exited the gardens through his gallery hall, and he tugged her into a tiny, vacant closet.

"Speak." He watched her as she tried to pull herself together.

"I... um... I..."

"Yes?"

"I asked Lady Carlyle to come to the gardens with some of her lady friends during the time when I arranged a meeting with you there."

Of all the things he thought this conversation would be about, this was the last thing he'd expected. Sebastian almost laughed at his own naivete.

"What for?" he asked drily. Of course, he understood what she meant right away, but he wanted to hear it from her.

She looked at him pleadingly but must have seen something in his eyes because she looked down and said, "I was trying to trick you into marrying me."

Sebastian pursed his lips. He thought he would feel anger, disappointment, or even disgust upon hearing the admission, but curiously, he didn't.

"You wanted me to marry you," he repeated slowly.

"Well…" Lavinia wrung her hands. "Yes, I did. I orchestrated all of this so I'd be caught in a compromising position… with you."

"So I would marry you."

Lavinia nodded. "It is not difficult to fathom, is it? You are handsome, rich, titled, and… tall. Any woman would be lucky to become your wife, but I couldn't do it. I couldn't do it to you, but also, I couldn't do it to myself. Conning someone into marriage, to live with such guilt upon my shoulders. *No.* I have enough guilt to carry into my afterlife." She paused and looked at him pleadingly. "But we get on quite well, don't we? Perhaps you would still… I know it is asking too much but—"

Sebastian would have laughed if the situation wasn't so dire. *What a cunning little vixen.* "Lady Lavinia, even your manipulation aside, I would not marry you. I would *never* marry you." He saw lights dim in her eyes, and he almost felt sorry for her.

And there he was a few minutes ago, intent on raising her

self-esteem, dreaming of making her feel desired. And in just a few words, he'd crushed it all. She deserved it, didn't she?

"But you were kissing me." Her voice was barely audible.

Sebastian rolled his eyes. "Yes. And I was quite enjoying myself. But I am not here to find a wife. My main priority—my only priority—is marrying off my niece. And once it is done, I shall return to the Continent."

Lavinia's eyes lit excitedly, and Sebastian couldn't help but step back from the glint in her eyes. "But we could go together. I do not want to stay in England any more than you do."

Sebastian frowned. "You want to leave England? But what of your friends, your family?"

"Trust me, nothing is holding me here," she said bitterly.

Sebastian suddenly remembered her heartfelt admission to the Duke of Kensington.

Of course. She wanted to escape her broken heart, and she saw Sebastian as a way to achieve it. Was last night a lie, too? Did she ask him to kiss her, to spend the night, in hopes that they would get caught? His heart gave a curious pang. "I know of your woes, Lady Lavinia, and as much as I sympathize, I cannot marry you."

"You know nothing about my woes," she said emphatically. "And anything you think you know, just multiply that by a hundred, and then perhaps you'd understand. Or perhaps not even then. The only recourse for me is to marry. But to leave this Godforsaken place would be even better."

Sebastian fell silent for a long moment, two people warring inside him. The sad truth was, he liked her. He felt comfortable around her. And perhaps of all the women who plotted to marry him, he would not have regretted marrying her.

But knowing what she'd done, knowing the love she had for the duke, and the attempt she'd made to ensnare him under false pretenses, using him to get what she wanted, just made him harden his heart to her.

"My apologies, but it'll have to be someone else."

If only Frau Elinor could hear him now. She'd slap those words right off his mouth and force him to marry this poor woman.

"If I do not find a groom, my guardian will marry me off to an old, widowed hermit. And that's not the worst of my fate," Lavinia said quietly, crushing the fabric of her gown beneath her fingers.

"I wish I could help you," Sebastian said just as quietly. Then he turned and left the room.

* * *

Lavinia's entire body shook, and her eyes filled with tears. She didn't even know what she felt. Was it frustration? Anger? Or disappointment?

Perhaps fear?

Either way, tears rolled down her cheeks, and she wanted to crush and destroy everything around her. Nothing had gone like it was supposed to. Everything was crumbling down around her, and there was nothing to hold on to anymore. She had no strength left in her, and all she wanted to do was cry into her pillow.

She leaned her back against the wall and sobbed loudly. Curse anyone who might hear her. Let them. What else did she have to lose?

Her dignity?

She snorted. What was her dignity worth when her life was ruined?

She wiped her face and stood there, waiting for her thoughts to catch up with reality. What was she doing here, at this house party? Who was she trying to fool? She would never be able to ensnare a husband. Her only option was to trap someone into marriage and truly, if she couldn't do it to Lord Roth, she wouldn't be able to do it to anyone.

Besides, living with a husband who resented her for such an entrapment wouldn't be better than living with an old hermit up North.

Actually, that might be the best solution yet. Why was she trying to outrun her guardian's plan? Yes, she knew of quite a few old, lecherous men her father owed money to. But could her life with such a man be any worse than her life was up until now under her father's roof? She could take Matilda with her as her companion. Or if all else failed, she'd have to rely upon Annalise's generosity to house Matilda.

But what of the note?

She straightened and paced the floor of the empty room. What of the note? So far, the person who'd written it hadn't even threatened her. It just said *I know what you did.* But it didn't say anything else.

Was it possible that she was overreacting?

She continued pacing back and forth and thinking about her wretched situation until her mind was muddled. But she did come to a final decision. Her time at the house party was over. She was going home.

Chapter 18

"I am going back to London," Lavinia said as her friends settled around her in a small drawing room for afternoon tea.

"What?"

"Why?"

"You can't!" all three said at the same time.

"Is it because of Kensington and me?" Caroline scooted closer to the edge of her seat.

"Does it have anything to do with my uncle? Because he left for a ride in a really bad mood just a moment ago," Victoria chimed in.

"You can't expect me to travel back when we've just arrived," Annalise complained.

Lavinia closed her eyes briefly, preparing herself for what she had to say. "No, Caroline, dear, it is not because of you and Dane… I mean… partially. But truly it is just because I am wasting my time here. My father is in London. He is dying. He could be already dead. And my stepmother is alone with him and my guardian. I left her there promising her a better life once I secured myself a husband, but the truth is, even if I marry, there is no guarantee it will solve any of my problems!"

She turned to Annalise. "I am sorry I dragged you all the way here in your condition, but I am certain you can stay and rest here for as long as you need, can't she?" The last she directed to Victoria.

"Of course," Victoria said immediately.

"You can't leave alone!" Annalise said sternly.

"No. But I am certain that Lord Roth would spare me a maid." Her voice hitched on his name. And then she added quieter, "I am sure he wouldn't want me to remain here, anyway."

"So, it *is* about my uncle!" Victoria exclaimed. "What did he do? Because if he hurt you in any way—"

Lavinia put up a staying hand. "It is not what he did… Rather, what I did."

Annalise frowned. Victoria glanced from one woman to the next, trying to figure out if they understood what Lavinia meant, while Caroline just raised her brow.

Lavinia cleared her throat. "I tried to… I tried to compromise him."

All three women blinked and looked at each other.

"Compromise what?" Victoria asked.

"She means she put them both in a compromising position, so he'd be forced to marry her," Caroline supplied.

Victoria turned toward Lavinia, aghast. "What did you do?"

Lavinia grimaced and looked away. "It doesn't matter. Either way, it didn't work. I-I couldn't go through with it, and I stopped anything from happening."

"Oh, darling," Annalise breathed.

"And I just… I need to get out of here."

There was a beat of silence.

"I can order for a carriage to be prepared," Caroline finally said.

Lavinia looked up at her. "Thank you."

"But before I do… Are you certain this is what you want?"

Lavinia nodded gratefully. "Yes, yes, it is."

"Very well. The carriage shall be ready tomorrow morning."

"Tonight," Lavinia pleaded. She could see her friends' worried faces, but she couldn't stay another night here. "Please."

Caroline nodded and stood. "Very well."

She walked toward the door, and Lavinia dashed after her. "Caroline, wait."

Caroline turned, her features expectant. Lavinia fiddled with her skirt, unable to meet her eyes. "I am sorry we drifted apart since your wedding to Dane."

Caroline shook her head. "It is my fault. I was rather abrupt the last time we spoke."

"Well, I wasn't gentle either." Lavinia finally looked up at Caroline as a nervous chuckle left her lips. "The truth is… I had this ridiculous idea that if I married Dane, I would somehow be happy, but it was never true. He loves me like a little sister, perhaps. He cares for me as a friend. But he would never love me as a wife. And knowing that, living with him and having that knowledge, would have crushed me. And I am glad you saved me from that fate. And I only hope that *you* can be happy with him. You are, aren't you?"

Caroline watched Lavinia carefully for a full minute, expressionless. Then she smiled, patted Lavinia on her hand,

and walked away.

Lavinia turned back to Annalise and Victoria, feeling completely wretched. Victoria stood and slowly made her way toward her. "You will speak to my uncle, won't you?"

Lavinia grimaced. "I don't think that's what he wants."

"I do not care what he wants; that's what he needs. You offended him. He is hurt. And not to sound egoistic, but I am afraid this will affect his mood when um… Well, my suitor decided to ask for permission to court me today."

Lavinia's heart lightened. At least there was some good news. "Oh, that's wonderful! To tell you the truth, I was beginning to worry that that man was just dallying with you. I am so glad that he will finally speak to him."

"Yes, he said he'll do it today, but I am afraid Uncle will say no."

Lavinia closed her eyes in agony. *How many people will I hurt with my thoughtless acts?* "Very well, I shall speak to him. But I am not certain that it will aid your cause."

* * *

Sebastian galloped across the field in short intervals for over an hour. His horse was tired, his muscles hurt, and he was dripping with sweat. He finally dismounted and let his horse graze by itself as he sat down in the grass while his breath normalized.

He ran through the conversation he'd had with Lavinia millions of times in his head, and he couldn't quite grasp what he was mad at.

He wasn't mad at her. Because she was right. In the society they lived in, what choice did she or any other woman truly have than to ensnare a husband? English gentlemen often accused women of being mercenary, but it was either that or being poor and unprotected.

In the society they lived in, there wasn't much choice for a woman. Unless, of course, she was a lucky one and managed to marry for love, and her love happened to be a man of means.

On the Continent, it was slightly different. Oh, there were still marriages of convenience, and the aristocracy still pursued marrying within their circle, but it seemed slightly different, nonetheless.

Divorce wasn't impossible, and it didn't effectively ruin a woman either. Hell, his cousin had divorced twice before marrying Victoria's mother.

There was something about England, and how it treated its women, that made those women calculating and mercenary. Because otherwise, they wouldn't be able to survive.

So, no. Sebastian was not mad at Lavinia but rather at society.

He wiped the sweat away from his face and studied the horizon. A lone horseman was moving swiftly toward him. Sebastian let out a groan. He didn't want company. But he couldn't as well run. So he sat there and waited for the lone rider's approach.

If he were honest, and there was truly no reason to lie to himself, he wasn't angry with the wretched English society either. He was mad at himself.

For what? That he couldn't figure out, no matter how hard he tried.

The rider came closer, and Sebastian could finally make out his form.

William.

Sebastian stood and walked toward his friend. William jumped off the horse before it had the time to stop and swiftly walked toward Sebastian.

"Bastian, I've been looking all over for you," he said with a grin.

Sebastian smiled. "Well, you've found me. What do you want?"

William took a deep breath and looked around before expelling it. "I needed to speak with you on a serious matter."

Sebastian chuckled. Right now was not the time for serious matters. But he was curious what William had to say. "Yes?"

"It's about Victoria."

Sebastian stilled. "What about her?"

"I know you said she is off-limits."

Sebastian took a menacing step, and William retreated. "What did you do to her?"

"I didn't do anything." William raised his hands in the air in self-defense. "I swear. But I wanted to ask your permission to court her."

"Out of the question."

"Bastian—"

"Are you out of your mind?" Sebastian cried. "I told you I would never let her be courted by a bastard!"

"A duke's bastard."

"Devil take you, even if you were a king's bastard! No. She is a duke's daughter, damn it! A princess! She wants to go back to Russia and help her sister rule. She'll be a Tsarevna. With a bastard, she is doomed. Anywhere."

William swallowed. A vein ticked at the side of his neck, and his fingers curled into fists. He was angry. Good. Sebastian could use a worthy opponent in a fight.

"She took a liking to me."

Sebastian took another step, his own fists forming by his sides. "Did you touch her?"

"She is an innocent. But don't you think she needs to have a say in who she wants to court her?"

Sebastian's rage died slowly. William was right. Sebastian looked at him for a moment before asking softly, "Did you tell her who you are?"

William didn't answer. He stood still. The only indication that he'd heard Sebastian was his accelerated breathing.

"Did you tell her you are a bastard or did you lie to her?"

"I am a duke's son."

Sebastian sniffed. "She will never have you. Even if I gave my blessing, which I won't… But that girl, my golden-hearted niece… She has an iron will. She will. Never. Have you."

William breathed deeply, calming himself, then turned on his heel, mounted the horse, and galloped away.

Sebastian was still following the tiny figure of his old friend as he disappeared behind the bend when something heavy landed on his head. He turned around, his vision blurry, and noticed two figures standing before him. One of them raised his hands and the next moment everything went dark.

Chapter 19

Lavinia packed all her valises in a matter of minutes and was ready to leave. But the carriage wasn't sprigged yet, and she had some time to spare. She'd already said her goodbyes to Victoria and Annalise. She'd even spoken to Mr. Townsend, who was nice enough to express his regrets about her untimely departure. But there was one person with whom she hadn't spoken yet, and she was arguing with herself whether she should have sought him out or not.

Deep down, she knew that Victoria was right. She needed to speak to him. She owed him that. But she was too scared. Of what? She didn't know.

She'd made a complete fool of herself with him, and she owed it to him to let him know of her defection. She couldn't just disappear without a word.

And also she needed to apologize to him.

She wasn't certain if it was her honorable side speaking, though. Because as much as she tried to convince herself that she was seeking him out for noble reasons, the truth was simpler.

She didn't want to leave without seeing him again.

She didn't want to leave with him thinking she was a mercenary, treacherous woman. She didn't want to leave with him thinking that everything between them was a manipulation.

The truth of the matter was, she didn't want to leave.

Just thinking about her dark, dank home was enough to make her skin crawl. But that wasn't it.

She didn't want to leave *him*.

For the first time in her life, she'd found a human soul with whom she could be herself and not feel judged or pitied.

Sure, she had her friends, but it was different with them. She still had to put up a facade, to pretend that everything was well when it wasn't. With him, she'd completely broken down, and he'd put her back together while talking and drinking a bottle of port. He'd put her back together while he painted her in the most beautiful way.

And then he'd told her that this was how he truly saw her!

She didn't want to leave.

She already missed his tender gazes and scorching kisses. And perhaps in her heart of hearts, she hoped that he would ask her to stay.

How pathetic.

Either way, she had to see him one last time before she left, or she would never forgive herself. So she asked the stable boy to saddle a horse and rode to where Victoria told her Roth liked to gallop in the field.

She took this opportunity to canter around the premises and take a last look at the beautiful land she was about to leave. She was certain she wouldn't see this place for a long, long time, if ever.

She took a roundabout way to get to the field, watching the beautiful sunset, saying goodbye to the Roth estate.

When she neared the field where the marquess's horse grazed peacefully, it was almost too dark to make out what was going on. Lavinia's vision was not perfect, and it was even worse during the twilight.

She dismounted and looked around once more. A few feet away, two men were walking toward the horses they had tied down and they were… carrying someone else?

Was it Roth? Was he hurt?

Oh, no!

The thought sent her heart racing.

Lavinia dashed toward the men, blood rushing in her head. "Wait! Stop!" she yelled as she ran after them. She tripped over something and almost fell, but quickly picked herself up and paused as she saw what she had tripped over.

A hat.

Lord Roth's hat. And was that blood on it?

Lavinia straightened, her hands shaking, as she finally realized what was going on. But it was too late. A tall, broad man in dirty clothing and a toothless smile towered over her.

"Open up!" he said and shoved a foul-smelling bottle into her mouth. Lavinia had no choice but to gulp it down.

The scoundrel pulled the bottle away and replaced it with a cloth, tying it behind her head. Lavinia tried to fight, but his hold on her was tight.

She fought nonetheless, trying to scream to no avail.

"This is a feisty one," the thug said. "Can I have her?"

Lavinia's eyes widened, and she stilled immediately.

"You can't have anyone, Doug. That's not why we're here!" the other man replied irritably. "Now help me load this man onto the horse."

The man called Doug tied her hands behind her back with a rope and walked toward the other man. They picked up Roth and hoisted him on the horse, face down.

"That'll have to do," the smaller of the two men said. "We'll get him to a carriage like this."

"What about her?" Doug asked.

Lavinia had a hard time concentrating. Her vision became blurry—even more blurry than before—and a slight buzzing in her ears was getting louder and louder.

"He said to take the marquess and no one else!" A man's unpleasant voice cut through her subconscious.

Lavinia continued hearing voices around her but couldn't distinguish who was speaking or what was going on.

"But he also said to harm no one!" She thought this was Doug's voice.

Lavinia squinted and tried to push herself up, but it was no use. Her head became as heavy as a boulder, and she toppled over.

"We can't leave her here like this. She's seen our faces!"

Blast! They will kill me. Damn Roth. Why did she have to go and seek him out? Why did she have to run toward him and scream like a bloody idiot instead of running away?

"Then we take her with us?"

Oh, no! Lavinia managed to raise her head slightly. "Take me where?" Or at least that's what Lavinia attempted to say, but what came out sounded something like, "Tlk m wl?"

"Bloody wench is still awake!"

Lavinia fell back down again. She shouldn't have made

herself known! But her brain wasn't functioning normally or was barely functioning at all. Now they were going to kill her!

"Damn it!" the other man grumbled. "Give her more laudanum then. And load her on top of the horse. We're taking her with us."

"No, no!" Lavinia tried to scream as loud as she could, but the strength had left her, and all she could do was just moan.

Collecting the last of her strength, she managed to twist and roll away, but fate was against her. The men reached her in two quick strides and fed her a few more drops of a vile drink before everything went dark.

* * *

There was a sound of horse hooves and a carriage moving. A quick flash of the sun in his eyes, and then someone poured water on him. Everything was as if in a daze. Sebastian could not comprehend what was going on around him.

The next moment he was casting up his accounts, and yet again, he was back swaying in the carriage as voices shouted over him.

The door banged closed loudly, and Sebastian struggled to get up, but the moon hid behind a cloud, and he fell back into bed.

None of it made sense. There was an echo of voices, and then her angelic face.

Lavinia.

Light flashed as if the candles were blown out by the wind, and then it was dark again.

When Sebastian finally opened his eyes, he stared at the

bed canopy above him. He blinked. His lashes stuck together, his eyes dry as a desert. He squinted at the canopy again.

It wasn't his bed canopy. It was dark blue, and… was it dusty?

Sebastian groaned as he tried to turn, but his limbs felt heavy. There was a whisper of an ache in his head, and he felt groggy.

What were those dreams he'd had? It was all very similar to a time when he was invited to a sheik's dinner party that concluded with their exclusive dessert, hashish.

His mind had become blurry, and everything seemed to proceed too slowly for Sebastian before the memories all blurred together and distant echoes of the world unknown started penetrating his mind.

Sebastian squeezed his eyes shut and opened them again, trying to concentrate. Now was not the time for pleasant reminiscence. He tried to get up, but his head was too heavy. Instead, he gingerly turned to the side and… froze.

He was not alone in bed.

Next to him, only a few inches away, lay the soft, rounded body of a woman. She was still clothed, although her bodice sagged, showcasing her undone corset and a cotton shift. Her long, wavy hair had escaped most of her coiffure.

The lady—for she was dressed like a lady—lay on her stomach, facing away from Sebastian.

"Please, be alive. Please, be alive!" Sebastian whispered to himself as he moved closer to her.

Heat still radiated from her body, but it could have just meant that she had been alive until recently. Sebastian gingerly nudged her on her side, and she murmured something in her sleep.

Alive then.

The last thing Sebastian needed was to be found in the bed of a murdered lady.

He moved closer and peered into her face. Her hair was in the way, but he truly didn't need to see her face. He'd recognized her.

And he would have recognized her even earlier if his mind wasn't playing tricks on him.

Lavinia.

She was in bed with him.

Was it one of her ploys to compromise him? Because if so, it was sure to work.

Either that or he'd gotten drunk and…

Sebastian looked down at himself. He was still clothed, his breeches fastened. Hell, he was even still wearing his riding boots!

Sebastian sat up and looked around the room. The outdated wallpaper, dusty corners, and the furniture still partly covered with a white cloth all made it clear that this room had not been used in a while.

Sebastian slowly stood and walked to the window. He looked out and blinked, not believing his eyes.

From the window, he could see the ocean!

The ocean, devil take it! How in the world did he get here?

Sebastian licked his dry lips and almost gagged. That terrible taste, sweet but bitter at the same time, was still evident on his lips. He knew that taste all too well.

It was laudanum. Someone had fed him laudanum and while he was unconscious brought him here, wherever here was.

Suddenly, things started making sense. The disjointed

memories of being in a carriage, of someone swearing, bringing him up the stairs. The scuffle in the field…

William!

Of course, it was the damned bastard! He must have anticipated that Sebastian would refuse to give him permission to court his niece. So he had his thugs waiting in the bushes, and the moment he left, they hit Sebastian over the head, and brought him to God only knew where. And now William had the liberty to seduce Victoria.

The bastard had the gall to accost Sebastian during his own damned house party and transport him hundreds of miles away!

Sebastian turned and studied the prone body of Lady Lavinia. What of her? Why would William bring her there?

Well, he wouldn't find any answers in this room. If he wanted to know where he was or why, he'd have to seek out the answers from beyond this chamber. He'd need to confront his attackers. If they hadn't killed him and had gone to all this trouble to bring him here, it meant they wanted something from him. And it was time to find out what.

* * *

Lavinia woke up with a terrible headache. For a moment, she thought Miss Gale was lying on her back because she felt a heavy weight on her. But after a few minutes, she realized that her limbs felt like they weighed a few stones. She groaned and struggled to turn to her back.

There was a movement in the room. *Beatrice*?

Then the bed dipped as someone sat beside her, but Lavinia's vision was too blurry to really make out who it was.

"Here, drink this."

Lavinia hastened to sit up, and strong hands helped pull her up and lean her against the pillows. Strong fingers took her hands in his and then handed her a glass of water.

"Drink," he repeated.

Lavinia gulped down the life-giving elixir and was finally able to breathe deeply. She felt a lot better. She handed the glass back and rubbed her eyes with her wrists. She raised her head and stared at the Marquess of Roth's deep emerald-green eyes. He was sitting beside her, watching her curiously.

"What are you doing here?" she croaked.

The marquess hid his smile. "Do you know what *you* are doing here?"

"Well, I just woke up…" Lavinia studied his enigmatic features, then looked around. "Oh my God! Where are we?"

Lord Roth nodded. "Apparently, we are in the small village of Watchet."

Lavinia scrunched up her face in confusion. "Where?"

"Yes. I went downstairs to look for our captors, but we are all alone in this house. I was forced to go out and seek some answers, but there were not many people about. I stumbled upon a fisherman who was kind enough to show me a clean stream, sold me a couple of fish, and told me where we are."

Lavinia placed her fingers against her temples. Her head started buzzing again. "What are we doing here?"

Roth's exhale communicated all the suffering of a man who'd been forced into a situation not of his own making. "I wish I knew. But I think it has something to do with the bastard who wanted to court my niece… And I refused."

A bastard wanted to court Victoria? What did that have

anything to do with them being in this strange house? A whisper of a memory nagged at her brain. Something familiar… But it was escaping her.

"But how did we end up here?"

"I was accosted." Roth rubbed the side of his head. "And I have a sizable bump to prove it."

"Oh, no!" Lavinia shifted toward him, but her own head felt like it was full of lead. She licked her lips, a lingering taste of something bitter making her grimace.

Suddenly, memories came flooding back to Lavinia. She was getting ready to leave the estate, and she'd witnessed Roth getting attacked. *Oh, Lord!*

"What I do not understand," Roth continued, "is what you have to do with any of it. Why are you here? With me."

Lavinia leaned back against the pillows. "Is there more water? There's a horrible taste in my mouth."

Roth nodded. "Of course." He poured some water from the pitcher and handed it to her.

Lavinia rolled the glass in her hand, watching the crystal-clean drink. The water was never this clean in London. She took a few sips and handed the glass back to him before speaking. "I sought you out."

Roth placed the glass on the bedside table and looked at her under furrowed brows. "Why?"

"I-I wanted to apologize for… well, you know… for trying to trick you into marriage." She grimaced, her cheeks growing hotter and hotter with every word. "I rode into the field, and I saw men carrying you. I thought you were hurt and instead of running away, I ran toward you. And well… Here I am."

She smiled awkwardly under Roth's penetrating gaze. There was a beat of silence.

"Well," he finally said. "I suppose you got your wish."

Lavinia blinked. "Pardon me?"

Roth smiled tightly. "After our adventures, I shall *have* to marry you."

Chapter 20

Sebastian sat in the small chair in the kitchen, gutting the fish, while he would have preferred it was William under his knife instead. All he wanted to do was find a horse, chase down the bastard, and kill him.

Sebastian knew William very well. The selfish reprobate would do anything in his power to get what he wanted, which meant that he could have dragged Victoria to some member of the clergy and married her while Sebastian was still jostling in the carriage the night of the attack.

Sebastian imagined going back, stabbing the bastard in his gut, and watching him drown in his own blood with satisfaction.

He had to relax his hand, for he had been squeezing the knife so hard his knuckles grew white. Yes, the time would come when he came back and made Victoria a widow. Of course, that would set Victoria free to go back to the Russian Empire as her sister wanted. But Sebastian would figure it out later. At the moment, his main priority was keeping Victoria away from the criminal that was William.

How stupid was Sebastian not to have realized what was going on?

William had been ogling her every chance he had. Sebastian should have paid more attention to Victoria, he should have made time to speak to her more, and he shouldn't have been too distracted by his own woes and selfish tendencies.

Clink.

His knife clattered to the floor, and Sebastian had to breathe in and out in order to calm himself. He needed to concentrate. There was nothing he could do about Victoria now. Not yet.

As much as he wanted to find a horse and gallop back to his country seat at the first opportunity, he couldn't leave Lavinia alone. She had spent most of the day sleeping. She still felt groggy and disoriented.

The darkness had descended on them, and to top it all off, they were both hungry. They would have to stay the night at this strange place before they tried to find a way to return.

William didn't know it, but snatching Lavinia had been a huge stroke of luck for him. Because it was the only thing holding Sebastian back. Without her, he'd be long on his way to gut the bastard.

"Do you need any help?" Lavinia showed up behind him.

"Do you know how to clean or fry the fish?" Sebastian asked without looking at her.

She heaved a sigh and settled in the chair next to him. "No."

One side of Sebastian's mouth kicked up in a smile. Of course, she didn't. She was a lady. "Then I don't think you can help me."

"How do you know how to do this?" She peered into his face, but Sebastian avoided looking at her. Instead, he concentrated on the fish.

"I was taught anatomy extensively. In fact, I was part of *L'Académie des Sciences*. That teaches one a lot about how to gut an animal… almost any animal." He finally looked at her and almost laughed at her aghast expression.

Almost. Because he became instantly mesmerized by her instead.

Lavinia had let down her hair, probably because her coiffure was out of place, and he doubted she had a comb with her to put it back to rights. Her hair fell in long waves down her shoulders, framing her face in golden brown locks. Her face was illuminated by the fire, reminding him once again of a beautiful angel. And then, whether it was from hunger or just the effect she'd had on him, he had an inexplicable urge to bite her apple cheeks.

He snorted to himself and forced his eyes back to the fish.

"Did they teach you to cook any animal, too?" she asked.

"Well, no. One of my mother's friends—lovers—taught me to hunt, which I am terrible at. But he also taught me to cook what I've killed. We'd spend days out in the woods on hunting expeditions. He was a soldier, and cooking what one caught is something that is looked at as being very valuable. When our countries are in constant wars, one has to be able to feed oneself and his comrades."

"Mm, well, in this case, I am very glad to be your comrade, as I am starving."

"You won't have to wait long." Sebastian took two rapiers, poked them through the fish, and held them over the fire.

"My lord—"

Sebastian let out a bitter chuckle. "*Ma petite…* I think we've gone through enough for you to be able to dispense with the formality. Please, call me Sebastian."

There was a beat of silence. "I couldn't."

"Of course, you could. I do not feel like a lord at the moment, and truly, I never liked this title. My friends call me by my name, and I think you should, too."

"Sebastian," she said softly, and everything inside him tightened.

Had he made a mistake insisting on her calling him thus? She held too much power over him as it was. This bit of intimacy tipped the power balance completely over to her side.

"I am truly sorry about what I did… before."

Sebastian frowned. "What do you mean?"

"Trying to trap you into marriage." She had a guilty look in her eyes as she bit her lip and looked at him from beneath her eyelashes.

"You didn't go through with it," Sebastian countered with a smile. "William managed to do what you couldn't without even trying."

She grimaced. "Who is this William person, and why did he do this to you?"

Sebastian slowly turned the fish to make certain they had browned on either side. "He is someone who doesn't like being told *no*. If you asked me earlier, I would go so far as to call him my friend. I knew him for a few years in France. A cunning fellow. Always gets what he wants."

"And he wanted to court Victoria?"

Sebastian nodded. "Yes. But he is a bastard and a criminal. As a bastard of a duke, he feels he deserves a lot more than what he was accorded in life. But as a bastard, he never truly had a place in this world, so he turned to criminal circles.

Based on *that* and what he did to us, you can understand why I said no to him."

"A criminal? What did he do? Aside from… this." She looked around with a grimace.

"When I met him in France, he was one of the body snatchers. You know"—Sebastian threw a meaningful look—"the one who robbed graves and provided bodies for anatomical studies. I suppose this doesn't make me look good either or the entire medical society, but William is a master thief. He can steal anything for anyone. And as long as he gets paid, he doesn't care who he hurts. Or I should probably say as long as he gains anything. And because of that, you are here. So, perhaps I should be the one apologizing to you."

She shifted uncomfortably in her seat. "If I didn't try to trap you into marriage, I wouldn't be coming to seek you out. So, I suppose the fault is still mine."

"How about we lay the blame where it deserves to be," Sebastian said, realizing they could be sitting there and apologizing all evening, and it would still do nothing. "At William's feet. Although, I have to admit, seeking me out in the field after dusk was not your best idea."

"Oh." Her skirts swished as she moved closer to him. "I couldn't wait. I was about to leave the Roth estate."

He turned to her sharply. "Why were you leaving?"

"As I said, my guardian has a marriage prospect selected for me."

"A widowed old earl?" He raised a brow.

She nodded. "I thought it was time I stopped fighting my fate."

"So, you were just going to marry him?" For some reason, the thought angered Sebastian. She didn't strike him as a lady who just gave up after one failed attempt. "What about Mr. Townsend? I thought you set your cap for him, and he liked you well enough."

"Not well enough. And I couldn't." She pursed her lips and shook her head. "I realized how hypocritical I was being. I didn't want to be trapped in a marriage not of my own choice, and yet I was about to do the same to you. Yes, I was going to try and be a good wife, but it doesn't matter, does it? You would always resent me for trapping you and—"

"And here we are trapped still," Sebastian finished for her.

She looked down at her hands. "At least, this time it's not my fault."

Sebastian chuckled. "Here's something you do not know, *ma petite*. If you had trapped me in that garden, if it were *you* who forced my hand into marrying you… I would never feel resentful about it."

"You wouldn't?" She looked utterly confused.

"No. You were right. Women have little choice when it comes to their life, and I can't help but admire those who push through the boundaries of society and make a comfortable life for themselves. I admire women who disregard the rules or even use those rules meant to keep them at bay and turn those rules around to get what they want—or need—in order to survive. My mother was like that. You remind me of her. And I have to say that I appreciate your integrity in not going through with your ploy, but if you had… that would not be the reason I'd resent you."

Lavinia's eyes darted from side to side in confusion. She clearly did not expect him to say that. "Um… thank you."

Sebastian turned back toward the fire. "What I would resent you for, however, is getting stuck with a wife who would never be able to love me more than she loves another man."

* * *

Lavinia raided the closets after their delicious fish dinner, looking for something, anything she could wear. She cleaned herself slightly with a pitcher of water and dusted her skirts, but her clothing was still remarkably dirty. She wasn't sure how she'd made the journey in the carriage to where they were now, but her gown was spotty, ripped in places, and it smelled of her unwashed body and sweat. And rubbing her dirtiest places with water did not help alleviate the feeling that she was the filthiest human on earth.

Roth—Sebastian—told her that there was a stream not far from the house where they could wash up, but the thought of having to don the same stained clothes afterward made her shiver unpleasantly. At the very least, she needed a clean shift.

She'd found clean linen bed sheets and towels in one of the closets, but there seemed to be no clothing in this entire house. With one more room to search, Lavinia walked into one of the smallest bedrooms and noticed a trunk in the corner. She rushed toward it, opened it, and was ready to dance in relief. There was a small collection of female clothing.

Granted the selection was limited, but the size was even larger than hers, guaranteeing to fit her comfortably. There were a few nightgowns, a shift, a couple of nightdresses, slippers of a slightly larger size than hers, and a few handkerchiefs.

After digging through more things, and finding a hair comb, soap, and a few other things necessary for human survival,

Lavinia revised her initial opinion of the house.

At first, when she'd just woken up, she thought this was an abandoned place the owners had left years ago. Now she realized she'd been wrong. This house was definitely still used by the owners from time to time. It just happened that the owners were not there at the moment. Perhaps they were in London for the Season.

There were no portraits or anything, truly, to indicate who this house belonged to, but she'd wondered if the villagers or the fishermen Sebastian had run into earlier had any idea who lived there.

Sure, Sebastian had made up his mind that William was behind their misfortune, but something didn't feel right.

This just didn't feel like a house the bastard of a duke would live in.

Sebastian entered the room and cleared his throat. "Are you ready?"

Lavinia turned toward him and nodded. "Yes."

She noticed he had a heap of linen in his arms, too. Apparently, he'd found something for him to wear as well.

"Let us go then."

They made their way toward the stream in quiet contemplation. Lavinia was thinking about the uproar she had probably caused with her disappearance.

Caroline had prepared her carriage to leave… What had she thought when Lavinia didn't show up? What had happened when they couldn't find her anywhere?

And poor Annalise! Lavinia closed her eyes and whimpered.

"Are you unwell?" Sebastian asked from her side.

Lavinia shook her head. "I was just thinking how much

stress I probably caused my friends by disappearing! Annalise is in a delicate condition, and I worry that I caused her a fainting spell. And poor Miss Gale!"

"Well, I can't reassure you about your friend, but you can be certain that my household would not let Miss Gale get into any sort of trouble. And don't worry. Tomorrow I shall find us a mount, and we will be back in no time. Watchet is only a few hours away from my country seat. We were probably only gone one night."

Lavinia turned to look at him, and she knew that he was just as worried if not more about the people he had left behind, especially Victoria, and she tried very hard to come up with something to tell him to ease his mind, but no words seemed like enough.

Soon they reached the stream, and Sebastian turned toward her with a slight smirk on his lips. "Do you want to go first?"

Lavinia looked at the running stream, and then at Sebastian, and she realized that she had not thought this through at all… She'd have to bathe with Sebastian standing right there on the bank! All manner of thought whirled around in her mind, but she finally decided it would be better if he was preoccupied with drying and dressing himself when she was in the water so he would not have any interest in peeking at her naked, unshapely body.

He was a connoisseur! He spent his time painting perfect, beautiful female bodies with thin waists, shapely breasts, and small bellies.

And although what she should have felt was shame about the prospect of him seeing her undressed, she hoped he would not see her because she was certain he would lose interest in her the moment he did.

She didn't want to disappoint him.

"Please." Lavinia waved a hand.

Sebastian shrugged and started disrobing right in front of her. Lavinia gasped and turned around. Although she was unwilling to look at him directly, now that she had her back to him, she became desperate to see his body.

Compared to her, he must have been built like a god. She lowered her eyes and concentrated on her bodice to take her mind off him.

"You shouldn't be ashamed," he said loudly over the noise of the stream. "We are to be married, after all. Might as well have a look now."

Lavinia peeked at him over her shoulder. The idea that he would be forced to marry her still didn't sit well with her. But the idea of being married to him somehow left butterflies fluttering in her stomach.

He sat on the rock, his front to her. His shirt was off, and he was only wearing his breeches while he tugged off his boots. His shoulders were corded with muscles, and as he raised his torso, she couldn't stop herself from admiring his flat stomach, the muscles on his chest, and then the V-shaped lines that drew the eye toward the triangle of hair disappearing under his breeches. He put his hands on his falls, and Lavinia immediately straightened, looking away.

He laughed. "You can look. I am not shy."

Lavinia gulped. "Well, I am. And I would prefer it if you didn't look while I was undressing, either."

"Why not take this opportunity to study the male form? We are going to lie together, eventually. You might as well prepare yourself for what's to come."

"You speak of it so casually," Lavinia noted. "But perhaps

we are not going to marry."

"Ah! Devil take it!"

Lavinia turned around at Sebastian's loud cursing.

He stood with his back to her, knees deep in the stream as he splashed water on his arms. His beautifully shaped buttocks and the wide expanse of his back were covered in goosebumps.

He was obviously uncomfortable with the cold water, but all Lavinia could think of was how gorgeous he was. She just wanted to walk up to him and plaster her body to his.

He looked so strong… She wanted to know what his skin felt like. Were those muscles as hard as they seemed? Were his buttocks soft or tight? Was he—

Splash.

Sebastian dived underwater and came up a moment later, his chest to her. He shook his head to dislodge the excess water and smiled. He looked so joyous at that moment that Lavinia couldn't help but smile.

By the time she finished undressing down to her shift, he had already made his way out of the stream, shaking like a leaf.

He started drying himself immediately, groaning and hissing.

Lavinia stepped into the water and hissed, too. Lord, the water was freezing! How was she supposed to wash herself?

"Just jump in full body and wash yourself as quickly as you can," Sebastian said from the bank. "Do not stop moving."

Lavinia nodded and ran into the water. When she was waist deep, she sat down so that the stream covered her entire body. She broke the surface with a yelp, for it was impossibly cold, and then soaped her hair and torso, before plunging under the frigid water again to rinse off.

It must have taken her all of three minutes to wash her entire body, which normally would have taken her over half an hour in a warm bath, and she was running out of the stream like the devil's hounds were on her tail.

The moment she reached the bank, Sebastian came up to her with the towel and wrapped it around her body. "We should have brought a blanket," he said as he rubbed her body, trying to warm her.

Lavinia was not self-conscious anymore. Or at least it was not a priority in her mind. She just wanted to get warm. So she let him hold her in his arms and rub her body with his warm hands.

His hot breath on her neck sent goosebumps down her length and not from cold but from pleasure. She became languid and rested her back against him, feeding off his strength and his warmth.

They stood like that; she leaning against him, him holding her in his arms and rubbing her body to keep her warm.

Lavinia didn't want that moment to end. It was so nice being held. When was the last time anyone had just held her like that? She couldn't remember.

He kissed her lightly on her ear—barely a kiss, more of a nudge, and moved away from her. He bent down and picked up a clean shift and handed it to her. "Get dressed," he said gently and turned around.

It took Lavinia a moment to realize what was happening. One moment she was wrapped up so safely in his arms and then the next, he was turning away from her, giving her privacy.

Part of her was glad that he'd remained a gentleman, but

part of her was heating up from the inside and hoping against hope that he would kiss her again.

She couldn't tell him that. If he didn't find her enticing enough to kiss in her wet night shift, she was not about to beg him for it. So she ducked her head and hurried to get dressed before she froze.

* * *

It took Sebastian all his willpower not to devour Lavinia when he wrapped her in his arms. She was so soft, so lovely. He wanted to run his hands all over her body and study all her curves. He wanted to weigh her breasts in his hands, circle her belly, kiss her neck, her shoulders.

But she trusted him.

The shy, innocent young lady, who had asked him just a moment ago to turn around and not watch her undress, the woman who was frightened to even watch him bathe, the one who blushed at the sight of nude art, leaned her half-clad body against him. She relaxed in his arms, trusting him not to hurt her.

He could not abuse that trust. No matter how hard and aroused he was, no matter that all his blood traveled from his body to his cock, making him doubt he could recall his name. He could recall the fear in her voice when she'd asked him not to look at her.

He wasn't certain what she was afraid of. He didn't want to think that someone had hurt her. He preferred to contemplate that she was just innocent, untried. And she was afraid of the greater intimacy between a man and a woman.

And yes, he wanted her. But he wasn't going to be pushing

her, either. If she had been bold enough to ask for a kiss when she'd wanted it, she was bold enough to indicate when she was ready to explore more.

So he pulled away from her and turned around, giving her the privacy she needed to get dressed.

When she was done, Sebastian wrapped his coat around Lavinia, who was shaking from the cold, and they set out back to the house a moment later.

Lavinia held her dirty clothing and riding boots in front of her, as she wore a ridiculously large nightgown and strange, old-fashioned slippers. She'd probably found those things in the house.

How strange. Would William have had such an item of clothing in his house? It probably wasn't even his. He must have rented it for the occasion.

"Sebastian," Lavinia said as they were nearing their tempo-rary home. "I've been thinking about our situation while I was bathing and..."

"Yes?"

"And I came to the conclusion that you might not need to marry me."

Sebastian raised a brow. Need? *No.* Want? That was a different question entirely. "Do enlighten me."

"I am quite certain that the moment Caroline found out I was missing, she took every precaution not to let anyone know. And she would have found out first because she was preparing a carriage for me to leave."

"Right."

Lavinia burrowed deeper into his coat as if from cold or uneasiness. "Caroline is a good friend. She would never let the world know about my plight, except for the people who could possibly help. So once we find a vehicle, we can leave for London and just explain it as if my guardian came to collect me, and that is why I left hastily in his carriage. My guardian is adamant about marrying me to one of my father's creditors. I am certain he would corroborate the story."

Sebastian slowed his step. "I admire your forethought about the entire situation. But I thought marrying me was something you wanted. You planned to trap me and then when you couldn't go through with it, you asked if I'd still consider marrying you. Now that the issue is our best, and dare I say it, the only way out, you are looking for an escape."

"An escape for you." Lavinia halted and looked up into his eyes. "As I said earlier, there is a reason I couldn't go through with trapping you. This is not who I am. I do not want a husband who is forced to take me against his will. And you said you would not resent me for it, but you aren't enthusiastic about marrying me either."

"No, that is not what I said."

"You said you'd resent me for loving someone else."

Sebastian didn't answer. Was she truly still in love with her duke? Certainly, those feelings didn't go away in a few days, but after all that they'd shared together, did she not even see a possibility where she could love him more? "I believe I said I would have resented you if you were the one who trapped me in that situation. But it is different now."

Lavinia shook her head. "It doesn't have to be. And I know that for you having a wife would be a burden... I don't want to burden you. And I suppose I don't feel right that you were forced into this situation."

"Aren't you forced into it?" Sebastian was getting angrier by the minute. That woman cared about everything else but herself, and, for some reason, she was convinced that was what she deserved. And that made Sebastian's blood boil.

"Yes… but—"

"But what? You are a woman, and so you're expected to be forced into situations you dislike?"

Lavinia exhaled a shuddering breath. "Yes. I am used to dealing with things that are out of my control."

Sebastian smirked. "And that is why—now I don't mean to be unkind—but that is why the man you're in love with is married to another woman. That is why your friends are living out their lives the way you've wanted to live yours. You think of everyone but yourself. Sometimes it pays to be a little selfish."

Lavinia looked away.

He'd said too much. Perhaps he'd hurt her. Well, the truth hurt, sometimes.

"I don't think I know how to be selfish. The only time I did what I wanted without worrying about the consequences, I was foxed." She chuckled, completely oblivious to the fact that she had just given a major revelation about their night together.

I did what I wanted, she'd said. And that gave Sebastian a glimmer of hope.

They reached the front doors, but instead of entering, Sebastian paused and turned toward Lavinia. "It seems like you just need some practice. And perhaps this is the best place for it. I mean, we are staying in this house alone. We are trapped here overnight, and you are about to marry someone soon, even if it is not going to be me. So why not make this night memorable? Dare I say… wicked."

Lavinia giggled and fiddled with the clothes in her hands.

"I am not good at being a wicked lady."

"Well, then you definitely need some practice, wouldn't you say?"

She raised her eyes to his, and Sebastian had to steel himself not to reel from the force of her gaze.

"What do you want?" he asked softly and tucked a loose lock of her hair behind her ear.

"I don't know… I don't think I *can* be wicked."

Sebastian chuckled. "You just bathed half-naked in a stream in the middle of the night with a man who is not your husband. You drank port in a small studio while alone with a gentleman and then asked him to kiss you. You interrupted a kidnapping and forced them to take you, too. And you told off a duke—*a duke*—when he was forcing unwanted attention on you. You, my lady, are wicked in the best meaning of the word. So please, do not halt now. What is it you want? Tell me, and I just might grant your every wish."

Chapter 21

⚜

I*'ll grant your every wish.*

Wasn't that something every lady dreamed of hearing at one point or another in her life? To hear those words from a handsome man, desirable by many, and the one who made her pulse race, was something out of a fairy tale. She had to blink a few times to make certain this was real. She wasn't dreaming, was she?

To be wicked for one night before going back home and confronting the nightmare that was her life was more than just enticing.

She wanted it. She wanted all of it. And she wanted it with this man.

Lavinia stepped toward him, only to roll her ankle on something.

A rock?

She heard a hiss, and something bumped into her leg as she reeled. Lavinia screamed and jumped, the borrowed slipper flying into the air.

"Ow!" Something sharp jammed itself in her foot. She cried out in pain while hopping on one foot and cursing the entire world.

What was happening? One moment everything was perfect, and now she had embarrassed herself again.

Now, *this* situation felt entirely too real.

This was her life. Not handsome men telling her they'd grant her every wish, but tripping on air, and making a fool of herself.

"Do not move," Sebastian said, holding his arms out as if trying to calm a spooked horse.

Lavinia lowered her leg and watched Sebastian as she tried to regulate her breathing.

"It was just a grass snake. Not venomous. Do not worry at all."

Lavinia's eyes rounded. *A snake?* "I stepped on something sharp," she said on a pathetic whimper. "It hurts."

Sebastian's features immediately changed, his brows furrowed, and his lips sat in a thin line. "Let me look at it."

He lowered to his haunches and raised her leg, forcing her to lean against his shoulders. Her heart beat loudly in her chest, and there was a ringing in her ears. The entire world felt off-kilter, but his solid presence and sturdy shoulders kept her steady.

"You split your foot with a sharp rock," he said. "It's bleeding, but it doesn't seem too bad. However, I won't know for certain until I examine it better." Sebastian straightened and dusted his knees.

"There are candles in the room we woke up in this morning," Lavinia said. "You'll be able to see better there."

She'd turned the entire house upside down looking for

clean clothing that day and found some interesting things. They were lucky the house was actually lived in, or they'd be forced to starve and sleep on dusty sheets. Lavinia was about to take a step, but Sebastian stopped her with a hand on her shoulder.

"It is better if you don't walk."

Lavinia frowned. "How am I to get inside the house?"

Sebastian raised his eyes heavenward. "I'll carry you."

He said that as if it was the obvious answer. Well, it wasn't. She was heavy and—

Sebastian bent down, and Lavinia hopped away.

"No!"

"I said not to move," he gritted between his teeth.

"I-It doesn't hurt that much. I do not think it is anything serious. I mean, it stings a little, but I can walk."

"Let me carry you." It wasn't a request, it was a statement.

"No!"

"Why not?" Sebastian threw up his hands.

"I-I am too heavy," Lavinia said, her cheeks burning.

Sebastian's expression turned from confusion to utter befuddlement and then finally to annoyance. He bent down and scooped Lavinia into his arms, not letting her dance away from him this time. He walked up the steps and entered the house without exhibiting great effort. But the stairs leading into the bedroom they both occupied were vast.

"Truly, Sebastian, I can walk. I don't want you to hurt yourself."

Sebastian paused with one leg on the stairs and started shaking with laughter. He leaned his back against the wall as he laughed, gulping for air.

Lavinia hit him lightly on his shoulder. "Why is this funny?"

Sebastian finally stopped laughing and looked Lavinia in the eyes. "Do I look like a feeble man?"

"No, but—"

"Then how about I worry about myself, and you worry about you?" He pushed off the wall, readjusted Lavinia in his arms, and proceeded to scale the stairs. "What is it with you and this fixation you have with your weight? And not only weight but your appearance. As if somehow you are less than perfect."

Lavinia scoffed. "I am *far* from perfect. And wouldn't it be better if I were like Annalise or Caroline and weighed like a feather, so you could easily carry me?"

Sebastian snorted. "No, I wouldn't enjoy a feather in my arms quite like I am enjoying having you."

Oh. Lavinia's blush deepened.

"Instead of dreaming of being thinner so some feeble man could carry you up the stairs," he said as he readjusted her in his arms once more, "why not dream of a stronger man to carry you no matter how heavy you get?"

Lavinia tightened her arms around his neck. "That sounds almost romantic."

Although she would never admit it, Lavinia realized that she *had* been dreaming of finding a better man—her prince—someone who would appreciate her the way she was.

Of course, she'd dreamed of it, but she'd never thought that those dreams would ever come true. They were always in her mind and to remain there while she lived her less-than-perfect life. She dreamed of this, but she never acted on those dreams and didn't fight for them to come true. Victoria's words echoed in her mind: *if you want to have something you've never had, you need to do something you've never done.*

Sebastian entered the bedroom, sat her down on the bed, and lit the candles around them. "Lie down, relax, and please do not move until I return," he said and disappeared out of the room.

He came back with a pitcher of water and a bottle of what looked like… gin?

"It's a good thing this house still has some alcohol left," he said as he placed everything on the bedside table and settled near her foot. He studied it under the light of a candle, and Lavinia tried very hard not to squirm.

She'd been examined by a male doctor from time to time, but this was the most intimate she'd ever been with a man if one excluded her drunken plea for him to kiss her.

"I need some clean cloth. Perhaps I'll need to rip these linen sheets—"

"Oh, no, don't. I found some handkerchiefs in the trunk earlier. I put them on the bedside table."

Sebastian took a handkerchief and proceeded to clean the wound. Lavinia bit on her lower lip to ignore the pain.

"You can scream if you like," Sebastian said with a smirk.

"It isn't the worst pain I've ever experienced," Lavinia said with a chuckle. She was just making a joke, but he threw her a dark gaze.

"What *is* the worst pain you've ever experienced?"

Lavinia clamped her lips shut. She shouldn't have said anything. "I fell a lot," she said quietly. And then in the attempt to steer the conversation away, "Does your promise to do something wicked with me still stand?"

Sebastian raised a brow. "The adventure of being bitten by a snake and stepping on a sharp rock didn't deter your wicked spirit? I knew I was right about you." He winked and continued wrapping her foot with a clean handkerchief as he grinned.

"Well, on the contrary. Perhaps I was reluctant about it, but this incident, however small, reminded me that… Well, life is short. Why not do something wicked while we can, right?"

Sebastian laughed and patted her foot. "All done."

Lavinia shook her head in wonder. "You are a wonderful painter, a good cook, and now a doctor? Is there anything you are bad at?"

One side of Sebastian's mouth kicked up in a smile. "Trust me, a lot." There was a pause. "However, I shall try to do my best in doing your bidding. So, tell me. What is it you want?"

Lavinia narrowed her eyes on him and chewed on her lip. "When I was looking for fresh linen today, I found a sketchbook and a pencil in one of the rooms."

Sebastian raised a brow. "And?"

Lavinia shrugged. "I thought perhaps we could use it."

A slow smile appeared on Sebastian's face. "I'll go bring it."

* * *

Sebastian found the sketch pad and the pencil and rushed back into the room.

Lavinia was leaning back against the pillows, her hair spilling about her shoulders, her hands demurely folded on her lap. She looked like a vision from his dreams.

He had dreamed about painting her, relaxed and scantily clad, since the first moment he had met her. And now that she'd finally allowed it, he bubbled up on the inside from anticipation.

It wasn't the excitement of simply painting again, or even

painting *her*. It was the anticipation of learning more about Lavinia, studying the crevices of her soul, and putting them up on the blank canvas.

Painting someone was the most intimate thing he had ever experienced. In a way, it was more intimate than making love. True, more often than not he ended up bedding his models, but that was more the extension of the intimacy they'd shared, the natural progression. Because once someone let one into their soul, it was easy to let them into one's body.

He stepped further into the room, and Lavinia looked at him shyly from beneath her lashes.

"Are you ready?" he asked.

"Yes." Lavinia's lips didn't move, but her eyes shone in a wonderful, secret smile.

Yes.

That's how he wanted to paint her. That little smile that so many people did not get to see, that confidence in her eyes that was so rare. Perhaps, if she saw herself this way, if she saw how beautiful she was, she would smile like this more often.

And then she did something he did not anticipate. She reached out her hand.

Sebastian raised a brow. "You want me to help you up?"

Lavinia shook her head, and now she was smiling in earnest. "No, I want you to give me the sketch pad and a pencil, and I want you to undress. I am going to sketch *you*."

It took Sebastian a moment to process her words before he broke out in laughter.

Oh, cunning little vixen. Well, he had encouraged her to be wicked.

He sketched a bow. "As you wish, my lady."

Lavinia grinned as she took the sketch pad. Sebastian held on to it for a moment longer, feeding off the feeling of her fingers on his. Then he took two steps back, looked Lavinia boldly in the eye, and started undressing.

Lavinia's eyes hungrily followed his hands and devoured every newly revealed piece of flesh. Sebastian dragged it out on purpose. He slowly undid the buttons of his shirt, then inch by inch drew it from his body.

Lavinia's mouth was slightly open as she watched him with rapt attention.

He put his hands on the falls of his breeches and paused. Lavinia caught her breath. Sebastian popped one button , and Lavinia leaned forward.

Another button.

She bit her lower lip.

Sebastian grinned openly, watching Lavinia mesmerized by his simple act of undressing.

It was flattering, to say the least, to witness the interest with which Lavinia was gaping at his body.

Finally, Sebastian took off his breeches and boots and stood in front of her, completely naked.

Lavinia's eyes immediately fell to his cock. She tried to raise her gaze, managing to look at his chest for a couple of moments, and then her eyes kept returning to his—by this time hard and aching—cock.

She tried to compose her features and licked her lips. His cock twitched and jumped, gathering uncomfortable sensations in his belly. Her eyes widened, and she licked her lips again.

Seriously, woman? Sebastian raised his brows.

Lavinia met his eyes, her cheeks red with embarrassment.

"Very well..."

She clenched the sketch pad in her hand, her knuckles white from the tension. And if she clenched her fingers on her pencil more, Sebastian was certain it would crack in half.

"Might I suggest that you start with my cock?" Sebastian asked playfully.

Lavinia looked at him, confusion obvious in her eyes. "With your... what?"

Sebastian glanced down, and Lavinia's face turned dark red. "Oh."

"I am not trying to make you uncomfortable," he reassured her. "Trust me. It's just that it is chilly in this room, and that part of the anatomy does not respond well to cold. Neither will it stay in such an... inflated state if it remains untouched."

"Untouched?" Lavinia asked softly. Her gaze dropped to his cock, and it jumped again. "Oh, my!"

Sebastian swallowed a laugh. "Yes, well... see... In its relaxed state, the cock is quite unimpressive. It grows and hardens when a man is... excited."

"Excited?" Lavinia seemed to be able to only repeat his words.

Sebastian swallowed a laugh. "Yes. It happens when a particular woman is in proximity."

Lavinia raised her eyes to his, her brows furrowed in confusion.

"A desirable woman." *You.*

Her breaths quickened, her chest rising and falling rapidly as she continued staring at him.

Sebastian smiled slowly. "Now, are you going to sketch me, or was it an excuse to ogle me? I don't mind either way, just let me know what you want me to do."

Lavinia swallowed a giggle, a mischievous light playing in her eyes. "Do not move."

Sebastian watched Lavinia as she concentrated on the sketchpad and started moving the pencil. Every once in a while, she would look up, her brows adorably puckered, her lips in a thoughtful pout, a secret smile in her eyes, and then go back to sketching.

It's been a few minutes, and Sebastian was getting bored. How did his models manage to sit or stand in one position for hours? It was odd that he'd never thought about it until he finally was in their place. Perhaps he should have chosen to sit. Or better yet, lie next to his artist.

To add insult to injury, it was getting really chilly.

Sebastian looked at his half-erect cock in chagrin. He grabbed it in his hand and stroked it gently to stimulate the blood flow.

Lavinia looked up just at that moment and froze.

Sebastian grinned. "Just trying to keep it upright."

Lavinia threw him a confused gaze, bit her lower lip, and went back to her sketching.

Sebastian watched her concentrated frown, her eyes glinting with candlelight, white teeth peeking out of her mouth just a little and biting down on her pink, soft lips. She was mesmerizing. The most charming woman he had ever seen.

Now, this was something he would never get bored with. Just watching her.

"All done," Lavinia announced with a cheerful grin.

Sebastian raised both brows. "It took you less than five minutes."

"I didn't want you to get fatigued." Lavinia's smile turned coy. "Or deflated."

Sebastian guffawed and approached the bed. He sat gingerly by Lavinia's side, leaning over her shoulder. He turned his head and inhaled a whiff of her hair. Perhaps it was standing in the chilly room all naked and exposed, or maybe it was something deeper, but sitting beside her, all warm and soft, and smelling of rose water soap, he suddenly felt extremely cozy.

He felt the same way in his Paris home, sitting in his large armchair by the fire, wrapped up in a warm blanket and reading a book. Comfortable. He felt comfortable with her.

She nudged him on the shoulder and held up a sketchbook for him to see. Sebastian squinted and laughed wildly as he saw her depiction of him.

She'd drawn a rather interesting collection of lines; what looked like two arms and legs, a muscled—at least, he imagined, that was what she was going for—torso, a round head, and a cock the size of his arm.

"At least you made me look very… um… well-endowed," he said, still laughing.

"It seemed very important to you," Lavinia pointed out. "What, do you not find your likeness very flattering?"

Sebastian took the sketchbook into his arms and studied it carefully. "I suppose I might look like this in the shadows. The lighting is truly terrible here."

"Aren't I the most talented?" she said with a laugh.

She was clearly joking, but Sebastian looked at her, at this shy, uncertain lady, who could make him laugh genuinely and feel so comfortable and couldn't help but feel the light coming from inside her. There was something about her, something inexplicable, that had drawn him to her from the first moment they'd met. "You are amazing," he whispered low.

Lavinia giggled. "I am a terrible artist. I am sorry for making you suffer through it."

"Oh, no. It was a pleasure. You can torture me anytime."

Lavinia turned toward him then, their faces only inches away. It would be so easy for Sebastian to dip his head and capture her mouth, and God knew he wanted to. But tonight wasn't about him. It was *her* wicked night.

"Did I deliver on my promise to your satisfaction, my lady?" he murmured.

Goosebumps stole over her skin. She nodded.

"Is there anything else I can do for you?"

Another nod.

Sebastian raised a questioning brow.

"Kiss me."

A sigh of relief whooshed out of his body. "Thank God."

Chapter 22

As warm lips pressed against hers, Lavinia couldn't help but let out a moan. Sebastian immediately wrapped his arms around her, holding her close as he traced her lips with his tongue. She wanted this.

She'd wanted this for longer than she could remember. And it felt serendipitous that both times she'd asked him to kiss her, it had been after one of them had painted the other.

There was something erotic about drawing the other person, whether clothed or naked, whether seriously or in a jest. It was like staring inside a person's world and seeing oneself reflected in the other's eye.

She wasn't a great artist, obviously. She wasn't an artist at all; she was terrible at it. But just earnestly trying to draw Sebastian, concentrating on his features, forced her to see him differently.

He was a handsome man, that part she'd always known. But as she looked at him over the sketchbook, she was not studying the shape of his nose or the arch of his brows. She wondered what thoughts lurked beneath his blazing emerald green eyes, what thoughts plagued that complex mind of his.

She did pay attention to his physical appearance, of course. It was impossible to ignore. But she had no dream of ever capturing the texture of his coarse, black hair or the perfect peaks and planes of his body. He was built like a god, all hard muscle and long limbs. And then there was the most exciting part of his body... his swollen, masculine length. It was angry red and covered with tiny veins, just as hard and captivating as the rest of him.

No, she would never be able to put that beauty on canvas. And she wasn't trying to.

Instead, she accentuated his eyes, because the first thing she had noticed about him was how they sparkled when he said something mischievous. She put a dimple in the corner of his mouth because it appeared there every time he smiled earnestly. She drew each of his elegant, long fingers because she would forever remember the warmth of his touch.

She wasn't a real artist. No. She couldn't dream of ever putting down on canvas his likeness the way he deserved. But if she looked at this sketch twenty years from now and could remember the shine in his eyes and the smile on his lips, she would consider her job well done.

Sebastian's hand traveled up her spine and cradled her head, his fingers sifting through her hair as he angled her for better access. He swept his tongue inside her mouth, and all thought fled her mind.

She was like a raw wound: exposed, bleeding, sensitive to his touch. His kiss aroused and soothed her at the same time. She felt vulnerable and also protected in his arms. How could one person stir such a wide array of emotions all at once?

Lavinia felt confused, and she didn't know how to respond to his passion. Her blood was rushing in her veins, making her hot and bothered. An uncomfortable feeling between her legs made her squirm. And as close as he was to her, she wanted him closer. She wanted to wrap herself around him and lose herself in him.

Lavinia ran her hands up his chest, wanting to explore the topography of his body, and he groaned.

Her eyes flew open at the realization that she had the same effect on him as he did on her. She had power over him. He was just as lost in their kiss, their connection, as she was. And he was just as exposed to her, maybe more so.

Lavinia closed her eyes and trailed her fingertips along his burning flesh. His muscles jumped beneath her touch, his breath hitching.

How lovely it was to feel wanted, needed. To feel control over another person, to bring him genuine pleasure while experiencing pleasure herself.

His tongue swept inside her mouth, tickling, stimulating, devouring her.

She wondered what he tasted like, so she touched her tongue to his.

The next moment, everything changed.

His fingers tightened in her hair, his other hand snaking around her waist, pressing her closer. He was like a hungry animal, lapping at her mouth, not able to get enough of her taste. And so was she.

His tongue rubbing against hers sent shooting sensations down her body. Her blood heated, and she wanted to be closer. Needed him closer.

Lavinia whimpered.

"Shh." Sebastian kissed down her neck. "Don't worry. I'll take care of you."

She moaned his name as he moved lower, kissing her collarbone, then the tops of her breasts. He licked around her round birthmark, then traced his tongue along the edge of her bodice. Sebastian dipped his fingers under the sleeves, then looked into her eyes.

His emerald eyes were blazing with passion. She knew what he wanted. He was asking permission to lower the sleeves and bare her shoulders. Lavinia's heart drummed in her chest at the idea of being more open to him. Bare to him.

What would he think of her?

Lavinia met his gaze and nodded.

Her cheeks burned, and her entire body stiffened as he slowly lowered the sleeves. He dipped his head and peppered kisses over her shoulders. He then hooked his fingers over the top of her bodice and raised his brow.

Lavinia licked her dry lips. Sebastian's gaze fell to her mouth, his eyes hooded, and he let out a shuddering breath. Did he truly crave her this much that his breath was ragged? Part of her couldn't believe this was real, that he was earnest.

She closed her eyes, and Sebastian immediately wrapped her in a warm embrace.

He was infinitely gentle with her without a trace of pity. No other man had ever looked at her that way, and it allowed Lavinia to be bolder, more open with her own needs. But the deep-seated insecurity was not easy to shake.

"We don't have to do anything you don't want," he said gently, though his voice was hoarse with passion. His hot breath worried the wisps of hair framing her face.

His manhood poked at her belly, both exciting and terrifying her.

"I don't want to disappoint you," she whispered back.

Sebastian eased her away and looked at her strangely. "That could never happen."

Lavinia smiled, although it was probably more of a grimace. "You don't know that. You don't know what I look like. What it'd feel like," she whispered.

"Do you?" His question was laced with something heavy, something Lavinia did not fully understand.

She shook her head.

"Then let's learn this together."

* * *

Sebastian burned to touch more of Lavinia's skin. His fingertips tingled in anticipation, and his breaths were coming in huge gulps. He wanted to see her body, to bathe in the light of her form, to sink his fingers into her flesh and squeeze, caress her mounds and peaks.

Her chocolate-brown eyes turned darker with passion, her gaze beckoning him to move closer, to touch her all over, to claim her as his. Her lips were wet and puffy, her skin abraded with his stubble. He'd staked his claim on her, and he wasn't about to stop.

Sebastian took her mouth with his and kissed her ardently. He licked the silky corners of her mouth, urging her to respond. And when she did, he felt as though he was floating among the stars, on the precipice of bliss.

His earthly body hardened uncomfortably, and he couldn't deny the need he had to enter her flesh.

He wanted Lavinia.

He wanted her more than he'd ever wanted anything.

His fingers traveled to the bodice of her shift, and he trailed the skin above, dying to dip his fingers inside, rip the cloth in two, and liberate her lovely flesh.

But she looked at him with eyes so vulnerable he didn't dare risk frightening her.

Instead, he dipped his head and kissed her nipple through the fabric of her shift. He licked the little hardened tip, and Lavinia instantly arched against him, feeding him more of her body.

Sebastian opened his mouth further, licking her, drawing circles with his tongue, as Lavinia writhed beneath him, moaning, begging for a release.

She was so passionate and so pliant in his arms. Her body, soft and biddable, was made for pleasure. And that's what he wanted to teach her. He wanted to bring her to the heights of pleasure where she'd never been before.

His hand inched down, exploring the expanse of her rounded belly, the soft curves of her waist. Lavinia ran her hand up his arms, chasing goosebumps with her touch.

With a groan, Sebastian lowered his mouth to hers, feasting on her lips. Her fingers tangled in his hair, caressing, tugging. It was a sensual dance of lips against lips, tongue against tongue, hands against skin.

Their bodies moved in rhythm to their kiss, arching and retreating, touching, feeling, thrusting.

Sebastian's hand traveled lower and cupped her between her legs through the shift. Lavinia gasped, and Sebastian plunged his tongue inside, claiming her mouth just like his fingers claimed her quim.

He caressed and circled her feminine lips through the wet

fabric of her shift, playing with her swollen nub, making her writhe beneath him in agonizing passion.

She breathed his name, her fingers curling into the flesh of his shoulders, her legs falling open wider.

Her scent drove him wild, making him crave her taste.

He ran his finger up and down, spreading the moisture and exploring her silky skin. He reached the apex of her sex and circled it. Lavinia moaned and raised her hips. Sebastian kept circling it as he held her down and watched her face.

She was thrusting in bed, her hair spread across the pillow, her face the grimace of passion. Her hips started lifting and falling in time with his motions.

Her moans became short and rhythmic. He could feel she was on the precipice of pleasure.

Sebastian growled and removed his hand.

Chapter 23

"Please!" Lavinia screamed the only word she was able to utter when Sebastian ruthlessly took away the pleasure he'd been building with his skillful fingers. When he'd started touching her between her legs, she was ready to die of embarrassment. But that feeling was quickly replaced by need, want, pleasure. Her hips moved rhythmically with his fingers, building toward something special. She didn't know what it was, but she knew it was there, waiting for her if she just chased the feeling.

Just as she was on the precipice of discovering what it was, Sebastian withdrew his hand and took it all away.

Lavinia's breathing was labored, sweat lined her forehead, and she was utterly frustrated.

Sebastian peppered soothing kisses down her neck. "I am not done with you yet."

Lavinia placed her palm against his cheek and looked into his emerald green eyes. Her breaths were getting more even, but the ache low in her belly didn't subside.

Sebastian kissed her lips, biting into her soft flesh, then soothed it with his tongue. Lavinia held him close, trying in her inexpert way to return his kisses.

"I want to see you," he said hoarsely against her lips, between the kisses. "All of you."

Lavinia squirmed on the inside.

She had never been naked around anyone before except for her maid. She was afraid he'd be repulsed by her naked form, because of course, he would. She didn't like her body. How could he?

She'd never felt beautiful even in her clothes.

Except for one moment...

That moment in Sebastian's little studio when he'd sketched her portrait.

Sebastian lowered his head and bit the upper slope of her breast. Lavinia arched into him, her body craving the closeness. The shift was sticking to her body and making her want to get rid of it. *Should I?*

He trailed kisses along her exposed flesh, while his hands roamed her body.

She trusted him with her pleasure, and she trusted him not to hurt her.

She trusted him.

But she wasn't prepared to see the disappointment in his eyes once he'd seen her.

"Douse the candles," she whispered.

Sebastian raised his head. He looked into her eyes, the question evident on his features.

"I want to feel you," she said. "But I don't want you to see me."

Sebastian's gaze slid along her body as if remembering her

form. He stood and doused the candles one by one.

When darkness enveloped them, Lavinia disposed of her shift in one quick motion. She climbed under the sheets, covering herself up to her chin.

Sebastian chuckled and sat beside her, rubbing his manhood in his hand. She watched him curiously in the dark. How did this perfect man, so strong and beautiful, end up in bed with her?

It was surreal.

"I wish you could see yourself the way I see you," he whispered.

I wish so, too.

Lavinia swallowed. She really wished she knew what he was thinking. About her and this entire situation. What he was feeling at the moment. What prompted his every action.

But he dipped his head and kissed her, and all her thoughts evaporated. Nothing mattered anymore except his kiss, his touch, and the passion between them.

In one moment, the sheet was off her body, and he was covering her instead.

Lavinia thrashed on the bed as he moved down, kissing her throat, her breasts, weighing them in his hands. His hands slid across her body, his fingertips circling her scars, sinking into her flesh. He didn't seem to mind either, he just studied every crevice of her body, kissed every hidden nook. Then he kissed across her belly and lower… until he pressed a kiss to her center.

"Don't move," he whispered and then licked across her feminine lips.

Don't move?

Lavinia's hips flew off the bed, and she cried out in pleasure.

Sebastian laughed before sinking his fingers into the flesh of her hips, holding her securely to the bed.

"Do not move," he growled and licked again.

And then again. And he continued licking, kissing, devouring her between her legs until she could not differentiate what he was doing.

The pressure built inside her again until she could not hold it anymore.

With a cry of pleasure, the world erupted around her into millions of stars. Lavinia's body floated among those stars before finally coming back to earth, her limbs languid, an indulgent smile on her lips.

It felt heavenly.

When she opened her eyes, Sebastian kneeled before her, his manhood in his hand. He rubbed his length, his face a grimace of pain.

After a few short moments, he let out a growl, and a creamy white substance burst from his length onto her belly.

With a sigh of relief, Sebastian fell to his back.

"You are magnificent," he said, staring at the canopy.

A small smile adorned Lavinia's lips. For the first time in her life, she believed that she was indeed magnificent.

* * *

Lavinia woke up and stretched in bed. She felt languid, her limbs relaxed and heavy. She needed to get up and walk around, but it felt so good to be in a warm, soft bed.

"Good morning."

Lavinia sat up at the sound of Sebastian's voice, clutching a bedsheet to her chest. Sebastian stood in the doorway, dressed in the clothing he'd been taken in. He looked fresh and ready for the day ahead.

"Good morning," she said shyly and looked away, the activities of the night before vividly playing out in her mind.

After the rigorous lovemaking, Sebastian had wet a handkerchief with the pitcher of water, cleaned her belly, and between her legs. He then climbed beside her, covered them both with a sheet, and hugged her tightly to him.

This was the first time she could remember that she'd spent a night with someone. And the feeling of being held so closely was the best feeling in the world.

Her only regret was not waking up next to him.

He crossed the room and stared out the window as if feeling her discomfort and giving her a bit of privacy. Lavinia started immediately brushing out her hair with her fingers.

God, it was like a bird's nest! She must have looked completely horrifying. Perhaps that was why he turned away.

"I went down to the village this morn to look for a horse for us, but I couldn't find anything." He sounded irritated. "I had to pay some boys to run down to the nearby village inn and bring us a ride. We might need to start our journey on horseback if you don't mind."

"I don't suppose I have a choice," she said quietly.

He turned toward her and smiled. "Not unless you want to stay here."

Lavinia's heart jolted in her chest. Was it the prospect of staying here with him that made her ache? Or was it the vision that he presented with his eyes glinting in mischief, a sweet smile on his lips, the sun playing with the strands of his hair?

Lavinia swallowed. "Well, then I better prepare for the day."

She scooted to the edge of the bed, still clutching the bedsheet to her chest. She was about to lower her legs to the floor when Sebastian stopped her.

"Wait," he said, forcing her to turn toward him. He had a frown of concentration between his brows. "The boys probably won't bring the horse anytime soon. Do you mind if I sketch you? Like this."

Lavinia blinked. This was the last thing she'd thought he would say. Her hair was still disheveled, she was wrapped up in a sheet, and she couldn't imagine that being sketch-worthy. "I do not think I look beautiful," she said, then cleared her throat. "Like this." *At all.*

"Beauty is bought by judgment of the eye," he said gently. "And my eye—the eye of a connoisseur—judges your form to be exquisitely beautiful."

"No gentleman has ever quoted Shakespeare to pay me a compliment," Lavinia said, feeling a blush creep up her neck. No gentleman had ever paid her a compliment at all.

"Well, they're all fools," Sebastian said dryly.

Lavinia chuckled. "Can I keep the sheet around me?"

It was truly foolish, considering the night before. But she felt more exposed now, during daylight, than she had felt under the cover of night and under the influence of all-consuming passion.

Sebastian cleared his throat. "Whatever makes you feel comfortable."

He picked up a pencil and a sketchbook and settled in the chair behind her. The pencil scratched against the paper as Sebastian started working. Lavinia looked at his concentrated face over her shoulder.

Whatever makes you comfortable.

She did feel comfortable with him. She did feel protected. Lavinia relaxed her hold on the sheet, letting it open further at her back, sliding against her skin and opening her bottom to his view.

Sebastian paused as he raised his eyes to look at her again and smiled.

It wasn't a predatory smile or a self-satisfied smirk. It was a smile of pride. Whether he was proud that she'd let go of her inhibitions, or that she did indeed feel comfortable around him, she didn't know. But it felt good to see that glint in his eyes, reassuring her that her trust was placed in the right hands.

She wondered if he could see her scars from his seat, and she hoped that he couldn't. He didn't give any indication that he did.

"Can I ask you something?" Sebastian asked, not taking his eyes off his sketch.

"Anything."

His smile flashed again for a brief moment, before he asked, "I understand being shy, but after what happened last night, I wouldn't think you'd be hiding your body from me."

"It was dark." Lavinia's tongue peeked out of her lips in a nervous gesture. "You didn't see me."

Another flash of a smile. "Oh, I saw you. I felt you. Tasted you."

Lavinia's cheeks burned, and she didn't quite know where to hide her gaze. It did seem foolish that she'd still feel shy, but that wasn't it, was it? She decided to be upfront with him. "It is not easy to open oneself up for another's scrutiny."

Sebastian paused and looked at her with a frown between his brows. "When I say I want to see you, I do not mean that I want to judge you. I want to see you, to learn more about you. To learn more about your body, your soul. Even if you were crippled, I would not care. That is not what I am looking for."

"What are you looking for, then?"

"I suppose I am looking for your trust in me."

There was a pause before he resumed his sketch.

"I do trust you," Lavinia finally said. "It is not you who is the problem, I suppose. I don't feel comfortable naked. I don't feel beautiful naked or even clothed. I know you will not judge me, but the words of those who did will forever live within me. Whispering to me when I'm at my most vulnerable."

"Who are the people who judged your beauty?" A scowl appeared on his face.

"Well… My father used to scold me for being too big ever since I was a child… For him, having a belly was an indication of his wealth. For me, it meant that I had no control, was sinful, and a glutton. Of course, that made me feel bad and, as a result, I just ate even more, became even bigger, and was subject to even more scolding. My stepmother… Well, she just didn't want to anger my father because then he'd just…" She cleared her throat. "And then when I started being overlooked by gentlemen in favor of my gorgeous friends, when I saw other ladies whisper behind their fans about me… There's only so many times one can hear that they are plain, unshapely, and a burden before one starts to believe it, I suppose."

"And how many times, then, do I have to remind you that you're beautiful and an inspiration until you start to believe *that*?"

Lavinia's cheeks burned, and she turned away.

"No, no, please, don't break the pose. I want to see your face."

Lavinia studied his face beneath her eyelashes. "How long does it take you to finish a portrait?"

"Hours. But this isn't a portrait, just a simple sketch. I shall be done in a few minutes. Later, when I am back at home, I can put it onto the canvas and paint it."

"Please, do not sell it," she said quietly. Her heart slammed violently into her chest at the thought.

Sebastian's pencil froze, and he looked up. "I would never let anyone see you like this. Your beauty is just for me."

Lavinia chuckled and looked down, tensing from the inside.

"I'd say this is progress. You are not looking away. The next step is accepting the compliment," he said with a grin.

Chapter 24

She had scars on her body.

All over her body. He had felt them last night on her arms and her belly, and now he could clearly see them on her back. From whips, burns, cuts, and something else he wasn't certain of.

It made his blood boil.

He was ready to break something. As it was, the pencil under his fingers almost snapped from pressure.

But Lavinia clearly wasn't ready to talk to him about it. She didn't want to be judged. And he was not going to pry.

From her brief recitation of her father, it was clear that he had been abusing her for years. He was the reason she was so certain of her unworthiness. He was the reason she viewed herself as a burden. He was the reason she hid in the shadows and had never pursued her happiness.

Her father had tried very hard to break her spirit, but he had not succeeded. It was a wonder she had trusted anyone at all.

It was a gift that she'd opened herself to him.

And Sebastian would spend the rest of his life cherishing that gift.

She was obviously still in love with her childhood friend, the Duke of Kensington. The love she harbored for him was doubtful to go away so easily, but Sebastian was not the kind to give up. Kiss after kiss, he was certain to break down her defenses and prominently lodge himself into her heart.

Because the moment she'd disrobed for him the night before, she'd become his, and he had no intention of ever letting her go.

Sebastian finished his sketch and looked it over. It wasn't perfect, but then he quickly realized that putting Lavinia down on canvas was not an easy feat. To relay her beauty, he would have to put down her soul. Perhaps in time, he would polish that skill, and he'd gladly spend the rest of his life doing just that.

"Do you want to see it?" he asked.

Lavinia's eyes lit up. "Please."

Sebastian moved to the bed and sat next to her. He showed her the sketch, and a look of wonder appeared on her face. Her mouth slightly opened, an adorable pucker between her eyes; she was completely flabbergasted by what she saw.

"I know it isn't perfect," Sebastian said sheepishly.

"Not perfect?" Lavinia sniffed. Her eyes glinted with tears. "How did you manage to do this? How did you manage to make me look so—" She swallowed, unable to finish the sentence. Tears slowly rolled down her eyes.

Sebastian tipped her chin and forced her to meet his eyes. "Is it so terrible?" he asked with a smile.

Lavinia looked into his eyes and he could see his reflection in her clear, brown eyes. "Is that how you truly see me?"

Sebastian shook his head. "I can't put to canvas what I see when I look at you. I do not have enough skill to portray that kind of beauty."

Lavinia closed her eyes, tears rolling down her cheeks.

"Don't cry, *ma petite.*" Sebastian kissed her on her forehead.

Lavinia let go of the bedsheet and wrapped her arms around him. Sebastian held her close, rubbing soothing circles on her back.

Lavinia kissed his ear, his chin. Sebastian gently nudged her with his nose and caught her mouth in a kiss. Her warm body pressed against his, made his body react instantly. His cock rose proudly in his breeches, demanding to be released from the confines of his clothes. His entire body tensed and heated.

His hands traveled down her body. He stroked her inner thigh, and Lavinia instinctively spread her legs wider.

The clatter of horse hooves and the loud conversation of young boys below the window quickly brought Sebastian back to reality.

Right. There was no time for one more tryst. They needed to go back to the Roth estate.

It didn't matter, though.

He'd have her for the rest of his life.

* * *

Lavinia wet the handkerchief wrapped around her foot and slowly peeled it away. The wound was closed, and she wasn't bleeding anymore. She could even step on her foot, although not without wincing. The ride on horseback wouldn't be pleasant, but she'd have to persevere.

A part of her wished she could have just stayed in this creaky old house with Sebastian till the end of their days.

She would get used to bathing in the freezing stream. She would even learn to cook the fish. This little adventure they were on was supposed to be a punishment, a torture. But in reality, these had been the best twenty-four hours of her life. And she dreaded what the future might bring her.

She looked at the bloody handkerchief in her hand and paused. There was a flower stitched at the edge of it, a rose. It looked oddly familiar. She'd seen this before, but she could not remember where.

"Are you ready?" Sebastian yelled from outside of the room.

"Just a moment," Lavinia called out. She left the handkerchief on the bedside table, wrapped her foot in a clean linen strip Sebastian ripped from the spare sheet, put on her riding boots, and walked out the door.

They had a long day ahead.

They mounted their horses, and Sebastian threw her an apologetic look. "I thought about your idea of going back to London and making it seem like your guardian collected you ahead of time, but we won't be doing that."

Lavinia raised her brow. "We won't?"

"No. Because as perfect as this solution would be for you, how am I to explain my disappearance from my house party? To go to London and then back would take way too long. And I have a bastard to kill and my niece to save."

"Then perhaps I can go to London and—"

"Don't even finish that sentence." Sebastian's face turned angry red in an instant. "I am not letting you out of my sight. So, we are going back to Roth estate and once I kill William, we are going to marry."

"But—" Sebastian spurred the horse into a slow canter, and Lavinia did the same. By his set features, she could tell that there was no arguing with him. She'd figure out the whole marriage business once they got back to the Roth country seat. "You are not actually going to kill him, are you?"

Sebastian just threw her a dark gaze, then turned back to the road and spurred on his mount.

The journey back to the Roth estate was exhausting. Lavinia had never spent so many hours atop a mount, and when they stopped for a break and a bite of food, she thought she'd never get back up.

The inn they stopped at didn't have any coaches, and they had to continue their journey on horseback. It was uncomfortable, to say the least, to ride in her worn, dirty gown, and more than that with her injured foot, her muscles aching and her back hurting after the hours they'd spent riding.

She knew she couldn't complain, because what else were they to do? They couldn't spend half a day languishing in an inn, sleeping and having a nice warm bath when Roth believed his niece was in danger. He was a man on a mission. He threw her worried gazes and asked about twenty times if she wanted to rest, but she forced a smile to her lips and always answered that she was not tired at all.

Well, that was a complete lie. And now, a few hours into their journey and several minutes past dusk, she was regretting it all.

Sebastian, who was a few paces ahead, as if sensing her despair, slowed his mount until Lavinia caught up with him.

"You are tired." That wasn't a question; that was a statement.

And Lavinia wasn't about to answer him, anyway. What could they do in the middle of the field with nothing but grass in sight? Lie down?

Sebastian halted and forced Lavinia to bring her mount to a stop, too.

"Come here," he said, with an utterly serious face.

Lavinia looked around. "Come where? I am standing right beside you."

Sebastian smiled. "Come and climb atop my mount."

"How will that help?" Lavinia was ready to cry from frustration.

"You'll be able to rest, relax your back. Come. You're about to fall over."

Lavinia would argue if he wasn't right. She felt herself almost toppling over as they spoke. But the idea of sharing a horse did not seem more comfortable to her. Still, she moved the horse closer to Sebastian's and then he leaned in, snaked his arms around her waist, and tugged her from her mount and onto his lap.

Lavinia landed on his lap with a loud plop. She looked at her vacated mount and then at her current place in wonder. How did Sebastian manage to transport her this easily?

Sebastian shifted his thighs, setting Lavinia between them, and then wrapped his arms around her.

"Sleep," he murmured, as he pressed her head against his chest.

Lavinia wasn't about to protest that either. She just closed her eyes and fell into a peaceful slumber.

* * *

It wasn't the most comfortable thing in the world to ride with a woman between one's thighs, but it was definitely one of the most pleasurable. Her hair was tickling his chin, and her soft curves hugged his body as Lavinia slept peacefully in his arms.

What a brave little thing she was. She hadn't once cried or given into conniptions upon discovering their situation. She'd bathed in the freezing stream, eaten his poorly cooked fish, and then joked with him while playfully sketching him.

She was extraordinary, and she didn't even know that.

Sebastian shifted in his seat. He felt acute discomfort between his legs. Because as many tender feelings as she coaxed out of him, he also had this visceral reaction to her closeness. There was nothing to do about it. From the first moment he'd seen her, he'd wanted her. And every time she was close, or every time he thought of her, his body reacted. He wouldn't be able to ride like that for a long time, and fortunately, he didn't have to. The Roth estate was just about an hour away.

He imagined the soft, clean bed waiting for him when he finally made it home and was tempted to whimper. He would love to slide between clean sheets with Lavinia, hold her close to him, as he was holding her now, and just sleep. He didn't need the kisses or erotic touches. Just sleeping next to her would suffice.

But he knew that was impossible under the current circumstances. He'd have to marry her first. And he would. No matter her protestations.

But first, he needed to deal with the bastard.

He looked at her peaceful form and tightened his arms around her.

Just at that moment, there was the rattling of a carriage and the sounds of horse hooves ahead. Sebastian squinted and finally noticed the lights of carriage lanterns.

Sebastian moved their horses to the side, not to get in the way of the carriage, but as the vehicle neared, it stopped just a few feet away.

Lavinia stirred in his arms. "What's going on?" she asked in a sleepy voice.

"I am not certain."

Sebastian lowered his hand and felt the dagger in his boot.

The doors of the carriage opened, and a slender woman with swishing skirts hurried toward them.

"Oh, thank God!" Caroline exclaimed from the darkness.

"Caroline?" Sebastian squinted at his cousin.

"John, Graham! Help Lady Lavinia off the horse."

Two liveried footmen appeared by their side and helped Lavinia down. The moment her feet touched the ground, Caroline embraced her fiercely.

Sebastian raised his brows. He'd almost forgotten that the duchess and Lavinia were close friends, despite Lavinia's affection toward her friend's husband.

He dismounted and was welcomed by a frosty gaze from his cousin.

"You shall explain in the carriage," she said sternly.

Sebastian blinked. And to think that he was her guardian for a few weeks upon coming to England. She'd settled into her role as a duchess quite comfortably; he supposed.

They climbed inside the carriage, Lavinia sitting next to Caroline.

Sebastian frowned. He'd prefer if she were by his side, but he realized that Lavinia must have felt uncomfortable, so he moved to sit across from them.

Once they settled into the carriage and Caroline stopped fussing over Lavinia, she looked at Sebastian. "Speak."

Sebastian raised a brow. "You know that tone is unacceptable, my dear cousin."

"When you drag my friend Lord knows where without saying a word and leave me to clean up after your disappearance, do you truly deserve a softer tone?"

"That's not what happened," Lavinia murmured. "He—We got kidnapped."

Caroline's mouth slightly opened. "By whom?"

"A man I am inclined to kill," Sebastian said darkly. "Where's Victoria?"

"She is at the manor. She doesn't know anything, and neither does Lady Elinor, or she'd have major conniptions."

"Annalise—" Lavinia started, but Caroline interrupted her swiftly.

"Do not worry. When you disappeared, I just told everyone that you went back to London as you planned. Annalise is none the wiser."

"Oh, thank God," Lavinia whispered, her hand to her chest. "How long were we gone? Two nights?"

Caroline frowned. "No. You've been missing for four nights."

"Four nights?" Sebastian barked.

"Obviously, it took us longer to get there than back." Lavinia had a worried plucker between her brows.

"What did you say about me?" Sebastian asked.

Caroline turned back to Sebastian. "When it became clear that you weren't at the estate either, I assumed you two ran off somewhere together or were stuck somewhere. Either way, to fend off the scandal, I told everyone that you fell ill and weren't taking visitors. So the duke and I took over running the house party while we searched all over for you."

Sebastian breathed out in relief. "Good. I knew you would keep everybody calm."

"But how did you even find us?" Lavinia interjected.

"Well, I did not." Caroline folded her hands on her lap. "Since the house party is in full motion, we could not send too many servants away to look for you without causing gossip. We asked some village boys to be on the lookout for two people with your description and sent some out to search for you but had no results. We were about to organize a search involving Kensington servants, but today one of the boys sent a missive that a lady and a gentleman matching the description we sent out were moving in the direction of Roth estate from the south, and I set out to look for you. I didn't have to go far, as you can see. But tell me, what happened to you?"

"The last thing I remember before waking up is speaking with William," Sebastian ground out.

Caroline frowned. "William?"

"Your brother-in-law," Sebastian said coldly.

Caroline reared back. "You are the one who invited him, cousin. But he was barely a part of the house party. I am not even certain how Victoria would have met him."

Lavinia turned toward Caroline. "Your brother-in-law? None of Kensington's brothers were at the house party. I believe the eldest is on a Grand Tour and the rest are too young."

Caroline licked her lips, visibly picking out words in her mind. "William is one of his numerous kin his family never acknowledged."

"A bastard." Sebastian supplied. "A duke's bastard, but still—"

"Oh, my God!" Lavinia suddenly exclaimed, horrified. "A duke's son!"

"What's wrong?" Sebastian immediately leaned toward her and placed his hand over hers. He caught a shocked gaze from the duchess, but he didn't care. They'd been ruined. Either way, let Caroline think what she wanted.

"I—Oh, Lord, Victoria's secret suitor is William!"

"What secret suitor?" Sebastian stilled.

"I am sorry. I should have told you, but I promised not to."

"She had a secret suitor?" Caroline looked quite shocked, too.

"Yes, I noticed a few days ago that she was being secretive and slinking away from the ball to meet a gentleman. She wasn't certain of her feelings toward him, so she didn't want any pressure from her family. But she assured me he was of noble blood. A duke's son."

"Oh, he is of noble blood," Sebastian growled. "The blood I'll be certain to spill once we get back to the mansion."

How did Sebastian not see this? The gentleman Victoria was in love with was William all along. He ground his teeth together, his jaw tensing.

Caroline seemed pained. "How did neither of us notice?"

"He is a conniving one, that's for sure," Sebastian grumbled.

"And Victoria has always been too trusting," Caroline said sadly.

Sebastian fisted his hands at his sides. "I hope she takes this lesson seriously."

Chapter 25

Kensington's fist connecting with Sebastian's jaw made a cracking sound before Sebastian lost his balance and the next thing he knew, he was sitting on the floor.

Of course, Sebastian saw the hit coming. His first instinct was to duck, but he also knew that he deserved it. So, he forced himself not to move until he had received his punishment.

"Dane, no!" Lavinia exclaimed, horrified, then ran toward Sebastian.

This was the welcome accorded to the master of the house.

The moment they had arrived, Caroline had led them into a study, where they were greeted by the duke. Now, Caroline was perched against the desk, watching the proceedings with a bored expression on her face.

At least, Sebastian mused, Lavinia had fierce protectors, and he couldn't be unhappy about that.

"You ruined her!" Dane growled.

"No! He saved me." Lavinia took Sebastian's face between her hands and peered at his jaw.

"Let us be honest, dear. I did deserve it," Sebastian said quietly.

Perhaps not for the reasons the duke had thought, but Sebastian did deserve a good punch to the jaw. And it felt good.

"No, you didn't!" Lavinia said emphatically, and then toward the duke, "He didn't!"

"You disappeared for four nights without a word! Then come home looking like beggars, and he does not deserve it? Oh, I beg to differ." The duke appeared calm, but his hands were still fisted by his sides.

Lavinia helped Sebastian up. "It is not like we chose to run off together."

"Did he marry you?" Kensington asked with a stony expression on his face.

Lavinia looked utterly confused. "I don't... Why would he marry me?"

"Then, he will now."

"Certainly," Sebastian murmured.

"If I might interfere." Caroline pushed off the desk and stepped closer. "They were taken from the estate against their will."

The duke clenched his jaw as he looked at Lavinia. "Were you harmed?"

"No... Well, not in any way that matters."

"I am fine, thank you for worrying," Sebastian said drily.

"Why would I worry about you?" Kensington looked disgusted.

"Perhaps you don't have to," Sebastian said, cradling his jaw with one hand, another on the small of Lavinia's back. "Or at least not about me. But you sure as hell have to worry about your brother because I am going to kill him. So, if we're done here…"

"We are not done." Kensington raised a staying hand. "What the devil are you talking about?"

Lavinia moved even closer to Sebastian as if trying to shield him. His own fierce protector.

"Your brother, William—"

"He is not my brother," the duke bit out.

"—is the one responsible for our predicament."

A blank expression overtook the duke's face. "How do you know?"

Sebastian's brow crimped, and his jaw tightened. "Well, let's see. He was the last one to see me before I was accosted. He asked permission to court my niece, which I denied. And he is the *biggest* scoundrel the world has ever known!"

A vein popped out on Kensington's forehead as he tried to rein in his temper. Oh, his bastard brother was a sore subject for certain. "I shall deal with him."

"Oh, no. You dealt with me quite splendidly. Your work here is done. Now the bastard is mine."

"No, wait a moment," the duke said before Sebastian could turn away. "We are not quite done yet. You might not be responsible for your predicament, but you did spend four nights alone with Lady Lavinia, did you not?"

"Unfortunately I do not remember half of them. But, yes, we did," Sebastian said with an indulgent smile.

Lavinia looked at him sternly as her cheeks covered with a blush.

"Then you *have* to marry her."

"Of course," Sebastian agreed, and Lavinia threw him a confused gaze.

"What do you mean, *of course*? Nobody, aside from people in this room, knows that we were together. People think I am back in London!"

"Did he hurt you?" Kensington asked.

"Of course not!" Lavinia spat irritably.

Sebastian squeezed her waist. He didn't want her to get too upset. Even if he did deserve the contempt from the duke, Lavinia did not.

Kensington's gaze followed Sebastian's hand, and his voice turned silky. "Did he do anything inappropriate?"

Lavinia's cheeks grew even redder as she shook her head. *What a poor liar.* Sebastian smirked.

"You are marrying her!" Kensington asserted once again.

"I never said I would not."

"Your Grace, Dane, nothing happened. At least nothing that would require a marriage," Lavinia assured. "You can't punish him just because we were both kidnapped—"

Sebastian raised a brow. "Punish me?"

Lavinia shushed him. She was so fierce in trying to get him out of this marriage that he started to feel insulted. "I will go back to London and—"

"No." Sebastian interrupted firmly.

Kensington looked from Lavinia to Sebastian, then back again. As he moved closer, he peered into her eyes. "If you despise him," he said quietly, as if imparting a secret, "I shall not make you marry him."

Oh, please. Sebastian raised his eyes heavenward.

Lavinia reared back. "I do not despise him."

"You don't?" The duke was the embodiment of concern. "It

just seems to me that you would rather be ruined than marry him."

"Oh, no, no. On the contrary," she said emphatically. "He is kind and gentle, clever and witty... And he is the most honorable man I know."

The duke raised his brows, and Sebastian swallowed a chuckle. *The most honorable, indeed.* Lavinia continued, not paying either of them any attention, her face getting a dreamy look. "He took care of me while we were away. Made certain I was warm and fed. H-He even carried me in his arms"—she said with a giggle and then cleared her throat as if just realizing that she'd lost the sequence of her thoughts—"Any woman would be so lucky to call him her husband. But—"

"Then the issue is settled," Kensington announced.

"Good." Sebastian nodded, gave a gentle squeeze to Lavinia's waist again, and turned toward the exit. "Because I have a bastard to find."

* * *

Lavinia rushed after Sebastian, only to be stopped by a gentle hand on her arm.

"Wait, Lavinia. You can't go following him around. Especially if you maintain that you don't want to marry him. You are not ruined just yet, but you will be if you run after him in the middle of the night," Caroline said.

"He is going to kill someone," Lavinia replied emphatically.

"I wouldn't worry about William," Kensington said from behind. "You have no idea how many other men he's crossed in his lifetime. And he is alive so far. Roth is not the first man to try to kill him, and he won't be the last."

"This is your brother!" Lavinia exclaimed as she turned on him. She felt as though she didn't recognize him. "Bastard or not."

Kensington gritted his teeth, his hands fisted at his sides. "Exactly. You don't know him as I do."

Lavinia was tired of this entitlement from him for one night. She never remembered him being like this. "First of all," she said, fisting her hands by her sides. "You do not get to decide who I marry. This is none of your business."

"Of course, it—"

Lavinia held up her hand. "Second of all, if anything is your business in this situation, it's finding your brother and dealing with him before Sebastian does!"

Kensington blinked, looking at Lavinia as if he were seeing her for the first time. "Very well. I shall go and make certain Roth doesn't do something he will regret. Your Grace." He tipped his head and threw a meaningful stare at Caroline before leaving the room.

Caroline immediately approached Lavinia. "Now that that's settled, let us get you into your bed. You need to rest"—she waved her hand at Lavinia's disheveled attire—"and change… Sleep! You look like you haven't slept in weeks."

Lavinia scrubbed her face. "Yes. You're right. I am extremely tired, to the point that I don't think I understand what I'm doing or saying. But all I know is that Sebastian feels the same. But his response to it all is heightened by the urge to protect his niece. I cannot just sit idly by when he is on a rampage. And poor Victoria! If she truly loves this… If she loves William, she will be devastated."

Caroline weaved her arm with Lavinia's. "You are right,"

she said as she walked toward the door. "Perhaps we can't do anything to help Lord Roth now. We have to believe that Kensington will do everything in his power to stop a tragedy from unfolding. However, there's something we *can* do. Let us go and check on Victoria. And while we are in the family wing, perhaps you'll reconsider going to bed."

Lavinia touched the tips of her fingers to her pulsing temples. She really didn't know what she was doing. She was not in a position to make independent decisions just now, her mind was so muddled. Without any other recourse, she nodded and followed Caroline out of the study.

As they made their way toward the staircase in silence, Lavinia thought about what poor Victoria would feel once she found out the truth about her beloved. She'd been so happy when she talked to Lavinia about love, so hopeful. And having experienced heartbreak, Lavinia didn't wish it on her mortal enemy.

Suddenly, the thought of leaving for London felt like a piercing blow. The idea that she'd leave Sebastian behind and marry someone else hurt her beyond measure.

She had to shake out her thoughts. When had she become so attached to Sebastian? Was it during their kidnapping? Or was it even earlier?

Her thoughts were tumbling one over the other, so when Caroline finally spoke, Lavinia jumped from fright.

"Lavinia, can I ask you something? Oh, pardon, did I frighten you?"

Lavinia forced out a smile. "I was so lost in my thoughts I forgot—Never mind. Please, what did you want to ask me?"

"It's about the marquess."

Lavinia turned toward Caroline, her concentration returning to the conversation. "What about him?"

"You seemed pretty adamant about not marrying him, although it seems like you get along pretty well… And dare I say you care about him."

Lavinia's cheeks heated again, as they did every time she thought of him. "It is because I care about him that I cannot marry him. He doesn't want a wife. He told me, very firmly, that it is the last thing he needs. He's been pushed to move to England against his will. He was pushed to join the aristocratic circle because of Victoria. And I shall not be the one to force him into an unwanted marriage. I've been a burden to my father my entire life… I won't be a burden to my husband."

"But with your father dying—"

"My guardian has a prospect for me," Lavinia said quickly. She didn't want to discuss this now. Her thoughts were in disarray. She knew the solution she came up with wasn't perfect. She still had a lot of issues to sort through. But she couldn't think about it now.

"If that's what you wish," Caroline said softly.

They made their way toward the family wing and reached Victoria's chamber pretty quickly, only nobody answered when they knocked. Caroline tried the handle, but the door was locked.

Caroline let out a frustrated breath. "She is either a very sound sleeper or—"

"Or she's not in the room," Lavinia finished for her.

"Yes, well… We can't be running around the entire estate in hopes of finding her. That is not productive."

"No, but we can't just sit here and do nothing. If she is with William, and Sebastian finds them—"

Caroline raised her brow before composing her features. "You are right. This can't end well." She chewed on her lip, such an uncharacteristic thing for Caroline to do, before she finally said, "I know this estate better than anyone. I grew up here. So, I shall go and look for them, but you should go to your room and rest."

"What? You can't possibly think that I'd do that!"

Caroline placed a calming hand on Lavinia's arm. "Lavinia, this is not your problem to deal with. I am certain His Grace will aid me in the search, and our servants—pardon, Roth's servants, too. It is our family's issue. And look at you! You are barely standing on your own two feet."

Caroline wasn't wrong. Lavinia wobbled from side to side, so tired she was. But she couldn't possibly sleep soundly when Sebastian was on a rampage. She needed to help him. But how? She definitely needed to take a breath and think things through.

"Very well," Lavinia agreed and walked toward her room.

She went to her dressing room and washed her face with a cold pitcher of water. That promptly woke her up as she shivered in a cold room. She remembered running into Victoria, all disheveled, in the gallery hall that led into the garden.

Perhaps that was a spot Victoria and William used to meet.

She perked up and dashed out of her chamber. She looked around before making her way to the servants' stairs. This was the shortest way to the gardens.

Lavinia rushed down the stairs and through the gallery hall. She needed to reach Victoria before Sebastian found them. She imagined that if Victoria and William were indeed in the garden, she'd find them in a compromising position. And she really didn't want Sebastian to witness that, nor Victoria to face such humiliation.

She dashed into the garden and immediately heard voices behind the rose bushes.

Lavinia turned the corner, prepared to see the worst, but what she saw made her heart soften.

Victoria sat on the bench, leaning her shoulder against a large, sinfully handsome blond man, her hand in his, a rose in her hair. She was smiling as she was saying something, and the man by her side watched her with a glimmer of adoration in his eyes. They truly seemed like a couple in love.

Lavinia's heart squeezed as she took a step and made her presence known.

Victoria raised her head, and her smile turned into a grin. "Lavinia! You are here! I thought you left for London!"

Right. Everyone thought she'd been gone. Lavinia licked her lips. "Victoria, there is no time to explain, but you need to leave."

They both stood. "Why?" asked the man, who Lavinia assumed was William.

"Because Seb—Lord Roth—is looking for you, and he is not happy."

Victoria shrugged. "Whatever he is not happy about is his issue," she said confidently.

William took her hand and squeezed. There was a gentleness in his eyes.

How could a man with such clear reverence toward Victoria have acted so despicably? "Victoria, your uncle shall not be happy to see you two together in the garden holding hands!" She turned to William. "And if you ruined her, he is going to kill you!"

Victoria looked at William with a grin on her face. "You don't have to worry, Lavinia! I am not ruined, and I shall never be ruined."

"Victoria—" Lavinia tried to interject.

"We might as well tell you," Victoria continued with a giggle. "We are already married!"

Chapter 26

"What?" Sebastian roared as he entered the rose bush alcove.

He had checked William's chamber, and when he hadn't found him, Sebastian remembered William roaming the halls at night, goading Sebastian about the ladybird he'd been visiting.

Had he been talking about Victoria all along?

In a fit of rage, Sebastian dashed toward the garden where he thought he might find them, and he did. Just in time to hear the words that easily escaped Victoria's mouth.

They are already married.

Sebastian had suspected that this was the reason for William's scheming all along. He'd anticipated it. And yet, expecting something to happen—dreading it—and hearing the confirmation, were two different beasts.

Blood boiled inside Sebastian's veins, and his vision blurred. All he could see was his sweet, innocent niece, holding hands with the worst scoundrel the world had ever known.

"You are not serious, Victoria!" he pushed through his greeted teeth. "Tell me you are not serious."

Victoria took a step back, and William shifted to shield her. "She is utterly serious, my friend. We are married."

"Then we'll get it annulled!" Sebastian took another step forward, his hands fisted at his sides.

"You can't." William's features were stony. "I made certain it's legal. There is nothing you can do."

"Well, then I'll have to kill you!" Sebastian growled.

"No, Uncle!" Victoria peeked from behind William's back, but the bastard moved to shield her again.

"Name your second," Sebastian said in a voice so low it was almost a whisper.

"Sebastian, don't," Lavinia warned by his side.

"You know very well I have no seconds in this house, Bastian." A light smirk appeared on his lips. "If anyone, you'd be the one standing by my side."

"Well, you forfeited my friendship the moment you seduced my niece!"

"He didn't seduce me!" Victoria peeked out again. "I married him willingly."

Sebastian watched her silently, waiting for his blood to cool. She didn't deserve his ire. She was innocent in this situation. "Did you, now?"

"I did. And I know that you dislike him and that you were against our marriage. That is why I had to do it in secret."

Sebastian's jaw tightened. "You shackled yourself to this—this criminal—on purpose? Why would you do this? You doomed yourself to be a social outcast! Do you know this? What about your aspirations of joining your sister in Russia and bridging our nations through advantageous marriage?"

"He isn't a criminal, despite what you might think."

Sebastian closed his eyes as the obvious answer dawned on him. He finally understood the only way she'd marry him willingly. He looked at William, a smirk of disgust on his face. "You haven't told her."

There was a beat of silence. Victoria stepped out from behind William, her features pinched with confusion. She swallowed before asking quietly, "What haven't you told me?"

William gritted his teeth, a vein popping out on the side of his neck. "You don't know what you're talking about, Bastian."

"Don't I? Then tell her. Now."

There was a long pause as Willam and Sebastian stared at each other under furrowed brows. William finally broke the contact and looked at Victoria. "I didn't lie to you about anything. Everything I told you is the truth."

"But you omitted some truths, too. Didn't you?" Sebastian gritted out.

William licked his lips. "Yes. I might not have told you the entire truth about the origin of my birth." There was a pause as he took a deep intake of breath. "I *am* a duke's son. A duke's bastard son."

Another long pause. Victoria looked from William to Sebastian and back again, her shoulders shaking on a nervous chuckle. "You must be joking."

William shook his head.

"Not just that. He is a criminal!" Sebastian growled. "A thief. He works with the king of London's criminal underworld, Hades."

Lavinia stepped toward him and placed a soothing hand on his arm, slowly shaking her head, as if saying, *Not now.*

Victoria's mouth was half open, her brows furrowed. She watched William as if she didn't recognize him. "How could you?" she said in a barely audible whisper.

"I can explain." William reached for her, but she stepped away.

"I told you about my dreams and aspirations!"

"You can still have all that!"

"I told you why I needed to marry a gentleman! And you *lied* to me!" Victoria cried, her pitch rising.

"I didn't! I never lied—"

"You tricked me! Humiliated me!"

Tears appeared in Victoria's eyes. She picked up her skirts and hurried away. William's eyes followed her every step until she disappeared behind the flowers.

Lavinia threw a devastated gaze toward Sebastian before rushing after Victoria.

"Do you think your relationship is perfect?" William spat. "Do you think you two have no lies between you?"

"It is a testament to how broken you are that you think comparing yourself to others is the only way to feel better about yourself."

"I *am* a bastard," William said bitterly. "Knowing that I am not the only one eternally damned regardless of the consequence of my birth is how I survive."

"It's a sad way to live."

"What would you know about it?" William gritted out, then shifted his gaze somewhere behind Sebastian.

Kensington stepped into the alcove at that moment, his gaze trained on William. "I see you managed to ruin everything again," the duke said softly.

"Not yet, *brother*," William said with a smirk.

"Kensington." Sebastian turned toward the duke. "Do you mind standing beside your brother at dawn?"

Kensington raised a brow. "A duel."

Sebastian nodded sharply. "Your bastard brother tricked my niece into a marriage. I do not see any other recourse."

"Name the weapon of your choice," William said nonchalantly.

"A sword will do." It was the only weapon Sebastian knew how to wield, and he wielded it better than most. He tipped his head. "I shall see you at dawn, William."

Sebastian rushed out of the garden, forcing himself to calm down. How did he miss the signs of Victoria being manipulated? He was supposed to be looking after her, and he'd failed.

And now he'd left Kensington to deal with William. The duke had no love for his bastard brother, but what if he helped him run off?

No. If nothing else, Kensington was honorable.

Sebastian turned the corner and stumbled upon a drunken Ian McAllistair.

"Oh, pardon," the man mumbled as he reared back.

Sebastian tipped his head and was about to pass him by, but he had a realization that he needed a second, too.

Sebastian did not have friends in England. William had been the closest thing he had to one, but he would be standing opposite him in a duel, so he needed to find someone else.

Since this was the middle of the night, he wasn't going to find anyone else. And he didn't want to delay the duel.

Sebastian turned toward McAllistair. "How drunk are you?"

The man shrugged. "I can find my room if that's what you're asking," he said in a drunken slur.

Sebastian nodded. "Very well. You'll do. I need a favor."

* * *

Lavinia followed Victoria to her chamber but didn't catch up to her. The girl was too fast, and Lavinia was too tired. Instead, she bumped into Caroline, and now both of them sat outside Victoria's room as the latter wouldn't let them inside. They could hear her crying, which turned into quiet sobbing.

Lavinia's heart squeezed, just imagining what it would be like to be deceived by a man she loved...

"It's all my fault," Caroline said quietly.

Lavinia furrowed her brows. "How is it your fault?"

Caroline smiled softly. "You and Roth were gone, and I was so preoccupied with looking for you and running the house party as if nothing was wrong that I didn't pay attention to Victoria at all. Lady Elinor is sickly, and she can't keep up with a young and boisterous charge. As a result, Victoria was left without a chaperone."

"I think you are setting unrealistic expectations for yourself. Nobody would be able to do everything you did and still be standing at the end of the night."

"Well, I *am* sitting," Caroline said with a chuckle.

Lavinia covered Caroline's hand with hers. "It's not your fault."

"I still can't understand how Victoria managed to sneak out and get married."

They sat in silence, each lost in their own thoughts for a moment. Lavinia contemplated Caroline's words. With so many things thrust upon her, she'd set such high expectations for herself that she thought a girl, who was not even under her care, getting married in a clandestine ceremony was her fault. And the ironic thing was if she had managed to catch Victoria before, if she had handled everything perfectly, nobody would be surprised.

"You know, Caroline, as much as I hate that this all happened, it is comforting to know that you are not perfect. That sometimes you can't do everything," Lavinia said.

Caroline looked at her, surprised. "I was never perfect."

"Oh, please, Caroline. You are beautiful, clever, and kind. You always know what to do in every situation. You know how to act and what to say. I've never once seen you make a single mistake. You are the embodiment of perfection."

"Except for today," Caroline said with a self-deprecating smile.

"If anybody else was left in charge after Roth's and my disappearance, the house would probably be on fire."

A chuckle left Caroline's lips, and she squeezed Lavinia's fingers. "Thank you. But I think you give me too much credit. I am far from perfect. But I truly appreciate your words."

Lavinia turned to Caroline fully, studying her suddenly sunken face. She seemed troubled, and Lavinia hoped she could say something to lighten her mood, but no words came to mind.

Footsteps echoed in the hall. Caroline scrambled off the floor and helped Lavinia up.

Sebastian approached them and glanced from one lady to the other, his gaze narrowing with concern. "How is Victoria?"

"She is devastated, as expected," Caroline said. "But I think she needs to spend some time alone with her thoughts. Let's let her sleep and… go have some rest, too."

Sebastian nodded. "Thank you. For everything."

Caroline nodded. "Oh, I've ordered a bath for you, Lavinia," she said, before turning away. "My lord, you can request one after her."

There was a long, charged silence after Caroline left, which was only broken once the footmen started bringing the bath and hot water into Lavinia's chamber.

"Well, I suppose I should go take a bath, now," she said but remained standing still. She couldn't make herself move away. Sebastian's presence beckoned her to stay.

He sucked in a breath. "Yes."

They stood there, not looking at each other but not willing to be the one to step away.

"You've been through a lot today," Lavinia said, looking at his disheveled cravat.

"As have you." His voice was hoarse.

Lavinia nodded. "So, you probably want to be alone."

Sebastian shook his head and bit his lip. "I really don't."

Lavinia raised her eyes to his. It took her a split second to make a decision. One quick glance at his pain-filled eyes, and she knew what he needed. What she needed—nay, wanted. Slowly but confidently, she extended her hand. "Then… stay with me," she said quietly.

A breath of relief left Sebastian's lungs with a loud whoosh. He smiled, just briefly, the corners of his mouth barely lifting, and took her hand.

Chapter 27

Then stay with me.

Those were the sweetest words Sebastian had ever heard. After the grueling horse ride, the tension-filled argument with William, and the soul-crushing moment of seeing all Victoria's dreams die, he didn't want to be alone.

He didn't want to be with anyone else, either. He just wanted her.

Lavinia.

The moment she took his hand, it was as if the fatigue had left his body. She filled him with strength and tenderness, and everything that was pure in this world.

In a few hours, the dawn would come, and he would fight a man he had once called his friend for the honor of his niece. He didn't know what to expect from that duel. He wasn't certain he was doing the right thing by calling William out.

Sebastian was not certain of anything, except for the woman who was holding his hand at that moment. And that was all he needed.

They made their way to her bedroom just as the last servants were leaving the room.

The bath was filled with steaming water; the towels lay on the chair nearby; the soap prepared. Everything was ready for Lavinia's bath.

Lavinia looked around the room. "Miss Gale is not here," she said.

Sebastian chuckled. "Do not worry. The servants probably took her when they realized you left." He locked the door and beckoned Lavinia closer. "Come here."

Lavinia obeyed, and he enveloped her in his embrace.

Sebastian burrowed his face in her hair and breathed in deeply. This, holding her in his arms, even just being in proximity with her, was his definition of heaven.

She slowly disengaged from him and looked up. She had to crane her head all the way back in order to look him in the eye. She was so tiny, his little muse.

"I need to take a bath," she said with a timid smile.

"Do you want me to leave?" He ran his hands up and down her arms in soothing motions. She shook her head. "To turn away?"

Her gaze was uncertain as she looked at him for a long moment before finally shaking her head again.

Sebastian gulped. She was trusting him again, and he couldn't quite describe what it meant to him. "Then let me help you undress, *ma petite*."

Lavinia nodded.

Sebastian carefully undid her bodice and let it fall to her feet. The stomacher and overskirts followed. Next went her petticoats.

That poor gown had truly suffered too much.

As Lavinia stood before him in a crumpled chemise, Sebastian wondered if she'd ever allow him all the way into her heart. He wished she would tell him about all her woes. He wished she'd stop hiding from him and open up to him completely.

Lavinia looked him in his eyes, her expression troubled.

"Is something wrong?" he asked and ran a finger down her cheek.

Lavinia gulped, her throat working on a swallow, and shook her head.

Then she bunched the fabric of her chemise in her hands and slowly took it off. Sebastian only had time to blink, and there she was, standing completely naked in front of him.

* * *

Lavinia didn't know what came over her. For some unknown reason, she just wished there were no barriers between her and Sebastian. For one brazen moment, she decided to bare herself in front of him and took off her chemise.

But as the moment passed and now, he was looking at her naked form, all doubts returned and started plaguing her anew.

Oh, no. What have I done?

The last time she was this naked before him, it was completely dark, and they were both drunk with passion. Now, as she shivered in a room full of candles, a fireplace burning and illuminating the room with a yellow glow, she was afraid she'd made a huge mistake.

She smiled sheepishly and covered her breasts with her arms. Sebastian stepped closer and kissed her softly on her lips.

Lavinia's eyes fell closed, and her body melted into him. When they kissed, nothing else mattered. It didn't matter that she was completely naked before him. It didn't matter that he was not. All the problems of the world had disappeared, and it was just her, Sebastian, and their kiss.

God, how she'd missed his kisses. It had been less than twelve hours since their last kiss, but it seemed like forever.

He snaked his arms around her waist and pressed her closer to him, his hard length pressing against her belly.

She chuckled as she pulled away. "I… um… Let me bathe first…"

Sebastian raised his brow. "First? And then what?"

She looked down, too embarrassed to meet his eyes.

Sebastian smoothed her hair on her head and pressed one kiss on the crown. "Come. I shall help you."

He held her hand as she stepped into the bath, hissing at the hot water. The cut on her foot burned, and her muscles ached, but the overall sensation was pleasant. She lowered herself fully into the bath and moaned.

Sebastian's gaze traveled down her body. He studied her breasts, her belly, then his gaze paused at the juncture between her legs. Lavinia squirmed uncomfortably.

"Do you mind passing me some soap?" Lavinia asked.

Sebastian's gaze returned to her eyes, and he smiled. "Of course."

He handed her the soap, then took off his coat and waistcoat, rolled up his sleeves, and crouched before her. "I wish the bath was large enough for both of us," he said, his voice hoarse. "I would have loved to join you."

Lavinia's cheeks were heated either from the hot bath or

perhaps from his words.

She started soaping her arms, hoping the soapy water would cover her form soon.

What devil had prompted her to disrobe in front of him? Granted, he didn't seem repulsed by her, quite the contrary. But her foolish heart was beating loudly in her chest, clouding any rational thought.

"You've been trying to paint me naked since we first met. So here I am, naked, and yet you're not painting me," she teased lightly, to cover up her discomfort.

A glimmer of a smile appeared on his lips. "I find I'd rather be right here. Close by. We'll have enough nights for me to paint you later. Provided I would ever choose not to be sitting by your side."

The smile left her lips, and Lavinia looked down. She wished his words were true. But it was unfair to promise him that, without telling him the full truth, the full extent of her troubles. "Sebastian, about our marriage—"

"There is nothing to say. The duke said it is settled," he interrupted softly.

"It is not his decision to make."

A coy smile tugged at his lips. "Well, did you have to sound so enamored with me when you talked about me?"

Lavinia's cheeks heated even more. "I did not sound enamored!"

Sebastian chuckled. "Oh, yes, you did. You said you'd be the luckiest woman on earth to marry me."

"I did not say that." She splashed water his way, a timid smile on her lips.

Sebastian turned away from the scattering droplets, then caught her hand and kissed her wrist. "Let us not argue about this anymore. Not tonight. I just want to sit by your side and watch you bathe."

Lavinia nodded. She soaped her arms, watching him from under her eyelashes.

Perhaps he was right. They'd had a difficult day, and they deserved a lovely, calm evening in each other's company.

She wanted him to kiss her again, but she wasn't about to ask. She'd asked him twice already. He knew how she felt about him. He knew that she craved his kisses. The next time, she wanted him to initiate their intimacy.

Sebastian watched her carefully, as she continued soaping herself, while he sat, relaxed, one hand in the bath, his fingers creating ripples in the water.

Suddenly, he stretched out his hand toward her. Lavinia raised her brow.

"Let me help," he said with a smile.

Shivers covered her skin from the mere thought of Sebastian's hands on her, his soapy fingers gliding down her wet skin… Lavinia had to bite her lip and clench her thighs together from the warmth enveloping her body. She slowly handed him the soap, her breath quickening in her chest.

Sebastian covered her hand with his. "Are you certain?"

She nodded confidently this time. "I think I prefer it…"

"Why, you are quite wicked, Lady Lavinia," he said with his boyish grin that made a dimple appear on his cheek.

Her face split in an answering smile. "I am."

Sebastian dipped the soap into the water, then ran his soapy hands down her arms. He massaged her fingers, and wicked sensations shot down her belly.

Lavinia moaned.

Sebastian shifted to sit behind her and started kneading the tense muscles of her shoulders. Lavinia dropped her head back with a moan.

Oh, that was a heavenly feeling.

Sebastian didn't pause. He washed her back, sliding his hot hands down her body as he carefully washed her, kneaded her aching muscles, and caressed her skin.

If only every bath was this pleasurable.

Sebastian helped her wash her hair. Then he shifted to sit beside her again.

He looked at the upper mounds of her breasts peeking out from the soapy water.

"Do you want me to continue?" he asked.

Lavinia shivered in anticipation. "Yes."

He smiled, soaped his hands, and slowly trailed them down her breasts.

Another moan escaped Lavinia's mouth as she arched into him, rubbing her beaded nipples against his palms.

Sebastian groaned. Then he trailed his hands lower, dipping them underwater, running his hands down her abdomen, her soft, rounded belly, the creases of her waist. He dipped his finger into her belly button, and she arched again.

He kneaded her hips, her thighs. Before she knew it, one of his hands traveled to the valley between her legs.

Lavinia let out an audible breath as he touched the sensitive skin on the inner side of her thigh. Sebastian trailed it higher but stopped just an inch from the patch of hair between her legs. He raised his eyes to hers.

"May I?"

Lavinia swallowed, her breathing labored. She looked into his eyes, which seemed darker somehow. He stared into her eyes, as his fingers played with the skin of her thigh.

He swallowed, and Lavinia's gaze followed the ripple traveling down his throat. Everything was erotic to her now. The tiny beads of sweat covering the skin of his chest were slightly exposed by his open shirt. The coarse hairs peeking out from under the neckline.

Everything about him seemed beautiful and sensual. Was that how he saw her, too?

It was better not to think about it.

It was better to surrender to her desires. With him, she wanted to be wicked.

Because with him, nothing was wicked. Everything was… just right.

Lavinia licked her lips, and his eyes darted to her mouth, burning with passion. And then she nodded.

Sebastian's finger ran along her feminine lips, and she gasped. He continued moving his finger as he stared deeply into her eyes.

The ticklish sensation rushed to her belly, and her mouth fell open on a gasp.

Yes! More, please!

She wanted to cry out loud to urge him on. Instead, she grabbed the bath by the edges and tensed, her knuckles whitening.

Sebastian leaned in and captured her mouth in a wet, wild kiss. Water splashed around them as he leaned in further, soaking the front of his shirt. His stubble abraded the skin around her mouth, but the burning sensation only intensified her wild passion. His arm, now wet to his shoulder, tensed, showcasing his beautiful muscles beneath the soaked shirt, as he continued working her center with his fingers.

Her hips moved in rhythm to his movements, her tongue

licking at Sebastian's lips. And then his finger plunged inside her.

She gasped, and her head fell back at the unfamiliar feeling. Sebastian kissed her neck, nibbled on her skin, the prickling of his stubble heightening carnal sensations. And then he soothed her burning skin with his tongue before devouring her mouth again.

Lavinia wrapped her arms around his neck, drawing him closer. Her muscles contracted as he worked his finger in and out of her, mimicking the motions of his tongue.

Sebastian plunged the second finger inside, while his thumb worked the sensitive, swollen bud at her center. Lavinia returned his kisses with all her ardor. She swept her tongue inside, craving the taste of him, wanting him even closer.

She whimpered and squirmed, needing more of him, more of his ministrations, more of everything. Sebastian bit on her lips before letting go of her mouth. "Don't fight it, *ma petite*. Tell me, what do you want?"

Lavinia took his free hand and pressed it against her aching nipple. "I want you," she whispered, not knowing how to properly express what she was feeling. "Everywhere."

Sebastian circled her beaded nipple with his finger, then squeezed her breast. He lowered his head and put her other breast into his mouth.

A scream left her lips, and her entire body grew taut. It was as if she turned into a being existing solely to experience the pleasure from Sebastian's lips and hands. His every touch just brought her to a new height of pleasure, wave after wave.

* * *

Sebastian didn't stop until the last spasms in Lavinia's body subsided. She sank fingers into his shoulders, her nails biting into his flesh in the throes of passion.

Sebastian loved seeing her like this, loved watching the grimace of pleasure on her face, loved hearing the sounds she made, and most of all, he loved feeling her inner flesh drawing his fingers in, contracting around him.

Only once she quieted down, and her breathing returned to a normal rhythm, did he withdraw his fingers and raise his head.

She watched him back with sparkling eyes. Her lips were wet, her cheeks cherry red.

Sebastian ripped the shirt off his back in one smooth motion. Lavinia's gaze followed him as if she wished to devour his form.

Good.

Because he wished to devour her, too.

Sebastian leaned down, wrapped his arms around her, and hauled her out of the bath. Water trickled down her body and onto the floor.

Sebastian didn't care; he wanted her and he couldn't wait any longer. He gingerly placed her on the plush rug by the hearth. He wanted her to be warm after the bath. He didn't want to soak her bedsheet where she'd need to sleep.

But mainly, he just wanted to see her illuminated in the warm glow of the fire. He'd seen her in the dark; he'd seen her obscured by the murky water. Now, he just wanted to feast his eyes upon her flesh without any barriers.

She looked like a goddess, with her inviting, round curves. He wanted to squish her soft flesh in his arms as he sank into her depth.

She propped herself on her elbows, thrusting her breasts upward, making his mouth water.

She didn't look shy anymore. Confidence shone in her eyes. Her wet skin glinted with fire, the droplets running in rivulets down her body. She was mesmerizing.

Lavinia watched Sebastian in return, unashamedly devouring his form. Sebastian slowly took off his breaches and unhurriedly kneeled before her. He held his cock in his hand, stroking it slowly, imagining how it would feel inside her.

Sebastian climbed on top of her and feasted on her body with his eyes, devouring every curve, every mound. He lowered one hand and ran his palm down her belly. "Are you not ashamed of being naked in front of me anymore?"

Lavinia bit her lip and shook her head.

He smiled softly, his hand traveling back up her body ever so slowly, causing goosebumps in its wake. "Why not?"

He ran his finger under her breast, making her arch. Then he cupped her breast and ran his thumb over her beaded nipple. His cock burned for her touch. He wanted to sink himself inside her right at that moment, but he didn't want to rush it either. He wanted to enjoy her.

"Because," she finally breathed. "When you look at me, you don't look at my body—"

"Oh, I look at your body," he said with a wicked grin. Then he lowered his mouth to her breast and licked her.

"Ah!" Lavinia arched again. She raised her burning gaze to his. "When you look at me, you see right through me. To my soul. It's as if you don't see the imperfections, you just… see me."

Sebastian met her gaze, his body heating even more from inside him.

"I don't feel embarrassed because you see... *me*," she repeated simply.

"I do," he whispered against her lips. "And you're the most beautiful woman in the world."

Lavinia arched and pressed her lips to his.

Sebastian kissed her deeply, his hands roaming her body, his cock burning against her skin. It would take one thrust, and he'd be inside her. But that was not what he wanted. That was not how he wanted her.

"If we do this," he said, his voice hoarse. "There will be no more discussion regarding our marriage. You will simply be mine."

Lavinia watched him as if mesmerized. Her mouth was slightly open, but she couldn't say a word.

"Say it." He bit her lip.

Lavinia blinked up at him. "Say what?" she whispered.

"Say that you're mine."

Lavinia's breaths quickened, and her body tensed. Her mind worked, and he could see all of the doubts plaguing her mind. "You don't know what you are getting yourself into," she whispered.

"I don't care. You're mine." He nudged her lips with his.

He wanted to kiss her. His lips burned for her touch. He wanted to be soothed by her kisses. But he didn't want to muddle her mind more than he already had.

"I'll be a burden," she tried again.

Sebastian shook his head. "Never."

Lavinia closed her eyes and ran her hands up his arms, then weaved them around his neck. "You don't know the full truth, and you might not want me after you do—"

"Nonsense."

"But I *am* yours," she said, her voice hitching on the last word. "And I will always be yours."

Sebastian wrapped his arms around her, pulled her closer to his body, and took her mouth in a long, slow kiss.

"Mine," he whispered against her lips, just so she wouldn't forget. "You're mine."

He rubbed his cock against her feminine lips, finding moisture there. She was ready for him, and he'd been ready for her forever.

He kissed her again. Rougher this time, biting on her plump lips, devouring her mouth with his tongue. She did not mind. On the contrary, she took his face between her hands and held him even closer.

Sebastian took himself in hand and pressed his cock against her center.

"Say it again," he whispered once more.

"I am yours."

Sebastian rocked against her, sliding inside her with the head of his cock. His eyes fell closed, and he groaned from pleasure.

Lavinia's hands slid lower, and her fingers dug into the muscles of his shoulders.

"Wraps your legs around me," he croaked as he looked up at her.

Lavinia's eyes were wide, her breaths coming in gulps.

"Don't be frightened," he whispered and nudged his nose against hers.

She shook her head. "I am not afraid."

Sebastian nodded and rocked again, thrusting a little more inside. Her breaths became ragged, her muscles contracting and refusing to let him in. She was tight and wonderfully hot.

But he could feel her confusion, her body's stress under him.

So, he stroked her body sensually with his hands and kissed her mouth again. She relaxed instantly, her muscles giving way. He thrust again and seated himself fully inside her.

An agonizing groan left his lips. It was the most wonderful feeling in the world, just being inside her.

"Lord, you're wonderful," he whispered and peppered her face with his kisses. "So beautiful, so lovely, mesmerizing, and absolutely mine."

He buried his face in the crook of her neck. "Hold on to me," he whispered against her skin.

Sebastian moved his hips away from her and then thrust inside again. She gasped at the contact, and he did it again.

The friction of their skin, the scent of their shared desire, and the sounds that she made all built toward the act of completion.

He continued thrusting in and out of her as he watched her face. Her eyes were filled with wonder, and her mouth was slightly open as she gasped with every thrust.

Their moans and groans melded together until time stopped and they became one, lost in the sensual dance among the stars.

Sebastian spilled his seed with a groan and collapsed on top of her, his heart drumming in his ears.

Mine, his heart sang with every beat.

Chapter 28

Sebastian watched Lavinia, quietly resting in his arms. Her breaths were even, as she snored softly. She was so warm, so soft and welcoming, that he never wanted to leave her side.

But duty called.

He couldn't ignore the duel he himself set up. So he crawled out of bed, got dressed, and with one last glance toward Lavinia's sleeping form, left the room.

The moon still shone in the sky, and he had a few hours before dawn to clean up and shave off his four days' worth of facial hair. He rang the servants' bell and leaned his back against the wall.

He hoped McAllistair passed down all the information into the duke's hands. His only job was to make certain the duel took place today, at dawn, at the Clover Close field. The rest, Sebastian was certain, Kensington would take care of.

Was he being foolish? Was the duel worth it?

He shook his head. Victoria had wonderful prospects. She

was young and clever, ambitious and lively. She didn't deserve to have all her dreams crushed just because a man had tricked her.

She was too trusting and naïve, and now she had to pay the price.

Well, Sebastian would have to pay the price, too. Because nobody had ever come out of a duel unscathed.

Was he truly going to kill William? The thought didn't sit well with him.

What if William killed him instead?

Sebastian didn't know how versed William was in the art of wielding a sword, but Sebastian was one of the best. He couldn't take any chances, though. Not after this night.

He went to his bedside table for a piece of paper, dipped the quill into the inkwell, and wrote out instructions to make changes to his will.

If he were to die, he didn't want to leave Lavinia with nothing.

What if she became with child?

Sebastian closed his eyes. He was definitely acting foolish. But was there a better way?

He hadn't slept properly for two nights, and perhaps his mind needed rest before making monumental decisions. But he couldn't let William get away with his wrong-doings. Because of him, Lavinia had been drugged with laudanum and carried away by the thugs! They could have hurt her. And that he could never forgive.

The servants came and, a few minutes later, bathed, shaved, and appropriately dressed, a riding crop in his hand and a sword hanging from his side, Sebastian was ready to leave.

He walked toward the grand staircase but paused by

Lavinia's chamber. He couldn't leave without seeing her. He didn't know what this day would bring.

Sebastian opened the door and walked in.

Lavinia still slept soundly, her chest rising and falling with her even breaths. Sebastian walked toward the bed and sat on the edge. He placed his hand on her side, a light touch, just to remember the feel of her for the rest of the day.

Lavinia moaned and opened her eyes. Her face immediately split into a smile. "Good morning," she said in a sleepy murmur. Then squinted at the window. "Is it morning already?"

"Not yet. Go back to sleep."

She turned back to him. "Why are you not sleeping? Why are you dressed?"

"I have to go," he whispered. "But when I come back, I shall make arrangements, and we'll get married."

Lavinia rubbed her eyes, then clutched the covers to her chest and perched herself against the bed rest. "Sebastian, we shouldn't get married just because you feel a sense of duty."

"Did it feel like a duty to you last night?" Sebastian raised his brow, drawing pleasure from her blushing form. "Besides, I think we covered it last night or did you forget? You told me that you're mine."

Lavinia's blush deepened. She leaned in and nudged his cheek with her nose. "I am yours. But before you make arrangements for this wedding, you need to know things… about me. I can't marry you in good conscience before I tell you what I have to tell you. Otherwise, I am just as bad as William."

Sebastian nodded. He had no idea what she would perceive to be as bad as lying about his true origins, but he wasn't about to argue with her. He kissed her lightly on her lips. "Very well. You'll tell me after I get back."

Lavinia reared back and furrowed her brows. "From where? Where are you going in the middle of the night?"

Sebastian gritted his teeth. He wished he didn't have to tell her. "A duel," he said simply.

"A duel?" Lavinia straightened, her voice a few octaves higher pitched than normal.

"Yes. With William."

"Are you out of your mind?" she gasped.

"No. And it's my duty to—"

"Your duty to kill your friend because he ruined your niece? Just like it is your duty to marry me?"

"One has nothing to do with the other, Lavinia." Sebastian stood and raked his hand through his hair.

Lavinia got out of bed, still clutching the bedsheets to her body. "Does Victoria know?"

Sebastian didn't answer. He turned around and walked toward the door.

"Of course, she doesn't! No woman in her right mind would allow that to happen. You can't kill him, Sebastian! Not only is it illegal, but no matter his deception, Victoria loves him!"

"Well, she'll have to fall out of love and quickly." His voice was hard and brooked no argument.

"What if he truly loves her, too? What if you're wrong, Sebastian. Don't you think you need to speak with him first?"

Sebastian halted and turned toward Lavinia. She almost ran into him, and Sebastian had to catch her by her arms. "He kidnapped you and me, stranded us in a decrepit old house without food or transportation so that he'd have time to seduce and fool my niece! Why in the world would I *not* kill him?"

Lavinia frowned. "Well, for the reasons I just said…"

"This is the only way to give her life back, her choices back, and her prospects!"

"What about your life? If you kill him, you will be imprisoned."

Sebastian scoffed. "Nobody would raise a brow if I rid this world of the criminal that is William. No one would care."

"Victoria will," Lavinia said heatedly. "You will. Other people might not care, but what about your soul? Can you live knowing that you killed another human?"

Sebastian took her face between his palms and kissed her savagely.

Instead of pushing him away as he thought she would, Lavinia weaved her hands around his neck and kissed him back. Gently. She soothed his anger with the tender touch of her tongue and the soft press of her body against his.

Sebastian pulled away, breathing heavily.

"Sebastian just—"

"Stay here," he growled. He walked to the door, grabbed the key, and locked the door behind him as he left.

* * *

Lavinia pulled on the servants' bell as hard as she could and scrambled to search for something to wear. There was nothing in the room except for the dirty gown she'd traveled in. So she ran, stark naked, into the dressing room. She picked up the first gown she could find and brought it over to her chamber.

There was a rattle of the door handle and a knock at the

door. Then came Beatrice's confused voice. "My lady?"

Lavinia rushed to the door. "Beatrice, it is me, but someone locked the door from the outside. Can you please unlock it for me?"

"Just a moment, my lady."

Lavinia heard retreating footsteps and let out a breath of relief. She returned to the dressing room and raided it, pulling out a chemise, stockings, a corset, anything she could find.

She pulled on her undergarments when the door handle rattled again. This time, the door opened and Beatrice entered the room.

"My lady! You are back from London so soon?"

"No, I haven't—it's a long story, but I came back."

"I thought it was odd how you left without your things and Miss Gale."

Miss Gale!

"I trust you took good care of her?" Lavinia asked as she started combing her hair.

"Of course, she is walking around the premises like she is the queen. All the servants adore her, although she doesn't seem to like men," Beatrice said with a chuckle.

"That she doesn't." Lavinia smiled.

"I'll bring her up to your room now if you want!"

"Yes, I'd love to see her, but later. I am in a bit of a hurry. Can you help me dress, please? And then I need you to go and wake the duchess."

Beatrice halted mid-step. "You want me to wake the duchess?"

Lavinia threw her an irritated glance. "Or ask somebody to do it, please. It's important."

"No one wakes the duchess," the girl insisted, still not

moving from her spot.

"Very well, then help me get dressed, and I shall wake her myself. But for the love of all that's holy, please, make haste."

Beatrice rushed toward the corset and helped Lavinia into it. Lavinia quickly got dressed with the help of her maid and fidgeted in her chair while Beatrice braided her hair. Before she could say she was done, Lavinia jumped up, rushed out of her room, and started frantically knocking on Caroline's door.

After what seemed like forever, the door cracked open, and Caroline peeked out, a worried pucker between her brows, a billowing nightdress covering her body.

"Lavinia? What's wrong?" She looked around the hall and then opened the door wider. "Please, come in."

Lavinia started pacing the moment she entered the room. "I do not know what to do. You always know what to do, so please, I need your help."

"Lavinia, please, sit."

"No!" Frustration, the sleepless night, and all the stress finally got to her. She could feel her body shaking as a tear slid down her cheek. "He is going to kill him!"

"Who?" Caroline walked toward the servants' bell. She rang it and turned back to Lavinia. "Who is going to kill whom?"

"Sebastian called William out on a duel last night—"

"Well, duels do not get arranged for days. We have time to—"

"No!" Lavinia threw her hands up. "He is gone. It is today. Now!"

"That's impossible."

"When Sebastian wants something, nothing is impossible," Lavinia said heatedly. And it was true. He always got what he wanted, and now he was on his way to kill the man his niece loved.

"Damn him and his hot-headed tendencies!" Caroline said as she paced into her dressing room.

Lavinia reached into her pocket for a handkerchief. "Perhaps if it was one or the other, but the fact that William hired thugs to kidnap us and put me in danger in order to take this time to seduce Victoria all made it too much of an unforgivable sin in Sebastian's mind."

"We could have discussed the marriage and come to a mutually beneficial decision," Caroline yelled from her dressing room. "Perhaps we could even send William away, threaten him with the magistrate for what he did to you and Roth—for the kidnapping."

Lavinia nodded as she wiped her tears with the handkerchief and folded it. "I know, I wanted to talk him out of it but—" She paused as she noticed the rose in the corner of the handkerchief. It was the same one as on the handkerchief Sebastian had wrapped her foot in while at Watchet.

Was it the same handkerchief? Had she taken it with her? No… It was all bloody, and she'd left it there. So then, where did this one come from?

"What's wrong?" Caroline came out of the dressing room with fresh garments in her arms. "What did Roth do when you tried to stop him?"

Lavinia shook her head. "No, it's not that. It's this handkerchief…" And then it dawned on her where she got it from. "My guardian gave it to me…"

"So?"

Lavinia raised her gaze to Caroline's. "I don't think William was the one who kidnapped us."

* * *

Sebastian didn't know what he expected from his second. He'd picked him out in the middle of the night, and he didn't care if he participated or not, because he knew that Kensington would arrange everything for the both of them. Yet there Lord McAllistair was, standing by Sebastian's side as he reached the dueling field.

William leaned his back against the tree, sipping from a flask with a bored expression on his face. Kensington stood a few feet away, as if unwilling to associate with his bastard brother more than he needed to. And then there was another man, sitting on the opposite side of the tree with a valise by his feet.

"Are you certain you want to do this?" Kensington asked as he approached Sebastian.

"If you were in my shoes, wouldn't you?"

Kensington shrugged. "There might be other ways, legal ways, to get out of this predicament."

"He kidnapped me. His thugs hit me over the head and drugged me. He put the woman I love in danger. All so he could seduce my niece. What are the legal ways to deal with this?"

Kensington raised a brow at Sebastian's choice of words, but he didn't continue arguing. "Fair enough."

Sebastian scanned the surroundings irritably, then tipped his head toward the man sitting by the tree. "Who is that gentleman?"

"The best doctor I could bring on such a short notice," Kensington grumbled. "You at least could've given us a day to prepare. I haven't slept, and poor McAllistair hasn't even sobered up."

"I couldn't risk the word getting out."

Kensington nodded. "Did *you* get any sleep?"

"No." Sebastian shook his head. "Did William?"

"I don't know." Kensington sighed. "But if you're ready, I think we can begin."

"Wait a moment. I know you're not my second, but under these bizarre circumstances, I do not think it matters. You are the only one I trust with this." He took an envelope from his pocket, sealed with his family crest. "This is a note to my solicitor about a change in my will. Just in case."

Kensington raised a brow. "Are you certain you want *me* to deliver it?"

"Nobody would argue with a duke. But it does have my seal on it. Besides, I know you will get the solicitor to take this seriously. Because you care about her."

Kensington took the envelope and twirled it in his hand. "It is about Lavinia," he said.

Sebastian nodded. "I do not expect to die today. But it is better to be prepared."

Kensington nodded. "I understand. And you have my word."

As the sun rose over the horizon, Sebastian stood opposite William, their swords crossed. It was an odd twist of fate. He'd never thought he'd end up across from William in a duel, but here they were.

They circled each other, neither of them willing to attack first. Sebastian had never fenced with William, and he had no idea how good of a fencer he was. He didn't want to underestimate him. But he wasn't about to circle around him all day. He lunged, but William parried it swiftly.

"Now, do not make it easy on me, Bastian," William said with a smirk. "I thought you were quite lauded for being an expert fencer. Unless you don't want to kill me after all."

"Oh, I shall kill you. Worry not," Sebastian growled.

"So, you are just playing with me?" William lunged.

Sebastian stepped back and counterattacked immediately. After exchanging a few blows, they returned to circle each other again.

"Does she know?" William asked. And then lunged again.

"No." Sebastian crossed the sword with William. He pushed with his entire body, making William jump back and stumble a few feet. "How did you even think you were going to get away with this?"

"I did get away with this." William straightened and took the proper fencing stance again. "She married me, did she not?"

"But she is not going to stay married to you," Sebastian retorted.

"Only if you kill me."

Another lunge. Sebastian parried the swing, pivoted, and thrust from above. William ducked and turned, staggering in the process, but quickly regained his pose.

"How did you think your life would proceed?" Sebastian gritted between his teeth.

"She loves me. She will forgive me sooner or later. And I'll have a lifetime to make it up to her."

"Oh, so you were just going to kidnap her? Like you kidnapped me and Lavinia?"

William paused, confusion lining his face. "I never touched either of you."

Sebastian snorted. "Right. Like you never lied to Victoria."

William attacked, forcing Sebastian to duck. As he was coming up from under his arm, Sebastian hit William's wrist, disarming him, and kicked him in the chest.

William fell on his back and coughed. "Not so honorable now, are we, Bastian?" he asked with a bitter chuckle.

"Enough of these games, William. You were after Victoria from day one. Tell me why."

A bitter laugh escaped William's lips. "The reason is as simple as it is foolish. I fell in love with her."

Sebastian snorted. "A soul as dark as yours knows not love."

"And does yours? Or are you playing with your ladybird?"

Sebastian pointed his sword at William's chest. "Do not speak of her this way. And tell me the truth. Why did you seduce Victoria? Why ruin her and her chances of marriage? Why kidnap me? What have I ever done to you?"

William scoffed and shook his head. "You and your illusions of grandeur. None of it had anything to do with you. Do you not think that perhaps I want something for myself? Something as good and sweet as Victoria?"

"Careful," Sebastian growled.

"All I wanted was Victoria. And I shall still get her one day. As for whatever happened to you, the kidnapping…" He shrugged. "It was a lucky coincidence. I had nothing to do with it."

"You are a liar."

William grinned. "I speak only the truth. I swear on my honor."

Sebastian stood over him, the tip of his sword pointing at William's chest. One plunge into his heart, and he'd be dead in seconds.

If Sebastian killed William, Victoria would be free to

remarry and do with her life as she pleased. If he killed William, he would be doing society a great favor by ridding them of a thief.

But what about your soul?

"You do not have an honorable bone in your body, William," Sebastian spat. His breath quickened as he watched William dare him to push the sword into his chest.

Can you live knowing that you killed another?

And not just another. A man he'd once called a friend.

Sebastian closed his eyes and threw the sword away.

William nodded and said so quietly Sebastian barely heard him, "You are right."

The next thing happened in a flash. William quickly jumped to his feet, a dagger glinting in his hand, and then a hot flash, followed by agonizing pain, brought Sebastian to his knees.

Chapter 29

Lavinia and Caroline were questioning Sebastian's valet, hoping that he knew where the duel was taking place. The lad was not helpful at all. And just when they were going to give up in despair, they were distracted by the hubbub downstairs. They rushed toward the noise and saw a horrifying sight.

Sebastian was undressed down to his breeches, one arm around Kensington, who was holding a bloodied piece of cloth to his shoulder. Kensington was shouting orders at the servants as they made their way toward the stairs. There were other people there, other men, but Lavinia didn't see anything else around her.

Sebastian was hurt.

She rushed toward him, paying no heed to anything else. "How badly are you hurt?"

Sebastian disengaged from Kensington and instantly wrapped his uninjured arm around Lavinia's shoulders. Lavinia enveloped him in an embrace and burrowed her face in his chest. Sebastian drew her closer and pressed a kiss to the top of her head.

"I am well. It's a superficial wound. Nothing to worry about." Did his words slur? She looked up at him and he smiled. "I didn't kill him, if that's what you're wondering," he said, and his warm breath, smelling of alcohol, hit her face.

"Didn't kill him? Oh, William." Lavinia shook her head. That question wasn't even on her mind. "As long as he didn't kill you, I don't care."

"Didn't you want to save me from damnation?"

"The room is ready," Kensington said by their side.

Lavinia jumped. She had completely forgotten they were not alone. Now she was acutely aware that there were people staring at them! And here she was, wrapped up in Sebastian's arms.

"Let's go," he said and kissed her on the forehead. He staggered, and then walked toward the stairs, not letting go of Lavinia.

She squirmed uncomfortably.

"Don't you think it is better to let me help you?" Kensington asked.

Yes. Probably best.

Lavinia was about to disengage from Sebastian's side, but he tightened his arm around her. "I am perfectly capable of walking on my own. But I'd rather *Ma Petite* is by my side."

Lavinia's cheeks burned. It was utterly inappropriate, but she couldn't seem to peel herself away from Sebastian even if she wanted to. And she didn't want to. For all her squirming and blushing, at the end of the day, she didn't care what people thought. She just wanted to be close to Sebastian.

They made their way upstairs, and Lavinia led him into his

bedroom. She helped him climb atop his bed, and Sebastian tugged her to sit by his side.

"Now, Doctor," he said. "I need you to open my wound further and clean it before bandaging."

"I will do no such thing," the white-haired old man said gruffly. "It is better to let the wound heal under scabs."

"I understand that this is a controversial subject, but I was part of *L'Académie des Sciences.* And I believe this is a more thorough way to heal the wound."

The doctor puffed out his chest. "I respectfully disagree."

Where did Kensington find this insolent doctor? "Since I am the one injured, I believe I should be able to make the final call."

"I can't in good conscience let you dictate to me what to do and then be responsible for your health after," the doctor said stubbornly.

Sebastian frowned. "Then you can go."

"Sebastian!" Lavinia exclaimed, horrified.

Sebastian took her hand and brought it to his lips. "Trust me, I know what I am doing."

"I do not doubt *you*, Sebastian. But who is going to help you?" she asked as the doctor collected his belongings and left the room, grumbling something under his breath.

"You. And him." Sebastian tipped his head toward Kensington.

Lavinia had completely forgotten Kensington's existence again. She looked at him and shook her head. "He is not a doctor. I am not a doctor either. We can't—"

"Step aside!" Caroline said to the servants as she entered the room. "What do you need?"

"See?" Sebastian asked. "We have all the help I need."

"You need a doctor!" Lavinia said emphatically.

"Come closer," Sebastian whispered.

Lavinia raised her brows in annoyance but leaned in still. "What?"

"Closer, damn it," he growled.

Lavinia leaned in a little more. Sebastian reached out, grabbed her by the nape, and brought her even closer until his lips touched hers.

It wasn't a light kiss. It wasn't soft or reverent. It was a kiss of desperation. He kissed her as if he wanted to possess her right there, in front of everyone. When he finally let her go, they were both panting.

"Do as I ask, *ma petite*. And everything will be fine."

Caroline delicately cleared her throat, and Lavinia might as well have burned from shame. Not even married people showed as much affection toward each other. It was indecent.

But Sebastian was hurt, and from the smell of alcohol on his breath, she concluded he was also drunk, probably from trying to dull the pain. He didn't know what he was doing.

Was that enough of an excuse for his behavior? Definitely not enough excuse for Lavinia's behavior.

"Anything we can do?" Caroline asked.

"Yes. I need you to bring a sharp, clean, preferably a never-before-used knife or a dagger to open my wound further."

"What?" Lavinia was horrified at what she was hearing.

"I have that," Kensington said and left the room.

Caroline followed his defection with narrowed eyes, then turned back to Sebastian. "What else?"

"Ask the servants to bring turpentine or vinegar. And clean sheets."

Caroline nodded and left.

Why is everyone so calm? Lavinia was shaking in panic. She looked at Sebastian's pale face and tried to collect herself. He needed her.

Lavinia touched his cheek. "What should I do?"

He took her hand and squeezed it tightly. "I have the most important job for you."

"Yes?"

"Stay by my side."

Lavinia squeezed his fingers. "I want to help."

He smiled, then brought her hand to his lips and kissed her knuckles. "You are."

There was a slight rap at the door, and Lord Payne peeked his head into the chamber. It seemed like the hubbub had awakened the entire house. "What is going on? There's so much noise. Annalise was afraid there'd been an invasion."

Sebastian chuckled and then hissed, his hand tensing on his wound. "Everything is fine. But we could use your help. Come in."

"Everything is fine?" Payne walked further into the room. "You're bleeding."

"Yes, well, at least, nobody is invading us."

"How is Annalise?" Lavinia asked.

Payne looked at Lavinia as if he'd just noticed her. "Lady Lavinia, we thought you'd left for London."

"I didn't make it far." She smiled sheepishly.

Payne's gaze fell to their clasped hands, and he raised a brow. "Annalise is well. But she would love to see you. She was worried."

Lavinia nodded. "I would love to see her, too."

Caroline returned just then with Kensington on her heels. "Here's turpentine," she said. "And clean sheets will be here in a moment."

"Good." Sebastian nodded, then turned to Lavinia. *"Ma petite,* for this one, I shall need you to look away. Can you sit by the window for a moment?"

"But you told me to be by your side."

"Yes... later. This one will be gruesome."

"I can ask Annalise to—" Payne started, but Lavinia shook her head.

"No. No need to disturb her. I"—she stood and walked toward the window—"I shall be here until you're done."

Lavinia understood that she would be in the way, but she didn't want to leave the room. She wanted to make certain she was by his side if Sebastian needed her.

So she stood by the window and looked on as Payne and Kensington held him down while Caroline cut open his wound and poured warm water inside.

The view was truly horrifying.

Lavinia would never forget Sebastian's red face, a piece of cloth between his teeth, every muscle in his body taut, and most of all, the roaring sounds he made. He had passed out before Caroline finished applying turpentine to his wound and wrapped it with fresh bandages.

Thank God. At least he wasn't in pain anymore.

"We should let him rest," Caroline said as the maids finished cleaning up the room.

Sebastian lay still in bed, his breaths even, his face relaxed.

"I'd rather stay," Lavinia whispered.

"There will be gossip," Kensington warned.

"We've already caused so much gossip this morning. My staying here will not change anything," Lavinia insisted.

"I do not think any of the guests witnessed anything. And

servants in this household do not gossip," Caroline said firmly. "Stay as long as you wish."

She patted Lavinia on her arm and left the room.

Lavinia sat on the chair by Sebastian's side and watched the even rise and fall of his chest.

Kensington dragged a chair to sit by Lavinia's side and shifted uncomfortably. "Lavinia, I've been meaning to speak with you for a while. Since—Since that day when you told me you loved me."

"Oh." Lavinia grimaced. "I am sorry. I shouldn't have said anything—"

"No." His expression was pained. "In fact, I think you should have told me earlier."

Lavinia turned toward him, surprised. "You do?"

He sighed. "Yes. I've always… Well, you know that I always sought to protect you. I cared about you, dare I say, even loved you."

Lavinia's eyes grew wider with his every word. Where had this conversation been when she'd needed it most? When she was desolate.

"Perhaps not in the way you wanted me to love you, but I did. I've had a great deal of time to think about this," Kensington continued. "And I think that yes, I would have—I would have married you had you told me this earlier."

Lavinia had to shake herself from the numb stupor she was in. "You would?"

"I would. I care for you, and marrying you would be better than—" He halted and grimaced. "Let me just say that it would have saved me from a few issues. And I do not think I would ever have been able to make you truly happy, but we would have been content."

Lavinia let out a disbelieving snort. "Why are you telling me this now? There is no use. You're married!"

"Yes." Kensington nodded. "And the reason I am telling you this is precisely because it is too late for us. I have not paid attention to you when I should have. And I think you are not paying attention to what is right in front of you, either."

Lavinia threw a glance toward the sleeping form of Sebastian. "Trust me, I pay attention."

"And I started paying attention, too," Kensington said with a sad smile. "He loves you, you know. And I can see that you love him, too. Not the way you loved me. Dare I say more fiercely than you ever loved me? And that is why I do not understand why you are resisting marrying him."

Lavinia chuckled bitterly. *If only it were that easy.* "There is more to this than you know. There are issues—"

"Does he know about these issues?"

Lavinia shook her head.

"Well, then tell him."

"I don't know if—"

"And you will never know. Not until it's too late. You didn't tell me about your feelings until it was too late, and it seems like that was the right choice for you in the long run, but… Do not lose this. Do not lose him, just because you're too late to tell him the truth." He shook his head with a chuckle. "Do not be William."

* * *

Sebastian opened his eyes and squinted at the canopy over the bed. His head hurt and when he tried to move—

"Ahh!" he growled and fell back against the pillows.

"What's wrong?" Lavinia's face appeared over him, and the pain in his body disappeared.

Well, not truly. The pain wasn't gone, but it was overshadowed by the pleasure of seeing her.

"Did I ever tell you," he croaked, "that I love seeing your face the first thing after I wake up?"

Lavinia pursed her lips to hold on to her smile, but it still managed to break out. She placed a hand against his cheek. "Does it hurt really bad? Do you want anything?"

He shook his head. "No, I think you healed me."

"Sebastian," Lavinia reproached. "Please, be serious."

"I am serious," he croaked. "But perhaps I can use a drink. Help me sit upright first."

When Lavinia leaned in to help him, Sebastian wrapped his arm around her waist and tumbled her into bed with him.

"Sebastian!" she chuckled as she raised her head, her coiffure tumbling over her face.

"Did you fall, *ma petite*? What a pity."

"If someone sees us—" she scolded softly.

"What? I might have to marry you?" Sebastian grinned, but Lavinia ducked her head.

She scrambled out of bed. "Let me get you a drink."

Sebastian sat up and leaned his back against the pillow, hissing. His shoulder ached and pulsed, but it wasn't an agonizing pain. Nothing to be troubled over. He'd had worse.

But he was still weak, and to be honest, he could use a bit more sleep. His eyelids felt heavy.

"Sebastian."

"Yes?" His eyes flew open.

Lavinia pressed a glass of water to his lips. "Drink."

Sebastian took the glass and sipped slowly. "Does Victoria

know what happened?"

Lavinia shook her head. "I do not know. I haven't left your side. Dane—Kensington—told me what happened during the duel… But I haven't seen Victoria."

Sebastian grimaced. He hated that she still thought of Kensington by his Christian name. "How long was I sleeping?"

"Not long. Half an hour, perhaps? I think you need more rest."

Sebastian nodded. His head was getting heavier and heavier with every second. "I think you're right."

"Sebastian. There are things I need to discuss with you."

There was a dull ringing in his ears. "Can it wait? I feel like I need a bit of sleep."

Lavinia nodded, but her face was troubled. "Of course."

Sebastian tried to get comfortable on his pillow. "Do you mind lying with me for a moment?"

Lavinia looked around. "Sebastian—"

"Just for a moment, until I fall asleep."

"Very well." Lavinia nodded and climbed into bed with him, perching her head on the uninjured side of his chest.

Sebastian hugged her tightly to his body and inhaled the sweet scent of her hair. He would stay like this forever if he could. And hopefully, soon he would. Just as soon as he got out of this bed and married his little muse.

Chapter 30

∞

Lavinia woke up to a light rap on the door. She sat up and looked around the room. The light streamed in from the windows, illuminating the entire room. What time was it?

Sebastian groaned by her side. He tried to turn to his injured side, then hissed and settled on his back again.

Oh, no! She was in bed with him.

The door creaked open.

Lavinia scrambled from the bed and dashed into a chair, palming her hair as she did so.

"May I come in?" Victoria asked as she stepped inside.

"Of course." Lavinia stood to greet her friend.

Lavinia's hair was disheveled, her gown was wrinkly, and she probably looked a fright, but Victoria didn't seem to pay attention. Her own face was puffy, and she looked pale, and frail for the first time since Lavinia had ever seen her.

She used to be so full of life. Lavinia's heart squeezed.

Victoria embraced Lavinia and then looked at her sleeping

uncle.

"It is all my fault," she whispered.

"No, it isn't," Lavinia said firmly. If anyone's, it was Lavinia's fault, and she wouldn't let anyone else take the blame.

Now that she knew that her guardian was the one involved with the kidnapping, it was obvious that she was the cursed one. She was the one who put the people she cared about in jeopardy.

Matilda would be homeless soon if Lavinia didn't marry. But how could she marry Sebastian now, after all this?

If it wasn't for her, they wouldn't have been kidnapped, and perhaps Sebastian would have stopped Victoria's wedding from happening. And the duel would have never happened.

And this was even before she took into account that someone was threatening her. If she married Sebastian now, who was to say that everything would not turn out worse than it already was? If she married Sebastian, there was no telling what her guardian would do next, either.

"It is my fault!" Victoria exclaimed, her lower lip quivering as she fought her tears. "Me and my foolish romantic fantasies. I was so certain that William was an honorable man, and now look at this! I brought this on my family with my foolish dreams and aspirations and now I can never—" She shook her head.

"It is not your fault, but William's." *And mine.* She took Victoria's hands in hers. "He was the one who fooled you, he was the one who stabbed Sebastian, and he was the one who caused all this. Not you. Do you understand?"

Lavinia didn't want Victoria to suffer because of her. She didn't want Victoria to feel guilt for her sins.

It would be better for everyone if Lavinia left and married

whoever her guardian had in mind. And she didn't even know *if* that man would take her.

She wasn't a virgin anymore.

And if that man found out and turned his nose away, she would be in a new kind of trouble.

"Poor Frau Elinor," Victoria whispered. "She was left to chaperone me when Uncle fell ill. And she is in frail health herself. I shouldn't have fooled her. I should have spoken to her. What a simpleton I am."

Lavinia hoped she could find the words to comfort Victoria, but she couldn't. Everything was spiraling out of control.

There was a beat of silence. "How is he?" Victoria finally asked, still staring at her uncle. "Will he be well?"

"Yes." Lavinia nodded as she let go of Victoria. "He said the wound wasn't serious and as long as he doesn't have a fever, he should be fine. He woke up for a moment, but he was too weak to stay awake for long. I hope he will be much better on the morrow."

Victoria nodded. "I am so glad that he has you."

Lavinia took a breath to answer, but there were no words.

She couldn't contradict Victoria at that moment. Sebastian did have her. And he would still have her, no matter what happened next.

"Do you mind if I sit with him for a while?" Victoria asked.

Lavinia looked at Sebastian. She was loath to leave him, but she understood Victoria's need to be with her uncle, too. So she nodded. "Of course. I could use a change of attire."

Victoria smiled. "And perhaps some food?"

Suddenly, Lavinia became acutely aware that she hadn't eaten anything since the night before. "You're right. But will you tell me when he wakes up?"

"Of course."

Lavinia left the room and wandered down the corridor to her chamber. She opened the door and instantly noted Miss Gale, in her usual spot, sleeping.

Lavinia dashed toward her cat and sat on the floor beside her. She'd missed her so much! She stroked her under her jaw, and Miss Gale stretched and yawned. She looked at Lavinia, turned around, and continued sleeping peacefully.

"I see you missed me, too, my loyal Galinthias," Lavinia whispered with a chuckle. She pressed her back against the wall, sitting by her cat, listening to her light purring.

A tear slid down her cheek, but she didn't even know why she was crying.

Everything had changed in just a few days. And yet again, everything was still uncertain. Miss Gale was her only anchor at the moment, her only constant in her life. And sitting by her side was just a reminder of that.

Lavinia's eyes started closing, and her limbs felt heavy.

She shook her head and forced herself to get up. She couldn't fall asleep on the floor. She needed to have some food and change. She needed to be ready when Sebastian awakened and called for her.

She walked to the servants' bell and pulled on it.

Beatrice walked in almost instantly. "Good evening, my lady."

Lavinia smiled. "Thank you for bringing Miss Gale back to me."

"Of course." The maid curtsied.

"Beatrice, I haven't eaten in what seems like forever, but I do not want to go downstairs. Can you bring me some tea and something to eat, please?" She couldn't face other guests in this house. Not yet.

"Of course," the maid answered, then hesitated. "Lady Payne asked me to tell her when you returned to your room. Do you wish me to tell her you're here?"

"Oh, yes. Please. And thank you."

The maid smiled, and then her gaze fell to the bedside table. "There is some mail for you on the table, my lady," she said and scurried away.

Lavinia had a sense of foreboding.

She walked to the bedside table and picked up a single envelope lying there. It was from Matilda.

There was a knock at the door, and Lavinia jumped in fright. *Will I ever stop reacting to sudden sounds like this?* "Please, come in."

Annalise peeked inside the room and then rushed in. Lavinia took a step to meet her, and the old friends embraced as if they'd not seen each other for years, and it truly seemed this way.

"Oh, my, Lavinia!" Annalise exclaimed, as she finally disengaged and studied her friend from head to toe. "You look like you've slept in this attire for days."

"Not for days, but I did sleep in this just now. Oh, Annalise, these were the most hellish days…"

"Were they?"

Lavinia let out a deep breath, motioned for Annalise to sit on the windowsill, and joined her. "I suppose parts weren't as hellish," she said slowly.

"Caroline filled me in a little, but she tried not to disturb me. I want to know everything!"

"I am afraid everything will take a lot of time."

Annalise gave Lavinia a stern look. "I can deal with a lot. I have nowhere to go."

Lavinia smiled and quickly relayed the story. She told Annalise everything, from her attempt to apologize to Sebastian at the field, to their kidnapping and escape. She told her about the duel and the subsequent revelation that it was her guardian who had orchestrated all of this. She relayed everything, since she had never held anything back from Annalise, including the kisses, but kept the more lurid details just for herself.

Annalise's face was animated throughout the story as she gasped or chuckled, or froze in a horror-stricken grimace. By the end of the story, she was holding on to her chest. "Oh, Lord! I've missed so much!"

"And I am glad that you did. I am eternally grateful to Caroline for keeping everyone calm during this bizarre situation. I do not know how she does it."

Annalise placed her hand on her rounded belly. "She is a gem. I don't know how I would have reacted had I seen it all unfold."

"And that is exactly why I am glad you didn't have the chance to find out."

Annalise cleared her throat and moved closer to Lavinia. "And so what... You do not love Kensington anymore?"

Lavinia heaved a sigh, remembering the conversation she shared with him in Sebastian's chamber. Finally, she said, "He's been there for me my entire life. He is my friend and I do not want that to change. Yes, I do love him. I think I always will—I hope, I always will. But perhaps the kind of love I feel toward him was never romantic. Sure, I wanted more closeness with him, but that was before I knew what closeness truly entailed."

A tender smile appeared on Annalise's lips. "And now that you do know…?"

"And now that I do," Lavinia repeated with an answering smile, "I can't imagine experiencing that closeness with anyone but Sebastian."

Annalise placed her hand atop Lavinia's. "So, you are going to marry him?"

Lavinia pursed her lips. "I… Honestly? I don't know anything else that would make me happier."

Annalise squeezed her fingers and laughed.

"I-I haven't said it to him yet, so I am not certain I should tell anyone else, but… You are my closest friend…"

"Yes?" Annalise prompted.

"I think I am deeply in love with him."

Annalise bit on her lower lip. And then tears appeared at the corners of her eyes. "Oh, my!" She searched her gown for a handkerchief and wiped at her tears.

"Oh, please, don't cry. Or then I shall cry, and we're going to sit here like two watering pots."

Annalise chuckled, wiping at her cheeks. "I am so happy that you've found love. That's all I ever wanted for you."

Lavinia nodded. "However—"

Annalise looked up at her in horror. "No, no howevers."

"I haven't told him about my guardian's schemes yet." *Or about my darker secret.* She swallowed.

"He shall not care. I am certain."

Lavinia lowered her gaze. She couldn't tell Annalise everything. It was too much. She hoped it wouldn't matter, but she was frightened out of her wits.

A knock at the door distracted them both. They turned to a half-open door, where Payne stood, watching his wife with hooded eyes. "My lady." He sketched a bow toward Lavinia. "Apologies. The door was open."

Lavinia smiled. "My lord. Please, come in."

He shook his head. "Thank you. But I came to collect my wife. Annalise, you said you wanted to have a walk before dinner. I suggest we go now before the sun sets."

Annalise threw Lavinia an apologetic smile.

"Please, go," Lavinia urged. "We shall have more time to speak later."

Annalise squeezed her hand. "Keep me informed of all the details."

"Of course."

As the door behind the Paynes closed, Lavinia remembered the letter from her stepmother. She walked toward the bedside table and picked up the note.

Dear Lavinia.

I am writing to inform you that your father has passed. Your guardian is making funeral arrangements, I am preparing to leave the townhouse, and the man who is to be your husband is in London. So, please, whatever you were going to do during the house party, do it now. And do not return to London until you're wed.

All my love, Matilda.

Chapter 31

❧

The flower in your bed is deadly. She murdered her father.

Sebastian reread the note a few times, wondering if he'd read it correctly.

He'd woken up a few minutes ago, feeling refreshed and rejuvenated. He had spoken to Victoria briefly. She had cried and begged for forgiveness in his arms, and then his secretary came by, forcing Sebastian to remember that he'd neglected some burning issues of his marquessate.

Victoria had left his side, leaving him to deal with his duties before he got too tired.

Sebastian's wound was not festering. It was healing nicely. Even so, he was still weak, and he would be for a few more days. But he was lucid, and he was in full possession of his mental faculties. Or at least he thought so until he decided to go through the correspondence and stumbled upon this cryptic note, signed with an indecipherable hand.

As a gambling man, if he had to put his money on a person to whom this note had alluded, he'd place all his bets on Lavinia. She was the only lady who could be found in his bed lately, and he hoped for the rest of his life.

But the note and its contents could not go uninvestigated. Lavinia was in trouble.

What should have disturbed him most was the idea that Lavinia could kill anyone, especially her sire. But that wasn't the part that stung. What disturbed Sebastian was that she hadn't confided in him.

He remembered her reluctance to commit to marrying him, he remembered every conversation with her insisting that she'd be a burden, that he didn't know the full truth. Well, he hoped this was what she alluded to. He hoped that this—the fact that she was in trouble—was the reason for her reluctance. Because *this* he could deal with.

The only thing they wouldn't get through was if she didn't love him back. Everything else was a hurdle they could hop over together.

Besides, he'd seen the burns and cuts on her body. He's seen her jump in fright at every little noise. Add to that the bits and pieces he'd managed to draw out of her, and he'd come to the conclusion that her father had been abusive.

He knew she didn't take murder lightly, even during a duel. So the conclusion was simple. *If* Lavinia had killed her father, it must have been in self-defense.

Lavinia did not have an easy life. And Sebastian was prepared to go through hellfire to ensure the rest of her life was nothing like her past.

He wasn't about to take the note as gospel. But it was obvious that Lavinia was hiding something.

The housekeeper entered his room with his supper and

placed it on his bedside table. "Do you need anything else, my lord?"

Sebastian nodded. "Can you please ask Lady Lavinia to come see me?"

The housekeeper pursed her lips and nodded. She wore a grimace of disapproval on her face.

It was obvious the older woman had heard all about the fact that Lavinia had spent most of the day in this room. She'd seen him kissing Lavinia upon returning from the duel, too, and she definitely disapproved.

But the Roth household was very loyal to their masters. No gossip left the walls of this house, and for that, he was thankful. As much as Sebastian didn't care if his house party guests got wind of this information and ran with it—he was going to marry Lavinia either way—he didn't want her to feel self-conscious about it.

Just then, Lavinia entered his room.

She still wore one of her worn, discolored gowns. Her hair was collected on top of her head in a heap of curls.

She paused at the door for a moment and then rushed toward him.

Sebastian smiled as she fell into his arms and kissed him soundly.

"Ow!" Sebastian hissed when she accidentally hit his injured shoulder.

"Oh, I am so sorry. Did I hurt you?"

Sebastian forced a smile through a grimace. "It was worth it."

Lavinia sat up but didn't leave his bed. She arranged her skirts around her, then looked at the bedside table. "You haven't dined yet. Do you want me to help you?"

"No." He took her hand in his. "I just wanted to sit with you for a while. Maybe experience your kiss again."

Lavinia smiled sheepishly. "I'll just end up hurting you again."

"You could never hurt me." Sebastian swept a lock of hair away from her face. She leaned into his touch like a cat. And just at that moment, through a slightly opened door, Miss Gale entered the room.

She meowed to garner attention for herself, then silently hopped onto his bed.

"Ah, I see you got your cat back."

Lavinia nodded. She stroked Miss Gale's fur, but the cat walked past her and climbed on Sebastian's chest.

He reared back with a grimace.

"Oh, she does that," Lavinia said. "She knows when people are hurting and lies on the injured part."

Sebastian raised his brow. How many times had this kitty "healed" Lavinia this way?

"Do you want me to collect her?" Lavinia's face was a worried frown.

"No, let her heal me." Sebastian was a man of science. But he didn't mind the warm body of a cat lying on his shoulder as long as she didn't rip the bandages.

Lavinia smiled her sheepish smile again. "You must think me a fool. But she truly does seek out the injured or ill people. Except, usually she avoids men. But you are an exception for some reason."

Sebastian grinned. "I am just that charming."

Lavinia burst out in laughter. Miss Gale raised her head in irritation but then continued to gingerly sit on his shoulder.

Huh. She did exactly what Lavinia said she would and sat

on his injury.

Now Sebastian half lay in bed with a purring cat on his aching shoulder. Lavinia's smile turned gentle. "I feel like she's in love with you. I don't think I can blame her."

Was that an admission?

Sebastian peered into her big, brown eyes, and he could feel the warring emotions inside.

He cleared his throat. "I don't suppose her presence will be a hindrance. I wanted to speak with you."

"Oh." Lavinia's face turned grave. "Yes. Me too."

Sebastian perked up. He didn't want to show her the note. He wanted her to confide in him all on her own. "Why don't you go first?"

A fortifying breath left her lungs. Lavinia looked down at her hands. "I actually have several things I want to discuss. And… most of them are about our marriage."

She said *our* marriage. Surely that was a good indication? "I am listening with rapt attention."

"Well." Lavinia shifted with visible restlessness. "Do you want to marry me only because you compromised me?"

"And by compromised you mean made love to you?" Sebastian smiled slowly, watching as her cheeks turned cherry red.

"Yes."

"Then no."

Lavinia blinked up at him.

"I *compromised* you because I'd already made up my mind about marrying you." He stared directly into her eyes to make certain she knew he wasn't lying.

"Then why do you want to marry me?" She looked earnestly confused.

As if she couldn't fathom that somebody would marry her out of their own free will. Or was it because of her secrets?

"Why do you *not* want to marry me?" he countered.

Lavinia heaved a sigh. "I want to. But I want to be certain of your motives. I do not want to be a burden—"

"I would never think of you as such," Sebastian said heatedly.

Miss Gale perked up her ears, but then resumed her purring, her claws working at his bandage above his injury.

Lavinia licked her lips. When she spoke next, her voice was strained. "You might change your mind."

This was getting tiresome, but Sebastian understood her anxiety. He wanted to soothe her, to let her know that none of it mattered to him. "I wouldn't."

"There are things I need to tell you."

Sebastian inclined his head. "Please."

"Firstly, I have no dowry."

Sebastian had to blink to make certain he hadn't misheard. "Does it look like I ever cared about that?"

"Secondly," Lavinia continued. "I have a stepmother who doesn't have a place to stay… I-I can't leave her behind."

"You can bring your stepmother to live with us. Hell, you can bring the entire household. I don't give a damn."

Lavinia nervously chewed on her lips. "There's more."

"Yes, you can keep your cat, too."

She chuckled. At least, she didn't seem as tense anymore. "That was not what I wanted to say, but thank you. Miss Gale would appreciate it very much. She seems to love you."

"Anything else. Nothing matters as long as I get you, you understand?" He squeezed her fingers.

Lavinia's eyes filled with tears. "You might hate me after this."

Sebastian's insides tensed. How could she even think that? "Never."

"It is about our kidnapping."

To say that Sebastian was taken aback was to say nothing at all. He expected her to say something about her father, but the kidnapping? "What about it?"

Lavinia fumbled in her pocket and then handed him a handkerchief, her hand shaking.

Sebastian looked at it, turned it this way and that before raising his eyes to hers. He wished he understood why she was so nervous. "A very nice handkerchief. Thank you."

"It's my guardian's," she said as if that was supposed to make any sense.

"And?" He furrowed his brows.

"When I hurt my foot on the rocks back in Watchet, you wrapped my cut in a handkerchief… with the same embroidery in the corner."

Sebastian squinted at her and then looked back at the piece of linen in his hand. "Are you trying to say that—"

"That house we were brought to was my guardian's. His mother's name was Rose. I suspect the handkerchiefs belonged to her."

"That doesn't make any sense." Sebastian shook his head. "Why would he work with William?"

"He didn't," Lavinia said emphatically. "He did it all himself."

This conversation made less and less sense by the moment. "But why? Did he want us compromised? In that case, I suppose I owe him a thank you."

"Please, be serious," Lavinia exclaimed. "He was the cause of all your troubles. If he hadn't done that, perhaps Victoria wouldn't have married. There wouldn't be a duel. Don't you understand? It's all my fault!"

"No, don't do this." Sebastian took her hands in his and squeezed. "Even if what you say is true, it is your guardian's fault, not yours."

"But it *is* my fault." Tears fell down her cheeks. Lavinia tugged her hands out of his hold and wiped her tears. "I told him… When I was still in London, he told me that he would marry me off to the man whom my father owed most—"

"The bastard," Sebastian growled.

He suddenly remembered that night in the gambling hell, where Atwood boasted about inheriting the Birch title and doing just that, gambling off his ward. Somehow, Sebastian hadn't made the connection until now. But that measly coward, Atwood, was Lavinia's guardian!

"I know most men my father owes money to. They are lecherous old men who always made it their business to make untoward advances toward me."

"Tell me who?" Sebastian was ready to rip them all apart, no matter his injury.

Lavinia just shook her head. "It doesn't matter. But I couldn't… I couldn't let him do it. So I lied." She closed her eyes, tears trailing down her cheeks. "I told him that I was already betrothed. To you."

It took a full minute for Sebastian to process her words. "When was this?"

"It was before the house party," she said as she looked at him again, a plea in her eyes. "Your name was the first one that came to my mind because of our accidental encounter at the ball. I didn't think anything of it. I just needed to ensure that my guardian wouldn't marry me right away. And saying your name gave me the perfect excuse to go to your house party and seek a better groom than what my guardian had in store for me."

Sebastian didn't quite know how to react. That was a lot of information to process. He scrubbed his face with his hand, trying to decipher what it all meant.

Now he started understanding why she was so insistent upon marrying him when she'd failed to trick him into marriage. That was why she'd pursued Mr. Townsend the first few days of the house party.

Did this information change anything? Certainly not. A lot had changed since then. Hadn't it? If she married him now, it wouldn't be for any other reason than love.

Except… she'd never told him she loved him.

Sebastian turned away. Miss Gale still purred on his shoulder. The sun bathed the room in a cheery glow. It was as if nothing had happened, yet there was a pang in his heart.

He wasn't about to give Lavinia up just because of this revelation. But it hurt to think that this would be the main reason she'd say yes to his proposal.

"It doesn't matter," he said, then cleared his throat. There was a slight ringing in his ears again. He was getting tired. "I still don't understand why he'd do this, but it doesn't matter. I'll deal with him upon our return to London."

Lavinia's head shot up. "Please, not another duel."

"Your guardian is Mr. Atwood, is he not?"

"Yes." She nodded.

"Then I won't need to duel. There are far more civilized ways to deal with him."

"Such as?"

Sebastian wished he didn't have to discuss this with her

now. He was getting sleepy again. But she was so concerned, he wanted to alleviate her fears. "He is in a lot of debt. And he shall inherit—or I suppose he *has* inherited even more debt now that your father is dead. A debtor's prison shall fit him nicely. I suppose that's why he wanted to get the two of us together? To get my money out of it?"

Lavinia frowned in thought. "I don't think so. I—" She clamped her lips closed and looked at him with narrowed eyes. "How do you know that my father died?"

Sebastian blinked. Did he just blurt that out? His mind must not be as sharp as he'd thought. But he also realized that the note didn't lie. Her father *was* dead.

Lavinia was looking at him with suspicion in her eyes. After all this time, she still did not trust him.

Sebastian shook his head. There were too many revelations for one day. But he couldn't keep the note from her any longer. "I received a note today. It's on the bedside table."

Lavinia stood gingerly, her eyes on the bedside table. She walked toward it as if something terrible awaited her there.

Then her face changed.

She stood there with a horror-stricken expression on her face, her hand hovering over the table, but her fingers frozen. Her mouth opened and closed a few times, her throat working on a swallow, but she didn't say a word.

Realization hit Sebastian unbidden. "You recognize the note," he said with a tone of resignation in his voice.

He didn't think he had a right to feel betrayed, but the feelings weren't rational.

It finally all made sense to him.

The secret she'd tried to keep from him, the burden she had on her shoulders, was not the fact that she had killed her father—if that was truly the case. No, her harrowing secret was that somebody was blackmailing her.

And for some reason, they'd decided to raise the stakes.

Lavinia didn't take the note. She didn't read it. She just nodded as she turned toward him, unable to meet his eye. "I was going to tell you."

"When?"

She swallowed. "Eventually." Then she looked at him with tears in her eyes. "It's not an easy topic to breach, Sebastian. But I wasn't going to marry you without telling you the truth."

"Is it true then? What the note says, is it true?"

Lavinia looked up at him with pain-filled eyes. "Yes."

Chapter 32

Lavinia expected anger and accusations. She expected slurs hurled her way, not because she'd ever seen Sebastian do this—no, he wasn't the kind—but because that was what she was used to. She didn't know there was another way to react to the revelation of her mistakes.

Even a small misfortune would earn scathing rebukes from her father. If he tripped, she was to blame for being in the vicinity. If men leered at her, she must have done something to provoke that behavior. And if they were lacking funds, it was her fault for needing gowns for the Season.

He would find a way to blame her for everything that happened around them, whether it was her fault or not.

And now there were actual, real things that she was to blame for. She *had* killed her father. His death *was* her fault.

She should have told Sebastian about this earlier. She should have told him so he wouldn't find out this horrible secret of hers via a note from the stranger. She shouldn't have withheld this information from him. If he knew that she was a murderer, perhaps he'd never have touched her…

And that was exactly the reason why she hadn't told him. She'd lied to him by omission, so she could keep him close to her. Lord, she was as bad as William.

Perhaps even worse.

Although she hadn't married Sebastian yet, she'd still managed to ruin his life and those around him. And it was all for naught. Because who would agree to marry a murderess? Everything that was awful in his life had been her fault.

Sebastian raised a hand, and Lavinia jerked, her eyes squeezing shut as her fingers curled into fists, and her entire body tensed. She was prepared to receive a blow, only it never came.

Lavinia slowly opened her eyes. Sebastian paused in the act of plucking Miss Gale off his shoulder. He frowned and placed her on the floor. The cat licked herself in irritation and then sauntered away.

"Did you think I was going to hit you?" Sebastian asked as he straightened.

Lavinia froze. Did she? "I—"

His jaw tensed, and a vein appeared on his forehead. "I would never lay a hand on you. *Ever*," he growled.

Lavinia nodded. "I know." And she meant it.

She had never been afraid of him. Not once. She had spent numerous times with him tête-à-tête, and she had never been afraid of him.

There was always trepidation when she'd danced with other men. She was always afraid to say something that would ignite their ire. Even with Dane.

Dane would never hurt her, she knew that consciously. But he was a powerful man. And that power ignited the sparks of mistrust within her.

Sebastian was powerful, too. Not a duke, but a marquess. Not as rich as Kensington, perhaps, but rich nonetheless. He was athletically built, strong, and yes, quite powerful.

Only she had never been afraid of him. Not physically. With Sebastian, she felt free to be herself.

Except for this little secret. And now she didn't know what to expect of him.

Sebastian patted a place beside him on the bed. "Please, sit."

Lavinia hesitated. She didn't want to be close to him. She didn't want to feel his heat, to smell his scent around her, only to see the disappointment in his eyes. Only to be rejected.

And yet, she moved toward him as if she were tugged by a thread. She sat by his side, her hands on her lap, her eyes on her hands.

"Look at me," he whispered.

Lavinia breathed out, preparing herself for the worst. When she finally looked at him, she didn't see any anger or disappointment in his gaze. How could that be?

Just kindness and something else, something unfathomable in the depths of his dear green eyes.

He raised his hand and reached for her with agonizing slowness. He didn't want to spook her. Lavinia leaned into him, unable to bear the torture of not feeling his touch on her skin. And then his finger trailed her cheek lightly, reverently.

"He hurt you," he said. It wasn't a question.

Lavinia's lashes fluttered down, just as the tears escaped her eyes.

"Tell me what happened," he prompted gently. "That day."

Tears freely rolled down her cheeks, and she had trouble collecting her breath. He cuddled her cheek in his hand, thumbing her tears away. Lavinia leaned into his touch, feeding off his calloused fingertips that scratched against her skin. She opened her eyes but didn't dare look at him as she spoke.

"My father had a habit of drinking. And when he was drunk, if he was lucid enough and could stand on his two feet, he always sought me out. He came up with some transgression I supposedly committed, whether that was true or not, and he punished me. It's been like this forever.

"Sometimes he didn't need a reason. The fact that I was a daughter, not an heir, was enough. The fact that I was clumsy and uncoordinated was enough. The fact that I was… well, me. It was enough."

Sebastian sat up, engulfing her in his reassuring heat. He cupped her face between his palms and placed a dry kiss on her forehead. Her lashes swept down again, her voice trembling as she spoke. "But when Matilda came into our household, things changed. For a while, he stopped drinking as much and he seemed… calmer. Dare I say, happy. I thought that maybe he'd changed. Perhaps we would become a family again. But my hopes were shattered when I realized why beating me was no longer his main amusement."

Lavinia shook her head, dispelling the horrible memories.

"Your stepmother." Sebastian's voice was hoarse.

He ran his hands down her arms in calming sweeps. Lavinia let out a shaky breath. She needed to continue. She needed to tell the story once and for all because she would never have the strength to do it again.

"She is only six years my senior, you know. When she came to our house, I thought she was a wise adult. But she was just a bright-eyed debutante. So young. And as years went by and she didn't provide him with an heir, things got incrementally worse every passing day."

She paused to regulate her breathing. It was getting difficult to speak. His reassuring caresses fell like lead on her arms because she knew they'd disappear as soon as she told him the truth. She looked past him with an unseeing gaze when she spoke again.

"A few weeks ago… It was just like any other night. He got angry with Matilda for making a conversation with some gentleman during a ball. He accused her of infidelity and took us home early from the function. It wasn't unusual. He was always like this. But that night, something was different. His eyes… he looked like a wild beast.

"When we came home, he hit her so hard that she fell against the stairs and hit her head. She wasn't moving. The terror I felt inside was something I never thought I could feel. My father didn't stop yelling at her. As if he didn't notice that she wasn't moving. He was standing over her—" A hiccup left her throat.

Sebastian moved to envelop her in his embrace but she reared back.

"No, please." She placed her hand on his chest, to keep him at arm's length, but couldn't take her hand away. The strong, reassuring beating of his heart calmed her rioting nerves. She curled her fingers into his shirt, drawing strength from him. "I thought he was going to kill her," she whispered.

Suddenly she was back in that hall at Birch townhouse.

Her father, menacing and large, threw a shadow over Matilda as she lay unmoving on the stairs. He kicked her in the stomach, as if not noticing that she wasn't moving. He continued yelling insults at her and threats.

One more blow and he'd kill her.

Lavinia's first thought, however selfish, was that if Matilda died, there would be nobody to draw attention away from her. As young as she was, Matilda was Lavinia's constant protector. Her only protector. If she died, Lavinia would be next.

Lavinia shook in terror, her feet frozen to the floor, but she knew she could not let Matilda die.

The next thing happened like in a foggy dream. Her legs moved of their own volition. Her hands picked up a decorative statue from the banister. And then she hit her father on the head.

He turned slowly and looked at her with fury in his eyes. Lavinia stepped back, tripped, and fell. The statue fell from her hands with a loud crash. She squeezed her eyes shut and covered her head with her arms, expecting her father to strike her. But the blow never came.

She opened her eyes and looked around. Her father had fallen down the stairs and lay in a heap on the stone-cold floor.

Lavinia stood and rushed toward Matilda. She was still breathing. She was alive. Thank God.

Matilda cracked open her eyes. "What happened?"

Lavinia looked back at the prone body of her father on the stone-cold floor.

"I killed him," Lavinia said to Sebastian as she concluded her story. Her mouth dry, tears were rolling down her cheeks.

The next moment, Lavinia was embraced in Sebastian's arms and cuddled to his chest. He caressed her hair, ran calming circles on her back, murmuring soothing nonsense in her ear. Lavinia cried, all her strength leaving her. She felt like a little girl who just needed to be held. That's it.

She didn't need reassurance or acceptance. She didn't need anything as long as she was wrapped in his warm embrace.

Nothing was expected of her at that moment. She didn't need to be brave or clever. She didn't need to justify herself or cry in anger that she did what she had to. For the first time in her entire life, she felt as though she was allowed to simply exist. Just be. And she still felt safe and protected. And she'd never felt this way before.

Sebastian kissed the top of her head. "You keep saving my soul, *ma petite*. Because if you didn't kill your father, I would have had to do it myself, for all the pain he'd made you suffer. And it wouldn't be an easy death either."

"He wasn't worth your soul," she whispered.

"No. But you are."

Lavinia looked up at him, and he swept the tears away from her cheeks. "Why don't you judge me?" And she honestly could not understand. This kind, gorgeous human being somehow accepted all her faults and didn't judge her one whit.

"It would be easy to just say I love you, and let you believe that is why," he said slowly. "And I do love you."

He loves me?

Everything inside Lavinia heated and tensed. *He loves me!*

"But that is not why I don't judge you. And I want you to understand this. None of it is your fault."

Lavinia looked up at him, confused.

"Your father beating you was never your fault. Your guardian's attempt to trick you into any marriage is not your fault—"

"But—"

"No. It simply isn't. You can't take responsibility for other people's actions. And I can't judge you for what other people did."

"But I killed him," she repeated again. "And not because I wanted to protect Matilda, but because I was afraid he'd kill me next."

Sebastian looked at her as if she were speaking a foreign language he did not understand. "*Ma petite,* perhaps your first instinct was to save yourself, but who can fault you for protecting your own life? If you didn't hit him, he would have killed Matilda. Would you rather you did nothing? How would that make you feel?"

Lavinia shook her head. "I would never have forgiven myself."

Sebastian rested his chin on the top of her head, and somehow this gesture calmed Lavinia as she cuddled deeper into his embrace.

"You are the most selfless person I've ever known." Sebastian's voice reverberated through his chest. "And yet, you are convinced you are the most selfish."

"I've made so many mistakes," Lavinia breathed.

"Haven't we all?"

Lavinia wanted nothing more than to sit like this, in Sebastian's arms, surrounded by his reassuring heat forever. But she could not forget that her mistakes had consequences. She disengaged from his embrace, wiped her tears, and looked up at him.

"What shall we do about the note?"

Sebastian smoothed her hair away from her face. "First things first. I'll get a license and we can marry today or tomorrow. I would rather we did it in a grand ceremony, but considering your guardian's interference, I think the sooner we marry the better. Then we travel back to London and deal with your guardian."

"And then?" Lavinia crinkled her brow. She wasn't about to protest a quick wedding.

"And then we ask for help."

<h1 style="text-align:center">Chapter 33</h1>

L avinia stood outside the door to her townhouse breathing deeply. She felt the same kind of trepidation that she'd felt every time she was on the doorstep of what had always been her house.

It had always been her house. But it had never been her home.

A warm hand landed on the small of her back. Lavinia looked up at Sebastian with a grateful smile. He knew how difficult it was for her to return to this house that held so many unpleasant memories. But with Sebastian by her side, Lavinia could face anything.

The butler opened the door, and Lavinia stepped into a dank, dark hall. God, she hated this place.

She swallowed a growing lump in her throat. "Is Mr. At—Lord Birch at home?" Her voice hitched at the title that used to belong to her father.

The butler inclined his head. "In his study."

"Thank you. No need to announce us," Sebastian said as

the butler made to move toward the stairs, then whispered against her hair, "How are you feeling?"

That wasn't an easy question to answer. Decades worth of anxieties were wrestling in her stomach. Lavinia looked at the floor where her father's body lay after she'd hit him in the head. "Everything will be better after today."

They made their way toward the study without speaking.

Lavinia was grateful that Sebastian didn't try to fill the silence. His warmth and his presence by her side was enough.

They paused by the doors to Lord Birch's study, and at Lavinia's nod, Sebastian knocked firmly.

"Enter." The new Lord Birch's voice sounded behind the doors.

Sebastian opened the door and held it for her to enter.

Lord Birch raised his eyes from the ledger in his hands as he sat behind the large mahogany table. There was another person in the room. He stood and turned toward Lavinia.

She recognized that man immediately. He was her father's solicitor.

Lord Birch also stood and smiled at Lavinia. "You missed the funeral."

"And you missed the wedding," Sebastian said as he joined Lavinia.

Lord Birch's eyes widened, his face taking on an ashen color. "My lord." He tipped his head, then turned toward his solicitor. "Please, leave us."

"Actually, I'd rather he stayed," Sebastian said. "There are things I need to say, and I'd be more comfortable saying them with a witness present."

Lord Birch swallowed, his eyes darting from Lavinia to Sebastian. "You couldn't have married."

"Isn't that what you wanted? Isn't that why you kidnapped us both and threw us into your old house in Watchet?" Sebastian seethed.

Lord Birch's face grew red. "I didn't do such a thing!"

Lavinia slowly drew out his handkerchief and placed it on the desk. "Your mother's handkerchief, wasn't it? And there are other things in the house that point to your involvement in the kidnapping."

Lord Birch fell into the chair, defeated. Certainly, the handkerchief wasn't enough evidence, but the man didn't seem to have the will to lie. Either way, he was about to go to debtor's prison. His only recourse was to plead. And that's exactly what he did. "I never meant you any harm! I placed you in my home, did I not?"

"Without food or other provisions!" Sebastian growled.

"I knew you to be a resourceful man. And I was going to bring you back in a few days. I truly was!"

"Why did you do it at all?" Lavinia cried.

"I just needed him out of the way, while I—" He raked a hand through his wig, dislodging it from the top of his head. "I timed it perfectly. The thugs were going to kidnap Lord Roth and at that exact time, I was supposed to arrive with Lord Pembroke and a special license."

"Why would you ever think I would marry Pembroke?" Lavinia shook her head, trying to collect her thoughts.

"I had everything planned out. I forged a letter in Roth's hand, saying he decided to elope with another. And I hoped in your heartbreak you would wed Pembroke instead. He is just as rich and just as influential. He would have convinced you to change your mind."

"Why let me leave for the house party at all?"

Birch waved a dismissive hand. "If you promised yourself to Roth, you weren't likely to break said promise. But if you thought he ran off, perhaps in your grief, you'd marry another. And I didn't want you to feel forced. I didn't need to make an enemy of you. Otherwise it would be easier to just kidnap you. I am not a villain."

Lavinia shook her head in disbelief, trying to ignore the large gaps in Birch's logic. She would have found out about the false nature of the letter. Especially since she wasn't truly betrothed to Roth before the kidnapping. But then, Birch didn't know that.

"Well, your plan didn't work out. And your thugs hurt Lavinia," Sebastian growled and took a menacing step. "And for that, you'll pay."

"I am not the villain!" Birch cried again. "They were never supposed to touch anyone else!"

Lavinia placed a hand on Sebastian's chest. There was no need for violence. There'd been enough of that. Debtors' prison would have to be punishment enough for Birch.

"I am not versed in things like this. But I had to do something! Only old Birch croaked the day of Pembroke's arrival, and we couldn't leave. And everything went wrong." He covered his face with his hands. "Now I am ruined!"

Lavinia and Sebastian exchanged a confused look. What now? This entire thing hadn't gone as planned at all.

The solicitor, who still stood by the desk, suddenly started rummaging through his papers. "I suppose this now belongs to you." He held out a piece of paper toward Sebastian.

"What is this?" Sebastian looked at the paper as if it was diseased.

The solicitor cleared his throat. "Lady Lavinia's dowry."

A high-pitched sob left Lord Birch's lips. Lavinia threw a concerned gaze toward her guardian. She shook her head from utter befuddlement and looked to Sebastian as if he could explain the situation to her, but he just shrugged.

Finally, Lavinia turned toward the solicitor. "But I don't have a dowry."

The solicitor blinked. "Yes, you do. Under threat from The Duke of Kensington, Lord Birch had left you a small, but lucrative, estate. He couldn't sell it or gamble it away until you turned one and twenty or until you married, but then the estate would transfer to your husband."

Sebastian shook his head. "I do not need that."

Lord Birch raised his head, hope glinting in his greedy eyes.

Lavinia jumped and took the paper in her hand. "I need it. It's mine... I never had anything that was mine before."

"Well, technically, you had it for a long time," the solicitor noted.

Lavinia studied the paper in awe. She had a small but lucrative estate. All hers.

But as much as she wanted to have something of hers, as much as she wished she could enter this marriage with Sebastian having something to offer, she knew she couldn't keep it. "Can I give it to someone else?" Lavinia asked the solicitor.

"It is your husband's to do as he pleases."

Sebastian squeezed her waist. "You can do whatever you want with it."

"I want to give it to Lady Matilda Birch. Please, can you arrange that?" She handed the paper back to the solicitor, then turned toward Lord Birch. "Where is she?"

He just shook his head. "She left right after the funeral. I know not where."

Lavinia let out a breath of despair. Why did everything have to be so difficult?

"We'll find her," Sebastian said against Lavinia's hair.

* * *

While the estate was rewritten as a gift for Matilda, Lord Birch collected his belongings, hoping to run away from the law. Sebastian didn't try to stop him. Instead, he helped Lavinia pack her things.

Once everything was taken care of, Lavinia and Sebastian descended the stairs, hand in hand. They had invited the servants to follow her into the Roth household and were just about to leave when there was a knock at the door.

The butler opened it, and Lavinia found herself looking at a tall, imposing, dark man. He commanded attention with his presence, and without even knowing his name, Lavinia understood that he was someone powerful.

He had gorgeous opaque gray eyes, a straight nose, and full lips. His hair—for he did not wear a wig—tied in an unassuming queue at the back, was dark black with a few silver strands showing. He stepped forward and sketched a perfect bow.

"Lady Lavinia, I assume," he said in a low, silky voice. Sebastian's arm hardened like steel beneath Lavinia's touch. The gray-eyed gentleman didn't even spare Sebastian a single glance. "Allow me to introduce myself. I am the Earl of Pembroke, at your service. I believe we are to be married."

Sebastian stepped forward, shielding Lavinia with his form. "Lady Roth," he said with such coldness that frost might as well have left his mouth, "is already married. To me."

Lavinia peeked from behind Sebastian. Lord Pembroke's brows drew over his eyes slightly. "Well, that's unfortunate," he said in the same matter-of-fact tone of voice. "It looks like I'll have to bankrupt the Birch title after all."

Sebastian and Lavinia bowed out soon after that, leaving the earl to deal with Birch.

"I thought he was old," Lavinia said in wonder. This was who Atwood had in mind for Lavinia to marry? "When he said he was a widower, an heir to a duke, and someone my father owed to, I assumed he was old, and lecherous like the rest of my father's acquaintances."

Sebastian paused before the carriage and looked at her with narrowed eyes. "And if you did know, would you have married him?"

Lavinia bit back a smile. "Perhaps. But I would have missed out on the grandest love I've ever known. I love you, Lord Sebastian Devis. And I would never change a minute of my life because it led me to you."

Chapter 34

Aweek later, as Sebastian and Lavinia traveled back to the Roth estate, they stopped in one of the Duke of Kensington's residences in Reading.

The duke wasn't in attendance, but they were instantly invited in to join the Duchess of Kensington for tea.

Lavinia surveyed the grand house, smiling at the memories of when she'd wanted to be the mistress of these estates. She'd dreamed of becoming the duke's wife, only to be happy now that it had never come to pass. How different her life would have turned out had she married him instead.

Would she still have met Sebastian then? Would they have fallen in love? Would she have regretted her fate?

Lavinia was glad that those questions would never be answered.

She leaned into her husband's side and whispered, "I love you."

Sebastian raised his brow and then grinned. "Happy you didn't marry the bore, aren't you?"

It was as if he'd read her mind.

Lavinia swatted at him playfully as they continued down the long corridor toward one of the grand drawing rooms.

Caroline met them inside, with a wide smile on her face. "Welcome," she said with a slight curtsy, and then, "Cousins."

Lavinia couldn't help but grin. They were, in fact, cousins with Caroline now, if only by marriage.

Once the greetings were over, and they sat at the table, drinking tea and eating pastries, the conversation turned to more serious subjects.

"Victoria is insisting upon leaving for Russia," Sebastian said. "Now that she is married, she is free to do what she pleases. But the political atmosphere is unstable there. As lovely as her sister might be, she is just as immature. I don't want Victoria to get caught up in more intrigue and scandal. And after what happened with William, I do not think it is wise to let her go there all alone."

"Why does she want to leave?" Caroline asked.

"Technically, there's nothing holding her here except for the maudlin memories and perhaps Frau Elinor, who by the way, is still insisting upon annulment."

"That would never be possible," Caroline said. "We all checked into it. William made certain the wedding was valid. Besides, even attempting to annul it would result in a tremendous scandal. At least now nobody knows that Victoria is even married."

"Not until William tells somebody," Lavinia chimed in.

Sebastian sighed. "A part of me still believes that he did that—married her—only to have something to hold over our heads, so he could blackmail us later."

"Speaking of blackmail." Lavinia glanced up at Sebastian.

After all, this was the real reason why they came to visit the Kensingtons.

"Right." Sebastian nodded. "We were hoping you could help us with something. Actually, we hoped to speak to your husband, but since he is not here, perhaps we can discuss this with you."

Caroline raised a brow, then carefully placed her cup of tea on the dish. "How can I help you?"

"We are not certain if you can," Lavinia said. "But it is not as if we have much of a choice."

Sebastian fumbled in his pockets and took out an envelope containing two notes. "Can you tell me if you recognize anything about these notes?"

Taking the envelope into her hand, Caroline glanced back and forth between Sebastian and Lavinia curiously before opening it. She picked out the notes and studied them carefully, her brows pinched in concentration.

"At first, I was convinced it must have been William's doing," Sebastian said. "But it doesn't seem like his modus operandi. And the signature reads—"

"Erebus," Caroline said evenly.

"Right." Sebastian jerked his head in a nod. "And with the rumors about the secret society called *Shadows*, and seeing how Erebus is the god of shadows, I thought it might be a coincidence."

"This is not them," Caroline said as she waved the notes in her hands.

"How do you know?" Lavinia shifted closer to Caroline.

"You said you wanted to show this to Kensington first, but you didn't show it to him yet, did you?" Her gaze was narrowed, calculating.

Lavinia threw a side-eyed glance toward Sebastian before answering. "You are the first person aside from the both of us to hold it in your hands."

"Good." Caroline stood resolutely. "Please, wait here."

She walked out the door, leaving Sebastian and Lavinia to exchange confused gazes.

Caroline came back a moment later and handed Lavinia a few envelopes, all addressed by Dane.

"What is this?" Lavinia shuffled the envelopes in her hands.

"Look at the handwriting. Especially the letter E. It's uncanny."

Sebastian shifted closer to Lavinia and took a few envelopes to compare the handwriting. "I suppose it is similar, but… What are you saying?"

"I am saying that this is Kensington's writing." Caroline nodded for emphasis before sitting down across from them.

"Do not be ridiculous." Lavinia didn't even want to contemplate the possibility. It was ridiculous. "Why would he ever do that?"

"Because… listen, this will be very hard for you to believe, but I spent months trying to figure it out. My uncle was always wary of Kensington. He did business with him, and he was mistrustful of him. When he arranged a marriage for me with Kensington, I was shocked. Until it all made sense."

"What made sense? Nothing is making sense."

Sebastian squeezed Lavinia's waist to keep her panic from rising.

Caroline licked her lips. "My uncle was also blackmailed and threatened with similar letters. All with the same handwriting, all going back for years. When he got ill, he became paranoid and obsessed with keeping me safe. And what is the safest way to ensure the blackmailer never targets me? To marry me to him."

"Why would that make sense?" Lavinia looked at Sebastian in confusion.

"The blackmailer would never destroy his own family," he supplied. "Or reputation."

"Or perhaps Kensington wanted my wealth. And black-mailed my uncle to get it. But Uncle realized exactly what Roth is saying. It was better to marry me to the devil himself than have the devil go after me once my uncle died."

"I don't believe this." Lavinia stood and started pacing.

"I understand your reluctance. But I've checked Kensington's finances—"

Lavinia rounded on Caroline. "Kensington's title was always well off."

Caroline shook her head. "He became a duke at fifteen. He had the title, but he didn't have the wealth. His father gambled it all away. Kensington was not well off at the time of the inheritance. And not for a few years after. How did he become so rich and influential in only a few years, Lavinia? Things do not add up."

"This is ridiculous. He has been helping me my entire life. Why would he want to harm me now?"

"Perhaps he was helping you and other people and was being altruistic so that nobody would suspect him. Or perhaps he was helping you to get out of the situations he put you in. Or perhaps he was helping you so he would have enough information about you that could potentially harm you in a way that would aid him in the long run. Or—"

"Please, stop." Lavinia raised her hand. "That is too many ors. None of it proves anything!"

Caroline nodded. "And that is why I agreed to marry him. To find the proof."

"With all due respect, Caroline," Sebastian intervened. "Isn't it more plausible that the leader of the *Shadows* secret society is the one doing this and not the most influential duke in England?"

Caroline straightened and took a fortifying breath. "No. Because I know who the leader of the Shadows is."

Epilogue

Four years later

Lavinia looked out the window at the narrow street. It was late, and she couldn't make out anything in the dark, but she was certain it was beautiful. After all, it was Sebastian's favorite city on earth.

Sebastian got used to their English life rather quickly, but he hadn't stopped telling her stories about his beloved Paris.

It took them a while to get here. But considering everything that had happened, four years after their marriage wasn't that long to finally have their wedding trip.

Sebastian wrapped his arms around her from behind. "Are you tired?" He asked, stroking her rounded belly.

"No." Lavinia smiled and shook her head.

"Liar," he growled in her ear, making her shiver.

"Maybe I am a bit tired, but I am equally as excited. We are finally in Paris!"

Sebastian kissed her ear, then down her neck. "You need to rest. It's been a long journey. And since our little one is asleep—"

There was a sound of footsteps behind the door, and then the loud knocking. "Mama! Papa!"

"Amelia, come back!" the nursemaid's voice sounded behind the doors.

"Asleep, huh?" Lavinia smiled at Sebastian and he hurried to open the door.

Amelia, their three-year-old daughter, rushed into the room and promptly plastered herself to her father.

"Pardon me," Beatrice, the nursemaid, said from the corridor. "She woke up and insisted on seeing you. But I didn't—"

"Do not worry Beatrice, go back to bed," Sebastian said as he picked up Amelia. He closed the door when the nursemaid walked away, and came toward Lavinia.

"I can't sleep," Amelia whispered. Then she turned to Lavinia. "I want sleep with mama."

Lavinia's smile deepened. It wasn't common for parents to sleep in the same room as their children, but considering her own childhood, Lavinia wanted to stay as close to Amelia as she could.

It was unheard of to be so attached to one's child. But Sebastian didn't mind. He spoiled his daughter more than Lavinia did, and neither of them cared about what others thought about that.

Lavinia rubbed her growing belly. She wanted to have a large family. And she wouldn't mind if all of them slept in the same bed. "Of course, dear."

All three of them went to the bed, and Sebastian tucked in his girls before dousing the candles.

"Are you excited about seeing Paris?" Sebastian asked as he settled beneath the covers and hugged both Lavinia and Amelia close to him.

"Very much," Lavinia said. "But you know what I am most excited about."

Sebastian smiled against her hair. "Yes, we finally get to see Victoria again."

The End.

Thank you for reading!

Loved the book? Sign-up to my newsletter to get a bonus novelette:

https://sendfox.com/sadiebosque

By signing-up, you'll also get new release alerts, bonus content such as extra epilogues, deleted scenes and other.

Caroline's story is next! Get it now: Taming His Wicked Duchess

Clandestine Marriages

Many avid historical romance readers probably know the rules a couple had to follow in order to get married in the 1800s. The Clandestine Marriage Act of 1753 stated that marriages had to be preceded by banns or a license (special or common), celebrated in a church before a priest and at least two witnesses, and if the bride or groom were under twenty-one, they should have had parental consent.

Well, before 1753 it was slightly different.

Parental consent was not required. And although one could marry without banns or a license in a clandestine marriage, it often resulted in a financial fine placed upon both the married couple and the member of clergy who married them. The latter could also find themselves incarcerated.

This little detail led to Fleet marriages becoming quite popular. Clergymen who were already in debtor's prison had nothing to lose, so they performed clandestine marriages for a fee.

Disgraced clergymen and criminals who pretended to be clergymen also carried out clandestine marriages outside of the fleet.

The other way to avoid banns was to request a marriage license. The common license was given to people who had a good reason for a hasty/secret marriage, including but not limited to: a pregnant bride, marrying a person of a different faith, age gap marriages, marrying a person of different social standing, being manipulated by one's guardian…. In short, if one could convince the local clergy that they required privacy or haste, they would be able to get it for a small fee.

If one wanted to go further and marry in a house or a private chapel they would apply for a special license which was a lot more difficult and expensive to obtain.

While Sebastian took the path of applying for a marriage license, which way did Victoria and William go? Let me know your guesses here: https://sadiebosque.wordpress.com/contact/

Read more here:

LASCH, CHRISTOPHER. "The Suppression Of Clandestine Marriage In England: The Marriage Act Of 1753." *Salmagundi*, no. 26 (1974): 90–109. http://www.jstor.org/stable/40535898.